TE

Everyone Dies

John Dolan hails from a small town in the North-East of England. Before turning to writing, his career encompassed law and finance. He has run businesses in Europe, South and Central America, Africa and Asia. John is the author of the *Time, Blood and Karma* series. He and his wife Fiona currently divide their time between Thailand and the UK.

Everyone Dies is the final book in the *Children of Karma* trilogy.

The *Time Blood and Karma* series

Everyone Burns

Hungry Ghosts

A Poison Tree

Running on Emptiness

The *Children of Karma* trilogy

Restless Earth

Two Rivers, One Stream

Everyone Dies

EVERYONE DIES

A tale of human mortality comprising a prologue, twenty-eight chapters, two interludes, and a Post Mortem Report

---

John Dolan

TENTION BOOKS

TENTION BOOKS

This book is intended entirely as a work of fiction. Although it contains incidental references to real people, this is solely to provide a relevant historical and geographical context. All other characters, names and events are fictitious, and any resemblance to actual events or persons living or dead is entirely coincidental.

All quoted words in this book are believed to fall under the category of fair use. However, the publisher is sensitive to the rights of copyright owners and should any such copyright owners have cause for concern please contact the publisher.

EVERYONE DIES published by Tention Publishing Limited

Tention Publishing Limited Reg. No. 8098036
Unit 4 Provender Mill, Belvedere Road,
Faversham ME13 7LD,
United Kingdom

ISBN 978-1-912361-05-2

For Fiona

In 2011, while living in Kuala Lumpur, I came up with the notion of writing seven novels about the adventures and misadventures of anti-hero Englishman David Braddock. With the publication of *Everyone Dies*, this project has reached its conclusion.

For the last eight years, my wife Fiona has supplied me with endless support and encouragement in this endeavour, all the while having to put up with a husband who was living much of his time in a fantasy world inhabited by gangsters, corrupt policemen, and disreputable ex pats. I take my hat off to her for her patience and understanding.

Thank you, darling. Maybe now, I can get all those jobs done around the house.

"By the sacred earth on which I kneel, by the shades that wander near me, by the deep and eternal grief that I feel, I swear; and by thee, O Night, and the spirits that preside over thee, to pursue the daemon who caused this misery, until he or I shall perish in mortal conflict. For this purpose, I will preserve my life; to execute this dear revenge will I again behold the sun and tread the green herbage of earth, which otherwise should vanish from my eyes forever. And I call on you, spirits of the dead, and on you, wandering ministers of vengeance, to aid and conduct me in my work. Let the cursed and hellish monster drink deep of agony; let him feel the despair that now torments me."

Mary Shelley, Frankenstein

"Death cures the hunchback."

Attributed to Nikita Khrushchev

Let's Start at the End, Shall We?

Have you ever wondered what happens when your heart finally stops beating?

Of course, you have. Everyone has.

There are only three things for certain that all members of the human race have in common, whatever our shape, size, sex or colour.

First, we fuck things up.

Second, we die.

Third, we worry about dying.

We don't fixate on this last item all the time, obviously. When we are kids, we have more pressing things to fret about than our mortality. And when we are grown-ups, most of our waking hours are spent working, fornicating, child-rearing, conversing, eating, and watching pointless television programmes or fiddling around on our phones.

Yet the joins between these activities are not perfectly sealed. Consequently, thoughts of death seep in between the cracks. At such moments, existential anguish rears up like a storm surge, sweeping all before it.

What happens to me after I die?

Over the centuries, the world's organised religions have systematically exploited the fear of the Great Beyond to keep their followers in line. There is nothing like the prospect of hellfire and eternal damnation to cower even the bravest among us. Moreover, the nature of such suffering is lovingly catalogued in graphic and precise detail.

Most Christian traditions have, at least since the Middle Ages, embraced the imagery of ever-burning sulphur, tormenting devils armed with pitchforks, and other unremitting punishments immortalised in Dante's

Inferno; while the Quran fills the febrile mind with similar flaming representations of the seven levels of *Jahannam*, each designed to reflect the relative severity of sins.

Judaism, Zoroastrianism, Hinduism, and virtually all of the other corporatised 'isms' have their own version of Hades.

Philosophers offer merely a fluffy counterbalance to this weight of horror. The great and grouchy Schopenhauer tells us that our post-death experience will be much the same as our pre-birth experience. Few are likely to find this much of a comfort.

Then there is the reverse of the coin, the destination of the righteous: heaven. The friendly carrot alternative to the scary stick.

The Islamic concept of *Jannah* envisages seven planes of reward, with descriptions in largely physical terms – flowing rivers and shady trees, houses of gold built by angels, sumptuous clothes and jewels, delicious food and drink. It is the land where every wish is instantly gratified, and all inhabitants are exactly thirty-three years old.

Christians, and especially Anglicans, have rather less to go on as to what delights await the pious deceased. Paradise, it turns out, cannot be so easily described by Jesus' priestly caste, especially as the text of the New Testament gives them so little to work on. There, vagueness is the order of the day. The specifics so characteristic of perdition are absent, and one presumes that the Western Churches continue to wrestle with the conundrum that one man's idea of bliss is another man's idea of everlasting tedium. It's difficult to draw up a marketing plan on that basis.

I once got into trouble with a vicar by asking him, "When I meet my grandparents in heaven, how old will they be?" After much throat-clearing, equivocation, and ingenious abstraction, he advised we should move on to the subject of flower-arranging for the Harvest Festival. Even after two millennia of Christianity, it seemed I would have to reach my own conclusions. And, I did.

Christians are not struggling alone with this, however. The adherents of many other belief systems have to draw on their own creative powers where celestial blessings are concerned. Some Buddhist teachings postulate only a form of extinction as the ultimate prize for good behaviour.

Atheists have it easy really.

Anyway, as it turns out, whether you have been naughty or nice, the Afterlife is nothing at all like you might have imagined. You can believe me because I speak from experience. Plus, I'm happy to take questions.

But before we get into that, there is a tale that needs to be told, and which should not be further delayed. So, if you are sitting comfortably, let's start with an introduction.

My name is David Braddock.

And this is the story of how I died.

1

"Every new beginning comes from some other beginning's end."

Seneca

Europeans tend to go mad in Thailand.

Fact.

For brief-stay tourists, the craziness is usually alcohol-and-lust-fuelled, and of a temporary nature. Normal brain functions are restored once the holidaymaker's plane completes its return flight to the West, at which point some mental switch resets to 'behave yourself'.

For us ex pat residents, however, the insanity is slower in taking root, and more insidious. Plus, once established, it is permanent. Our particular brand of folly manifests in various ways, but it always involves mania, a dissolving of behavioural boundaries, and a lack of moderation. Indeed, *moderate* is not an adjective you hear often in Siam.

It is certainly not one you would use to describe the rain that falls on my adopted home of Koh Samui. Our island's micro-climates, resulting from the presence of central mountains and periodic changes in wind direction, mean that cloudbursts often occur over a limited area. In other words, it can be pissing it down here, yet sunny in Chaweng.

And right now, it *is* pissing it down here.

From the sheltered balcony of my Mae Nam apartment, I can see that, after only two hours of this particular deluge, the bottom road is already flooded. Folks have given up trying to ride their motorbikes, and instead are wading knee-deep through the water as it plummets from the sky and rushes down from the already-saturated hills. There is no wind, so the downpour is dropping in sheets. The sea, only half-a-kilometre away, is invisible behind this dense aqueous curtain. It must have been on a day such as this that Noah looked up and thought to himself, "Yup, I was right to build that ark. Better get the elephants inside quick."

When I elected some years ago to swap the cold December drizzle of England for the warm winter inundations of Thailand, I hadn't appreciated that gills would be needed if I ever wanted to venture out. The general state of the infrastructure here doesn't help. At this time of year – thanks to the lack of properly-sized drains and the woeful road maintenance – sinkholes appear, surfaces break up and wash away, and parts of the main route around the island resemble canals. You could waterski outside Samui's biggest supermarket. If this were the UK, Health and Safety would require they employ a lifeguard.

But this is not the UK.

Anyway.

Secure from the descending torrents and warmed by several generous measures of Bells, I am experiencing a rare moment of serenity.

Wayan, my Balinese housekeeper, has retired to her room to watch Thai soap operas on her TV. Relations between us are strained these days, and we only communicate when necessary. This state of affairs is not attributable to any ill-will on either of our parts, rather to *circumstances.*

And these circumstances are difficult.

Allow me to expound.

Last month, in England, my daughter Katie disappeared, murdered on the orders of her former father-in-law and Russian oligarch, Grigory Polzin. The background to this lethal directive was that Katie had been tried at the Old Bailey on the charge of unlawfully killing her abusive husband Alexander – Polzin's younger son. After her acquittal, disgruntled Polzin Senior took matters into his own hands, commissioning a professional hit man to assassinate her and ensure her body was never found. The hired gun in question is known to Interpol as *Captain Nemo*, and he is suspected of being responsible for several vanishings over the years. Conversely, he is known to Wayan as Robert Buchanan, and he was her lover.

My God. When I summarise it like this, it reads like the plot of a pulp fiction novel. Except ... it's not. Not unless I have finally taken complete leave of my senses, and am not, in actuality, on my balcony, but rather in some padded cell, straitjacketed, drooling and howling at the moon.

No. I'm not that lucky. I'm stuck with this version of reality. The one in which my daughter is dead.

Now you know why my housekeeper and I tiptoe around each other. She is not in any way to blame for what happened, having been oblivious to her paramour's occupation. But guilt hangs heavily on her despite my best reassurances. The ease between us that we both took for granted has gone. Possibly forever. Once Christmas is over, we have agreed she will go back to Bali for a month or so to give us both some space. Whether Wayan will actually return to Samui after her home visit is uncertain. It may be too painful for her.

In the spirit of full disclosure, I should add that there is no actual proof that my daughter is dead; nor that Buchanan killed her; nor that Polzin was behind her disappearance.

But I *know*. I don't need proof.

Katie had no reason to vanish, and Polzin had every reason to make sure she did. The Russian is a vile, vindictive bastard, and one who considers himself beyond the reach of the law. Well, that's as may be.

So, while the British police and Interpol continue to flounder and chase shadows – spurred on by my regular phone calls demanding updates on their progress – yours truly is back in the Land of Smiles, working out the best way to give Grigory Ilych Polzin's karma a shove in the right direction. I am not about to rely solely on the Boys in Blue to deliver a result. That would be altogether too passive a route to follow.

Hence, my current interlude of calm is a *rare* one.

I light a Marlboro and splash the rest of the bottle of Bells into my glass. I have two more bottles in the kitchen cupboard, so no sweat if the rising waters keep us indoors for a day. After that, I can always swim down *Soi* 7 to the convenience store if necessary.

The light is fading. A car has got stuck on the bottom road. I can't tell whether the driver is waving or drowning. Either way, his problem is not my concern.

I have quite enough on my plate, thank you.

Justice walks into a bar, carrying a sword in one hand and a set of scales in the other.

"I can't serve you," says the barman.

"Why not?" she asks.

"Because you don't exist."

I've just put the phone down after a call from my UK-based step-mother, Nang.

She's worried about me.

She thinks I talk too much to dead people.

Which is ironic, as Nang has been pressing me for months to read my late father's memoirs of his time in Malaya. Now, if that's not a conversation with a dead person – albeit a one-way exchange – I don't know what is. I have, however, no intention of opening Edward Braddock's manuscript which is currently mouldering in the bottom of a drawer. I should throw the damn thing away. It's not as if Nang would ever find out. But, somehow, resolve is lacking.

My energy is being conserved for a more momentous undertaking.

I probably shouldn't have mentioned to Nang the occasional reappearance of my deceased wife, Claire. Even though she has told me she has regular dialogues with her departed husband, it seems the fact that Claire is *visible* to me during our discussions causes her concern.

"Look, Nang, it's not as if I don't know she's not real," I said during the course of the call. "Visual hallucinations are not uncommon where someone is under a lot of stress. Google it."

"How much are you drinking at present, David?"

"Why?"

"Your voice sounds slurred."

"It's a bad line. Also, I have a spot of toothache, so I'm talking out of the side of my mouth."

"Is that true?"

"Cross my heart."

"Then, go and see a dentist."

"Hey, that's a good idea. Why didn't I think of that? Thanks, Nang."

"Don't be rude. It doesn't suit you."

"Sorry."

"Have you spoken to Natalie recently?"

"A few days ago. I'll phone her after we're done."

"See that you do." A pause. "Anything from the police?"

"No. Nothing."

"Keep at them."

"I do."

After that, we moved onto less weighty topics, namely the current weather in England, the commercialisation of Christmas, her gardener's hernia, and the despicable actions of the Labour Government headed up by the unforgivably-Scottish Gordon Brown.

I should have asked her how she was.

Damn.

Simple courtesies slip my mind these days. It's a capacity question, I guess.

Still, she sounded like she was OK.

I smoke a cigarette while I look at my cell phone and wonder whether I can face the usual stilted conversation with Natalie. All my calls to Claire's mother invariably follow the same format. I enquire about Jenny, my niece. Natalie gives a brief response. We compare the weather on Samui with that in London. She asks hesitantly whether there have been any developments with the police on the search for Katie. I say no.

I don't tell her that her dead daughter has been turning up for chats in my Samui apartment. Even I am not that tactless. Plus, if I did, she might query whether her other departed daughter – Anna – has been here too. And, given that she holds me responsible for Anna's death, any such confab would be bound to end badly.

I stub out my Marlboro, think *fuck it,* and call her.

As it turns out, no extinct persons feature in our talk. Natalie even wishes me Happy Christmas, in case we don't speak again in the coming days.

That's my family stuff done for now.

Despite everything, the *David Braddock Agency* continues to function. Not that we have much competition for private investigation services on the island. Indeed, we have none. Even so, the fact that the *Agency*'s principal owner – me – shows only a passing interest in the business' solvency these days, and that male tourists wanting someone to spy on their local girlfriends are currently in shorter supply than in former times, does make it surprising that we are still going.

But maybe it's not *that* surprising. We do have something that no-one else has: Da Pintaraporn. My partner at the *Agency* will never let us go under so long as there is breath in her body. She toils tirelessly in marketing and in ensuring our clients are happy, and this year she has been conducting surveillance assignments herself, despite having a husband and young child to look after. Normally, she would be making me feel guilty that I am not pulling my weight. In the past, Da was never slow to criticise me. *Au contraire*. She was always pretty bloody fast, elaborating on my shortcomings with a gleeful enthusiasm that most women reserve for disparaging their spouses. Moreover, her disapproval was never restricted to purely professional matters, but covered pretty much every aspect of my lifestyle. But, knowing what she does about my recent troubles, she is cutting me some slack. Her patience, however, will only extend so far.

We are enjoying a brief respite from the rain as I drag myself up the stairs to the *Agency*'s offices on the first floor of our bland building in Chaweng. Pimpim, our receptionist, greets me with a wide smile.

"Is Da in?"

I already know the answer to this, but I don't have the energy to come up with anything original to say. My formidable partner is always in early, come rain or shine. Her time-management skills are depressingly good. It's sobering to reflect that when I hired Da some years ago, it was on the basis that she spoke excellent English and had beautifully-shaped breasts. Little did I suspect what other talents lurked beneath that cool exterior. Ah, well.

"*Khun* Da is with a client," Pimpim replies, and offers to make me a coffee.

We talk for a few minutes about nothing in particular. Since Da's door remains closed, I retire to my office, shut myself in, and top up my coffee with a dash of Bells from my stash.

A few minutes later, I hear my partner's voice bidding goodbye to what sounds like a German customer. There is a guttural laugh, then a phlegmy cough, followed by heavy footsteps descending the stairs. A minimum fourteen stone, I'd say. A smoker. He wants to keep tabs on his Thai inamorata because of Teutonic pride rather than through any deep affection. Otherwise, he wouldn't be laughing. Da's not that funny.

And here she is, leaning against my door jamb, regarding me with the same sort of expression that a female biology teacher might have when she is about to dissect a frog: that frown of concentration before she reaches for the scalpel.

She is dressed in a crisp white blouse, a savagely tight blue skirt, and shoes with heels. Her dark hair is bound in a ponytail. Lately, Da has started wearing black-rimmed glasses. Not because she has sight issues (the lenses are plain glass), but rather because she believes they give her a professional air. Personally, I think that, in combination with the ponytail, the spectacles make her look like a college student: the type of student who causes young men to indulge in inappropriate thoughts. And not only young men.

But what do I know?

"You're in early," Da says. "I'm impressed."

"That's good. It's important to me to have your approval."

"Huh."

My witty rejoinders no longer have the impact they once had. But sarcasm is a habit that's hard to break.

However, what my fearsome partner *has* been impressed about is that in all the months the leggy Pimpim has been working for us, I haven't made a pass at her. Da has postulated that I am at last approaching some kind of belated maturity – although she did add that it might be that Katie's disappearance has temporarily suppressed my libido, and therefore I am as emotionally stunted as ever. In fairness, she didn't phrase it in *quite* those terms, but I could tell what she was thinking.

Da's speculations about the state of the Braddock psyche are usually eerily accurate. But in this instance, they are wide of the mark. When one's focus is on murdering someone, the proximity of female legs – even if aesthetically pleasing – hardly registers.

"What's happening today?"

"Why, *Khun* David? Are you considering doing some work?"

"Only if absolutely necessary."

"Well, somebody has to go and see the accountant today."

"*Today?* Does it have to be today?" I catch myself whining.

"Unless you have something more important to do. In which case, tomorrow will be fine."

She says this sweetly enough, but I am attuned to the terrifying undercurrent.

"No, fair enough. I'll go today. Let me finish my coffee first."

"Have you put whisky in that?"

"Only a drop. Pimpim's coffee always tastes a little bitter. But I don't want to upset the girl as she's doing so well."

While I am bullshitting, Da is silently closing my office door. Unfortunately, when it's closed, she is still on this side of it. I sense a Little Chat is coming. Much like my stepmother, Nang, Da is at her most intimidating when she is quiet and reasonable.

She bends over my desk and takes a sip from my mug. I note two things. One, her breasts haven't lost any of their shape and fullness since she gave birth to Pratcha. Two, she has left a lipstick stain on the rim of the mug.

I deem it prudent not to mention either of these observations.

Da sits down and gives me one of *those* looks. You know the sort of look I mean: the sort that shrivels testicles.

"More than a drop," she says.

I light a Marlboro, but otherwise don't respond.

"I couldn't help noticing that you now have three bottles of Bells in here, one of which is currently half-empty."

"What do you mean, you *couldn't help noticing*? Have you been going through my drawers again?"

"I regularly go through your drawers," she replies coolly.

In the face of this blatant truthfulness, all I can manage is, "Well, you shouldn't."

"It's not good for our clients to have you smelling of whisky. And it sets a bad example for Pimpim."

"What? Am I supposed to be a role model for our receptionist now?"

"I don't want her thinking all Western men behave like you. She should be able to keep her illusions alive a little longer. She's still young."

"Disillusionment should start young. It stops you from becoming bitter when you're older."

Da doesn't say anything. She maintains eye contact and waits for me to break.

I break.

"All right. Point taken. I'll run down my stock of Bells and keep it at a single bottle. Happy?"

"Only if you run down your stock of Bells *slowly*." She softens somewhat. "*Khun* David, please don't think me unsympathetic. I am aware of your personal troubles. But, if I don't speak up, nobody else will. You are drinking too much. And we do have a business to run."

I hold out my pack of cigarettes as a peace offering. Usually, she doesn't take one, but today she does. I light it for her.

"I'm sorry," I say.

We smoke in silence for a while. I let my coffee get cold as a sign of my good intentions. She removes my mug when she leaves as a sign that she doesn't believe my good intentions.

"Call the accountant first," she fires over her shoulder.

I have another Marlboro before calling the accountant.

The conversation with Da has depressed me. Correction: it has depressed me *further*.

But worse than that, it has made me reflect.

Other than my talent for cynicism – which some might argue is not a talent at all – my skills are deserting me.

Let's review the list.

We'll start with a minor one. I was formerly a passable saxophone-player. Hardly a virtuoso I should add, but I could stand on stage and blow without people throwing things at me. Today, that prospect would be nerve-racking. Indeed, the very idea of appearing in any kind of public performance is daunting. Consequently, my instrument hasn't been out of its case in a long while. I've given up on it. Or it has given up on me. One of the two.

Moving up a gear, I used to have a reasonable counselling practice that sat alongside my PI work. For a brief period, I was judged to be *the* person to talk to on the island if you were having an emotional crisis. But those glorious days are long gone. Bit-by-bit, I have progressively driven away all my old therapy clients; and new ones don't show up too often. Even people in the grip of despair can recognise that I am unsuitable as a sounding-board for their problems. They see in me not some empathetic healer, but a thing of ice, responding mechanically to their pain.

Then there is the other side of the *David Braddock Agency*. I once considered myself – immodestly, perhaps – a half-decent private investigator. A few complicated knots were untied during my watch. But most of my recent forays into serious detecting have ended in failure. Cases in point: Trask and Fosse. I was unable to track down the American former soldier, Sam Trask, whom one must now presume dead somewhere in Bangkok. Despite my promises to his sister Becky that I would keep looking for him, I have not. I did give a copy of his photograph to my gangster-relative Nathon Lamphongchat and asked that his guys keep their eyes open, but he took it reluctantly. It's understandable that I've heard nothing back. It is a hopeless task, more so now that any trail is long cold. And what of the psychopath Jim Fosse? Do I believe the account of his nemesis Jedediah Reichenbach that Fosse is not, in fact, dead, but has reinvented himself as his brother and is now hiding out somewhere in South East Asia? Where would I even begin to search for him, assuming I was motivated to do so?

The questions are academic. Those files are closed.

But, worst of all, I am no longer either a husband or a father. Such skills as I possessed there are redundant. And why? Because my family consists of a still-born son, a dead wife and a dead daughter.

Residues.

Around me, everyone dies.

And Katie is the most recent addition to the ever-growing list of misplaced Braddocks. The newest exhibit in my display case of loss. The bill-topping finale.

Katie, Katie. Where are you now?

Oh, my daughter.

What miserable, unidentified grave enfolds your remains?

I sit in my study, my fingers moving over the keys of my laptop. It is night, and the rain is back.

As I squint at the screen, Claire hovers over me. By this, incidentally, I mean that she is looking over my shoulder, not that she is floating under the ceiling like some Hollywood travesty of a ghost. No, my wife's spirit has more respect than that for Newton's law of universal gravitation. Although, given that she has no mass, it is not obvious why her feet *should* be on the floor. Regardless, they are. She is also, as usual, wearing her favourite gardening gear: one of my old work shirts, denim jeans, and galoshes. Not the perfect get-up for indoors, but it's pointless asking Claire about it: this is my projection, after all.

"How's it going?"

I push back the chair and crack my knuckles. My neck feels stiff, and there is a troubling numbness in my fingers. "Given that the bulk of human knowledge is supposed to be accessible on the Internet, not so good. Though I've found plenty of cat videos."

"Are you surprised? Did you think researching Grigory Polzin was going to be a simple matter of using Google? He doesn't strike me as the sort of man who would publicise his affairs. He must have many enemies. He's not going to make it easy for them – or for you."

"Well, there are lots of newsfeed pictures of him pressing the flesh with famous people, and some infamous ones. So, he's not *entirely* averse to having his ugly mug out there if it promotes his businesses. It's just –"

Claire perches on the corner of my desk. I'd love to reach out my hand and touch her. But I can't. I would grasp nothingness. And then the illusion that she is actually here with me would be shattered.

I light a cigarette instead, and am careful not to blow the smoke in her direction, since I don't want to see it pass through her.

"How am I going to kill him, Claire? It's one thing to bluff my way through being a private detective, but quite another when it comes to planning and carrying out a murder. That requires real proficiencies, such as our friend Robert Buchanan possesses."

"It's a shame Buchanan's on your blacklist, David. You could have hired him to shoot Polzin for you. That would be much easier."

"Can you pay an assassin to kill one of his own clients? I'd have thought they might have some kind of honour code about that kind of thing. But maybe not. Unless they have a special premium rate.

"Plus, Buchanan's gone invisible again. Nobody could survive in the game as long as he has without being able to vanish into thin air. Anyway, I'd rather Interpol found him – preferably dead – than have him on my payroll. Even though Polzin gave the order, he is the man responsible for what happened to Katie, don't forget."

"I haven't forgotten."

"Besides, I don't want Polzin dispatched by remote control from a distance. I want to look him in the eye before he dies, and do the bastard myself. Up close and extremely personal."

I suck deep on my Marlboro.

Claire waits a few seconds before she asks, "So, how are you going about your research?"

"I started with the usual search engines, plus online newspapers. I've hit upon some good translation software so that I can look at Russian websites and blogs. It recognises Polzin's name in Cyrillic script, highlights it, and points me at the relevant article."

"And what have you discovered so far?"

"There's little information about his companies. Which is to be expected. Corporate Russia is notoriously secret where its dealings are concerned. I am pleased to see, though, that despite their success in the Georgian War this year, the Russian economy is in trouble. In the last few months, the price of Urals heavy crude oil has collapsed, losing seventy-per-cent of its value. That must be hurting Polzin. He has a number of oil and gas pipeline contracts, and many of these are being renegotiated. The ruble's down by about a third against the dollar. That's the reason so many Russkis are cancelling their winter holidays on Samui."

"Spare me the macroeconomics, Mr. Keynes," she says. "What else?"

"Well, Polzin has a sizeable stake in a Macau casino, and he's trying to get traction on building a new gambling joint near the border in Cambodia. But, for reasons that are unclear, that's not taking off."

"All terribly interesting, David, but I don't see how being *au fait* with his commercial interests helps. Have you found out anything of *practical* use? Like, where he lives? What his routines are? How he spends his time? Does he always have bodyguards with him? Those are the sorts of things a professional hit man like Buchanan would be delving into."

"I am well aware of that, Claire," I say, annoyed. "But I have to start somewhere."

She raises an eyebrow.

"I do have the address of his Moscow house. I found that out by rummaging through Katie's papers before I left London. It's a big, tasteless heap - much like the man himself - in one of Moscow's better districts. Crawling with security, no doubt. And the offices of his corporate HQ, ditto."

"Have you considered hiring a Moscow private detective to do some digging for you?"

"I have."

I snuff out my cigarette and am about to take a gulp of whisky. Claire is staring at me disapprovingly, so I pull my hand away from the glass and light another Marlboro instead.

"The problem is, it's impossible to know who is connected to whom in Russia. Or whom to trust. I don't want Polzin to have the slightest whiff of what I am up to. Right now, he probably regards me as some ineffectual, grief-stricken moron, who is incapable of acting. I want him to go on thinking that way. But I haven't completely dismissed the idea of using a Russian private dick if my own efforts come up empty."

"Though, if Polzin is found dead and some Moscow gumshoe has been collecting personal data on him, that gumshoe might be inclined to rat out his foreign employer to the Russian authorities. Then, you'd be squarely in the frame."

"That too. Murdering someone is one thing. Getting away with it is something very different."

"I'm relieved you're planning that far ahead, my love."

Wayan puts her head around the study door.

"Mr. David? I heard your voice. Were you calling me?"

In my surprise, I drop my cigarette. Ash and sparks fly everywhere as I brush at my trousers.

Shit. Have I been talking out loud?

"No – no, Wayan. I'm, um, writing a report, and I was reading it back to myself to make sure it's OK. Sorry, I was – uh – no. Ignore me. I'm fine."

I attempt a smile.

Claire is staring at me, a worried expression on her face.

My housekeeper nods and disappears.

"Be kind to Wayan," my dead wife says. "Whatever else, be kind to her."

I squeeze my eyes closed. When I open them again, Claire has gone.

I am alone. There is only the sound of the rain. And the slug slime of hatred coating my mind.

A voice in my head tells me that my enemy's enemy is my friend.

I knock back a whisky while I try to work out what this means.

Then I check for hairs on the palm of my hand.

As I said, Europeans tend to go mad in Thailand.

Fact.

Claire was a mite hard on me.

The fruits to date of my Polzin research cover several pages: scribble which even I can barely read. My handwritten notes have deteriorated to the point where you'd conclude a doctor had written them. But somewhere in there, amongst the spidery trails, crossings out and starred or underlined items, are details of flights to and from Moscow, addresses, hotels, upmarket bars, businessmen's clubs, transport links and taxi stuff, visa information, weather, and various dos and don'ts gleaned from travel guides.

Useful, but not adequate.

I'm lacking any insight into Polzin's personal schedule. Unless I can find out where he's going to be at a particular time, I'm going to be wandering around his known hang-outs in his home city hoping to bump into him – while sticking out like a sore English thumb. That's not a plan, that's a *hope.*

Then there is the little matter of exactly how I'm going to kill him. Puffing cigarette smoke in his face until he contracts lung cancer would take too long. As would reading him James Joyce's *Ulysses* until he has a bleed in the brain. And, much as it would be satisfying to strangle him with my bare hands, he's a big bastard. Although he's overweight, he's built like a brick shithouse. It would require a large stretch of the imagination to believe I would be able to overpower him physically. A knife? No. Too much blood, too close up. Too *Psycho*. Though death by stabbing would at least be consistent with how his odious son met his end.

Katie ...

No.

Concentrate, Braddock.

Plus, I'm unlikely to find Polzin alone. Unless I can contrive to murder him in his sleep. Even then, he might have some flinty-faced Svetlana in bed with him, if not his blimp of a wife.

And when Polzin is not in the Land of Nod, he's usually accompanied by bodyguards. *Armed* bodyguards. Two of them, perhaps? Or three? He may even be packing a piece himself. It could be like the Gunfight at the OK Corral, but with one significant difference: I've never fired a gun in anger before.

It's going to have to be a gun, though, isn't it? I don't have the wherewithal to execute an effective bomb plot. Not unless I'm going to join the Taliban or ISIS for a crash apprenticeship.

How am I going to get hold of a pistol and ammunition in Moscow?

How am I going to make my escape after the deed is done?

Does it even matter if I do escape?

Ah, the subjugating power of thought. So much to consider. And the more I contemplate my to-do list, the longer it gets. I feel crushed beneath the chariot wheels of my own logic.

I must not become discouraged.

Instead, I will have another Marlboro.

My enemy's enemy is my friend. This phrase keeps chasing around inside my head, searching for a home.

Hmmn.

A man like Polzin must have many enemies who hate him as much as I do. Well, maybe they don't hate him quite so much. But perhaps they hate him enough to be an ally.

That's what I need: help. Of a particular type. Someone who can furnish me with the sort of on-the-ground information which it is difficult for me, an outsider, to access. Someone motivated to assist me.

I stub out my cigarette, leave the Bells alone, and go back to my laptop.

Tap-tap-tap.

See, I don't *always* require alcohol to function.

2

"Calm, gentle, passionless as he appeared, there was yet, we fear, a quiet depth of malice, hitherto latent, but active now, in this unfortunate old man, which led him to imagine a more intimate revenge than any mortal had ever wreaked upon an enemy."

Nathaniel Hawthorne, The Scarlett Letter

It's four-thirty in the morning when I finally switch off my computer.

I light a Marlboro and have the whisky that I've been denying myself for the last few hours.

My time on the Internet has been productive. The tell-tale sign of that, is that although I am barely capable of coherent thought, my head is still buzzing. A minor breakthrough has been achieved, which may turn out to be a major one, though much research remains to be done.

After focusing my search activities on Polzin's domestic competitors, one name has come to the fore: *Fyodor Orlov*. The relationship between these two oligarchs, so far as I can tell, is not one of simple business rivalry. If reports are to be believed, they loathe each other. The fact that they operate in the same niches, and compete for the same state favours, does not fully explain the mutual animosity. Something personal must have happened for them to want to use every opportunity to undermine each other. I've not been able to uncover what that is. Maybe further digging will throw up the cause.

But one significant factor gives me reason to home in on Orlov. *I've met him.*

Some years ago, my Russian kick-boxing chum, Vlad, asked me to act as an interpreter in a business negotiation between Orlov – Vlad's boss – and Thongchai Rattanakorn, Samui's top Mafia Godfather. The purpose of the meeting was for the Thai and Russian partners to see each other face to face. The project they were seeking to get off the ground was the construction of a new jetty at Na Thon, as a prelude to a hoped-for investment in an airport on the Surat Thani mainland. As it turned out, the scheme never made it off the ground and I didn't have to participate further. That was something of a relief to me since my relationship with Rattanakorn was, shall we say, complicated, and not helped by the fact that Rattanakorn's wife Nittha had a crush on me at the time. Had the Samui gangster ever had wind of *that*, he would also have had a crush on me – but his would have involved the use of several tons of concrete.

Anyway.

That gathering of the great and the bad was one of those cat-and-mouse affairs where each side knows exactly what is going on, but they want to see the whites of each other's eyes. Doubtless, this is to assess how skilled their chosen associate is at close-proximity lying.

I puff my cigarette, and try to visualise Orlov. I remember him as a man in late middle-age, well-preserved, slicked-back hair, sharp-suited and sharp-witted. Intelligent. Crafty. A sense of humour tending towards the lethal. Excellent command of the English language. (Unlike his local boy Vlad. Although, in fairness, Vlad's Anglo-Saxon speaking skills have improved as a result of his squiring innumerable European Muay Thai groupies and some of the more educated Thai bar girls – who, no doubt, taught him more than English.)

I wonder.

I wonder if Orlov would be prepared to help me plant Polzin in the ground. If I can persuade him to trust me enough to co-operate, that is.

But first, I will speak to Vlad.

No. Second, I will speak to Vlad.

First, I'd better get some sleep. I am powering-down faster than a laptop with a flat battery.

It's started raining again, and I'm faffing around at the *Agency*.

Naturally, I got in late. But I sidestepped the wrath of Da by volunteering to debrief a client on our surveillance of his Samui girlfriend: good news for him, for a refreshing change. Da had sniffed my breath and concluded I would just about pass muster, so she handed me the baton and retired to her office.

Now that our happy customer has left, I'm on the Internet behind my closed door, swotting up some more on Fyodor Orlov. The Bells has worked its way out of my drawer and is pouring itself into my coffee mug while I pretend not to notice.

Today's copy of the *Nation* is unread on my desk. Since the main headline is about a train derailment near Bangkok where nobody was hurt or injured, it's a fair bet that there's not much happening in Thailand at present. Thai trains generally trundle along so slowly that nobody commits suicide by throwing themselves underneath one. Not if their intention is serious. And, if all they're doing is seeking attention, posting a politically-incorrect tweet would do a better job.

My concentration is not great. Hardly surprising, since I've had little sleep.

Memories of Katie are floating around in the semi-derelict warehouse of the Braddock brain. I let the current carry me.

The projector cranks up, and the screen reveals me in London, earlier this year, accompanying Katie to the opening night of a production of Shakespeare's *Richard III* at one of the capital's less-frequented theatres. A friend of Katie's was appearing in a small part in this underfunded extravaganza and she had been supplied with complimentary tickets, presumably so there would be at least *someone* watching when the curtain rose. *Dickie 3* had always been one of my favourite Bard plays, but I suspected that this performance would put me off it permanently, or at best give me the hump.

As I feared, the house was somewhat sparsely populated as a rather pudgy guy wearing too much stage makeup started swinging around on crutches and declaiming on loured clouds and the Yorkist sun. Katie's rather fey amigo – as the Duke of Clarence – was good at rolling his eyes and his arse but rather less accomplished in rolling his *r*s. Happily for all of us, the good duke was soon submerged in a barrel of Malmsey, and thereafter we proceeded at a lame and unfashionable pace towards Dickie's interment under a Leicester car park. But not before the devious monarch had shouted himself hoarse demanding a horse.

"It wasn't *great*, was it?" Katie had asked afterwards, with a click of her tongue.

"Well, it was their first night," I said charitably.

Since then, I have been officially *off* Shakespeare.

The film changes to one of our many arm-in-arm walks around London, then inexplicably flips back to footage of a seven-year-old Katie at a petting zoo; then to my sobbing daughter with a grazed knee; then to that courtroom at the Old Bailey where ...

I take a swig of my laced coffee.

Enough.

Time to make my excuses to Da and go to see Vlad – titled *The Impaler* by those who have been unfortunate enough to encounter him in the ring. Or in the bedroom.

Pimpim informs me that *Khun* Da has slipped out for a while.

Good. That's one less lie I have to tell.

Although Vlad does his fighting at the Chaweng Muay Thai Boxing Stadium, he trains at a practice ring in Lamai. The Lamai facility is popular with the more muscle-bound kick-boxers, since the owner is good at getting his hands not only on dodgy steroids, but on other chemical performance enhancers too. I understand that his prices are reasonable and, as he has a cosy relationship with local law enforcement, if you buy from him you're unlikely to be busted. The proximity of a cornucopia of girly bars doubtless adds to the attraction for those wishing to wind down after a heavy practice session.

I park my jeep in Lamai town centre, where they are starting to set up for the night market, and proceed on foot to *Punchy Joe's Gym*. I've tried ringing my Russian friend to let him know I'm coming, but he's not answering. As it's afternoon, it's unlikely he's still nursing a hangover or screwing anyone. And although it's possible Vlad is at the *Muscovite Girls* nightclub discharging his managerial duties, he's more likely to be at *Punchy Joe's*. When he's at the gym, he can bask in his minor celebrity status while giving his body an adrenaline workout, whereas at the club all he would be able to do at this time of day is check whether the morning cleaners have done a good job hosing down last night's excesses. And that's not really his thing. Doubtless, he'll have delegated that job to some underpaid flunkey.

It's no longer raining, but in the potholed dirt side road to the gym the water is still lying in deep puddles, requiring some careful footwork to avoid having my shoes and chinos coated in red mud. The neighbouring girly bars are in restocking mode – that's alcohol, not girls, you understand – and the garish signage is switched off to save power; the interiors dark apart from the glow from the fridges. The tatty drinking establishment next to *Punchy Joe's*, I note, has a cage out front for one of its exotic dancers to writhe around in. *Tasteful*.

An old Thai guy is leaning on a mop by the entrance.

"Is Vlad around?"

"I haven't seen him," he says, and returns to his doleful contemplation of the floor.

I catch sight of Ivan, one of Vlad's buddies, in the gloom at the back of the gym, so make my way towards him. Ivan is from Saint Petersburg, and is another Muay Thai fighter. He once made the mistake of allowing his weight to stray into the Heavy Weight Class, and subsequently had his butt kicked savagely by Vlad. Since then, he's been careful to ensure he remains in the Cruiser Weight Class to avoid further painful, and potentially life-threatening, humiliations.

Ivan is chatting to Ariel, a Norwegian boxer of Amazonian proportions. She appears to be taking time out from teaching two female *farang* students how to avoid losing teeth. Vlad once told me that Ariel has a tattoo of a seashell on her inner thigh, and that if you press your ear to it you can hear the sea. "And smell it," he added, somewhat unkindly.

Ariel has been smoking but, as I approach, she puts out her cigarette and instructs her quaking charges it's time to get back to work. One of them climbs gingerly into the ring with her. I think of lambs and slaughter.

"Afternoon, Ivan," I say, lighting a Marlboro.

"Ah, Braddock." He smirks at me, then performs three rapid air-punches right in front of my face. "The famous Samui private ear."

"Private *eye*."

"Whatever."

"Is Vlad here?"

"No."

"Can you be a little more specific? Or helpful?"

"He's in Moscow. Flew there last week. His uncle has died."

"Oh, I'm sorry to hear that." I truly *am* sorry to hear that. But not for compassionate reasons. For purely selfish ones. "When will he be back?"

Ivan shrugs. "I don't know. Could be some time."

"Who's taking care of *Muscovite Girls* while he's away?"

"I am," he says proudly, and sticks out his chest.

"Congratulations, Ivan. An excellent career move for a Cruiser." I consider patting him on the shoulder, but he's smelly and perspiring. Though it's not just him. The whole place reeks of sweat and testosterone. It's enough to put a drinking man off his Bells. Well, nearly.

"Do you have a phone number for Vlad in Russia? I need to speak to him."

"Is it urgent?"

"Yup."

"Can I help?"

"Nope."

"It's not about drugs then?"

"Not this time."

He pulls off his gloves, digs a cell phone out of his bag, and gives me *The Impaler*'s number.

"Are you coming to the Stadium this Saturday, Mr. Private Eye?"

"Do you have a match, Ivan?"

"Yes. I'm up against a Georgian. Top billing. He's one of the best –"

"Probably not, then," I say. "But good luck. Though I'm sure you won't need it."

He snorts.

"Thanks for the number."

I find a nearby bar that doesn't have a cage outside it, and order a beer from a large Thai lady who winks at me and tells me she is off work at seven. I express my regrets that I have a prior engagement, then buy her a drink.

I check my watch. It's late morning in Moscow, so it should be a reasonable time to call Vlad. I hope he's not at the funeral.

He answers after a few rings.

"Hello. Vlad speaking."

"Hi, Vlad. It's Braddock."

"Ah, Braddock. A surprise." He sounds half-asleep. Or stunned.

"I'm sorry to hear about your uncle. My condolences to you and your family."

"Thank you. It was expected. He has been sick for a long time. But still a shock."

"I understand. Is there a lot to do?" *Hurry up and get back to Samui.*

"Yes. A lot. My uncle was my mother's brother. He has been taking care of my mother for many years – ever since my father died. My mother is also not so healthy."

"I'm sorry to hear that too." *Hurry up and get back to Samui. I have a Russian to kill.*

"My uncle was a good man. But not so good with money. So, I have many things to sort out. And I have to make sure my mother is OK. It has hit her hard."

"Do you have any brothers or sisters who can help?" *So that you can get back to Samui quicker.*

"No, only me."

Shit. "So, you could be some time in Moscow?"

"Yes."

"But you don't know how long?" *This is not sounding particularly empathetic, Braddock.*

"No."

"Listen, Vlad, I don't want to intrude on your grief." *Better, Braddock.*

"Is OK."

"I do need to talk to you, however. About your boss, Mr. Orlov."

"I can talk now. I have time. What about Mr. Orlov?"

"No, it's not something I can speak about over the phone."

There is a pause. "Ah. I understand."

I'm sure he does. The circles Vlad moves in, he appreciates some things should not be discussed over an open phone line.

"Good."

"Then, we will talk as soon as I am back on Samui. Best I can suggest."

"It can wait." *It can't, but it will sodding have to.* "Do what you have to do in Moscow. Family is important."

"Yes. Family is the most important. I will let you know when I am coming back."

"Thank you. Please give your mother my best wishes."

"Did Ivan give you my number?"

"Yes."

"He is a good man, Ivan."

"He's all right," I say.

I'm parked outside *Wat Son*, the Old Monk's former temple. It's more run-down than it was in his day. The existing senior monk lacks his predecessor's iron discipline on housekeeping matters, and evidently does not inspire the same fear in his colleagues. Or, I should say, respect.

I miss the grumpy old bugger. I miss him cadging my cigarettes, and spouting incomprehensible phrases on the nature of reality. Most of all, I pine for his barbed comments, his never-ending criticism of my personal behaviour, and the deadpan irony with which he used to describe me as the *White Tathagata*. Under his unforgiving tutelage, I made some progress in understanding what Buddhism is really about, and in finding some inner peace. Fat chance of that now.

Spirituality is something else that I've flushed down the toilet in recent years. Though it's hardly surprising I've lost my faith in the retributive power of karma. If karma does work, then it works in a bloody strange way, and too slowly for my liking. So many good people I loved have met with horrible, undeserved deaths – Claire, Anna, and Katie, to name a few. Meanwhile, the planet's scumbags go about their toxic business as usual. Like Grigory Polzin and Robert Buchanan, for instance. And Jim Fosse, if Jedediah Reichenbach's theory is correct.

Accordingly, I'm not about to rely on the universe, the British police, Interpol, the Flying Spaghetti Monster, or the vagaries of chance to put right the wrongdoings of evil men. I'm not waiting on the dock for the boat to come in: I'm going to swim out to meet it. And I'll be swimming out *armed*.

Wat Son appears sad in the rain. Its paint is peeling, its gravel unraked, its shrubbery run amok. One of the *nagas* is missing part of its head. Sections of the monks' dining hall roof are being consumed by moss. There is an air of slow collapse about the whole place.

Hardly anybody is about. A *soi* dog chews its hind-quarters. An orange-robed monk whittles wood beneath an awning. Two young *farang* women, huddled under a faded hotel umbrella, hurry past my car in search of shelter, their flip-flops sloshing through the water. As I watch their disappearing backs, I see they both sport Siamese blessing tattoos on their shoulders, and wonder if they have a clue what the Thai letters mean. One rather mischievous island tattoo artist of my acquaintance used to engrave all manner of rude words on the bodies of clients who upset him, or who haggled too hard on price. Sadly, he's moved away. You have to get your fun where you can.

What am I doing here?

A kindly interpretation would be that I am gathering my thoughts after my disappointment at learning of Vlad's prolonged absence.

But that's not it.

I'm procrastinating, delaying my return to the office.

And, perchance, indulging in a little sentimental reflection on the good old days: the days when I still harboured hope for the future.

I ram my jeep in gear and skid off into the rain. The *farang* girls get splashed as I drive by them.

Life's a bitch, ain't it?

On Christmas Eve, I receive a call from Hitomi Tanaka in New York.

Hitomi is a petite, sexy Japanese-American, and another of my inconclusive cases. Her husband Akira vanished last summer in Dubai while filming a documentary about Russian money-laundering. The working hypothesis is that he was assassinated on the orders of some Russki or Arab who had a lot at stake. *My* further hypothesis – though Interpol is not convinced – is that the man who carried out the killing was Captain Nemo aka Robert Buchanan aka Some Other Bloody Alias.

But not only have I failed to find her husband, I have also failed to seduce her. Fortunately, carnal pleasure is not high on my priority list at present. In fact, it doesn't feature. And it is a long way to New York, even for what I'm sure would be a memorable session.

"I figured I may not be able to get hold of you tomorrow, David," she says. "So, I'm ringing now to wish you a Happy Christmas."

"And to you, Hitomi. Your first Christmas without Akira." She doesn't respond, so I continue. "I presume you haven't heard anything?"

"No. Nothing."

"I'm sorry, sweetheart, this must all still be fresh for you. Are you spending the day with relatives and friends?"

"No. I can't face the hugs, the concerned looks, and the expressions of sympathy. I'm spending tomorrow on my own in my apartment with a bottle of something and a pack of cigarettes."

"Sounds like the perfect Yuletide to me."

"To tell you the truth, I was half-minded to jump on a plane to Thailand and have Christmas with you. But then I thought that might be inappropriate."

"It would hardly be the most inappropriate thing I've done."

She giggles at this. "It would hardly be the most inappropriate thing I've done either. What are you doing now?"

"Drinking whisky."

"Me too."

"You're starting early."

"It's not so early. Are you smoking one of your Marlboros?"

"Of course."

"Wait a second, and I'll join you. Though I don't have Marlboros so we can't be in perfect synch."

"I've always considered simultaneous orgasm overrated anyway."

I hear her light up. Then she says, "How are you coping, David? About Katie, I mean."

"Some days are better than others. But, I guess, I'm still pretty raw. I hassle the police every few days, but that's more out of habit than out of a belief that anything will come of it."

"We have a lot in common."

"Yes."

A beat.

"I wish I'd taken that flight to Thailand a few days ago."

"So do I."

"You still fancy me, then?"

Later, Claire mimics her. "*You still fancy me, then?*"

I don't say anything.

"I don't like that Tanaka woman."

"You astonish me."

"How long were the pair of you on the phone?"

"About an hour."

"Did she make you hard?"

"Not really."

"Liar."

Christmas morning, I'm wide awake at five o'clock, and fidgeting. So, I get up. Dawn is still an hour away, but it looks like it's going to be a sunny day. The island can dry out. I, on the other hand, have no intention of drying out.

Wayan hears me banging around in the apartment, and appears in her robe.

"Is everything all right, Mr. David?"

"Yes, fine, Wayan. I can't sleep any more. But you go back to bed. It's early. I'm going out for a few hours. We'll exchange presents after lunch, if that's OK with you."

"Would you like me to make you some breakfast before you leave?"

"Nah. I'll have something at the Belgian bakery. They're open at six. Then I might go to the beach or the temple. Don't worry about me. I'll see you later."

She comes over and gives me a hug. "Happy Christmas, Mr. David," she says.

I squeeze her and tear up a little. If only things could be different. Or how they were before Robert Buchanan stepped back into her life. If only I were adequate to the task of assuaging her guilt. *So many if only*s.

I kiss her on the top of her head, and wish her a Happy Christmas in return. It's all I can trust myself to say. A dam may burst otherwise.

I drive down to the main road. In a few minutes, I'm at the Chinatown part of Mae Nam, where on Thursdays they hold a Walking Street Market which is popular with tourists: cheap cocktails, bugs on sticks, coconut ice cream, flaccid pizza, and all manner of Thai tat. But this morning, almost every building is shuttered.

I park the jeep in the cul de sac where the *Boulangerie Belge* is sited. The bakery is starting to stir, despite the fact that it's not yet six and the sky is only now beginning to pale. The smell of fresh-baked bread fills the air: the baker will already have been up for hours, Christmas or not. While the tables are being laid out, I light a Marlboro and embark on a short stroll to the nearby twenty-four-hour *Family Mart* where I restock on cigarettes and whisky. I buy two bottles of Johnny Walker and clear them out of Marlboros. I dump these in the back of my jeep before taking a seat at one of the *Boulangerie*'s outside tables.

Malee appears to take my order. She is the Belgian owner's live-in girlfriend. Although she is in her early thirties, if it weren't for the dark morning rings under her eyes, she could pass for sixteen. Her tight, petite body is clad in an equally tight black lace-trimmed dress, and she has a set of red felt reindeer antlers pinned in her hair: befittingly seasonal. I had occasion to sleep with her once, and I remember the event for two reasons. One, her breathtaking bendiness. And, two, the constant stream of words that flowed from her mouth, before, during and after. Malee keeps up a ceaseless internal dialogue - apparently in English - which regularly spills out into the external world, regardless of the topic and whether anyone is listening. Despite her language skills, I suspect that her IQ only barely creeps into double figures, which makes me wonder whether our lovemaking can be properly described as consensual on her part. Not that she appeared in any way unhappy about it. Hard to tell though, as she never either frowns or smiles. She simply – talks.

She says, "Ah, David! Sàwàt-dii khâ. Happy Christmas for you. My first customer, khâ. Khop khun khâ. I no see you for long time, khâ. I kiss you?"

"Yes."

"Khâ."

She kisses me enthusiastically. The scent of frangipani wafts off her, subtly enhanced with base notes of butter, dough and chocolate.

To business: she brandishes her order pad. "What you want?"

"Are you on the menu, Malee?" I say.

"Yes." She nods solemnly. "My boyfriend Louis in France for Christmas. So, you can have me if you come back eleven o'clock, *khâ*. After close. Finish early today. Have room upstairs."

"Right." Not the sort of conversation one expects to have on Christmas morning. This definitely wouldn't happen in England.

"You have condoms, khâ?"

"I ... I can get some."

"Condoms good. You want breakfast? Coffee?"

"Er, yes, please. Black coffee. And croissant."

"You want fruit also?" she continues in the same serious stream-of-consciousness tone in which she enquired about the condoms.

"Yes. Why not? I'm having everything else."

Malee jots down my order. Then she says, "Have to finish in bedroom at one o'clock. OK?"

"OK. Yes. Fine. One o'clock finish."

I light another Marlboro and wonder where I can buy a gag.

On the grass verge opposite the bakery, some fighting cocks are strutting around in their cages. They appear unconcerned by the presence of a black cat grooming herself under a cashew nut tree. The area is strewn with polystyrene food containers and empty water bottles. When Louis is around, he is scrupulous about cleaning up any litter. I guess standards have slipped since he boarded the flight to Brussels.

I suppose I should feel guilty at the prospect of seducing his girlfriend. If seduction is the right word. Malee evidently puts copulating in the same pigeonhole as selling a baguette: just another transaction. Besides, I tell myself, if Louis had had the foresight to engage the *David Braddock Agency* to keep an eye on his errant inamorata, then professional ethics would have prevented me from shagging her. So, it's his own fault, really.

And, by the way, I don't think I'll be the only one.

Other customers begin to arrive, and Malee buzzes around addressing them in her flat monotone. Her figure, I note, is not unlike Hitomi's. Later, if I'm having trouble maintaining an erection, I can close my eyes and pretend Malee is speaking Japanese.

Enough of that.

My breakfast turns up, and I begin ripping croissants apart.

EVERYONE DIES

After I've paid for my *petit déjeuner*, Malee hands me a slip of paper which reads: *11.00am, 2,000 Baht.*

When I return to the *Family Mart* to purchase a box of extra-safe prophylactics, I bump into Jules, a crusty, unmarried Frenchman in his sixties, who owns a café bar in the Chinatown street of Mae Nam. He is also buying condoms. (What has Christ's birth come to?) As, like myself, he has nothing much to do for a while, he invites me to walk back with him to his place and crack open a bottle of something. The bottle in question turns out to be a 12-year-old Glenlivet. And over the next few hours, we drink the lot.

I've been acquainted with Jules for several years. He is short, has a mournful, ruddy face, a nose like a rambutan, a shaved head, and a stomach you could rest your pint on. He hates a wide variety of nationalities and cultures, but views the Thais and British as acceptable provided they make an effort to speak his *lingua franca* – which I do. When he's in a good mood, as he is today, he's the perfect host. When he's not, he's irascible and mean. One of these days, I tell him, he's going to land himself in real trouble.

And the most likely source of that trouble will be the pistol he keeps under the bar, 'in case any Arab comes in'.

Before we've had too much to drink, I ask him about his gun, and he gives me a lesson in assembling and disassembling it, and some pointers about how not to blow your own head off. I may need to talk to him again when we're both sober, although I doubt he's going to be able to help me lay hands on a firearm in Moscow. Still, you never know.

Since I don't think I am capable of talking to Wayan over the phone without slurring my speech, I send her a text message to say I won't be home until around one-thirty.

The alcohol consumed has thus given me a double dilemma. Will I be able to perform with Malee? And will I be able to appear adequately sober over lunch with Wayan?

By the time ten-fifty has come, Jules and I have set the world to rights and decided that the *Entente Cordiale* remains intact. Moreover, I have convinced myself that I can manage both Malee and Wayan – though for different things, obviously.

Before I leave, Jules confides to me that he is seeing Malee at one-thirty, so he'd better sober up.

"Don't you feel awkward about sleeping with Louis' girlfriend, Jules?" I ask him. "Louis is a near-neighbour of yours, after all."

He makes a typical Gallic movement of the shoulders. "If he leaves a girl like that on her own, what can he expect? Anyway, he is from Belgium. That's not even a proper country."

Malee greets me with a cup of coffee, locks the street door and leads me upstairs. While I'm sipping my coffee, she tells me how her morning went, what time they sold the last croissant, what sort of a year it's been, and how much the rents are going up in Bophut. Then she takes my coffee cup, and we strip off. I ask her if she wouldn't mind not talking during sex as I've been drinking whisky and I will need to concentrate. She tells me that's OK, and she is as good as her word, only picking up the topic of Bophut rents after we have our clothes on again.

By that time, we've been at it off-and-on for nearly two hours, including cigarette breaks – which is pretty astonishing when I consider the whisky that's chugging around inside me. And it was really rather pleasant. When Malee is silent, she is great company. Plus, she was every bit as elastic as I remembered. I hardly needed to fantasise about Hitomi at all.

I leave her three thousand Baht, and she tells me that she will be out this evening, but if I want to come back her pretty auntie will be here, and she only charges one thousand Baht. I thank her, and say I will think about it.

I wonder if she will have time to change the sheets before Jules arrives.

Now, there is probably something awfully sacrilegious about all this on the day of Our Lord's birth – on a par with being fellated by your married cousin in the back of the hearse after a relative's funeral – but, given what else has been going on in my life recently, a spot of illicit horizontal jogging hardly registers on my morality meter.

Sod it.

I'll repent later.

Wayan and I have Christmas dinner together. The only thing that's missing from the traditional plate is Brussels sprouts, and that's no great loss since it means I won't be farting tomorrow. All-in-all, it's a pretty impressive effort considering it's been prepared by a woman from Bali who is more comfortable with rice and noodles.

After my assignation with the limber Malee, I drove home along the back road *very* slowly, and I sucked my way through half-a-pack of mints before I entered our apartment. Then, after a hurried hello to Wayan, I dived straight into the shower, so that when we sat down at table, I was both presentable and passably coherent.

If Wayan did notice anything untoward, she was diplomatically mute.

Once we've cleared away the dirty dishes, we swap presents. She has bought me a flashy, old-fashioned lighter, and a Panama hat to replace my old one which would not look out of place on a scarecrow. My gifts for her are, as ever, unimaginative – several shop-wrapped boxes of body lotion, hand cream, perfume, shampoo and conditioner, all purchased on the advice of commission-hungry salesgirls.

After the wrapping paper has been binned, Wayan says she is going out to pick up some groceries as we are running low on fruit and vegetables. This is fine, as it means I can bring the bottles of Johnny Walker up from the jeep without her seeing, and tuck them away somewhere for later. Later, Wayan is going over to Da's for the evening (I was invited too, but politely declined), which means I will have a few hours to myself.

Perhaps I will drop by the bakery and see Malee's auntie if I'm still sober enough to keep my jeep on the road, and if I can remember where I put the opened box of condoms.

Comes the nightfall, comes the rain: but only a light spattering. Not enough to prevent Wayan jumping on her bike to go to Da's.

I'm sitting on my balcony with a fresh pack of Marlboros and one of the bottles of Johnny Walker to keep me company. I light a cancer stick with my new lighter whose cover closes with a satisfying click.

My hands have a slight tremble, and even relaxing my shoulders and arms has no noticeable effect. Despite the air-cooling effect of the drizzle, I'm sweating and my heartbeat is a tad irregular. Not sufficient to give me any serious concern for my well-being, but enough to make me reach for another dosage of therapeutic whisky to help me relax. I believe the term is 'self-medication'.

I am glad I made my Christmas well-wishing phone calls earlier, because now I couldn't face the prospect of any *faux-jolly* conversations over a crackly line. My concentration is shot, and I wouldn't be able to sound even vaguely normal.

My call to Natalie was cordial, and she put Jenny on the phone to thank her kindly uncle for his presents, one of which she had been allowed to open on Christmas Eve. The contrast of my little niece's experience of today with mine brought tears to my eyes, and has no doubt contributed to my current depressed mood. Misery is always uncomfortable around happiness.

Nang was remorselessly chirpy during our obligatory chat, until we reached the part where she began hectoring me about the fact that I haven't read my father's manuscript.

"And it's not like you don't have the time," she said. "What on earth do you do with yourself when you're not at the office?"

I could hardly explain that planning the killing of a Russian oligarch eats up a lot of my hours, and the rest of my time is spent either gossiping with my dead wife or trying to drink myself unconscious. So, I told her that I'd been a mite emotional lately, and that I thought re-opening my family's history might be too much for me. She was rightly suspicious of such a candid declaration of feeling from her closed-off stepson but, this being the season of goodwill, she let it go.

I stub out my Marlboro and light another one.

Claire is with me on the balcony, observing my movements with barely-disguised concern.

"It might be a good idea if you went out, David. This brooding alone isn't helping matters."

"It's raining."

"It's not raining that hard."

"Where would I go?"

"You can always pop over and see Malee's auntie for an hour or two. That might cheer you up. And her prices are reasonable."

I cough. "Listen, Claire, about Malee this morning –"

Claire shakes her head and says, in a kindly voice, "You are a disgusting animal, David Braddock. You are so fortunate that I still love you."

I take a deep breath, then two quick puffs on my cigarette. This just about forestalls any sobbing.

"I miss Katie, Claire. Of all the people I've spoken to today, hers is the voice I truly wanted to hear."

"That's how sorrow seizes us, David. Grief is not the presence of some red-clawed monster, looming up at us in the night. In point of fact, it's not a presence at all. It's an absence. The absence of something good."

"And a permanent absence."

"Yes."

"I wish I could hold you, Claire. I wish I could hold *someone.*"

"Now you really do sound like a sad drunk. I'm a ghost, my love. You can't touch a ghost. Pull yourself together. You have things to do."

"Like what?"

"Like learning how to fire a gun."

3

"People pay for what they do, and still more for what they have allowed themselves to become. And they pay for it very simply; by the lives they lead."
James Baldwin

It's one of those days at the *David Braddock Agency.*

Belgian Louis pitches up in an agitated state, and asks to see me. Pimpim shows him into my office and exits, taking her long legs with her.

The citizens of Flanders not being renowned for their small talk, Louis speedily proceeds to the nub of his visit.

"I want someone to keep an eye on Malee for me."

"Put her under surveillance, you mean? I'm guessing she doesn't need a nanny."

Even with Louis' firm grasp of the English language, my subtle wit is wasted on him, so I snuff out my Marlboro and attempt to look businesslike.

"Fill me in."

"I'm suspicious. Malee's been going out a lot recently. Supposedly with her girlfriends. But, naturally, if something *is* going on, they'll cover for her.

"Also, she seems to have a lot of cash on her these days, and I don't think it's coming out of the till."

"I see."

"I have to go to Bangkok for a few days, and I want you to watch her for me – follow her – while I'm away. Tell me what she gets up to. Whom she meets."

"Right."

"Can you do that? I leave on Wednesday."

"The only problem, Louis, is that my work diary is clogged at present. You're lucky I had a spare half-hour to see you this morning."

"Oh."

I tap the side of my head for a few seconds, as if I'm deep in thought.

"Can you wait a few minutes?"

"Yes."

"Let me talk to my partner. See what we can do."

I leave Louis sitting there, and go into Da's office, closing the door behind me. She peers up from her papers.

"Yes?"

"Louis from the Belgian bakery is next door. He wants us to watch his girlfriend Malee for him for a few days while he's in Bangkok. He's worried she might be fooling around."

"So? You can handle that, David, surely. Or are you concerned it will interfere with your drinking?"

"It's not that." I scratch my chin, and weigh my words carefully. Da's stare is making me nervous. "Let's say, I have a conflict of interest so far as Malee is concerned."

"Are you screwing her?"

"No, I'm not," I reply. "At least, not since Christmas Day."

Da raises her eyebrows. "You have an unusual way of celebrating one of your major religious festivals, I must say. Did this event happen while Wayan was at my house?"

"No. Before lunch, if you must know."

"Did you pay her?"

"Certainly *not*," I say, with as much indignity as I can muster. She maintains unblinking eye contact, so I add, "I may have tipped her afterwards. But that's not the same thing."

Da sighs like the worst kind of ham actress. "I had begun to hope, with everything that has gone on, that you might be attaining some sort of maturity in your relationships. It's disappointing that you are regressing."

"Not that it's any of your business, Da, but for your information, that was the first and only time my genitals have seen any action since German Gretchen left the island, over a year-and-a-half ago."

She raises a hand. "Please, don't make me contemplate your genitals, David. I haven't had lunch yet." A loud outbreath of resignation from Mrs. Pintaraporn. "Very well. Send Mr. Louis in to see me. I'll pick it up from here."

"Thank you."

"After all, we can't have you grappling with an ethical dilemma, can we? You're not equipped to handle it."

As I reach the door, she says, "David?"

"Yes?"

"Is that true? About there being no-one since the German woman?"

"Yes," I reply gruffly. "Why?"

The ghost of a shrug from Da.

"Interesting."

Her eyes sparkle. She's not smiling. But she is really.

After I've given Louis the glad tidings and ushered him into Da's office, I phone Jules.

"Just to let you know, Jules, that Louis is asking my *Agency* to put a tail on Malee. He's fretting that she might be seeing someone. So, if that's *you*, you might want to lie low for a while, starting today. Especially avoid her while he's in Bangkok. We don't want an international incident in Mae Nam."

"I am grateful for your advice, *mon brave*," he says. "I owe you."

"Good. Because I need your wise counsel on the subject of guns."

"I am happy to talk about *pistolets* any time. Come over and we'll have a drink or three."

"I will."

Koh Samui has three shooting ranges. Thais love their guns, and there are plenty of tourists who fancy themselves as Liam Neeson. Blowing the crap out of targets makes a change from loafing on a beach, and, for the adrenaline junkie, it's a step up from the island's go-kart racing.

Jules recommended I try the one outside Chaweng, as they have knowledgeable staff, a wide array of weaponry, and thus far no-one has been killed there. Not officially, anyway.

It's a start. I want to have a few more conversations with my French friend on the subject of firearms, but I need to take it steady. If I appear too keen, he might begin to wonder about my sudden interest in matters of death-dealing.

I'm now back at the range for my eighth session, and Udom, my designated instructor, greets me with a cheery wave.

My initial visit here was daunting. Did I want to learn how to fire a pistol, or a revolver, or a rifle? Or perhaps I'd like to have a try with a semi-automatic? When Udom indicated the guns behind the glass, my stomach knotted. The enormity of what I was planning to do hit me properly for the first time.

I'm going to kill a man in cold blood. And these are the tools of my new trade.

A wave of nausea broke over me, and I experienced some difficulty keeping my twitching hands still. Udom looked worried at my reaction.

"You're sweating, *Khun* David," he said. "Are you all right?"

"I have a slight fever," I replied. "Nothing serious."

He must have smelled the alcohol on my breath, because he said, "As this is your first time with us, maybe not the semi-automatics. Safer with one bullet at a time."

"Agreed."

"What about a rifle?"

I want to shoot Polzin at close range. "No. A hand-gun."

"OK. As you can see, we have a .357 Magnum, or a .44 Magnum. Hand cannons. Like in the *Dirty Harry* movies. Enormously popular. How about one of those?"

"Something a little less Hollywood, Udom. I'm not proposing to demolish a building."

He muttered something to one of his colleagues, and a sleek black pistol was passed through the window-hatch. Udom checked it wasn't loaded, then gave it to me.

"How about this one?"

I turned it over in my hands and felt the weight. Despite the heat of the day, the metal was cold.

"What's this?"

"A Glock. Nine millimetre."

"How much?"

He consulted his chart. "With ten bullets, fifteen hundred Baht."

"Good."

Now, I'm familiar with the drill. How to stand. How to load and hold the weapon. Where not to point it. How to deal with the recoil.

But shooting at a human target will be vastly different from firing at a paper one.

Half of January has gone.

As has all of Wayan.

She's in Bali, and will be there for several weeks more. Or forever. My estimate is that it's fifty-fifty as to whether she comes back to Samui, even though I've told her I want her to.

"After we've had some space, some healing time, things will be different," I said.

"I hope so, Mr. David."

Wayan has been such a central part of my existence for so many years. But the mist that has come down between us is proving difficult to dispel. As Claire advised – not that I needed the advice – I have been gentle with her. I have sought to reassure her several times that, had Robert Buchanan never stepped back into her life, the result for Katie and for me would have been the same. On each occasion, she nodded politely, but could not meet my eyes.

Our parting at the airport was difficult and strained. We both put on a brave face. We hugged for a long time. Then she walked away.

Graceful as ever. Even in the depths of sorrow.

There's still no date set for Vlad coming back.

I have continued my research on Polzin and Orlov, but there is a sense of diminishing returns. Also, I have a growing conviction that I am relying too much on my kick-boxing friend and his boss to help me solve my problem. If Orlov is not interested in what I have to say, and accordingly declines to assist, I will have wasted a lot of time. Momentum is leaching away from me.

Should I simply hire a hit man, and have done with it?

No.

For one thing, there's nothing 'simple' about engaging a professional assassin. It's not as if they take out classified ads in the newspaper.

Although, if I did have to go down that route, I could pick Nathon Lamphongchat's brains. He *is* family - albeit distant - and my Bangkok gangster relative knows some lethal characters. Indeed, it's impossible to be in the drugs business and *not* rub shoulders with the more violent members of society.

But to make use of a gunman would be to forego the pleasure of squeezing the trigger on Polzin myself. The thought of being close up to him, in the moment, as my gun discharges, of watching his viscera splat against a wall, is better than sex. It's better than anything.

So, paying for a hit on the Russian is my least-preferred option.

Ahead of that in the priority order of things, is my flying to Moscow and hanging around in dubious bars and nightclubs in the seedier parts of the city for as long as it takes to find some unprincipled thug who will sell me a gun and some ammunition. After which, I'll linger around Polzin's main Moscow office during daylight hours - hopefully avoiding the attention of the police and security services - until an opportunity arises to plug him.

Admittedly, it's not the most detailed and meticulous scheme ever devised for an assassination, but it might work. And more likely to succeed than trying to get into his heavily-secured private residence to do the deed. I'm not the SAS.

Of course, in this scenario, assuming I'm not immediately mown down by Polzin's bodyguards, the odds of my making a successful getaway afterwards would be close to zero.

But does that even matter?

After all, it's not as if I have any compelling plans for what remains of my life.

I've stopped food shopping altogether. It's easier to dine out.

With no Wayan to attend to my nutrition, my eating patterns have taken a turn for the worse. My breakfast is either a Full English at one of the local greasy spoon cafés, or none at all on the mornings I opt for lie-in. I skip lunch about every other day, since Pimpim's coffee can see me through to sundown. After that, it's usually some rice dish which can be easily sluiced down with beer.

Consequently, and in spite of the best endeavours of the whisky manufacturers to keep something in my digestive system, I'm losing weight. The diet gurus should take note. An obsession with revenge might not be great for your mental health, but at least it's calorie-free.

My apartment, meanwhile, is still on affable terms with hygiene and tidiness. This is due to the efforts of one of Da's cousins, who comes in twice a week to change the bedding, do my laundry, and give the place a dust. It's not up to Wayan's standards certainly, but it's good enough for me. My contribution on the domestic front is limited to remembering to flush the toilet and put out the rubbish. Which, as it's mainly empty bottles, is no great hardship.

Da has proposed she drop by and check that I'm not living in complete filth between her cousin's visits. It is an offer that I have refused politely but firmly. Though I suspect she lets herself in anyway and pokes around when I'm out. That would be typical of the woman.

This evening I threw up over my balcony.

Must have been a dodgy prawn.

It's a bit of a low point for me, to be honest.

Claire does not approve, and tells me so.

I smoke, then take out the empties.

Must remember to buy some Bells tomorrow. Johnny Walker is just not the same.

Can't be bothered to switch on my laptop.

Da pushes my ashtray aside and drops a newspaper on my desk.

"One of our clients is dead," she announces.

"Who?"

"Mr. Louis."

"Luckily, he's already paid."

"Huh."

"It must have been a great comfort to him in his final hours that your surveillance statement vindicated Malee of any wrongdoing."

"Your friend Jules shot him."

"Jules?"

"You'd better read the report. It's on page two. I'm going to grab a coffee. I'll be back in a minute."

I flip open the paper and am confronted with a photograph of a sullen, cuffed Jules standing in his bar surrounded by uniformed policemen. He is re-enacting his crime for the cameras, as is the Thai way.

The reportage calls the shooting a crime of passion – the lethal result of a love triangle involving Jules, Louis and *femme fatale* Malee. The wording is sensationalist and likely inaccurate. It says Malee is twenty-two, for a start. It also describes both men as French, which will have Louis spinning in his grave.

Da has sat down with her cup of coffee.

"You were lucky not to get a mention," she says.

"Why would *I* get a mention?"

She shakes her head.

"Jules is in the Monkey House on remand. You'd better pay him a visit."

"To make sure there's not going to be any collateral damage for the *David Braddock Agency*, you mean?"

"Exactly. I don't want the fact that we gave Malee's behaviour a clean bill of health to become public. Bad for our reputation."

"I don't see why that should happen. You didn't spot Malee getting up to anything while Louis was away, did you? And it was only for a few days. She might have been resting or having her period. We can't be held accountable for what went on after that."

"You tipped Jules off, didn't you? That's why I didn't see anything."

"That's an outrageous suggestion."

"You did though, didn't you?"

"Of course, I did."

"Why?"

"You know me. I hate conflict."

Da stands up.

"Go and see Jules."

"OK." I reach for my Marlboros.

"Now would be a good time," she says. "Right now."

The Monkey House is the locals' nickname for Koh Samui's prison, which squats on a rise off the main ring road in the south of the island. From a distance it appears impressively modern and well-maintained. From close up, not so much.

After the expected nonsense getting inside, I am granted access to Jules, who has been summoned over the P.A. system from the *farang* recreation area where he was playing *petanque*.

We sit in our allocated booth and stare at each other for a few seconds while we adjust to the altered situation.

"So, how are you?" I say.

"I have been worse. Apart from the bites of the mosquito, everything else is bearable. Up at dawn, singing the Thai National Anthem followed by Buddhist prayers at eight. Six head-counts a day. Quiet time at nine. Don't ask me about the nights: the lights are left on."

"How about food?"

"You ask a Frenchman about *food*? It's shit. All the Europeans send out for food. Though that's shit too. But at least it's European shit. I would kill for some decent paté."

"Speaking of killing, what happened?"

"About Louis, you mean?"

"Unless you've killed somebody else too, yes. How did he find out about you and Malee?"

Jules scratches under his armpit. "She told him. Yelled it at him, he said. They had a big row and she got angry."

"That's hard to imagine. She's always seemed so ... docile."

"She told Louis about you too, David. You would have been his next stop after me."

"Well, I guess I should consider myself lucky you shot him."

Jules becomes agitated. "He was like a crazy man. He had been drinking. These Belgians, they can't drink. He came at me with a chair."

"So, you shot him."

"No choice, *mon brave*. I am an old man and he was a young, angry one."

"I told you keeping that gun under the bar would get you into trouble one day."

He gives another of his shrugs and spreads his hands. "What can I say? It is *regrettable*."

"You are surprisingly unruffled, Jules, considering the circumstances."

"It is all fixed already. I have a good lawyer."

"You have a good fixer, you mean."

"A fixer, yes. The Thais are not interested when one *farang* kills another, David. You know that. It means more money for them, that is all. I shall be out of here next week."

"How much is that costing you?"

"A lot. Lots of people to pay."

"I'll bet."

"And I will have to leave Thailand. That is the saddest thing."

"Where will you go?"

"Perhaps I will open a restaurant in Cambodia, or somewhere else. But not in fucking Belgium, that is for sure."

"Quite."

Jules leans forward, and says confidentially, "*De toute façon*, David, you have nothing to worry about. Nobody knows about you and Malee, except for her and me. And she will not say anything. And neither will I. What would be the good?"

"Thanks, Jules."

He sits back again and yawns.

"Do you need anything?"

"No. But if I do, I will be in touch. *Merci*. Thank you for coming. I always said the English are not so bad."

"With regard to Jules, we're in the clear. He'll be gone from Samui shortly, and Malee is keeping her mouth shut. Nothing to worry about," I tell Da.

"Right," is all she says. She keeps her eyes on a file in front of her.

"Are you OK? I'd expected an acerbic come-back, followed by a lecture."

"There's no point."

I hover, uncertain how to proceed.

"Is there something on your mind, Da? Something else?"

"Nothing that needs to concern you."

When I still don't leave her office, she says, "Close the door on your way out, would you? I have work to do, and don't want to be interrupted."

I may not be the most insightful of men, but this is not the Da I know. And when I think about it, there's been an *oddness* about her behaviour recently. Subtle, but noticeable. She's less frank and combative with me. On occasion, she doesn't hold my gaze – and she has *always* been able to stare me out. It's not a furtiveness exactly, it's more like ... hmmn ... hard to put into words. Maybe I've finally worn her down. But I don't believe that's it.

Perhaps it's that my perception is clouded at present.

Yes, that's probably it. Nothing else.

It's me, not her.

One o'clock in the morning. All is quiet.

I've had an email from Wayan. She's OK.

Still nothing from Vlad.

I switch off my laptop, make a few notes, dilute my Bells with a couple of ice cubes, and light a Marlboro.

Orlov has lost another contract to one of Polzin's companies.

The Russian economy's still in bad shape.

Good.

The Samui weather has picked up. No rain for a bit.

But my nausea's back.

I should eat something.

A phone call from Hitomi. We are both down-in-the-dumps and fail to cheer each other up. Neither of us has anything to report. We are stuck in limbo.

Afterwards, I can't even summon up the enthusiasm to masturbate about her.

Certainly not with Claire watching.

Pimpim delivers the bottle of scotch I'd asked her to pick up for me. I slide it in my desk drawer and hand her the empty one that she's reluctantly agreed to dispose of when Da isn't around. She is uncomfortable in her complicity, but offers a resigned smile and toddles off to get me a glass of water. I can't drink any more coffee today or I'll be clinging to the ceiling.

I'm making an effort to appear calm. Prem sold me some marijuana, which I hoped might take the edge off things, but the weed has instead ramped-up my arrythmia and sensations of paranoia. So, I've binned it and reverted to plain old Marlboros which will disassemble me at a slower rate.

I'm doing a surveillance job for Malte, a Danish fitness instructor whose girlfriend Ting Saksri has worked for the *Agency* on honeytrap assignments.

Therefore, as Miss Saksri and I are more or less old friends, we're indulging in a little chess. She knows I'm watching her and I know she knows I'm watching her. *Catch me if you can. Musical beds. S&M Cluedo: Colonel Mustard in the Library with a Rope.*

We are both aware of how it will end, but in the meantime we're both playing the game. Yesterday evening, as she didn't have any customers, I took pity on her and bought her a drink. By way of thanks, she pinched my arse.

"Got any good photos of me with men yet, *Khun* David?" she said.

"Not yet, no."

"Want me to give you some? Then, you can stay home and still charge Malte for your time."

"That would be highly unethical."

She giggles. "You make me laugh. Spill my drink."

"Glad to be of service."

So, as I was on beer last night, I don't have a hangover today. Merely shaky hands and some acid reflux.

I'm still losing weight. I should buy a new belt. A smaller one.

"We need to talk, Da."

"About what, David?"

"You." I sit and face her across her desk.

"Why? Isn't my work satisfactory?"

"It's not your work I want to talk to you about. It's what's going on outside work."

She studies me for a moment.

"You haven't been drinking," she says.

"No. Not today."

"Congratulations."

"Don't try to deflect. There's something strange about you at present, but I can't put my finger on what it is. You're not the same."

"Maybe that's because you're sober today. Is it because I'm in focus?"

"It's not only today. Look, Da, if you have any personal issues that are –"

She cuts me off.

"David, I am not going to discuss my private life."

"You're quite happy to discuss *my* private life," I snort.

"That's entirely different. You don't *have* a private life. Everything you do is public. It's all *out there*."

"Fair point. *But*."

"But *what?*"

What, indeed? I am disgracefully unprepared for this conversation. How many years have Da and I worked together? Yet I know so little about her and her family. And that's because I've never been sufficiently bothered to ask. I should have shown more interest. I have been derelict in my duties. She must think I don't care.

"I care about you, Da. You might not believe it, but I do. And I don't want you to believe that I don't care. I must appear to you as a self-absorbed prick most of the time. I get that. But talk to me now."

This outpouring disconcerts her. She is about to speak, but then decides to stay silent. She drops her head.

"Perhaps you think I'm a blabbermouth and can't be trusted," I offer.

"It's not that." Her voice is quiet. "You are usually discreet, in fact."

"Then, what is it?"

A beat. She meets my eyes.

"For as long as I've known you, David, you've had demons to exorcise. You still have. This is not about trust. There is only so much you can take onboard.

"I don't pretend to understand what's going on in your head now. The loss of Katie. Your drinking. Your mood swings. Who knows what else?"

"You're saying you can't talk to me because I can't handle it?"

"I'm saying that my problems – such as they are – are small compared to yours."

There was a second there when I almost got through to her: I sensed it. But now the wall is back in place.

"So, please don't ask me about this again. I'm fine. Really."

I've missed my chance.

Today's encounter with Da has convinced me that sobriety is not the answer – whatever the question.

I'm not terribly coherent when I ring Nang, and she calls me out on it. Or rather *bawls* me out on it.

"If you can't handle your drink, David, then stay off it," she says with ferocity before slamming the phone down on me. I chew over ringing her back to apologise, but things might spiral even further, so I have another drink instead.

I'm celebrating the fact that Da's cousin has been in to clean today, and the apartment is spotless. All my shirts are neatly ironed and hung up in the wardrobe. Any excuse for a celebration.

But I must make sure I'm in a fit state before my next conversation with Natalie. That way, maybe she'll put Jenny on the line.

"David, you're a mess," Claire says.

She's usually right about most things.

I light a Marlboro and contemplate doing some more research on Polzin.

But I don't think I'm up to it.

No. Definitely not.

But soon.

Saturday: gun practice is planned for this morning.

However, it is not to be. At the firing range, Udom takes one glance at me and decides it would not be safe to let me shoot.

"There are children here," he says. (Why they allow kids as young as ten to let off firearms seems to me to be the real question, but we are not about to get into a debate on that.) He indicates my trembling hands, and tells me not to return until I can hold a pistol without shaking.

Return when you are sober, is what he actually means, but is too polite to say.

He does have a point. I shouldn't have started drinking so early, then everything would have been fine. But there's no sense in crying over spilt Bells. I'll just have to come back tomorrow.

Meantime, I have a free day, until I have to check on Miss Ting this evening. She's already informed me that tonight she will be plying her carnal trade at the *Mosquito Bar* to save me the trouble of having to search around. Bless her. She is consideration itself.

I grab a late breakfast of noodles in a cheap Thai establishment overlooking Chaweng Lake. Bacon, eggs and sausages would have been a better choice, but the mere thought of all that grease sliding its way down my throat makes me queasy.

What now?

I suppose I could go home for a few hours, but the prospect is not appealing. So, I make my way on foot to the *Mosquito Bar*.

Might as well find myself a good table.

Miss Ting doesn't pitch up until after nine, by which time I've done half a bottle of Jim Beam, and a couple of Changs for the sake of variety. Even so, I'm still sufficiently *compos mentis* to say no to the proprietor's suggestion of a pizza. The *Mosquito Bar*'s pizzas kill more tourists each year than the local Mafia.

Ting sits on my knee and asks me if I'm inebriated enough to buy her a drink.

"Only *one*," I say.

"How is *Khun* Da? I not see her for long time."

"As insufferable as ever," I reply. "And will you remove your hand from my trousers, please, Ting. I'm supposed to be working."

She winks at me. "I work too."

"Right, Ting. But not on me. Look. Here are some young guys. Do your stuff on them. They're up for it, I'm sure. Especially the spotty one."

"You no fun, *Khun* David."

"Yes, that is the general opinion. Now bugger off. And ask the barman if he wouldn't mind turning down the music. It's making my ears bleed."

I continue drinking and smoking. For the sake of form, I use my camera phone to snap a few shots of Miss Ting draped over some guy. In one of the photos she is giving me the finger, but in a friendly kind of way.

By eleven, the music doesn't seem so loud. Even when I knock over somebody's beer on my way back from the toilet, the crashing of glass sounds like the soothing tinkle of wind-chimes. I wave away his complaints airily and fish out a one hundred Baht note. Not without difficulty.

I am assisted back to my table, where I demand a large Jim Beam.

I resolve not to look at my watch again. It doesn't matter what time it is.

Why would it matter what time it is? It's not as if I have to be anywhere.

A happy shout goes up from the pool table.

My ashtray is overflowing, and is replaced with an empty one.

Empty, empty.

There's nothing sadder than an empty ashtray. Except for an empty glass.

Where the hell is my Jim Beam?

You just cannot get the service these days.

I think I might be laughing, though God knows why.

A barmaid places a generously-filled whisky glass on my table. No ice. They remembered, yay. The girl whispers something to me.

I can't make out what it is she is saying, so I decide to nod. This satisfies her, and she goes away.

The brown liquid hits my throat.

No burning.

Warm.

Fuzzy.

And rather floppy.

"I am deliciously floppy." Not sure if I say this out loud.

What was it I was so depressed about, anyway?

4

"Work is the curse of the drinking classes."

Oscar Wilde

What the hell place is this?

I am lying fully-clothed on a mattress in a small room with yellow walls. My head feels like somebody has been rubbing the inside of my skull with sandpaper, and there is an acidic taste in my mouth.

"Hello!" I call. No reply. I increase the volume, then wish I hadn't, as the sandpaper mutates into an angle-grinder. Pain flashes behind my eyes.

The door swings open, and Da enters carrying a glass containing a green, frothy liquid. It looks as if it might be radioactive.

"It's about time," she says.

"Where am I?"

"You're at my house. Sit up and drink this."

"How did I get here?"

"After you passed out at the *Mosquito Bar*, Ting called me. I drove over and got a couple of the guys to help me bundle you into my car. Then two of my neighbours unloaded you at this end. Now, sit up."

I comply and lean against the wall. She hands me the glass.

"What's this?"

"It will do you good. Drink it."

"Is that vomit on my shirt?"

"Yes."

"Is it mine?"

"Who else's would it be?"

"That's pizza, isn't it? I didn't eat any pizza."

"I doubt you remember half of what you did last night."

"I didn't make a pass at Ting, did I?"

"No."

"Well, that's something."

I sniff the limey liquid that she has given me.

"Did I make a mess of your hallway?"

"You did. And the back of my car. And my front steps."

"God. Sorry."

"It's all cleaned up now."

I swallow some of Da's concoction. It's foul.

"All of it," she says.

I drain the glass.

"Horrid."

"Don't be such a baby. You need to shower. You smell revolting. Wait here, I'll get you a towel."

I appear to have lost my watch. "What time is it?"

"A little after ten."

"Can I have a cigarette first?"

I pull out a crumpled pack of Marlboros, and rummage around in my trousers until I find the lighter that Wayan gave me for Christmas.

"On the porch. I don't want you smoking around Pratcha."

"Isn't he at school today?"

"It's *Sunday*, David. You haven't been passed out *that* long."

I rise unsteadily to my feet and she leads me outside. There is way, way too much sunlight. I plop down on a wooden chair and light up.

"Could you manage some breakfast after your shower?"

"Ugh, no. Some water would be nice, though. I should rehydrate."

She goes back into the house. Pratcha puts his nose round the door to stare curiously at the stinky, unkempt visitor who has invaded their home. Deciding the sight of my dissolution and ruin is not for her impressionable son's eyes, Da pulls him away and gives him some instruction in rapid-fire Thai.

I gulp down the water. That and the cigarette dilute the taste of Da's homemade hangover remedy, though some of the sludge remains stuck to my gums.

"Take off your shirt," she says.

"Da, it's flattering that you are still so sexually attracted to me even in my current state, but aren't you worried that Tong will walk in on us? Not to mention little Pratcha. What will he think?"

"Very funny. We're going to the temple as soon as you're presentable, so I want to sponge out your sick while you're in the shower. Anyway, Tong's not here. He's in Bangkok."

"What's he doing in Bangkok?"

"Just take off your shirt, David."

I do as I am told. Remarkably, my hands are not shaking.

"Why are we going to the temple?"

"Because you need to get yourself straightened out. And that's as good a place to start as any."

I shower and reflect that this is only the second occasion I've ever been to Da's house. Moreover, I've met Tong in person no more than three times. However, Da *is* rather a private person, and does tend to deal with me on a need-to-know basis. So, my ignorance of matters Pintaraporn is not all down to Western indifference. But I'm making excuses for myself. I'll stop now.

Da throws my shirt at me as soon as I'm dry. There is a wet patch where the pizza used to be.

"How long is Tong away for?"

"Why do you want to know?"

"Well, I was going to borrow a razor, but there wasn't one. And, I couldn't help noticing the complete lack of any male toiletries in your bathroom.'

"You'll have to go to the temple with stubble." She examines me. "You don't look too bad. Considering."

I am handed my wallet and keys, and told that Pratcha is at his auntie's house.

"Let's go. I'll drop you at your car later."

I don't pursue the topic of Tong further. I'm already in the doghouse, so I keep my lips zipped.

When we arrive at the temple, Da buys some incense and tells me to pray.

"For what?" I ask.

"Do you still talk to your dead wife these days?"

"On occasion."

"Then, pray for her. In any event, be quiet and still, and try not to throw up again."

"I have nothing left to throw up."

"And, starting tomorrow morning, you're going to the gym before work."

"Yes, mother," I say.

Rhino's Gym is a mere five-minute drive from my apartment. The sign outside declares that membership guarantees I will 'Look Amazing Naked', which must count as the most mendacious marketing slogan ever. If we were in the UK, it would definitely qualify for a strongly-worded letter to the Advertising Standards Authority. The last time I looked amazing naked, I was a baby. And I wasn't that stunning even then.

The equipment located within is of such antiquity that in all likelihood it meets the requirements of a World Heritage Site. The most technologically-advanced pieces of apparatus are the ceiling fans. And not all of those work. *Rhino's Museum* would have been a more appropriate moniker. A first glance suggests that most of the customers are of a similar vintage.

It's seven-thirty in the morning. I'm honouring my promise to Da to be there at opening time. Well, near enough. I note it's been open for half-an-hour already, and some old boys are wheezing their way around the rusty weights and pulleys, while a Thai lady with a broom makes a half-hearted attempt to dispel the dust which has blown in from the two sides of the gym that are open to the elements.

I pay for a month's membership and have a cigarette by the desk while I stand self-consciously in a pair of shorts, an old tee-shirt, and flip-flops, wondering where to start. No cardio stuff, that's for sure. Bugger that. I'll just lift some weights and see where that takes me.

Twenty minutes later and I'm coughing my lungs out. Up comes some green phlegm, which has the same phosphorescent hue as that shit Da made me drink yesterday. Perhaps it's the same stuff. Fortunately, I'm by the gym's only toilet so, after some further abysmal hacking, the goo ends up in the bowl. I catch sight of my flushed face in the sink mirror. Thus far, I don't look amazing, even in clothes.

I stick it out for another fifteen minutes, by which time my heart is thudding like the bass of a seventies disco track, and I figure I've lost a kilo in sweat. *Sweat is the pain leaving your body,* I tell myself. It's unconvincing. Everything aches.

That's enough for my first session.

One of the regulars takes pity on me, and invites me to join him and his two buddies in the Gentlemen's Parlour for coffee. The Parlour comprises a corner of the hut in which there are three round plastic tables and an assortment of chairs, only some of which have four legs. The table adjacent to the worn-out Muay Thai training ring is designated for ladies. Mixing of the sexes is not encouraged at *Rhino's*. The sole concession to liberalism is that there is no 'WHITES ONLY' sign. Hey ho. I sit down gingerly.

"First time?" asks one of my new companions.

"How could you tell?"

"The blue lips are a bit of a giveaway."

"It doesn't get any better either," offers one of the others. "And if you think the exercise is bad, wait till you taste the fucking coffee."

I taste the fucking coffee. He's right.

Introductions are made. The guy who invited me over is Shane, a bald Kiwi of Sumo wrestler proportions who used to own a hamburger franchise, and presumably ate all the profits. Noah, a skinny former advertising executive from Nebraska, has a beard like Moses and a lazy eye. Tim – or Timothy St. John Jennings R.N. (Retired), to give him his full designation – completes the group. He has a severe crew-cut, and boasts two missing toes as the result of a motorbike accident.

All Three Musketeers are over sixty, which makes me the baby of the ensemble.

I tell them I'm a Private Dick.

"That makes a change," says Noah. "Most of the dicks on Samui are public. And the biggest ones are on the ladyboys."

"One of my Aussie buddies recently lost his Thai girlfriend to prostate cancer," announces Shane. "Terribly sad. Especially when you consider how much the boob job cost."

Tim splashes a large measure of Thai rum into my mug. "This will help counteract the worst effects of the brown muck. Otherwise you'll be growing hair on your teeth before you get home."

"You blokes come here every morning?" I ask. The coffee is much better with the SangSom in it.

Shane nods gravely. "Every weekday morning. Noah and I have Thai wives, so it gives us an excuse to get out of the house for a couple of hours. God knows why Tim's here. It's not like he's married."

"I'm here for the witty banter," says Tim. "I live in hope that one day I'll hear some."

This is what I've come down to.

I send Wayan an email, sticking to 'safe' subjects.

She replies within the hour.

She's fine.

All is well.

Except, it's not.

My nicotine intake is up, but I've been dry for three days. Dry, that is, if you don't count my morning snifter, my nightcap, and the Thai rum that Tim pours into the *Rhino Gym*'s frightful coffee. (Despite his bike accident, Tim is not discouraged from riding his bike while under the influence. The smell of alcohol clings to him like the smell of Marlboros lingers around me. And he starts early – way before the sun is over the yardarm, or whatever the nautical expression is. A kindred spirit, one might say. I mustn't spend too much time in his company or all my good intentions will come to naught.)

"Only a few days of working out, and I've already got chest pains," I complain to Da. "This fitness is killing me. Maybe that's what you had in mind when you corralled me into exercising. It's your revenge for all the wrongs you imagine I've done to you."

"Wayan has mollycoddled you over the years. That's your trouble, David. Anyway, nothing wholesome ever comes of revenge. Karma has a way of biting you on the bottom, if you reason like that."

"Are you speaking from experience?"

She is about to elaborate, but thinks better of it.

"No."

"So, you've never been bitten on the bottom? You've missed out. I'll talk to Tong about it. Encourage some healthy experimentation."

Her voice has a sudden edge.

"Stay out of my private life, David. I've told you before."

I raise my hands in apology.

"OK, OK. It was only a joke, Da. No need to rip my head off."

She has had her fill of the conversation.

"I have work to do. If you're worried about chest pains, you should see the doctor. Have a word with him about your hand tremors too."

"That's the alcohol withdrawal. I've read about it."

"How can you be suffering from withdrawal symptoms? You haven't stopped drinking."

"I've cut down," I reply guardedly.

Pimpim appears in my office doorway. She brandishes a pair of scissors and a towel.

"What's this?" I ask.

"If we can't sort out your insides, then we'll do our best with your outside. You need a haircut."

"A haircut? Here in the office? *Now?"*

"Pimpim used to work in a spa. She'll sort you out."

As usual with Da, resistance is futile.

"Do your worst, then," I say.

She's right about my hands, though. The steadiness was short-lived.

"And go and see a doctor. We don't want you dropping dead in the office."

"Bad for business?" I ask.

"Yes. Bad for business."

Da leaves the room and Pimpim drapes the towel over my shoulders.

I stare at my hands.

See a doctor?

Hmmn. Well. Maybe.

"Ready?" says Pimpim.

Revenge.

What made Da mention that? Because I mentioned it earlier?

I have a scotch, and ruminate on the matter.

No obvious explanation presents itself, so I have another scotch.

Then I ring Nang for a chat.

Bad idea.

I've switched off my laptop for the night. Apart from a recycled Russian newspaper article about Polzin's interest in buying into a proposed casino in Cambodia, there's nothing new. And zilch on Orlov either. I flick through my copious written notes on the two oligarchs to find something I haven't already memorised.

I spoke to Natalie earlier in the day, before I opened a new bottle. We had an amicable conversation, for once. About nothing profound. Every cloud, silver linings, etcetera.

Anyway.

We are into February. My daughter has been dead for over two months. Ten weeks, to be precise. Still I remain on hold while my Russian kick-boxing friend does what he has to do in Moscow. In the meantime, I am a character in a Samuel Beckett play.

But I am waiting for Vladimir, not for Godot.

My phone rings.

On the line is Thaddeus Thor, a partner at the London law firm that handles Katie's property and testamentary affairs.

What sort of parents would call their child *Thaddeus*, I wonder? People obsessed with the writings of Charles Dickens or George Eliot, perhaps? Or maybe people who didn't want any kids – as a not-so-subtle act of revenge.

There's that word again. Funny how often it crops up.

"Mr. Braddock, I'm sorry to disturb you, but there are some issues I need to talk to you about, and I'm afraid they won't wait."

"In that case, Mr. Thor, you'd better disturb me."

"As you are aware, apart from some small dispositions to her niece, you are your daughter's sole beneficiary. And Ms. Braddock had the foresight to appoint you to manage her assets in the event that she – um – could not be contacted."

"Yes, I'm aware of all this."

"Well, a decision has to be made with regard to the proposed sale of Ms. Braddock's Shad Thames apartment. The sale agents have been contacting me, and I require instructions as to what to do."

"Take it off the market for now."

"But they have a potential buyer –"

"Just take it off the market." I can't deal with the selling of property now.

"Very well. And there are costs to be discussed. Not only my fees but ongoing expenses for the apartment."

"Tell me how much you need and I'll transfer it to your client account. Give me your details."

He coughs politely.

"If we are to act for you, Mr. Braddock, there are certain formalities to be gone through. Identity verification and so on to do with money laundering regulations, and there are our firm's policies on accepting new clients –"

"Send me over the paperwork and I'll fill it in."

"Ah, thank you." He sounds relieved. *Lawyers.*

I ask him a question I don't really want to ask.

"What is the legal situation with regard to Katie's disappearance, Mr. Thor? Is there anything else we should be doing? With regard to her estate, I mean."

He chooses his words with care.

"On the question of *death in absentia*, English law generally assumes that, after seven years and in the absence of any evidence that the person is still alive, they can be declared legally dead. However, we can make an application before that time to obtain probate, for instance, if we can demonstrate that there is a probability –"

I cut him off.

"No need. Seven years sounds about right to me. Thank you, Mr. Thor."

I will Claire to appear and join me on the balcony of my apartment, which she promptly does.

"You rang, m'lud?" she says.

"Yes, I did."

"And you're talking out loud to me now?"

I give the kind of Gallic shrug that the now-deported Jules would be proud of.

"Wayan's not here. The neighbours think I'm crazy anyway. Who's it going to bother?"

"Nobody, I suppose."

I light a Marlboro. My exhaled smoke passes right through Claire. It's rather unnerving.

"I want to ask you something, O Wife of Mine."

"What's that?"

"How come I can see you and talk to you, but I can't conjure up Katie?"

"Perhaps it's because there's a part of you doesn't accept that she's dead."

"Then, why am I doing all this preparation to get rid of Polzin? No, I know she's dead, Claire. I may be delusional, but I'm not *that* delusional."

"You should try meditating. You always used to find it a help."

I shake my head. "Doesn't work anymore. Like most things. At the rate all the crap runs through my brain, it's like trying to herd sheep with a tortoise."

"A legless tortoise."

"I'm hardly legless."

"Not yet, you aren't. But you're getting there."

I set down my glass.

"Seriously, David, are you entirely convinced our daughter *deserves* to be avenged? Because you will be putting your life in danger to achieve that. Katie was a would-be murderess. She would have killed Alexander if circumstances hadn't intervened. Planned his death, and carried it out."

"I don't need doubts, Claire. I know what I have to do. It's the *only* thing I have left to do. That's why tomorrow I'll be at the shooting range again."

"If your hands aren't shaking too much."

Something lurches in my stomach. There is a hint of acid in my mouth and a twitching in my chest which grows steadily worse.

"I feel slightly sick."

"You are sick, David. You're very, very sick, my darling."

I sit still until my heart regains a regular rhythm, by which time Claire has gone.

That was a bad one. If I were sensible, I'd see a doctor.

If.

I throw the rest of my whisky over the balcony, and go to bed.

5

"I have no desire for others to take it on themselves to analyze my thoughts. I am without thoughts. I have never, not even once, acted on the basis of any doctrine or philosophy. I am convinced that those people whom the world considers good and respects are all liars and fakes. I do not trust the world."

Osamu Dazai, The Setting Sun

Nathon Lamphongchat rings me.

"How are things with you, David?"

"As delightful as ever, Nathon. Most of the time, I struggle to contain my joy at all the gifts that life has bestowed on me. To what do I owe this pleasure?"

"I need you to fly up to Bangkok for a few days to help me out on something."

I am indebted to Nang's nephew for a heap of past favours, but it is unusual for him to request my assistance, so my suspicions are instantly aroused.

"I'm not an expert on selling drugs, Nathon. Are you sure you called the right number?"

"Hilarious. This is a legitimate deal, and on the other side of the negotiating table are three English businessmen. I'd like your opinion on them."

"You're perfectly capable of haggling with some of my countrymen without me stringing along. What's this really about? You've had Nang bending your ear, haven't you? This is her doing."

"She's concerned about your mental health. She said the last time the pair of you spoke, you were drunk. Nang thinks you need something to distract you from your troubles."

"And to keep me away from the bottle."

"That too. But, seriously, I would like your input. When you're sober, you're quite perceptive. We're selling one of our hotels and ... Oh, never mind about the details. I'll explain later. Also, Jingjai is performing in a concert, and she'd like you to come along. She'd welcome the moral support. Next week. What do you say?"

"I'll consider it."

It occurs to me later, when I'm at the firing range, that Nathon might know something useful about Polzin's casino venture in Cambodia. Or he might know somebody who knows. His network is large. Thus far, I've eschewed calling on the gangster branch of my family for aid in the matter of Grigory Polzin. But, with no sign of Vlad's imminent return to the island, I should reflect on other avenues.

Besides, the distraction might be beneficial. Start my grey matter working. Wake me up. Blow away some of the fug. *Why not?*

My hands are reasonably steady today. Consequently, Udom is less anxious. Though my shooting skills still leave much to be desired, it has to be said. And it's not as if these targets move – unlike people.

Polzin will not be so obliging as to remain motionless for me while I fiddle with my pistol. Given my poor aim, best if I shoot him from a yard away, or with the gun muzzle pressing against his body. Two bullets to be sure. If I have time.

Close enough for me to smell him.

There's an unappealing thought.

I tell Nathon I'll fly up to Bangkok on Sunday evening.

I email some trivia and island gossip to Wayan, Nang and Natalie.

Pad Thai for dinner.

After five trips to the gym, there is still no sign of my developing ripped abs. I am also disappointed that my biceps – which I had expected would be of Schwarzenegger-like-proportions by now – are not noticeably bigger. The only thing that is growing, in fact, is my level of fatigue. And, possibly, my frustration.

While I cool down after a forty-minute session on the weights, I complain to the Three Musketeers about this establishment's promotional blurb.

"Veeti's advertising can't be trusted," opines Shane. "He told Tim that if he worked out regularly, his two missing toes would grow back."

Veeti is *Rhino's* Finnish owner. If the boys are to be believed, he won the place in a poker game. He only visits Samui a couple of times a year, and when he's not around, Noah keeps an eye on his investment for him. Judging by the state of things, it must be his lazy eye. On his last trip here, Veeti unblocked the toilet and upgraded the equipment by buying two new plastic chairs for the Parlour, but unfortunately didn't fix the leaks in the roof. After last night's downpour, a woman is endeavouring to mop away the pools of water before the mosquitoes take up residence. The rowing machine is out of action until the flood in the far corner subsides.

I am informed that Veeti spends most of his year in Manila, trafficking Filipina maids to the Middle East. Apparently, there is an arrest warrant out for him in Finland. He is thus typical of the white-skinned European flotsam that washes up on Samui. Hydroponic vegetables bobbing on a foreign ocean, seeking land. Either pursuing an unattainable dream or being pursued by the authorities of their home country. Or both. Robert Buchanans all, but without his lethal talents or gift of invisibility.

As for *Les Trois Mousquetaires*, I have learned that they fill their hours outside of gym-time in a variety of ways.

Most days, Shane locks himself in a spare bedroom which he has converted into a 'study', and watches sport and porn on an oversized TV screen. When the Internet goes down, or he suffers a power cut, he sits in the dark listening to 80s hard rock on his smart phone until the battery gives out. After that, he just sits in the dark.

Noah has a pool maintenance company, and when he is not haranguing his Thai workers, he is cruising the island finding anonymous places to park his truck so that his wife won't know which girlie bar he is drinking at.

In keeping with his history as a Royal Navy man, Tim has a boat moored at Bang Rak, which he spends hardly any time sailing but a lot of time cleaning. Wednesday evenings, he goes to a pub quiz in Bophut, so on Thursday mornings at the gym he tries to remember some of the questions so his buddies can test their wits. Sometimes, he even recalls what the answers were.

This morning, Tim is regaling me with tales of his experiences as a navy diver during the Cold War, while our other two companions appear suitably bored. They've had all this before. Since Tim's stories always involve, in one way or another, stuffing the Russians, they have a certain appeal for me. Plus, I'm not hearing them for the umpteenth time.

"I shouldn't tell you this," he says, as he always does, "but one of my best memories is of the special job my team of divers did in the North Atlantic." He pauses for effect while Shane rolls his eyes. Noah rolls one of his eyes.

"Sounds promising. But drip some more SangSom in my mug first, would you?"

Tim tops us all up before continuing.

"We sunk a Russian submarine," he announces.

"The *Kursk*?" I raise an eyebrow.

"God, no. The Russkis did that all on their own without our help. Besides, that was in 2000, and I was retired. This was in 1983."

"I'm all ears."

"The Americans had intelligence –"

"That's hard to believe," interjects Shane.

Noah gives the New Zealander a withering look from his good eye, while Tim begins again.

"The Americans had intelligence that the Russian submarines were using a particular deep ocean trench so they could move around the North Atlantic undetected. They had set up sonar buoys and they would use the soundings to avoid the risk of their hitting rock.

"Now, the Yanks will always use Brits to do the dirty work, if they can, so they passed the info on to us. I went down with my team, and we moved the Russian buoys. Not too much, otherwise they'd have realised something was wrong. But *enough*. Long story short, one of their nuclear-powered attack subs – the *Akula* – snagged on the rocks and tore a hole in the port side."

"A big hole?"

"Substantial enough to sink 'em. Pressure tank breach, you see, compromises the buoyancy. The whole crew died."

"So, there's a crippled nuclear submarine that's been leaking radiation into the North Atlantic for over twenty years?"

"Yes."

"I don't recall ever reading anything about the sinking of the *Akula*."

"It was never publicly reported. Not in anybody's interests, you see. Most of the Cold War was like that, David. Successes and failures of both sides were kept secret. And *everybody's* touchy about nuclear accidents. We only found out about it from the Americans who were tapping into the Russian naval communications system at Vladivostok."

"Impressive stuff," I say.

"Tim won most of the Cold War single-handed," chimes in Noah. "Even more impressive when you realise he has a prostate the size of a grapefruit."

"Speaking of which," says Tim, rising, "excuse me a minute, will you?"

The Englishman makes his way to the toilet. He still has a military bearing, despite his imbibing habits and his shortage of toes. Though it's early in the day. The sight of Tim speeding around on his motorbike after dark may be an altogether more concerning prospect.

Shane and Noah are meanwhile staring at two Thai girls doing stretching exercises on the floor mats. They have been nicknamed the Panda and the Gopher by my new friends, since one has dark circles around her eyes and the other displays an unfortunate overbite. However, these facial characteristics are not sufficiently off-putting to protect them from a certain amount of ogling.

"Anyone want another coffee?" I ask.

There are no takers.

It's been a few days since I've pestered the City of London Police for a progress report on the Katie investigation, and an item on BBC News has whetted my appetite for a conversation.

I get through to DI Zachary, who greets me with the world-weariness and resignation that has become standard in our interactions. At the beginning of our relationship, she was professionally-guarded about what she told me, but over the weeks she's come to share more with me than she ought to. Anything to prise me off her back.

"I suppose you've seen the TV report and that's why you're calling, Mr. Braddock? The female body we discovered in the disused stone quarry in West Yorkshire?"

"That's right."

I hold my breath.

"It's *not* Katie. I would have called you immediately if there was any chance of that."

I breathe again.

"This is all provisional at this point, but ... We believe the remains are those of a woman in her late thirties or early forties. Judging from the condition of the body, she's been there for somewhere between eight and ten years. Forensics are working on identifying her now."

"Cause of death?"

"You do realise, I'm not supposed to talk to you about this, Mr. Braddock. This is an ongoing investigation, and it *doesn't* concern Katie."

"Come on, DI Zachary. We're practically old friends. If I was in the UK, we'd probably be sleeping together by now. Besides, who am I going to tell?"

The Detective Inspector clicks her tongue.

"Gunshot to the head."

"Ah."

"We'll speak again in a few days, no doubt," she sighs.

"You can count on it," I reply.

Friday. Weekend looming.

I'd like to think I've made a valid contribution to the running of the *David Braddock Agency* over the last few days.

Inter alia, I've written the report on Ting's naughty doings for Malte and sent it off to him. Before I did so, I met up with Ting for lunch and ran through it with her to make sure I had all my facts correct. I want us to stay friendly in case the *Agency* requires her again for a honeytrap job. Plus, she did me a good turn ringing Da when I passed out in the *Mosquito Bar*. Fair's fair.

"No problem, *Khun* David," she said.

Miss Saksri already has a new sponsor, so she's not too concerned. Her latest sugar daddy is in his mid-seventies, so she's keeping her fingers crossed for a payout in the not-too-distant future. Then, she says, she will screw me for free. I can hardly wait.

I tell Da I'll be in Bangkok for a few days next week, doing some work for the Lamphongchats. She'll hold the fort in my absence. I promise to reciprocate if she needs some time off. Because I'm like that.

"Is this *paid* work?"

"Regrettably, no."

I brace for the tirade, but nothing happens. She appears tired again. Not interested to engage in banter. *Resigned*, in some way.

One of her fingernails is chipped, I notice. Da *never* comes to work without perfect fingernails.

"Try to stay off the booze in Bangkok," she says.

"What about girls? Am I allowed girls?"

"Whatever you like," she replies with a dismissive wave.

The chipped fingernail bothers me.

EVERYONE DIES

A cigarette smoulders in the ashtray.

I am in the *Sports Bar* in Mae Nam, and night clouds are scudding across the sky. They are so low that they appear almost to skim the rooftops. Rain is coming again. The weather can't make its mind up.

I used to drink here sometimes in the old days, when the former Samui Police Chief Deng 'Papa Doc' Charoenkul and I locked horns. In a strange way, I miss the wily stitch-up artist since his promotion to Bangkok.

But I pine more for the Old Monk's company. I'm sure he'd sort me out if he were here. He'd advise the *White Tathagata* on what to do.

I recall a chat with him one time while he sat puffing his way through a pack of my Marlboros, when I proffered the opinion that smoking was going to kill him. He'd looked at me like I was an idiot – a not uncommon occurrence.

"You forget," he said, "we are Buddhists. There is no death. We are, both of us, immortal."

But, we're not.

Not when it comes down to it.

We're not immortal at all.

6

"My family is my strength and my weakness."
Aishwarya Rai Bachchan

I am wearing the new Panama hat that Wayan bought me for Christmas, a crisp pair of chinos, a fashionably-creased dark linen shirt, and have squeezed my feet into a pair of smart deck shoes. Mirrored Ray-Bans camouflage my red eyes.

I am suitably decked out for the capital.

My flight this morning from Samui to Bangkok was almost full: a ratio of approximately one private detective for every one hundred and thirty other passengers. I was seated next to a sweet old dear from Oklahoma who talked incessantly while showing me photographs of her grandchildren. Two cans of Singha beer were required to keep me engaged until we touched down at Suvarnabhumi Airport.

A battered taxi carries me out to the city's suburbs. The driver is apprehensive when he is told his destination is the Lamphongchats' compound. I don't get overcharged.

After a thorough frisking from Nathon's gate security – which stops just short of an anal cavity search – I am escorted on foot to the big house, then out into the back garden where the head of the family is enjoying drinks with his wife under the shade of a large umbrella. I leave my suitcase on the verandah.

It is a while since I have seen Samorn, and her appearance comes as a shock. The wasting disease that is consuming Nathon's beloved spouse has speeded up. Her once-beautiful face is haggard, her cheeks sunken, and her body skeletal beneath the folds of her clothing. *A frail starveling.* The hands that grip the glass of fruit juice present as claws. Despite the heat of the day, a blanket covers her legs. I bend over to kiss her, and she offers me a wan smile. Nathon pointedly asks a maid to bring me some water.

The three of us chat for a few minutes. My hosts express their concern about Katie's disappearance, enquire how I am coping, and gently probe as to whether there have been any further developments. I pretend the water is gin, and utter platitudes. This is not the time to be maudlin.

Presently, Samorn declares herself tired, and leaves us. She leans on the maid's arm as she walks back to the house.

"What do you think?" Nathon says.

"She's a fighter. That's what I think."

"Yes." He strokes the rim of his glass. "It's amazing she's lasted this long. I count every hour as a bonus."

"At least she has her family around her. That must be a great comfort. Speaking of which, how are Niran and the girls?"

"Niran takes a lot of the weight off my shoulders these days. He's very involved in the business now. Kanya is expensive, but no trouble. She's started a design course which keeps her busy and out from under my feet."

"And Kanikka?"

"Hmmn. Yes, Kanikka."

"She and Sinchai Sangukhon are still an item?"

"Sadly, yes. He's actually not a bad kid, but ... Let's talk about something else."

"Wedding bells on the horizon soon?"

"David –"

"You'd better start writing that father of the bride speech."

"If I supply you with a whisky, will you talk about something else?"

"If you'd got me a whisky to start with, I wouldn't even have mentioned it."

Nathon beckons to a flunkey and a large Laphroaig Single Malt materialises at my elbow. It has ice in it as a concession to sobriety.

I decide to defer the topic of Grigory Polzin until later. After I've been *useful.*

I light a Marlboro.

"So, Nathon, what's this pseudo-job that my wicked stepmother has persuaded you to give me, to keep me out of trouble?" I swallow some of the Laphroaig. It goes down smoothly.

He watches this, concerned.

"Nang is upset about your drinking. You do know that, don't you?"

"Don't worry. I'm always dry when I work. Let's get to it."

"All right, then. We're selling one of our Bangkok hotels – the *Shanghai Crown Palace* in Chinatown. The timing is right. It will require a major refurbishment soon, so I'd like to offload it now."

"Exactly how many Bangkok hotels do you own?"

"A few," he says, casually. "But, that's not important. A Chiang Mai businessman named Yosboon has been trying to buy the *Palace* from us for several years. For reasons I won't go into – suffice to say, they are personal – I do not want it to fall into his hands."

He expects me to ask for details of his feud with Yosboon, but as I am being uncharacteristically incurious, he continues.

"The company that we are negotiating with to buy the *Palace* is British. *Anglo-Thai Property Investments.* Naturally, we've carried out a due diligence exercise, and there is a prohibition clause in the draft contract stopping them selling on to certain named individuals. But, even so –"

"You're worried that they might be acting as a front for Yosboon."

"Just so."

"Their negotiating team are all British?"

"The main man and his sidekick are. Their finance guy is Indian, but he only crunches numbers. Jason Underwood is the CEO, and he's the one who's been doing the talking. So, if there is anything fishy going on, he's party to it."

"Have you checked him out?"

"Naturally. He's mid-fifties, and on his third wife. From an old English family. Went to Eton, and spent some years as a trader in the City of London."

"I hate him already. Does he have any money troubles?"

"No. He's loaded. But that doesn't mean anything, and it certainly wouldn't keep him honest. The wealthy always want more."

"Well, you should know all about that, Nathon."

He gives me a sideways look, but doesn't respond.

I stub out my cigarette and light another.

"What's your plan?"

"I'm meeting their team at our city office this afternoon to discuss some tax issues."

"You want me to attend the meeting? I've packed a suit."

"No. I don't want him to associate you with me. You'll watch the meeting in an adjoining room through a CCTV link. Afterwards, you can give me your impressions."

I frown. "That's nowhere near as effective as my being there in person. That way, I can pick up on his twitches and tells. Plus, I won't get to ask him any questions. Why does it matter if he realises I'm batting for your team? You can tell him I'm an advisor."

"Well –"

"Or is it that you expect I'll turn up rolling drunk and embarrass you?"

Nathon sighs.

"Nothing of that sort, David."

I puff at my Marlboro in an attempt to head off my rising annoyance.

"Enlighten me, then."

He spreads his hands on the table.

"Underwood and his men are staying at the *Palace*. I gave them complimentary rooms as a gesture of goodwill, and so I could keep an eye on them. The CEO has been put in our best suite."

"I assume you have bugged their rooms?"

"Of course. But they'll have anticipated that, so I don't expect to learn anything useful."

I'm calming down.

"Go on."

"I am dining with them in the hotel restaurant later this evening. Afterwards, I'll leave them in the bar with two bottles of champagne."

"And you want me in the bar – as some unconnected, visiting British businessman – to strike up a conversation with them. Have a few drinks. Bond as we're all Brits together in a foreign land. Maybe buy some chasers. See what I can extract from Underwood."

"You're way ahead of me."

"Well, I like the part about having a few drinks, anyway."

"I thought you would. Probably best if we don't mention the alcohol part of the plan to Nang. For both our sakes."

"Agreed."

I finish the Laphroaig.

"What if Underwood won't tell me anything?"

"Then, I'm no worse off. All it's going to cost me is your bar bill."

"Which might be considerable, by the way."

Nathon finishes his fruit juice.

"Have you booked a hotel room yet?"

"Not yet, no."

"I'll put you in one of ours. The *Garuda Mansion* is only a half-kilometre walk from the *Palace*."

"You mean, a kilometre walk."

He knits his brows in puzzlement.

"After a few whiskies, Nathon, I tend to zig-zag."

I have been parked in a side-office with a jug of water and a coffee machine. On the desk in front of me is a large video screen, split into four – each picture taking a feed from cameras in Nathon's conference room, with each camera giving me a slightly different angle view of the *Anglo-Thai Properties*' negotiating team. All I can see of Nathon and his men are the backs of their heads. Which is fine: I saw quite enough of Nathon's fizzog this morning. Earphones are clamped to the sides of my head, relaying through the discussion clearly but making my hair itch. My scalp is sweaty despite the heavy pumping of the room's air-conditioner.

I have been instructed not to smoke as it will set off the fire sprinklers. Much as I am tempted to test this assertion, I have opted for discretion rather than valour – though that may change if the meeting drags on for too long. They've already been in there for an hour-and-a-half. If my Thai employer had given me warning that I would have to be without my treasured Marlboros for any length of time, I would have covered my arms in nicotine patches.

It's bad enough having to forego alcohol, but cigarettes too? Consequently, my right leg is jiggling up and down and my hands are not sure what to do with themselves. Not the ideal set-up for prolonged concentration, but hey ho.

Jason Underwood sits at the centre of his side of the conference table, flanked by his lieutenants – Roy Hampton (Underwood's bag-carrier and whipping boy, in my estimation) and Prakash Patel (the numbers man). Hampton is nondescript in appearance, wears a boring tie and a grey suit to match his grey hair. Patel is lanky, bespectacled, and carries the solicitous air of an undertaker. He is bald on top, but his side lengths of hair have been dyed and combed-over, like bootblacked Shredded Wheat. Neither of the flunkeys says much, but then it looks like it might be difficult to squeeze in a word when their boss is holding court.

Underwood is one of those loquacious, droning characters, profoundly in love with the sound of his own voice. He waves his hands around a lot, and uses the word 'I' in every sentence. A man to be avoided at the water cooler. He'd keep you there for hours boasting about his many successes, and occasionally patronising you with a question – though he wouldn't be paying any attention to your answer, since he'd be too busy weighing up which of his incredible achievements he was going to tell you about next. In short, I'd sum him up as the sort of arrogant English twat you see lining the back benches of the Parliamentary Conservative Party. The type who fiddles his expenses, and who meets his partners at rubber fetish parties.

Still, that's only my opinion. Though it's the opinion I give to Nathon after the conference has finished.

We're on the roof garden of the office building and I'm gulping down lungfuls of Marlboro smoke to eradicate the taste of Nathon's coffee. I have still not been offered any alcohol, so I'm scratchy and can't keep my legs still.

"Leaving aside your prejudices against all things Etonian, David, what else do you think?"

"I think if I can get some booze down Underwood's neck this evening, any discretion he has will evaporate. If he is pulling a fast one on you, he'll be gagging to boast about it to somebody. And I might fit the bill."

"Good."

"Can I have a proper drink now?"

"No. This is a dry office."

"You sodding cheapskate."

I'm in a suit and Bangkok is lit with neon. Sin and shitty Western music once again invade the capital, hunting for custom. Drab Doctor Jekyll has performed his daily transformation into wrinkled Mr. Hyde, Thai-style. The city rears up on its hind legs and howls. Everyone counts their blessings. Then they count their Baht and head for the bars.

Unlike on Samui, night usually falls fast here. At the first whiff of evening, the Bangkok day turns pale, punches its clock-card, and scurries off like a chastened cur, surrendering the streets to darkness. Whereas, on Samui, pinkness often lingers in the sky, as the sun lowers itself slowly into the sea like a hemorrhoid-sufferer easing himself into a bathtub.

It's a little after nine.

I'm sitting at the bar at the *Palace*, cradling what is only my second Singha of the evening. Yes, I'm behaving.

Nathon and his two associates have only recently departed, leaving Underwood, Hampton and Patel at a corner table with two complimentary bottles of champagne on ice. Patel – evidently not a drinker – quickly makes his excuses and leaves. I wait until one of the bottles of bubbly has been consumed, and red flushes are spreading across the happy faces of Underwood and Hampton, before I make my move.

"Excuse my interrupting, gentlemen," I say, using my plummiest voice, "but I couldn't help noticing the English accents. One longs for the sounds of

Blighty when one has been in the Far East awhile. Are you, by any chance, celebrating?"

"We may be a little premature," responds Underwood, "but we're close to clinching a deal, so we're letting our hair down."

"Congratulations. I've concluded some successful business of my own today, but sadly I have no-one to make merry with. Would it be terribly forward of me if I were to offer a couple of additional bottles of champers in exchange for joining you for a little while?"

"An English businessman is always welcome at my table," says Underwood, waving his arms expansively. "Especially when he brings bubbly."

Hands are shaken. I introduce myself as James Fosse, Consultant, and tell them my cover story – an abbreviated rehash concerning a commercial deal that the real Mr. Fosse concluded in the Philippines. God, it must have been ten years ago that the Artful Jim spun me that yarn. How time flies when you're not having fun.

Having checked my minor public school credentials, Underwood launches into his reason for being in Thailand, how his company is growing, what fantastic business he's doing, etcetera. Hampton agrees enthusiastically with whatever his boss says, and I pour Moët & Chandon liberally into our glasses to keep Jason (yes, we're already on first-name terms) oiled. His words flow smoothly like diarrhea round a U-bend.

After an hour of fizz and bull, Hampton is fading. Underwood upbraids him for his wimpishness, before shaking his head sadly.

"You get off to bed, then, Roy. I don't want you falling asleep tomorrow. Jim and I have some more serious drinking to do yet. Eh, Jim?"

"Absolutely, Jason. Let's have a couple of whiskies before we open the next bottle."

Hampton makes his escape.

Our session continues.

The CEO of *Anglo-Thai Properties* can hold his drink.

So much so, that I'm wondering if I'm going to be able to outlast him.

It's a race to the bottom.

The champagne has all gone, and we're both on our fourth whisky. Underwood has even had the presence of mind to take two calls on his cell phone, without even breaking stride. But even though my vision is a trifle blurry, and background noises sound muffled, my brain is relatively sharp. So far.

I tell myself that no matter how pissed I become, this is all in a good cause. I am working, after all. It goes with the job. Today at least, I have no need to be burdened with drinker's guilt. I'm glad I had that rice and meat dish before I left my hotel: it must be soaking up some of the alcohol. I wonder if I'll see it again later. Half-digested pork is not an agreeable sight to behold. Especially when it is coming out of your gullet at speed.

"Tell me about this latest deal of yours, then."

"It's our first major hotel acquisition in Bangkok," he effuses. "I'm very excited about it."

"The property ownership thing is tricky here in Thailand. Do you have a Thai partner to help you out with that?"

For a moment, I suspect he's going to clam up on me. But then he grins and taps the side of his nose.

"Just between you and me, this is. It's not *official*, Jim. I don't officially have a partner here. But I do have a Thai investor who's putting money in through offshore channels. And I've managed to negotiate a free one-year option to sell our share onto him at a profit via a Hong Kong company. So, it's win-win, this one."

"Is it a two-way option? Can he buy you out within the year too?"

"Yes. That's the way these things work. But he'll have to pay a pretty penny if he wants to get his hands on the *Shanghai Crown Palace* as sole owner."

"Some local bigwig connected to the government, I'd guess?"

"I can't tell you his name, Jim. It's more than my life's worth. He is an important person in Chiang Mai though, I will say that."

I clap his shoulder. "Hey, your secret's safe with me, Jason, don't worry. I don't know anything about fucking Thai hotels, anyway."

"I bet you know a lot about fucking *in* Thai hotels, though, eh?"

We both laugh uproariously at this.

Another double whisky, and *finally*, all of a sudden, Underwood is rat-arsed. I tell one of the staff to help him up to his suite, but not before I've pocketed his cell phone.

The walk back to my hotel is not a kilometre, but it's not far off. People keep bumping into me and muttering things. I drop two cigarettes. Then I drop the packet. My hands are trembling too much for me to open a new one.

Claire is waiting for me in my room, but I can't talk to her until the pork and rice has been flushed down the toilet.

Even then, the conversation is brief, and I have no idea what she's on about.

Something about family, blah blah, something else.

No idea what time it is.

The couple next door are having noisy sex, but that's not going to keep me awake.

I switch out the light.

7

"I always take Scotch whiskey at night as a preventive of toothache. I have never had the toothache; and what is more, I never intend to have it."
Mark Twain

Surprisingly, when the bedside alarm goes off, I don't have a hangover. Unsurprisingly, however, it feels like my insides have been scraped out, and last night's projectile vomiting has rendered my throat bruised and sore. My liver and kidneys hurt, and there is a sensation of tightness in my chest.

I need food inside me. Even more than I need my first cigarette of the day. A big plate of eggs and bacon, fruit juice and coffee to sort me out. And sod the medical experts.

Yum.

While shoveling this greasy fare into my mouth, I reflect that in the last few hours I have been more effective at getting stuff done than in the previous three months of faffing around over my Polzin dilemma. Horses for courses. Set a thief to catch a thief, and set a drunk to catch a drunk. Perhaps I work better inebriated these days, or maybe it's that my temperament is better suited to evaluating people and extracting information than to planning a killing. Though it's more likely, all earthly things considered, that the Man Upstairs is having a laugh at my expense before doing something more extreme, like setting off a hurricane or wiping out a village with a landslide, for instance. God's perverse like that. He gets bored easily. Needs constant entertainment.

I push away my plate. That's better. My watch says eight-fifty. One of Nathon's drivers should be in the lobby now, waiting to spirit me off to the Lamphongchats' suburban compound.

A Marlboro or two first, though.

I check my hands. They're only trembling a little.

"You are in better shape than I expected," says Nathon.

I drop into an armchair.

"English resilience. It's what made the Empire great."

We are in Nathon's study. The French windows are open onto the sunny garden. A red squirrel scampers across the lawn pursued by one of the Lamphongchat dogs, then flies up a tree. The dog barks awhile, then gives up.

I light a cigarette, and Nathon hands me an ashtray.

"Do you have anything for me?"

"Underwood definitely has a Thai backer, though he wouldn't disclose his name. Plus, two-way options relating to ownership once the deal is done. He said the local investor was Chiang Mai-based, which may point to it being Yosboon."

"I see."

"Anyway, I stole his cell phone, so you can have one of your guys hack into it and see whom he's been calling, and who's been calling him."

I fling the phone over to my surprised companion.

"You have hidden talents, David."

"Champagne and whisky tend to uncover them. Do you want me to observe your next meeting with Underwood? Though, if you do, I shall require something stronger than coffee and water to see me through. And I *will* be smoking, regardless of your fire sprinklers."

He ponders this, then says, "No, you've done your bit. I hadn't expected it would happen this fast, to be honest with you. I thought you'd need at least a couple of drinking sessions with Underwood before you won his trust."

"Bubbly and chasers are great levellers of the defences. Especially for the braggart. We aim to please."

"Hmmn. It will be better if you don't meet him again. I'll have one of my people work on his cell phone today. By this evening, I'll know where I stand. Although even if Yosboon isn't involved, the fact that Underwood hasn't disclosed his backer is enough to make me want to pull the plug. I do have another potential buyer on the sidelines, though I won't get as much for the *Palace* if I go down that route. We'll see."

"When are you next meeting the wonderful Jason?"

"At one o'clock. It's a Buddha Day today, so I'm going to the *wat* this morning after we're finished here."

"Somehow, Nathon, I find it difficult to picture you at a temple bowing and *wai*-ing, burning incense, and generally being righteous – while all the time your pushers are out on the streets selling drugs to children. How do you square your apparent religious devotion with what you do for a living?"

"We *don't* sell drugs to children," he retorts angrily. "And as for my supposedly contradictory behaviour, it's no different to your swilling down whisky to convince yourself you're not a drunk. We humans have an endless capacity for self-deception and self-justification. If you'd paid any attention at all to the teachings of Lord Buddha, you would know that."

"Yeah, I used to be familiar with all that stuff." I yawn. "But since my spiritual advisor upped sticks and went to live in the north of the country, I've been somewhat lacking in the virtue department."

Nathon makes to stand, but I forestall him.

"Before you go, there is something I want to talk to you about."

"Oh, yes?" he says, suspicion invading his eyes. "I don't suppose this is anything to do with your father's manuscript? Nang told me to encourage you to read it. She seems to think it essential that you do."

"No, it's nothing to do with that."

"I didn't think so. That would be much too simple. But I thought I should ask." He sighs. "What is it, David?"

"What do you know about Grigory Polzin?"

His face becomes hard.

"The man who ordered your daughter's ... disappearance? Not much. *Why?*"

"Because I want to kill him."

There is silence for a few seconds.

"You mean, David, that you want me to put you in contact with a professional hit man? Well, I suppose I can –"

"No, that's not what I mean, Nathon. I want to kill Polzin myself, and I need some information to be able to do that."

"*Kill him yourself?* You don't have the skills. I understand that you want him dead. But – *Polzin*. That's a job for an experienced assassin."

"Nevertheless, I want to be the one who pulls the trigger. Now do you have any info that would be useful to me? Insider stuff. Intelligence about his dealings in Asia? His Macau casino, the proposed gambling investment in Cambodia? Anything that might help me get close?"

"You are not a gunman," he says flatly. He crosses his arms.

"Supposing, instead of it being Katie, it had been Kanikka or Kanya or Jingjai. What would you do? Contract it out?"

Nathon examines his hands and shifts in his chair.

"In that case, I would want to look him in the eye, then shoot him. Personally."

"So, what's the difference?"

"The difference, David, is that *I* could do it. I doubt you can. You'll die in the attempt."

"That's not such a big thing at this point, Nathon."

He rises.

"I have no useful insights to give you about Grigory Polzin," he says. "But, if you decide you want a third party to do the job, then I can help. Think about it."

"If I hit a wall, then that will be my last resort. But *only* if I hit a wall."

He purses his lips.

"What shall we say to Nang about the last twenty-four hours?"

"That I observed Underwood for you, got talking to him at the hotel, and unearthed some useful information about his backer. She doesn't need to know about the drinking, or the stolen phone. Or our chat about Polzin."

"All right." His tone changes. "Are you coming to Jingjai's concert tomorrow evening?"

"I promised I would."

"Good. How will you fill your time until then?"

"Oh, I'll find things to do. This *is* Bangkok."

"Think hard about the Polzin business, David."

"I think about little else, Nathon."

I have an entire afternoon and evening to kill. A night to get through, then tomorrow morning and afternoon to fill.

That's going to be nigh impossible without booze.

In my early days in Thailand, now eight years distant, there was no problem in finding ways to pass the hours. Particularly as my first months were spent in Bangkok. I used to blot out the painful memories of Claire's death by burrowing like some nocturnal mammal into the bodies of young Thai women. I can't tell you how many women, nor even recall most of their names. They all smiled, though, I do remember that. There was a Mod, a Ying, a Pichaya, several Nanas, and even a Da – though she lacked the testicle-shrivelling intensity of her namesake on Samui. Back then, I drank a lot too, but that was par for the course. You can't hang around in girlie bars without drinking or folks will either think there's something wrong with you or that you're a tight *farang* bastard; and probably Scottish.

Perhaps a trip down Memory Lane is called for while I'm in the capital with nothing useful to do. After all, who can say whether I'll ever be back here again. If I end up getting myself killed while trying to assassinate Polzin – as Nathon believes is likely – then this may be my last chance to say goodbye to the City of Angels.

We'll start slowly.

I ring my former partner Asda, with whom I once owned an antiques business, before I sold him my share. He, his wife and family are 'normal' people, and, in the past, they have often asked me to join them for a family dinner: invitations rarely taken up. OK, *never* taken up. To my shame.

But Asda is out of town on a buying trip, so that avenue is closed.

I have a leisurely lunch by the river while I contemplate what to do next.

Visibility is not great today. The heat and lack of rain has allowed the city's dust to rise into the air. Consequently, Wat Arun looms on the opposite bank as in a mist. The Chao Phraya is heavy with traffic. The river heaves, its brown and green waters sluggish but sure. Rusting barges plough a frothy furrow through the central channel. Locals – their stares carrying the sightlessness of routine – jump on and off the Express Boats that temporarily hug the piers before releasing with an engine snort. The wash against the piers is garnished with thick weed and floating trash.

I wonder how many corpses have been fished out of this waterway in the last twenty-four hours. A few, for sure. Usually unidentified.

The contemplation of a body count inevitably turns my thoughts to Katie, then that leads on to a further meditation on killing Polzin. Then Vlad and his tardy return to Samui. Then ... Whenever it starts up, this whole revenge circus whirrs round and round in my head, ceaselessly. I have been here before, countless times. It's hard to turn off the mechanism.

The assignment I've carried out for Nathon has at least had the virtue of giving me a brief respite from my obsessional behaviour, along with a vague but welcome sense of accomplishment. However, now that's done. So, at this point, the only thing that's going to stop the wheels clanking in my head is a drink and a friendly face.

And I know where I can find both.

But first, a Marlboro.

And, yeah, I'd better pay my lunch bill too.

Patpong feels quiet.

The world economic meltdown has been hard on the Asian tourist trade. And Bangkok needs tourists. More specifically, it needs their cash. So, I am guaranteed a jolly greeting at *Siam Welcomes You,* the bar-cum-brothel where I was once a regular. I climb the steps – which are rickety and more stained than I remember – and open the door.

I need a moment or two for my eyes to adjust to the dusty gloom of the interior. The Mama-san squints at me as I pull up a stool at the bar. Despite the fact that I haven't set foot in the place for a long time, she recognises me. Her memory for names and faces is encyclopedic.

"*Khun* David, no see you for long time. I like your hat."

"Christmas present, Mama-san."

I remove my Panama and gaze around. There's only one other customer. He's sitting on a corner sofa having his crotch stroked by one of the girls. The three other young ladies of *Siam* are swiping on their smartphones. They look up at me expectantly. None of them is familiar, but that's hardly surprising. The meat turnover here is fast. They wear out quickly. Much quicker than the furniture, which has been here forever. Like Mama-san.

"Slow day?" I ask.

Mama-san wrinkles her nose, and her plump Oriental features take on a more piggy air.

"Nobody loves us any more."

"I'm sure that's not true."

"You want a girl? Maybe two? Best room free upstairs for you. Special price for old friend."

"Not now."

Her face falls, so I offer to buy everyone a drink. This cheers her up. A smidgeon. She rings a bell, and a young bearded *farang* appears.

"You have a Western barman now, Mama-san?"

She barks drinks orders at him before sliding onto the stool next to mine.

"He cheap," she whispers confidentially. "I think he have no papers. And customers like American barman. Can talk about burgers and baseball when they finished with the girls. Stay longer." She winks.

"What's your name?" I say to Mama-san's latest wage slave.

"Chris."

He pops the top off a Singha and sets it in front of me.

"What brings you to Thailand, Chris?"

He gives a shrug, and places a large whisky before his employer.

"Long story."

"Chris good with the girls," Mama-san chimes in. "No pinch bottoms or boobs. Very nice boy."

As the barman ferries drinks across to the others, she adds slyly, "Perhaps he gay." She puts a hand on my leg and squeezes. "You not gay, *Khun* David."

"Certainly not."

I light a Marlboro.

"Keep my stool warm for me, would you, Mama-san? I have to make a call to my office."

"You come back?"

"Five minutes."

"OK." She reluctantly lifts her hand off my thigh. "I wait for you."

An old Burmese is pissing in the alley outside, and a cat is screeching atop a faded awning, possibly in protest at the heat of the afternoon. It's approaching four. It will be at least another three hours before the area starts to come alive. Until then, it's only stalls and street food and the occasional reprobate. I may as well be here as anywhere else.

I phone Da.

"Hi, Da. The Lamphongchat business is all wrapped up, but I still won't be back until the day after tomorrow. I have Jingjai's concert to attend."

"So, you're slobbing around."

"You could say that. If you wanted to be especially unkind."

A sigh.

"Where are you?"

"In Patpong."

"I don't suppose you're shopping for nice shirts at Jim Thompson's?"

"No. I'm at *Siam Welcomes You*. I've just stepped outside."

"Is that one of the blow job bars in *Soi* 1?"

"It's not a blow job bar. It's more of a foreign gentlemen's club."

"In *Patpong*?"

"All right, yes, they do have girls."

"And booze."

"And booze, yes. But it's not what you think. I have my trousers on and I'm only having a Singha."

Another sigh.

"So, what are you calling me about?"

"A work matter."

A few minutes later, I go back inside. Mama-san's face bears an expression of relief. The other customer has gone. As he didn't pass me on the stairs, he must be in one of the top bedrooms having an oil change. Or a full service.

"You want a girl now, Khun David?"

My phone trills. It's Nathon.

"I have to take this. Would you turn the music down, please?"

I carry my Singha to a table away from the bar.

"Hello, Nathon."

"Underwood and his team have left. We checked out his phone. Calls to and from Yosboon on there, as suspected."

"Then, the deal's dead?"

"It certainly is."

"Does Underwood know?"

"Not yet. We'll inform him tomorrow. He can waste another day here, the bastard."

"Seems fair."

"Speaking of tomorrow, you are coming to Jingjai's concert, aren't you?"

"For the hundredth time, Nathon, yes. I won't let your niece down."

"It sounds like you're in a bar."

"Yes. In Patpong. But I've already had this conversation with my office. I'm not drinking –"

"I'm not your mother," says Nathon Lamphongchat. "You're a big boy. See you tomorrow evening."

I down half the bottle of Singha and light another Marlboro.

My phone pings. It's the expected message from Da. I go back to the bar.

"My girls are bored," says Mama-san, despondently. "You have one of them now, *Khun* David? Before you drink too much?"

"I'm not going to be drinking too much," I tell her. "But I would like to have a word with your barman. Ask him to join me at the table. And put another round on my tab."

"My barman working." She crosses her arms.

"He's not working. You don't have any customers. I only want him for a few minutes."

A crafty expression flits across her face.

"Ah, I understand. You want gay man? Try something new?"

"No," I say firmly. "I only want to talk to him. And, incidentally, simply because a man doesn't want one of your girls, it doesn't make him gay."

The barman makes his way across to my table. He is wiping his hands on a tea-towel, and trying to appear casual, though his eyes are wary.

"You wanted to talk to me?"

"I notice you have a slight limp, my friend. I expect that's from your time in Iraq."

"*Iraq?* No, I've never been to Iraq."

"You look different with a beard, Sam. And you've lost weight."

"You've mistaken me for somebody else. My name's Chris –"

"No, your name's Samuel Trask. Formerly Private First Class of Charlie Company in South Baghdad. And more recently employed by Jedediah Reichenbach of Greensboro to carry out surveillance on one James Fosse. I just had one of my people send me through your picture. I thought it was you, but I wanted to be sure."

I hold out my cell phone for him to see the head-and-shoulders photograph that has come through from Da. The American's face is expressionless.

"Who are you?"

I offer him a chair.

"Maybe you should sit down."

"Who *are* you?"

"Well, I'm not the police. So, sit down, Sam. *Please.* We don't want a scene in here, do we?"

He sits.

"My name is David Braddock, and I'm a private investigator based on the island of Samui. I was employed by your sister Becky to track you down."

"You've been looking for me for two years?"

I scratch my chin.

"Not exactly."

"How did you find me?"

"That, Sam, is a trade secret." I'm not about to admit it was pure blind chance. "And, anyway, it doesn't matter. What I want to know is, what the hell have you been doing, and why haven't you been in touch with your sister? Have you any idea how out of her mind she's been with worry?"

His head drops. I light a cigarette and let him stew.

"How is Becky?"

"Happily divorced and still in the property business. But haunted by her brother's disappearance, and unable to mourn him properly." *A feeling I can relate to only too well.*

"What did she tell you about me?"

"That you were a lost soul, suffering from combat stress. And that you had some obsession about medieval chivalry – knights and damsels in distress or some such crap – likely stemming back to an incident during your posting in Iraq."

"My need to rescue women." He laughs bitterly. "Oh, yes, that."

"What happened, Sam?"

He exhales and steadies himself.

"My 'obsession', as you call it, almost got me killed."

"Go on."

"I was following Jim Fosse here in Bangkok, as you seem to know, on Reichenbach's instructions. And there was this girl." He stops briefly, then ploughs on. "A young Thai girl. Shuang was her name. She was working as a prostitute, and not willingly. She needed help. And I wanted to assist her to get away. After what had gone on in South Baghdad. What I witnessed there ... What I did nothing about. I felt the need to ... to *atone*. To put *something* right."

I'd like to press him on the triggering event in Iraq, but I don't want him to clam up. Instead, I light another cigarette while he tussles with his guilt. He must have done this on countless occasions: I can see the anguish in his eyes. He's had lots of time, and yet it's still there. A troubled man. Possibly a mentally ill one.

"Anyway, I messed up. The gangsters who were trafficking Shuang caught me and beat me up. Really badly. Lots of broken bones and internal bleeding, but I won't bore you with the details. To this day, I don't know why they didn't kill me.

"They dumped me in some dirt-poor suburb. It was only because some old Thai guy and his wife took me in and patched me up that I survived. No police. No ambulance. Only the three of us in a wooden shack by a canal. And no talking: they didn't speak English anyway. Me being fed soup. I have no idea how long I was there. I was dazed. In shock. I had no money, no credit cards, and no passport. They saved my life. And I have no idea why they did that."

"Why didn't you go to the police, or to your embassy, or ring your sister?"

He looks me squarely in the eye. "Because I'm fucked up, Mr. Braddock. Well and truly fucked up. I was almost murdered over a girl I didn't even know. And all because I saw another girl die in Iraq – one I could have saved, maybe. One whose face I can't shift out of my head. So, idiot that I am, I tried to rescue Shuang. To make amends somehow by riding in on my white horse. And do you know what? If I had the chance, I would do it all over again. And again. And again.

"I figured it would be better for all concerned if the earth swallowed me up. If every trace of Samuel Trask vanished. I toyed with the idea of suicide, but somehow that seemed too easy. Too much of a let-off."

"How have you lived since then?"

"After I left the old couple, initially by begging. A few cash-in-hand jobs from foreigners who felt sorry for me. Keeping out of the way of the authorities. An Australian bar-owner let me sleep in a room at the rear of his premises. Slowly, I got back on my feet. Managed to eat properly, clean myself up. Then I became a barman here. I'm not exactly awash with cash, but I'm surviving."

"What happened to the girl? *Shuang*, was it?"

"I went back a few times to the bar she worked at. Discreetly, as you can imagine. If I'd been recognised, well, I wouldn't be here now."

"And?"

"She'd gone."

"Did you hear about Jim Fosse? See anything in the newspapers or on TV?"

He shakes his head.

"For the first weeks after the gangsters trampled all over me, I wasn't interested in the news. I can't honestly say I've thought much about Mr. Fosse. Or Mr. Reichenbach, for that matter."

"Fosse's dead."

"Ah."

"At least, he might be dead. There are conflicting opinions on the subject. You could have been a suspect, at one point. But fortunately, the police fitted up somebody else for the crime."

"Fosse was another abuser of women. I'm not sorry if he's dead."

"I'm with you on that."

He stares at me, resignedly.

"So, what happens now? Do you get me fired from here? I notice you're pretty thick with Mama-san. And are you going to call Becky and tell her you've found me?"

"Well, for a start, I have no intention of getting you fired."

"But you *are* going to call Becky."

"No. *You* are going to call Becky."

I hand him my cell phone.

Despite my assurances to Da, I spent the rest of the day and some of the night becoming properly rat-arsed at *Siam Welcomes You*. Having promised on the lives of all the saints that he would not do a runner, and that we would meet again tomorrow, Sam loaded me into a taxi.

I stumble entering my hotel room.

"Look at the state of you," says Claire.

"Hey, don't be too hard on me. I found Sam Trask today. Another success for the *David Braddock Agency*. Even if it was by luck."

"It's not luck."

"Then, what is it?"

"Karma," she says, decisively.

"Whatever."

"The threads of karma lie everywhere, David, don't you know that yet?"

"Huh."

"When I was alive, I was forever telling you *things happen for a reason*. Your meeting Sam Trask today has significance, and not only for him, but for you."

"In that case, why isn't karma intervening to help me kill Polzin, eh? It's not as if he doesn't deserve it."

"Perhaps it is. You just haven't realised it."

"Whatever, Claire. I'm afraid I've grown out of my mystic stage. I have more urgent concerns at present."

"Like what?"

"Like the pain in my chest and down my left side, for instance. And the fact that I don't have proper control over my speech. Can we stop talking for a minute?"

"Would you prefer it if I left, so that you can pass out in peace?"

"That would be good, yes. Thank you."

8

"One of the advantages of being disorganized is that one is always having surprising discoveries."

A.A. Milne

The following morning, I am rudely awakened by hammering on the door of my hotel room. I pull a towel around my waist, and am confronted by two khaki-clad Thai policemen, and a cowed member of staff.

"Yes?"

"You come with us," says the uglier of the coppers. "Colonel Charoenkul want to see you."

"About what?"

"You come with us now."

"Let me put some clothes on, then."

I pointedly leave them standing in the corridor while I dress.

Half-an-hour later, after an uncomfortable ride in the back of a police car, during which neither of my escorts say a word, I find myself in the office of Colonel Deng Charoenkul.

'Papa Doc' sits at an oversized desk in his oversized office. The shelves to my left contain his golf trophies and a couple of token books. A picture of the King hangs on the wall behind him. These necessary items aside, the room is almost bare.

Charoenkul is his customary well-groomed self, though he's acquired further weight since I last saw him. It makes his sly face more porcine than before. I am not offered a chair. The policeman who drove me here hovers unseen at my back.

The Colonel looks up from his phone.

"Ah, Braddock. It's been a while. You might have shaved for the occasion."

He studies me with a slightly bemused expression on his fleshy features.

"I wasn't given the opportunity. Your boys were too anxious to get me in the car."

"Indeed? Well, I never fault an officer for his enthusiasm."

"What am I doing here, Chief?"

Charoenkul interlocks his fingers.

"You were observed visiting the Lamphongchat family compound two days ago, and again yesterday morning. Would you care to tell me what that was about?"

"No, I wouldn't. Family business. Which is to say, none of your business."

The Colonel gives a small nod and something hard smashes into my left kidney. I pitch forward onto the desk, temporarily winded. When I glance back, Neanderthal Man is holding his truncheon, apparently keen to use it on me again.

I straighten up with difficulty, and am momentarily seized by an angry urge to tell Charoenkul that I used to screw his wife. But I think better of it. So long as I require at least one functioning kidney, it's better that he remains ignorant of the bedroom gymnastics that Kat and I got up to.

"I notice you've modified your interrogation technique since your Samui days, Chief," I say. "You appear to have abandoned the psychological warfare approach in favour of something more direct."

"I'm busier now, Braddock. I don't have the time I had before. Bangkok is a fast-moving city. It demands a different style of policing."

He tilts his head to one side, and says kindly, "Perhaps we should start again. Why don't you take a seat?"

I lower myself onto the proffered chair, trying not to give him the satisfaction of knowing I'm in pain. Even though the bastard knows anyway.

"Now." He places his palms on the desk. "Why did you go and see Nathon Lamphongchat?"

"He's considering selling one of his Bangkok hotels to a British company. He called me in as a consultant to observe the other side's negotiating team, and to get their CEO drunk. That's all."

The policeman's eyebrows wrinkle.

"Which hotel?"

"The *Shanghai Crown Palace.*"

"Why does he want to sell it?"

"Something about its needing refurbishment soon. He doesn't want to spend the money. He'd rather have the cash."

To pay his bribes to you, I don't add.

Charoenkul looks disappointed.

"So, it's a legal deal?"

"Yes. All above board as far as I can see. I suppose Nathon must do *some* legal transactions. For the novelty, if nothing else."

The Colonel's eyes become slits.

"You wouldn't be lying to me, Braddock, would you? Because that would be unwise."

"Have you ever known me to lie to you, Chief?"

"I've never *caught* you lying to me. But then, with you, it's always the things you *don't* say that concern me."

I panic for a second that he is aware of my affair with his late wife. Though that cannot be. If he was in possession of intel on those sticky extramarital liaisons, this interview would have been conducted in the cells. With a cattle prod.

"What's the name of this British company?"

"*Anglo-Thai Property Investments.*"

It seems safe to tell him the transaction may or may not go ahead because of financing complications, but I don't mention the name of Yosboon. That would be giving the bugger too much, and he might start digging deeper. He scribbles a few notes on a pad. Then he sighs, and the energy goes out of him.

After what I hope is a respectful period of silence, I say, "Is that all, Chief? Can I go now?"

He waves me away.

"Stay out of trouble, Braddock. If that's possible."

"Can I get a lift back to my hotel?"

"No. That would be an abuse of police resources. Use a taxi."

Once I'm on the street, I call Nathon.

"Colonel Charoenkul pulled me in for an unfriendly chat; wanted me to tell him why I'd been to see you. He must have people watching your compound."

"That comes as no surprise," is Nathon's untroubled response. "What did you tell him?"

"Only the basics about the hotel sale. What I thought he needed to know without embarrassing you. I didn't mention Yosboon."

"Good."

"Why does he have you under surveillance? Are you having difficulties with him?"

"No more than usual. He wants to retire soon, so he's trying to get as much leverage as he can with his 'clients' to squeeze more money out of us. Also, he's recently taken up with Mananya Som, the Thaisom heiress, so he's keen to show he has cash to throw around. Maybe you remember her?"

"Oh, yes. The Toxic Princess. Over-entitled diva and fashion snob. Not averse to a spot of violence towards the less privileged, if the rumours are correct. You surprise me. Charoenkul and Mananya make an odd couple, I must say."

"They're in a position to scratch each other's backs. And fuel each other's vanity. Let's leave it at that, shall we?"

"OK. Have you given Underwood the glad tidings yet?"

"I'm just about to. See you this evening."

"Looking forward to it. But, listen. Before you go, I need to smuggle an American who has no papers out of Thailand and back to the US. Do you have someone who can help?"

"Yes. Of course. But it won't be cheap. Not once I've factored in my commission too."

"I'm sure you'll be fair, Nathon."

"You'd better give me the details. My man will contact you later today."

"Perfect."

Next, I phone Da.

"Re the photo you sent me yesterday: it was Sam Trask. I've had a little talk with him, and he's spoken to his sister. We should have some money coming our way once he's back in the States."

"Good."

"And I'll be back tomorrow morning, as planned."

"Right."

She doesn't seem inclined to prolong the conversation, so I say, "Are you all right?"

"Yes. Why?"

"Well, you're being uncharacteristically disinterested in my news. And monosyllabic."

"Am I?"

"Yes."

"Well, I'm not sure how to break this, David, but not everything in my life is about you. Sorry, but I have to go. I'll see you tomorrow."

I open a new packet of Marlboros, and muse on the strange resignation in Da's voice. Perhaps she has finally given up on me. Or given up on *something*.

I certainly expected her to quiz me on whether I'd been drinking yesterday. And unless she asked specifically – which she didn't – I wasn't going to volunteer the information.

Charoenkul is right about me in that respect.

It's not the things I say that you have to worry about.

It's the things I don't say.

My left kidney has stopped throbbing, and my stomach has been filled by a McDisgusting Burger and cripplingly-salted fries. Since Wayan has been in Bali, my food intake has been about as healthy as that of a *soi* dog. I have thus far avoided rooting around in refuse bins, but the processed crap slithering its way through my tubes can't be doing me a lot of good. I'm amazed I'm not putting on weight. Maybe my body is drawing the line at the mechanically-recovered meat, cow brains, sugar and verminous additives that I'm stuffing in my mouth, and expelling the lot unprocessed. Or perhaps alcohol makes calories evaporate. If it's the latter, it's a selling point the whisky companies have missed.

Noon has come and gone, and I'm back at *Siam Welcomes You*.

"I wasn't sure I'd see you again today," says Sam Trask, presumably referring to the condition in which I last left this establishment.

"I wasn't a hundred per cent sure that you'd still be here either. Despite your conversation with your sister, I reckoned there was at least a one-in-four chance you'd do a runner."

"I said I'd go back to the States, and I will. Though, I am going to need your help, Mr. Braddock."

"Stop calling me Mr. Braddock, Sam. It makes me sound ancient."

"David."

I'd like to believe it was my persuasive skills that convinced this former grunt to stop feeling sorry for himself and to return to the bosom of his family to face the music. But I know it wasn't. He'd already had a bellyful of living like a demented beggar in the City of Angels before I rolled up, and all that was required was for someone to point it out to him. The emotional phone discussion with his sister Becky effectively sealed the deal. When she spoke to me later, she said she wanted me to get him home whatever the cost. Evidently, money is not a problem since she shafted her ex-husband for alimony.

Which is just as well.

"Have you told Mama-san you're leaving?"

"Not yet. Though she suspects something is going on."

Mama-san is eyeing us suspiciously, though she breaks into a grin readily enough when I wink at her.

"Then, don't. Best if you simply don't turn up again after today."

"So, what happens now?"

"I've spoken to one of my contacts. The wheels are already turning on organising you some false papers and a plane ticket to the Land of the Free. Someone will be in touch in the next day or so. They're going to need a passport photograph of you, so I suggest you shave off that beard. It'll make you look more like the naïve American prat that you actually are."

"What's the name of this person?"

"Never mind their name. They have your cell number: that's all that's important. You should be back in Hicksville in a week, probably less."

"*Greensboro*," he says, needled.

"I've been to Greensboro," I tell him. "I know exactly what it's like. Do you have any money?"

"Not really. And I don't suppose I'm going to be paid for my work here, am I?"

I slip him some notes. Surreptitiously, so that Mama-san doesn't see.

"Here's twenty thousand Baht. That should keep you going until your flight. If not, call me and I'll arrange some more for you."

"Aren't you staying in Bangkok?"

"No. I have to be back on Samui tomorrow. Don't worry. You'll be taken care of. I'll cover the cost of your papers and the rest of it."

He stares at me earnestly.

"I'll repay every last cent to you, David."

"No need. I'll be billing your sister. She's my client. Take it up with her."

He is crestfallen at this, and I see the self-reproach nibbling away behind his eyes. Maybe I shouldn't be so hard on the chump, even though my inclination is to give him a good slapping. I put on my therapist's voice before continuing.

"Sam, have you given any consideration as to what you're going to do when you're back home? I'm not talking about jobs. I'm talking about who might be able to offer you emotional support – aside from your sister. What's your relationship like with your parents?"

"I'll build bridges there, but I'm not going to lean on my family." He pauses. "I was thinking about this last night when I couldn't sleep. There *is* someone I am going to reach out to when I'm back in the US. Someone I met here in Bangkok before everything fell apart. A lady from New York. Hitomi is her name."

"She sounds Japanese."

"Japanese-American. Hitomi Tanaka. She was on holiday here, and we ... connected."

I don't like the way he says 'connected'.

But no. It *can't* be the same Hitomi Tanaka. That would be ridiculous. "A single lady?"

He blushes.

"No."

"You don't strike me as the sort of guy who would chase after a married woman."

"Ordinarily, I wouldn't. But there is something special about Hitomi."

I wish he'd stop using her name. I smile benevolently. The urge to slap him is almost overwhelming.

"Don't get me wrong, David. I don't hold out much hope. She as good as told me there was no future for us when she left. She said – much as Becky did – that I needed to rescue a woman. And that she wasn't that woman. That she didn't need rescuing."

Well, she might need rescuing now, Sam. Now that her husband's dead.

I say, "Uh-huh."

"She was incredibly perceptive. But ... What the hell? After what I've been through. It gives me something to focus on."

"Stalking a married woman, you mean?"

He snorts.

"Hardly that."

I should leave this subject alone.

Hitomi.

For God's sake.

Hitomi.

Talk about something else, Braddock. He's wondering what's going on.

"Do you still have the need to save some maiden in distress, Sam? Or has that moment passed?"

He considers the question carefully before responding.

"What I witnessed in Iraq will plague me for the rest of my life, David. If I could do something to redress the balance, even to tip it a little, yes, I would. You might think that childish. Foolish, even. But guilt is hard to live with."

"Yes, it is."

"Maybe I'm unhinged, do you think? Fixated, even?"

I study him. I understand his remorse and shame, because I have known it myself. I still know it.

"Supposing, Sam, that I could help you sort your head out."

"What do you mean?"

"If I knew of some woman who had been victimised; where redress was called for against the person who had hurt her. Would that be of interest to you?"

"What exactly do you have in mind?"

He sounds eager.

Too eager.

Bad idea.

Let's close this down.

"I can't tell you at present. It's something I'm working on, and nothing may come of it, but it concerns an abused woman."

"Then, in principle, yes. But you'd need to be more specific."

I conjure up an image of Hitomi Tanaka, and I can't talk to this man any more. Is this some stupid jealousy, or what?

Sam and Hitomi. Together. Sweating naked beneath her sheets.

I need a drink.

"For now, forget I spoke, Sam. I probably shouldn't have mentioned it."

"But, if something does develop, you *will* get in touch with me?"

Now, Hitomi dissolves, and Jedediah Reichenbach's face looms up. His zealot's stare. That sinister grinning skull. The visage of a man possessed by a single purpose.

Did some of his employer's mania rub off on Sam Trask?

Did some of it rub off on *me*?

Do I come across like him? A man fixed solely on revenge?

How depressingly similar we all are. And how inexplicably connected.

I pat Sam's shoulder in reassurance.

"Yes, Sam. I will get in touch. Trust me."

Ha.

Trust me.

The last plea of the cornered charlatan.

Two whiskies and one beer are all I've drunk today, yet my hands refuse to stay still. If the withdrawal is going to be as bad as the addiction, then it's not much of an incentive to quit.

Abstinence is a right royal pain in the butt. Virtue is such a swindle.

However, I've resolved to be temperate for Jingjai's concert, so I'm making up for the lack of malt by chain-smoking Marlboros. At this point, as I shower and shave for the evening festivities, I estimate my body is about five per cent nicotine, and I must smell like the aftermath of a forest fire. On with the deodorant and Hermès. Teeth scrubbing and flossing. Mouthwash until I gag.

I set my Panama hat at a jaunty angle, and inspect myself in the mirror. Linen-clad, and with my feet in a pair of sturdy brogues, I look like an absconder from a Graham Greene novel. The Englishman abroad. All I need to complete the outfit is a cigarette holder, a monocle, and a bare-breasted native beauty on my arm.

I'll do.

Now, where's that driver?

The venue for Jingjai's gig is a new performance space in Chatuchak called the *Voice of Youth*, so I expect to be the oldest person there.

Inside, it's huge. The main space has a ten-metre-high ceiling, and there are banks of stage lights everywhere, along with rotating spots, a hydraulic stage, smoke machines ... Well, you name it. It's also packed out: there must be a thousand people here. I had no idea Jingjai and the *Silk Thais* were so popular or so successful. The event is being filmed for TV.

I stand (yes, *stand* – there is no ruddy seating) next to Nathon, and his daughters Kanya and Kanikka. Kanikka's boyfriend Sinchai has been dragged along, though he appears cheerful about it. Half-a-dozen of Nathon's gorillas form a human barrier around our party: wealth does have its privileges. Nathon's son Nithin, I gather, is backstage with the leading lady. Samorn, sadly, is not up to the trip.

After a half hour set from the warm-up band, Jingjai and the *Thais* mount the stage to a huge cheer. The girl with the diamond in her tooth is dressed in a long, tight silver dress split to the thigh. She waves and welcomes us in Thai and English before taking her seat at the piano. They launch off into a set of cover versions comprising a mixture of rock, jazz, and popular ballads. It's so good – and the reception from the crowd is so enthusiastic – that I forget my troubles for the next hour, and sweat and sway along with everyone else. Jingjai has recovered fully from all her injuries sustained during the Lamphongchat-Sangukhon drug war. She is a little star. Perhaps soon to be a big star. And to think, she used to be my receptionist at the *Agency*. Her voice is like liquid chocolate with a hint of smoke.

Afterwards, we all go backstage. Once the hugs and congratulations are over, Jingjai takes me aside. There is no trace of diva in her. She is still the same unaffected girl who used to make my coffee.

"Thank you *so* much for coming, David," she says, throwing her arms round my neck. "It's made my night. I'd have understood if you didn't show. With Katie, and everything. It's so sweet of you."

"I wouldn't have missed it for the world, sweetheart."

"Da tells me you've been depressed recently. I'm so sorry."

"*Da?*" I say. "You're in contact with Da?"

"Yes, we talk on the phone regularly. Have done for ages. Didn't she tell you?"

"No, she didn't."

"She's a great source of advice. Always kind and understanding. And she's worried about you, despite her own problems. Well, her one problem in particular."

"What problem?"

"Maybe I've said too much."

"What problem?"

She mimes drawing a zip across her mouth.

"It's not for me to say, David. If she wanted you to know, she'd have told you herself. Please, forget I spoke. Do you want a Pepsi?"

"Don't you have anything stronger?"

"For you, no. Sorry."

"Da has briefed you well, hasn't she?"

When I arrive back at my hotel in the wee small hours, I am stone cold sober. It's not a nice feeling. I am about to raid the mini-bar, but Claire tells me not to.

"Have one night off the booze, eh, David? You'll sleep better."

But I don't sleep better.

I wake at four o'clock, convinced there is someone in my room.

But there isn't.

There's nobody.

Not even a ghost.

9

"I am all in a sea of wonders. I doubt; I fear; I think strange things, which I dare not confess to my own soul."
Bram Stoker, Dracula

Koh Samui again. My trip to Bangkok is now a distant dream.

No rain, so there's a lot of dust in the air.

Vlad is still not back, and my patience is wearing thin. If he's not here in the next week, I'm switching to Plan B.

I've received a gentle prod from Thaddeus Thor that I have not completed the paperwork he sent me so that he can act on my instructions. So, I've done what any lazy ex pat would do: I've dumped the lot on my Thai lawyer's desk and told him to sort it out.

There is one bright spot on the horizon, though.

Wayan returns to the island today. I'm collecting her from the airport this evening.

When I pitch up at the *Agency* after a liquid breakfast, Da is grumpy and out-of-sorts. I'm not sure whether it's because she is on surveillance duty tonight and tomorrow night, or whether it's that I'm having trouble standing up. I suspect it's the latter, because she sends me home in a taxi to stand under a cold shower and drink a couple of cups of black coffee.

I have been instructed to be back at the office by eleven o'clock smelling fragrant, as I have a rare therapy client whose appointment has already been postponed twice. I just make it.

Da inspects me and removes some loose threads from my shirt. Then she smells my breath while Pimpim pretends to be busy.

"You'll do."

Normally, she would give me a much harder time than this, but today her mind is elsewhere. I haven't mentioned Jingjai's slip of the tongue about her 'problem' because I'm waiting for her to be in a more receptive mood. Which at this point, isn't happening. When I reflect on the historical dynamic of our relationship, I would categorise it as two punch-drunk boxers circling in the ring, each waiting for the other's legs to give out. But now, it's different. We're not even in the same ring. She's put up a wall.

We need to talk. But I have to speak to her alone, and that requires me to come up with a reason to get Pimpim out of the office. Then I'll attempt to prise open the oyster. I doubt that will prove easy.

"The client is in your office."

"Don't worry. I'm on my best behaviour."

"I've stopped worrying, David. Life is too short."

With that, she turns on her heel and walks into her office, closing the door quietly behind her. Pimpim offers me a sad look, and I wonder if she's been told anything.

I'll talk to her later. Discreetly.

As irony would have it, the client has come to see me to discuss his heavy drinking. Now, I might have my faults, but I'd like to believe that hypocrisy isn't one of them. Accordingly, I refer him to Samui's alcoholics group and give him the contact number of the island's Austrian psychiatrist Braun, who treated me some years back – although it didn't feel like much of a treat at the time. He's fat and jolly and bloody annoying, but he knows his stuff, dammit.

I don't charge the client and, as we're both at a loose end, I treat him to a lunchtime beer at the Irish Pub.

While we're having our second Singha, I make the decision that I will not take on any more therapy clients. Not unless I go and see a therapist first to sort myself out, and that's not going to be anytime soon. Not until after Grigory Polzin is dead.

I trudge back to the *Agency*. The one o'clock sun is searing and I'm glad I'm wearing my Panama hat. I might moan occasionally about the rain, but I wouldn't mind some now. While I walk, I smoke. My chest is tight, and I seem to have developed a cough. Perhaps it's the dust in the air. Yes, that's probably it. No reason to work myself up.

I am about to knock on Da's door when Pimpim forestalls me.

"Khun Da is not there," she says. "She left a note for you."

She hands me a folded piece of paper. It reads:

David,

I have to go home this afternoon. No more appointments in diary for today.

See you Monday.

Da

"Did she say why she had to go off?"

"No, *Khun* David. But she did have a phone call soon after you left."

"From whom?"

"I don't know. She took it in her office. But she seemed upset."

I scratch the back of my head and re-read her note.

"Does Da seem different to you at the moment?"

"How do you mean, *Khun* David?" she says cautiously.

"Not her usual bustling, efficient self? Like something is troubling her?"

Our receptionist answers noncommittally.

"She's quieter."

"Hmmn. But she hasn't said anything to you?"

Pimpim shakes her head.

I light a Marlboro.

"Take the afternoon off, Pimpim. Nothing's happening. We might as well close the shop."

"Are you sure?"

"Yes. It is Friday, after all. Off you go. Have a good weekend. I'll lock up."

She grabs her bag and hurries down the stairs before I change my mind.

As soon as I hear the front door close, I go into Da's office and rummage around in her desk and filing cabinet.

I'm not sure what I'm searching for, but whatever it is, I don't find it. All I discover is yet further evidence of my colleague's tidiness. And some hand cream.

No condoms or cocaine.

In fact, nothing of a personal nature at all save for a framed picture of Da with Pratcha. No photographs of Tong. Though, I could swear she used to have one on the top of her filing cabinet.

I secure the premises, climb into the jeep and consider my next move.

It doesn't require too much thought.

I'll drive to Da's place and, if she's there, I'll insist we have a conversation. Or rather *the* conversation. The one I've been putting off.

I clunk my vehicle into gear and switch on the air blaster. I would like to listen to some heavy rock, but the jeep's music system isn't working. My ride also has four bald tyres, and more scratches than paint on its bodywork. It needs some TLC. Like most of the objects and people in my life, it's been neglected while I seesaw around the Grigory Polzin project. But, let's not get into that now.

Focus, Braddock.

Da first. Murder later.

So as not to give Da notice of my arrival – which would give her the opportunity to come up with an excuse as to why she can't talk to me – I leave my jeep in the road next to hers and take a cut-through on foot.

Two police cars are parked outside Da's house. A stern-faced policeman stands guard on the porch.

Nosy neighbours are standing around in groups, having animated discussions and gawking. My initial impulse is to stride up to the front door, knock loudly and demand to be told what is going on. On this occasion, however, moderation prevails. If Da is in some sort of trouble, the last thing she needs is me making an exhibition of myself.

As the *soi* is generously endowed with foliage, I position myself behind a clump of dense bushes to observe proceedings. Nobody pays me any heed. I'm the least interesting thing around.

After a couple of minutes, my coworker appears, closely flanked and proceeded by officers of the law. She holds her hands down and in front of her, but from this angle, my sightline partially obscured by people and by one of the police vehicles, I cannot tell whether she is cuffed. Her face, like that of her escorts, is grim. A friendly soul asks about Pratcha, and Da calls back that her cousin will pick him up from school. Without more ado, she is deposited into the back of one of the cars, and two of the policemen gruffly tell the onlookers to disperse. They do so with reluctance.

Da doesn't see me, concealed as I am in the greenery. Her eyes are fixed downwards. I fancy there is something akin to shame in them. The cars drive off. There are no sirens or flashing lights. Within moments, the scene has returned to that of a normal Friday afternoon.

Should I head over to the police station or to Da's cousin's place to ask some pertinent questions? The Braddock of Old would certainly have done so. But there is nothing certain about this Braddock. I can't even prioritise properly between killing myself with alcohol and killing Grigory Polzin with a bullet. All is prevarication and excuse.

Here I am, furtively lurking. Like a stalker among the branches. Wondering what I need more: a cigarette or a drink.

Something fundamental has occurred. Da – these days, my principal emotional crutch – has been taken away by the police. And I have no idea why.

I sense that a floor has given way inside me. The last pillar has tumbled. No walls remain standing. There is nothing left to support the roof.

But never mind about *me*. It's *her* I should be worrying about.

Da, what on earth is going on?

I go back to my jeep and light a Marlboro.

I double-check that my phone is switched on.

Da will call me if she needs me, I tell myself.

But – *will she?* What am I, these days, when all is said and done, but an unreliable drunk? Why would she put her faith in me?

I need time to decide what to do. From now until tomorrow – unless Da rings me in the meantime – I will do nothing. If I haven't heard from her by, say, eight o'clock tomorrow morning, then I will call her. And if I receive no response, I will ring round her family members, drive over to the police station, do whatever has to be done ...

No, wait. A better idea. Once I've collected Wayan this evening, I'll keep checking back here to see if Da's home. Say, every hour. I can say to Wayan I'm on a surveillance job.

If Da isn't back by eleven, I'll call her cousin, then I'll go to Bophut Police Station and raise hell.

She's not spending a night in the cells if I have anything to do with it.

Good.

That's more like it, Braddock.

It's at seven that I am scheduled to collect Wayan at the airport.

My joy and relief at her decision to return to Samui is tempered by a nervousness as to how we will respond to each other. I want things between us to be as they were before our disastrous trip to London. Or as close as we can achieve to that. I miss the ease and trust, the humdrum, straightforward interactions we used to have. The days before guilt took her over. Before the gaping sense of loss and the fixation with payback took *me* over.

However, to wind back the clock to that untroubled time requires both of us to revert to our former selves. And, unfortunately, bad experiences are not so easily erased. They become part of who we are, burrowing into our flesh – into the deepest parts of us – like determined bloodsuckers. It becomes a struggle between the parasite and the host as to who is the most resolute.

In my case, it is a battle I am losing.

My housekeeper, though, looks more serene than she did at our last parting. And, despite the sadness that I can yet detect in her eyes, she appears to have made some kind of peace with herself. As she walks through Arrivals, there is less heaviness in her gait. She smiles at me, and I can't help smiling back.

We hug briefly, and I pick up her suitcase.

During the drive to Mae Nam, we keep the conversation light. I feel relief flood through me. Wayan is back, and whatever notions she may have had about staying in Bali are now irrelevant. They don't matter.

"I've missed you," I say.

"I have missed you too, Mr. David."

She briefly rests a hand on my arm, and I have to suppress a catch in my throat.

"How is the apartment?"

"Clean and tidy. Never fear, you're not coming home to a slum."

Coming home. How reassuring those words sound.

"But I'm afraid I am on surveillance duty this evening, Wayan. I will have to love you and leave you. Clients are *such* a nuisance, aren't they? We can get back to normal tomorrow, after you've unpacked and rested from your flights."

"No problem, Mr. David. Your work has priority. Do we have food in?"

"Yes. The larder and fridge are fully stocked."

"Then, I shall cook you a full English breakfast in the morning."

"Excellent. It's not been the same without your cooking."

"You have lost weight."

"Well, I probably needed to."

"And how is Da? We haven't messaged for a few days."

"She's OK. Well, you know Da. Same old, same old."

Except that she isn't the same old Da. But until I understand what's going on, I'm not about to burden Wayan with speculation. Let her settle in before the next catastrophe strikes.

More concealments by yours truly.

Has my life *ever* been straightforward?

I am reluctant to leave Wayan at the apartment. The sense of lightness that is infusing me is like a tonic, and it more than compensates for the dull pain in my chest that came on this afternoon, and which is stubbornly refusing to leave. I shall continue to ignore it.

And – water aside – I shall *not* be having any drinks this evening. I might even cut back on the fags as my breathing is a bit raspy. I need to be clear-headed, and with working lungs. I might be visiting the police station in a few hours, where some indignant shouting may be required.

Eight o'clock.

I drive up Da's road.

Her house is in darkness, so I turn my jeep around, pick up some bottled water at a nearby *Family Mart* and head to one of the small beaches at Mae Nam to do some thinking. I switch off the engine, plonk myself down on the sand and rehydrate. The Marlboros stay in my pocket.

It's quiet. Nobody is about except for a couple of ancient Thai woman who look like they have been carved from teak. They offer me toothless grins as they plod by. Under the bright moon, the flat sea is an aquarelle wash. It is at times like this that Claire tends to show up, but tonight she is otherwise engaged. Either that, or she is giving me some space. Which is to say, *I* am giving me some space.

At this point, it would be beneficial if I could meditate awhile, so I give it a go.

No chance.

My attempt is half-hearted and feeble. I give up. Were he here, the Old Monk would be suitably disgusted by his ineffectual protégé. But I do have a reasonable excuse: I am too preoccupied with Da.

Her uncharacteristic remoteness and self-absorption.

Her atypical disinterest in business matters.

The absence of Tong.

Her being driven away in a police car.

I don't like where these thoughts are headed, so I light a cigarette.

This brings a resurgence of chest pain which helps to drive away an unwelcome notion that has been circling me.

The notion that my trusted coworker may have killed her husband.

10

"People aren't either wicked or noble. They're like chef's salads, with good things and bad things chopped and mixed together in a vinaigrette of confusion and conflict."

Lemony Snicket, The Grim Grotto

Saturday morning, and I'm on my balcony sitting down to a cooked breakfast. Wayan has joined me, and she is sipping a pineapple juice. We're talking about inconsequential stuff, and the whole tableau is joyously domestic and normal. The pain in my chest has gone away, even though I smoked more cigarettes last night than intended. I did *not*, however, drink anything other than water. A minor success, then. Some remnants of my willpower remain.

While Wayan removes the plates and cutlery, my mind flips back to yesterday.

Da's place was still dark during my circuits at nine and ten o'clock. After my first drive there, I decided it would be better if I parked in the next street and walked along the cut-through. Otherwise, Da might spot my distinctively-decrepit jeep – which would lead to a whole new conflict situation.

At eleven, the downstairs lights in Da's house were on, and I could see her walking around inside. Her movements looked stiff and twitchy, and her face was an unreadable mask. But she wasn't happy, that's for sure.

Of Tong, there was no sign.

Having satisfied myself that Da was safely home, I made my way back to the jeep. A *farang* on his own hanging around for too long might result in a meddlesome neighbour calling the cops, and then *I* would be the one spending the night in a police cell.

In the bright light of day, my speculations on whether Da might have done away with her husband seem absurd. She and Tong were childhood sweethearts, devoted to each other. In all the years I have known her, I have never detected even a scintilla of discontent in her marriage. Quite the reverse. It says more about my current mental state than it does about my coworker's character that I could suspect - even for a second - that she would be capable of such an act.

True, Tong is obviously not around at present, and Da is not being open about his absence. At least, not with me. But there could be a whole host of explanations for that state of affairs, not all of them sinister. Da is a private person. Whenever difficulties crop up, she is used to sorting them out herself. Some embarrassing family issue might have arisen; one she is not keen to make public. Moreover, I may have misremembered there being a photograph of Tong in Da's office. It must be admitted, my memory is not always reliable, especially when I am preoccupied - as I am now - with other concerns.

Then there is the little matter of the police taking Da away. That happening might be completely unrelated to Tong. Connecting the two events is something *I* have decided to do, and it's not necessarily valid reasoning. Possible Braddock confirmation bias at play. Not *every* occurrence is a link in some karmic chain of causation, despite what the Old Monk and my dead wife might say. Plus, Da is not under arrest and incarcerated at Bophut Police Station. She's at home.

The above thought-stream offers me a degree of comfort, but it doesn't actually explain anything. I am no nearer to understanding what is going on in her head. To unearth the truth or truths, I need either to confront Da, or to do some clandestine digging. My natural temperament favours the latter course. I can always *ask her* if all else fails.

And, yes, I am fully aware that I may be using this as a diversion to delay my getting on with the business of dispatching Grigory Polzin. But, at present, Vlad's sojourn in Moscow provides me with a valid excuse for inaction. For a while longer, anyway …

Wayan interrupts my cogitations.

"Mr. David, there are one or two things that we need. If it's all right with you, I would like to go out and do some shopping."

So much for my making sure our supplies were in order. Though, in fairness, I've never claimed to be an expert on the mechanics of housekeeping.

"That's fine, Wayan. Let me give you some cash."

"And – while I am out – I wondered if it would be all right if I called in to see Miss Da? To say hello."

Perfect. If I can't find out what's going on with Da Pintaraporn, perhaps Wayan can.

"That's fine. Take as long as you like. I have a few things to do myself, and I'll be going to the shooting range later. I probably won't be back until late afternoon."

"Is there anything special you would like for dinner?"

"As long as we are eating together, I don't care what we have."

That's not me being smarmy. I mean it.

I am *so* glad Wayan's here.

My first port of call in unravelling the Pintaraporn mystery is Tong's workplace. I drive over to Chaweng where he owns and runs a repair shop at the bottom end of town.

Correction: *owned and ran.*

The place is closed. The tell-tale signs of disuse are on full display. The metal shutters at the front have faded event flyers from months ago pasted on them. The concrete hard-standing is dotted with sausages of dogshit, some of them rather hairy and white.

I squeeze down the alley at the side of the building, and squint through the dirty windows at the back. As my eyes become accustomed to the dark interior, I can make out the hallmarks of abandonment. No computer equipment or phones. No desks or chairs. Old papers and receipts all over the floor. Peeling paint on the walls. An empty noticeboard.

Nothing has been going on here for some time.

I make enquiries of the neighbouring shopkeepers. All they can tell me is that *Tong's Repairs* has been shut for some time and that, no, they don't know if he's moved somewhere else. The question, *When did you last see Khun Tong?* meets with the same response from everyone: a blank expression, and the words, *Long time.*

The next stop is *Fergie's Tattoos.*

Now, I might not have shown much of an interest in Da's husband over the years, but there are one or two things about him that I do recollect. The first is that Tong enjoys fishing when time permits, and the second is that he likes watching televised English Premier League matches at the *Chaweng Mega-Screens Bar.* (You will note at this point that I am still using the present tense when I speak of Tong. Call me sentimental.)

While Tong is nonpartisan in his football viewing – professing only the desire to see a 'good game' – his old school chum who accompanies him to the aforesaid bar is anything but nonpartisan. Kornkan Phanthusim is a diehard Manchester United fan, even going so far as to name his tattoo business after the Red Devils' long-serving manager. Accordingly, most people simply refer to him as 'Fergie', a label with which he is more than content. I guess if my parents had lumbered me with the handle *Kornkan*, I'd have been glad to grab at any nickname that came along. Even *Tiny Dick*.

Sporting impressive dreadlocks, reeking of weed, and with much of his body covered in football-or-dragon-themed ink, Fergie is unquestionably the possessor of great artistic talents in the sharpened bamboo department. He also has the reputation of being an unpredictable nutcase – which may be down to his legendary consumption of cannabis-based products. He once famously claimed that his tattoos come alive on your skin. *Well, maybe they do for you, Fergie*. I find it surprising that Tong, who has always struck me as strait-laced, would have such a character for a bosom buddy. But bonds formed in childhood can be difficult to break. Shared history, and all that sappy nonsense.

The tattoo parlour – situated on a Chaweng side-road, and hemmed-in by shops displaying original paintings, and stalls flogging unoriginal sarongs and beaming monkeys made from coconuts – is open. But Fergie has no customers to adorn at present. I discover him lounging on a chair, drinking some dubious tea from a chipped mug, and muttering to himself. A faded Man Utd banner hangs from a beam and a mangy dog is curled up in the corner. The walls are covered in photographs of happy sunburned Europeans displaying the proprietor's handiwork.

His bloodshot eyes narrow when he sees me.

"Hello, Fergie. How's business?"

"Quiet," he answers cautiously.

"I suppose it's too early in the day for pissed tourists wanting tattoos."

He grunts.

"What do you want?"

"I'm looking for Tong. Do you know where I can find him?"

"Tong's wife works for you, doesn't she?"

"Or I work for her. It's rather ambiguous these days."

"Then, I suggest you ask *her*."

"I'm asking you."

"I have nothing to say."

"Come on, Fergie. I'm sure it's not a state secret. I'm only asking for a little information."

"Go away," he replies. There is an edge to his voice now, and his eyes are defiant. "I'm busy."

"No, you aren't."

Silence.

"Have the police called on you about Tong?"

"Close the door on your way out. You're letting the heat in."

He rises, and disappears into the back room.

As Wayan's cooked breakfast is still sledging its way through my entrails, I forego lunch in favour of a couple of Marlboros and a cold Chang.

The Tong conundrum is becoming curiouser and curiouser. So far, I've drawn nothing but a big fat blank. That's both annoying and concerning in equal measure. It crosses my mind to drop by the police station and see if I can glean anything there. But I've used up most of my goodwill with the local boys in blue (or rather, khaki), and I'd rather stay below their radar for the time being. I resolve to put Tong out of my head for now. Perhaps Wayan's visit to Da will throw up something.

Later, Braddock.

Meanwhile, I go off to the shooting range. Polzin's not about to blow his own brains out, and it's time I got back on track. Back to what really counts. I have allowed myself to become distracted – sidetracked, one might assert – by non-Russian matters. That needs to stop.

I pop off a few dozen rounds, each time firing five shots in quick succession. The results are variable, and I can't blame it on quavering hands because I'm steady today. I'm just shit with a pistol, that is all. I wish it were possible to buy grenades over the counter in Moscow. That would be *much* easier.

When I arrive home, Wayan is not yet back, so I refresh my memory on my Polzin and Orlov notes, and do a few Internet searches on things Russki. Nothing new.

Hurry up, Vlad. This is wearing.

There is an email from Becky Cates telling me that her brother is in Greensboro. She acknowledges my efforts on her behalf, and requests that I send her my invoice. *Don't worry if it's a big one,* she adds. *It's worth it to have Sam safe. Thanks again, David.*

Ah, well. At least somebody's happy.

I hear the sound of keys, and a few seconds later Wayan's head appears around the door.

"Sorry I took so long, Mr. David," she says. "Can I get you anything?"

"No thanks, Wayan. I'm good. How is Da?"

I close my laptop and swivel around to face my housekeeper. There is an evasiveness in her eyes, and she doesn't reply immediately.

"I've been rather worried about her lately, you see," I explain. "She's not been herself. But that's Da. She's not exactly forthcoming."

"No. She isn't."

I had hoped for rather more than this, so I plunge in.

"Did she talk to you about what might be bothering her?"

"She does seem *down*, Mr. David. As you say, not herself."

At this point, I can either grill a reluctant Wayan, or I can remind myself that my Balinese Princess has only recently returned, and that it is imperative that I don't make her uncomfortable or stressed. Otherwise, she might jump on a plane back to Denpasar. And I do *not* want that.

"Maybe I should talk to her."

"Yes," she says, relieved. "That would be best, Mr. David. Would you excuse me now, while I unpack the shopping?"

"Unpack away."

"Will dinner at seven be all right?"

"That will be fine, Wayan. And don't tell me what we're having. I'd like it to be a surprise, OK?" I smile as reassuringly as I can. The subject of Da is dropped and the tension dissipates.

"OK."

There was a time – not so long ago – when I could persuade women to open up to me. But not now, it seems.

There's another skill I appear to have misplaced.

Have I altered that much?

After dinner, I drive to the office and reacquaint myself with the case Da is working on. I flip open the thin file and leaf through the notes.

Our client is an Italian-Swiss pastry chef, Mateo Moretti, from Lausanne. We have a photograph of his potentially-disloyal squeeze, coyly holding up a cocktail glass for the camera. Pla Parwinuk is tall, slim and bony, and apparently recently-arrived on Samui from Isaan. If that is correct, it is helpful for my purposes. After several years on the island, my face is well-known to many of the bar girls and, if they spot me, they realise the game is up. PI Braddock, remorseless pursuer of unfaithful females, has become too familiar a presence to remain incognito. One might say, I am a victim of my own success.

Anyway, that's the excuse I use these days for dumping most of the surveillance jobs on Da. She appears to accept the reasoning, even though it interferes with her sleep.

If our notes are correct, the svelte Pla should be spending this evening drinking with a couple of her female buddies at *Roxy's* in Chaweng Noi. She should also have been there yesterday evening when Da was supposedly on duty – but was *not*.

I replace the file in the cabinet, lock up the office, and climb back into my jeep.

It's half-past nine.

My plan is initially to watch Da watching Pla. And, as and when the opportunity presents itself, to talk to my partner about her baffling behaviour. But, business first. Let's see if Miss Pla is being good, or whether her boyfriend's suspicions are well-founded.

As expected, Da's bike is standing outside *Roxy's*. I park my vehicle down the road in a dirt side-turning.

The place is busy. *Good*. I spy Da perched on a stool at the bar, and with her back to me. To her left is an overweight Western man whom she is studiously ignoring. To her right is a table with several young laughing Thai women, one of whom I recognise as our target. I look around for somewhere to sit where I will be out of Da's sight-line.

I locate a small bench squeezed into a corner, from where I should be well-positioned to view surreptitiously the unfolding of the evening.

But, before I can sit, a fracas erupts. I watch, temporarily transfixed, as Da throws her drink in the face of the *farang* at her side, before slipping off her bar stool and giving him a hearty slap to the side of his face. She screams something at him, and everyone turns to goggle at this free, unexpected entertainment. The man's face darkens in anger, and he takes a step towards Da.

I am there in a flash. As his hands grab at her, I twist him round and plant a satisfying right hook to his jaw. He staggers backwards, and several glasses go flying. Caught unawares, the man loses his footing, and lands heavily. There is a sickening thud as his head makes contact with the floor. At first, I think he might have been rendered unconscious, but after a moment he pulls himself up. He is groggy and shocked. I become aware that Da is gripping my arm.

"What are you doing here?" she says.

I don't reply. I want to see if this fat bastard has the stomach for a fist-fight.

He doesn't.

Cursing, he rises to his feet, yells something at me in Cockney-English, then elbows his way out onto the street.

The customers go back to their drinks. One of the bar staff produces a dustpan and brush, and starts sweeping up the mess of glass and liquid. He appears unfazed: another normal evening at *Roxy's*.

I grasp Da's hand, and unceremoniously drag her out into the car park. Her face is flushed.

"I had it under control, David," she asserts, recovering her composure. "There was no need for that. He'd been coming onto me for the last half-hour and –"

"You did *not* have it under control, Da. He was a big bugger and he might have hurt you. You *lost* it."

I release her hand.

"Go home," I tell her. "We'll talk about this later. I'll take over."

"I am perfectly capable –"

"No, Da, you're *not*. You can hardly maintain a discreet presence here after what's just happened."

"Well," she says defiantly, "neither can you. You've thumped a customer, and almost knocked him out."

Her logic is sound, but I'm not about to agree with her.

I treat her to one of my stern stares. "That's *my* problem. Go home."

"What are you doing here, anyway? Checking up on me?"

"Go. Home. Now."

She acknowledges I am not about to budge. This detective's not for turning.

"I need to pay for my drinks first."

"I'll sort that out."

I fold my arms, nightclub-bouncer-style.

She musters her dignity, and walks slowly to her bike. She doesn't turn around.

I wait until she has ridden off before lighting a Marlboro.

Shit. What now?

I return to the bar, and receive some appraising glances. An understanding barman waves away my apologies, explaining that the oaf in question had it coming. I settle Da's bill and carry a draught Singha to the corner table. The tailing operation is now a farce – my coworker was right about that – but I need a few minutes to gather my thoughts: none of which are about *Agency* business.

I've finished half of my beer and smoked another Marlboros, when I become aware that someone is standing in front of me.

"That was a nice punch," says the tall Thai girl.

"Thank you," I reply. "I try not to make a habit of whacking people, though."

A giggly laugh.

"My name is Pla. What's your name?"

"David."

And your bloke is paying me to follow you, I don't add.

"Was that your girlfriend?"

"No. Only a friend."

"Ah. Do you have a girlfriend?"

"No. Not at present."

"A wife?"

"Not when I last checked."

She weighs this up.

"Can I join you, David?"

Sure. Why not? I can just picture my report to Mateo Moretti. It would run something like, "I observed Pla on Saturday, and she chatted up a Western man. Then they went off to a hotel together and had sex. I know this to be true because I was the man." Evidentially, that would be compelling, but we probably wouldn't get our invoice paid.

Instead, I reply, "I'm flattered, Pla, but I have to be going in a minute."

She wanders off.

The remainder of this assignment will have to be delegated to our young, sometime-associate, Prem. He's finished with school so, when he's not peddling drugs, he has time on his hands. And he's rather expert at stalking women. By now, he may even have a police record to that effect.

I drive back to Mae Nam slowly, my mind clogged with contemplations of Da.

Missing husband.

Police.

Now this.

Oh, Da.

What on earth has happened to you?

11

"I believe that every human has a finite amount of heartbeats. I don't intend to waste any of mine running around doing exercises."
Neil Armstrong

Sunday morning.

In that ambiguous land between sleep and waking, I feel Claire's hand stroking my cheek. But when I open my eyes, I am alone. Since I neglected to close my curtains before turning in, the sunlight is streaming through my bedroom window, painting the room a bright orange. Even so, my dead wife's touch lingers on my skin.

Great. My hallucinations are now no longer only visual and auditory. They have become tactile too. And I can't even blame it on alcohol, since all I had to drink yesterday evening was *one* Singha.

Perhaps it was the lack of malt whisky coupled with the weird happening at *Roxy's* that have not only ramped up my delirium, but also caused the psychedelic dreams that thundered through my defenceless grey cells during the night.

Dead women, everywhere.

Claire, Anna, Kat – all meeting their respective ends. While in the background, like a kind of hellish soundtrack, the voice of my sometime-psychiatrist Braun intoned, *Women die around you, Braddock.* Interspersed with these scenes of loss, like some dismal advertising break, was the repeating vision of a pale, gowned Katie wandering through a graveyard, searching the headstone inscriptions for I know not what. But the most disturbing feature of these images was that, while they supposedly represented deceased family members and lovers, I could sense the presence of Da. The eyes of the other women were somehow *her* eyes.

If I were the superstitious type, I would fret that I was witnessing some kind of portent. An omen. Luckily, I'm not fixated on magical auguries. I'm just a guy who might have a drink problem. Plus, evidently, a problem when I don't drink. *Bummer*. Heads you lose; tails you still bloody lose.

However, if my unquiet slumber has done nothing else, it has reinforced my belief that I must talk to Da today. No more prevaricating.

Well, I say that, but first I require breakfast. Furthermore, a trip to the gym would seem to be in order. That way, over croissants I can mention to Wayan that Da had a meltdown last night, and she might get the hint and call her while I'm pulling weights. That will give us both time to think of what we want to say to each other.

This is *strategy*, by the way, not *procrastination*. I'm done with procrastination.

At least, I will be later today.

Besides myself, Tim is the only other member of the Parlour Gang to make it to the gym this morning.

We unadvisedly decide we should have a 'proper' workout, and I overdo it. Also, my right hand is swollen from last night's punch, and even a SangSom-fortified coffee can't anaesthetise the pain. I'm so short of breath I daren't light a Marlboro for fear of asphyxiating like the unfortunate crew of the *Akula*. Now, aching muscles are one thing, but when it comes to not being able to smoke, it's time to call it a day.

"Did I tell you the story of my little escapade in Berlin in nineteen-eighty, David?" Tim asks.

"No," I reply.

He has, in fact, already recounted the tale, but it's easier to hear the anecdote again than to try and take part in a conversation – an activity that would require me both to breathe *and* talk at the same time.

"Well, I shouldn't really be saying any of this but ... Anyway, the Yanks asked if my team of divers would come in and move some anti-personnel mines in the River Spree, so they could smuggle some spy out from the Russian sector of Berlin. This was in November, and as you can imagine ..."

As Tim burbles away, I come to a decision. *Screw this exercise lark*. It's not as if I'm going to wrestle Grigory Polzin to death. I only need to be fit enough to fire a gun. And giving myself a heart attack in a vain effort to be buff is not going to help matters.

Ergo, I quit. Consider the towel thrown in. Time to leave the ring.

So, it's goodbye to early mornings, to *Rhino's Gym*, to unpalatable coffee, and to Tim's rollicking yarns.

I've heard them all anyway.

I arrive back at the apartment sweaty and sober: an unattractive combination.

After I've showered and changed into something more suited to a man of my age and fitness level, I speak to Wayan.

"I think I'd better ring Da. See what all that kerfuffle was about last night."

"Actually, Mr. David, Da called while you were at the gym. She wanted to give you a heads-up that she will need to book leave for tomorrow."

"She called *you*? Why didn't she call *me*?"

But I know perfectly well why Da phoned Wayan: to judge the temperature of the water. To ask my housekeeper what kind of mood I was in, and to find out what I had said to Wayan about the fiasco at *Roxy's.* My housekeeper is too honest for her own good. And for my own good.

"Never mind," I say. "I'm going to my study."

"Do you want some lunch, Mr. David?"

"A sandwich, maybe. After I've called Da."

I close the door to my study and smoke a Marlboro before I select Da's cell number.

"Hello, David." Her tone is difficult to read. "Did Wayan pass on my message? Will it be OK with you if I book tomorrow off? I have some family business to attend to, and there's not too much in the appointments diary."

"We can talk about that later today, when we meet *in person*."

"Ah," she says. "In person."

"What time are you free this afternoon?"

"I'm afraid I have some things I have to attend to this afternoon. Sorry, David. Would it be all right if we got together this evening?"

"Yes, very well. Eight o'clock."

"At the office?"

"No. I'll book a table for us at *Valentino's*."

"*Valentino's?* That place where young couples meet? Why there?"

"Well, it's not because I want to whisper sweet nothings in your ear, Da. It's because the tables are private. Plus, the presence of other people might help me restrain my urge to throttle you."

"Ah, I see."

Now, she sounds suitably abashed.

"Eight o'clock, then."

The hours tick by.

I get caught up in an article on an Internet site which explores the *modus operandi* of Russian spies operating abroad and their killing methods. It's not directly relevant to my Grigory Polzin project, but any information about assassination may give me one or two handy pointers. Though I don't know how I would go about laying my hands on any radioactive material, or the other sorts of unusual and lethal gadgetry the Kremlin churns out for its boys. In his book *Aquarium* – the article goes on – the defector Viktor Suvorov catalogues the Russian state's barbarous ethos, and says it never forgives a betrayal. The man himself expects to spend the rest of his life looking over his shoulder, and talks of deep cover operatives living in the UK.

How deep a part of the Russian state is Polzin? I wonder.

Hmmn.

Food for thought.

I stub out my cigarette: it's seven-thirty, and I haven't reached for the bottle all day.

Before I leave the apartment, I have a brief conversation with my housekeeper.

"Wayan, I realise that you and Da are close friends, and that you don't want to break any confidences. But, is there anything I should speak to her about while I'm meeting her in private? Anything – *important?*"

She hesitates before answering. Then she nods resignedly.

"Tong," she says. "Talk to her about Tong, Mr. David. It's time."

Even though I reach *Valentino's* ten minutes early, Da is already there. She has a glum expression on her face, and is cradling a glass of soda water. I sit opposite her. She is like a naughty schoolgirl who has been summoned to the headmaster's office.

"Are you going to sack me, David? Is that what this is about?" she says without ado.

"Do you think I *should* sack you?"

"I was unprofessional. If our positions were reversed, I'd probably fire you."

"Yes, but you're heartless. I'm not."

"So, this is only a telling-off?"

"No, this is not a telling-off."

A waiter has appeared, and he asks if I'd like to order a drink.

"Bring us a bottle of white wine and two glasses. Also, a jug of iced water."

"White wine, sir? We have –"

"I don't care. Just a decent bottle of anything dry. So long as it's not French."

He slips away.

"Am I going to need something stronger than soda water, then, David?"

"You *like* white wine, don't you?"

"Yes."

"Then stop grumbling."

I stare at her for a few seconds. I hope I look stern.

Then I say, "I want you to tell me about Tong."

"Tong?"

"Yes, Tong. Your husband."

"Has Wayan said something to you? Because –"

"Wayan hasn't said a thing to me. She's too loyal to you for that."

She squirms satisfyingly in her chair.

"I don't see how this is relevant."

"Quit stalling, Da. We both know it's exceptionally relevant. So far as I can gather, no-one has seen Tong in months."

I reach over and take her hand. This unexpected show of affection catches her by surprise, though she doesn't try to pull away.

I say softly, "Talk to me."

Desolation rises in her eyes, but she fights it back.

"Have you killed him, Da?"

Now she pulls away. The desolation is gone in an instant, and in its place anger flares. Her mouth becomes a narrow, disdainful slit.

"Have I done *what?*" Her words are cold and contemptuous. "You think I've murdered Tong? Is that why I'm here? You think me capable of *that,* do you, David?"

"No."

"Then, why would you ask me such a thing?"

I give it a second or two before replying. "To get a reaction, Da. To try and unlock those lips of yours that are so firmly sealed. You have not been straight with me."

I let this sink in. She seems inclined to accept my speech at face value. Her ire fades, and she swiftly surveys the restaurant to see if anyone is listening to us. It appears that nobody is. She sighs.

"Talk to me. Please. Tell me what's going on."

Da bites her lip and stares into my face as if for reassurance. One more little sincere shove should do it.

I place my hands on the table.

"I do realise that I'm not the most sensitive of people, Da. But you are an essential person in my life. And, all banter aside, I do care about you. A lot. So, trust me. Mmn?"

As Da gathers her thoughts, she spots the swollen knuckles of my right hand.

"That was quite a punch last night," she says. "Really, quite impressive. Does your hand hurt?" She strokes the inflamed skin gently with her fingertips.

"A bit. Long time since I've done any boxing. Frankly, I'm surprised I didn't shatter some bones. My bones, not his."

There is silence as the waiter returns and dribbles some wine in my glass. I taste it and indicate my approval. He pours for both of us and inquires if we are ready to order.

"Are you hungry?" I ask my coworker.

"Not much."

"A selection of starters, then?"

"Yes. That will be fine."

Our waiter scribbles on his pad and withdraws. Da downs a mouthful of wine, then sets her glass aside.

"So, you want to know all about Mr. and Mrs. Pintaraporn, do you, David?"

"I do."

"I must warn you, it's not pretty."

"Life seldom is, my dear."

Da takes a deep breath.

"About fifteen months ago, Tong and I started having problems."

She pauses, so I prompt her lightly.

"You and Tong always struck me as being devoted to each other. What happened?"

"Tong's gambling happened. He'd always liked playing cards. But he'd always kept it under control. Then it got *out* of control."

She dabs her lips with a napkin.

"You are aware that Thongchai Rattanakorn runs about twenty illegal gambling houses on the island?"

"I am."

"Tong started playing serious poker. For serious money. And, as you might expect, he lost. *Big*. The next thing I knew, we were up to our ears in debt. There were dreadful rows, as you can imagine. But I won't dwell on *that*.

"Anyway, to cut a long story short, we had to sell all of our family land, including Tong's family's land here and on Koh Phangan. We only barely managed to keep our house. All of our savings went. At the same time, Tong's business took a downturn. If it hadn't been for my salary… Well, I'm not sure what we would have done."

"Jesus, Da. Do you need money now? Because if so –"

"No, David," she says firmly. "I can cope. Things are stable now. Our debt is paid off."

"And Tong?"

Da takes another deep breath.

"Last September, I told him I wanted a divorce. I threw him out of the house, and his parents took my side.

"He closed his shop and informed me that, as he wasn't wanted, he was going to live in Bangkok. I pleaded with him to stay on Samui for the sake of Pratcha, but he was determined to leave. And he did."

Da has another mouthful of wine. I top up her glass.

"Tong had changed, you see. The gambling obsession changed him. It ate him alive, hollowed him out. The sweet man I'd loved was still there, but his addiction and his shame drove him away from me. Perhaps I shouldn't have kicked him out. If I hadn't …"

She is close to breaking down.

But the story isn't finished.

I let her compose herself before I ask, "What were those two police cars doing at your house on Friday?"

She stares at me, aghast.

"Who told you about that?"

A couple at an adjacent table are taking too much of an interest in our conversation. I glare at them, and they return reluctantly to their meal.

"Nobody told me, Da. I was there. I saw the police take you away."

"You've been *spying* on me?"

"Hardly *spying*. I was concerned for you, that's all. You've been acting odd lately."

"Yes," she says. "I suppose I have."

I wait.

"The police came to my house and asked me to go to the station with them.

"A man had been found dead in Bangkok. Murdered. The body had been provisionally identified as that of my husband. They wanted me to look at some photographs. Tomorrow I have to go to Bangkok, to the morgue, to formally identify him. But I already know it's Tong. It seems he was killed after a fight at a poker game."

"So, that's why you want to have tomorrow off?"

"Yes."

"Would you like me to come with you?"

"That's not necessary, David. Tong's mother and father are accompanying me. One of my cousins will look after Pratcha for the day. And, of course, I will have to book some leave for the funeral in due course."

"That's OK."

"Thank you."

I digest this information, before saying, "Why couldn't you tell me any of this before? You must have been in a terrible state for months. Don't you trust me?"

"It's not about trust, David. I *was* going to tell you. But you had your own crises. And then, when Katie disappeared in November ... Well, let's say there has never been a right time."

"Huh. You still should have said something," I grumble.

"Maybe. Well, you know now."

I scratch my head.

"And why the hell did the Samui police send *two* cars to pick you up?"

She shrugs.

"I guess they haven't had a lot of excitement on the island recently. Figured they'd make a show of it. No doubt, it will be all over the local paper tomorrow."

"Uh-hu."

Da studies me.

"Is that why you thought I had killed Tong? Because of the police cars?"

"For heaven's sake, Da, I did *not* think you had murdered Tong. That's ridiculous."

But I had thought *just* that. For a brief time, yes. But the notion had undeniably gone through my mind.

Our food arrives, and we become mute while we pick unenthusiastically at the *Valentino's* offerings. It's not that there's anything wrong with the food. It's *us*.

Well, in truth, it's *me*.

My head is totally bollocksed. I see death and bad intentions everywhere. For me, everyone is either a killer or a victim.

The sooner I get rid of Polzin, the better.

As if she has a direct line into my neural network, Da says, "Anyway, you've been preoccupied lately too. And I'm sure it's not only that you're mourning. I have the impression that you're planning something unwise."

"Like what?"

She doesn't reply directly. Instead, she says, "Nothing good ever comes of revenge, David."

I make no comment.

Now it's her turn to put her hand on mine.

"What will it take for you to stop drinking?"

The death of Grigory Polzin. Nothing less.

"I don't know," I say. "Shall we order another bottle of wine?"

12

"Oft have I heard that grief softens the mind,

And makes it fearful and degenerate;

Think therefore on revenge and cease to weep."

William Shakespeare, Henry VI Part 2

"Da has told me everything," I inform Wayan over breakfast. "I'm up to speed on her situation."

My housekeeper is visibly relieved. Wayan is a straightforward person and therefore uncomfortable with deception. It's an admirable trait, and one I wish more people shared. People like me, for instance. Though I can hardly make public my current project. That would defeat the object.

"I am glad that Da's story is out in the open, Mr. David. It's good that there are no secrets between you."

Well, that might be expressing it too strongly, but I nod anyway.

Above all, I want Wayan to be comfortable. I *don't* want her to feel that a permanent return to Bali is in her interests. Because – leaving aside my own selfish position – I genuinely believe it is better for her to be here with me. At least, I'm fairly sure I genuinely believe it.

Let's move on.

Now that my assignment for Nathon has been safely filed away, my delusions about gym exercise put to bed, and Da Pintaraporn's personal mystery resolved, I can concentrate my efforts entirely on becoming a ruthless killer.

And, the timing couldn't be better. Before I turned in last night, I received some positive news at long last: a message from Vlad saying he will be back on Samui today. I can *finally* get this show on the road.

Time to think on mortal matters. Before I act on them.

Yeah, let's do that for a minute or ten. It's too early to go into the office anyway, and Vlad will be uncontactable until this afternoon.

Good old Death.

And, while I'm contemplating this topic, I elect to treat my abused lungs to some ironically appropriate carcinogens. To kick-start my wits, you understand. For the moment, I'm striving to keep my alcohol intake to a reasonable level, so I need to poison my body with something else instead.

I light a cigarette and, from the vantage point of my apartment's balcony, I watch the mottled clouds form and reform over the island. There is a chill in the air today. My blood is not so overheated, and neither is my brain.

Tong, believed alive, is dead. Sam Trask, believed dead, is alive. And as for Jim Fosse, well, his current state of being is uncertain. The damned American is the human version of Shrödinger's cat, both alive and dead at the same time. Until we open his box, we can't tell for sure. And we don't even know where his box *is*. There's the uncertainty principle for you in a nutshell. But then, Fosse has always been something of an enigma wrapped in a paradox, as Mr. Churchill might observe were he not pushing up the daisies himself.

I take a deep drag on my Marlboro and contemplate the Grim Reaper.

We anthropomorphise *la mort*, don't we? From our formless dread, we fabricate a fleshless human skeleton draped in black. And we do this both to induct our children into the league of fear, and to comfort ourselves that Death is a person, and therefore we can reason with him. But Death is not a person. It is an end. It is the curtain coming down at the conclusion of a Shakespearean tragedy, informing us that the story is over and it cannot be re-run. The Hunchback King will never receive a fresh horse. Desdemona is still stifled. Ophelia is still drowned. Tamora's children remain cold cuts wrapped in pastry. Nobody is writing a sequel.

All is now past. There is no present and no future.

We're done.

Cheery.

I bounce around inside my skull for a while, trying to find some comfort in *bon mots* to lift the gloom.

I fail.

So much for the consolations of philosophy.

But then, philosophers are more into abstruse thinking than happiness, aren't they? With them, it is all about depth. This intellectualised but unperceptive approach more or less guarantees that they will end up either insane or abysmally soured. In this respect, the over-educated and overly-reflective have learned nothing from their predecessors. Profundity, it seems evident, does not bring contentment. Whereas a lifelong commitment to superficiality, on the other hand, appears to foster naïve joy and serenity. Perhaps it is better to be the froth on the cappuccino than the bitter grounds at the bottom of the cup.

I check my watch.

Time to move. I'm holding the fort at the *Agency* today. By now, Da is on her way to Bangkok for a viewing of her husband's corpse. After which, my coworker will officially be a widow.

Fortunately, she looks good in black.

That's enough of that, Braddock.

Pimpim places a coffee in front of me while I open the newspaper.

As Da predicted, she is in it. On page two. There is a photograph of her, dazed and vulnerable, and flanked by serious-faced policemen. Who needs a court system, eh? At least there is no suggestion that Da might be in some way responsible. That would be going too far, even for the shit-sucking journalists of Koh Samui.

I close the paper in disgust and throw it in the trash bin.

Then I top up my coffee with a glug of Bells.

"It's sad about *Khun* Da, isn't it, *Khun* David?" says Pimpim.

The morning sidles by.

I phone Prem. I tell him to come into the office so that I can instruct him on taking over the surveillance on the Mateo Moretti job. He turns up twenty minutes later, in high spirits, and smelling of weed. I give him the file on Pla, along with some verbal instructions, and he goes off cheerfully even though he wasn't able to interest me in a purchase of marijuana.

Shortly before noon, Pimpim relays through a call from Da. I close my door.

"It is Tong," she tells me. "I knew it would be."

"I'm sorry, Da. Is there anything you want me to do?"

"Not right now, David, but thank you."

"Listen, you don't have to come in tomorrow. It's too soon. I can –"

"No. I'll be in tomorrow afternoon. I'm flying back in the morning."

"Da –"

"Please, don't say anything. I'm only just holding it together. If you start being nice to me, I'll fall apart."

"OK. Well, in that case, make sure you're not in too late tomorrow. There's work to be done."

She laughs.

"You are such a bastard, David Braddock. And, I'm grateful you are. Today, at least."

"Take care."

"You too."

After lunch, a distressed Canadian lady pitches up at the *Agency*. She has recently retired and become resident on the island; she informs me. However, the Fates have dealt her a cruel blow. Her beloved poodle Fufu has gone missing, and she fears the animal has been kidnapped, or worse.

"Some Asians eat dogs, you know, Mr. Braddock," she quavers.

I resist the urge to ask whether she has checked out the food stalls to see if any Fufu-sized comestibles are available for purchase.

"Does your company investigate this sort of thing?"

"We investigate anything and everything," I reassure her.

I am halfway through a speech to the effect that the chances of finding her missing canine are small, but that I will mobilise a troupe of cash-hungry street urchins on her behalf, when her cell phone barks. (Yes, *barks*.) It is the lady's husband telling her that Fufu has reappeared, muddy and flea-ridden, but otherwise none the worse for her adventure. I charge the woman five hundred Baht for the consultation. She is so relieved that she pays up without a murmur.

At four o'clock, I decide to make some calls of my own. I tell Pimpim she can go, and then settle back in my chair with a Marlboro.

First up, Vlad.

"Hello, Braddock," he says.

Though Vlad's English has come on by leaps and bounds since I first made his acquaintance, his accent remains thick, and he still pronounces my surname as if it is two words: 'bra' and 'doc' – which makes me sound like a physician attending to a woman's support garment.

"Can we meet, Vlad? Are you over your jet lag?"

"Sure. Eight o'clock tonight at the Irish Pub?"

"Perfect. I'll buy you a Guinness."

"No, you'll buy me a vodka."

"Whatever."

My phone conversation with Nang is rather longer, and I suspect from the outset she is listening closely to me for any signs of slurring. But detecting none – and, let's face it, I have been depressingly dry for hours – she relaxes. We discuss my time in Bangkok working for Nathon, and she comments that her nephew was well-satisfied with my efforts on his behalf.

"You saved him some trouble, David. He's very grateful to you."

So grateful he was economical with the truth to my step-mother. Something for which I am grateful to him.

"Have you started reading your father's memoirs yet?"

"Not yet, no."

She clicks her tongue.

"When are you going to start?"

"It's difficult at present, Nang. Da's husband died suddenly last week, so we're short-handed in the office. I'm working days and evenings while Da is off making the funeral arrangements. And, as you can imagine, little Pratcha is beside himself."

OK, this is laying it on rather thick, and I do experience a twinge of guilt at using Da's private life to justify my unfilial behaviour. But, hey, one has to make use of the tools to hand.

Nang's inherent decency prevents her from pursuing the reading topic further at this stage. Though I'm sure she won't let it rest until I have ploughed my way through Edward Braddock's damned manuscript. But, for now, I am reprieved – if not pardoned.

"Was it an accident or –"

"Tong was attacked and killed in the street."

Close enough to the truth to give me plausible deniability later. And suitably shocking to prevent Nang going into the prurient details.

"That's awful, David. The poor woman. And so cruel on the child to lose his father like that. Please give Da my sincere condolences."

"I will. I expect to see her briefly tomorrow."

"Anything new from the police on Katie?"

"No. I'll be calling them again after we've finished."

"Good."

After Nang's usual condemnation of misguided British Socialism, she rings off.

My call to Natalie goes unanswered. *Ah well.* Perhaps I'll try her again this evening.

Last up, DI Zachary. It's been some time since I've bugged her, though I doubt she's missed me.

"Mr. Braddock." It sounds like a sigh.

"Do you have anything for me?"

"No, and I'm rather tied up. Can we talk some other time?"

"How about that body you found in the quarry? Any news there?"

"I've already told you, it's not Katie."

"I'll be off the line faster if you give me some details."

"The information has only come in a short while ago. We haven't even released it to the press yet."

"Well, I'm not going to tell anyone."

I sense her shoulders drooping, then hear her flicking through some papers.

"The deceased woman was one Monique Fosse, originally from London. She was reported missing about ten years ago."

Interesting.

"Was she living outside Leicester at the time of her disappearance?"

"Yes," she says, surprised. "How did you –"

"And, let me guess, when you tried to contact her husband James, you discovered that he too was dead. He died in Bangkok a couple of years ago, right?"

"How do you know that?"

"Because I identified his body. Plus, I was living in Leicester when Monique vanished."

"Oh. You knew them both?"

"Yes, I did. Have you spoken to our friend Banks at Interpol about this?"

"No. Why would I?"

"Because he was the local investigating officer at the time." I give her a moment to digest this, before adding, "Small world, isn't it?"

"And getting smaller by the minute."

I hear her scribbling something.

"Tell me, when do you plan to be back in the UK, Mr. Braddock?"

"I have no plans. Why?"

"Because I would like to talk to you. *Properly*."

"Are you asking me on a date, DI Zachary?"

"No. Definitely not."

"Then, why would you want to talk to me?"

"Well, you appear to be awfully well-informed about UK missing persons. It seems to me that people disappear or die around you with remarkable regularity."

"Alas, that's true. Especially women."

Monique Fosse is officially added to the body count.

On occasion, over the years, I've wondered what became of her: Jim's inconvenient wife.

Hmmn.

Karma.

Or six degrees of separation.

Or coincidence.

Or maybe – because Jim Fosse has had his dirty hands in events – *inevitability*.

But I must not allow myself to be distracted.

Not now that Vlad is back.

Nope.

The Russian is a few minutes late arriving at the Irish Pub. I've managed to procure a table where the Ronan Keating songs whining their way out of the music system aren't too intrusive. We really should have picked a less *Celtic* venue. Any minute now, I expect someone who thinks he's Michael Flatley will start performing a jig.

Vlad gives a weary wave as he spots me. He drops his musclebound body onto a chair. The hitherto jolly giant emanates fatigue. Even his tattoos seem faded. Plus, his usually-shaven head is not so smooth as when I last saw him. It's spiky, making him hedgehog-like – if you can visualise a hedgehog that can lift one-hundred-kilo weights.

"I need a drink," he says.

"You and me both."

I order a double vodka with ice for my companion, and a small Singha for yours truly. I need to pace myself, though I *will* hit the spirits if I hear any tunes from *Riverdance* this evening.

"First of all, Braddock, I want to say I am sorry to hear about your daughter going missing. I didn't talk to you about this on the phone because I was worried it would be insensible."

"You mean, 'insensitive'?"

Perhaps Vlad's English hasn't improved so much as I thought.

"Do I?"

"Yes."

"Ah, OK." He downs the vodka in one and clicks his fingers at one of the staff members to signify he requires a refill.

"Well, thank you, Vlad. But before we say anything further on that subject, let me express again my condolences to you. Were you close to your uncle?"

He slaps a mosquito on his leg before responding.

"Yes. He was a kind man and has supported my mama ever since my father died. A long time ago now. Over twenty-five years – in nineteen-eighty-three. I was only four when Papa passed away, so I don't remember him."

"Ah."

The big hunk looks like he wants to reminisce awhile, so I take a mouthful of Singha and remain silent while he blathers on. I'd guess that, for his mother's sake, Vlad has had to be relentlessly cheerful over the last few weeks. So, this may be the first opportunity he has had to offload and to have his turn at being miserable.

Vlad recounts his family's woes in mind-numbing detail. It's all so depressing, that I catch myself half-listening to Ronan Keating. Vlad's paternal grandfather had spent ten years as a *zek* in a Siberian labour camp, surviving in the freezing wasteland on a diet of bread and thin vegetable stew. I gather this was for daring to voice criticism of 'Uncle Joe' Stalin. His other grandfather – falsely accused of theft – had not been so lucky, and had perished in one of the gulags through a combination of overwork and starvation. His maternal grandmother committed suicide as a result. So, Vlad's father had been handed the responsibility of restoring the family's fortunes – a task which he seems to have accomplished admirably up until the time of his demise.

"Papa was in the Navy," he says. "Everyone was proud of him. He was handsome and strong. I have photos of him in his uniform. Mama says I look just like him." He grimaces slightly. "Then he was killed by the Americans. I've hated Americans ever since."

"Killed by the Americans? How?"

"He was an officer on a nuclear submarine during the Cold War. The Americans sent down divers in the Atlantic to move some – how do you say – *sonic buoys*? Yes, I think that is right. Sonic buoys, or sonar buoys." He shrugs. "We used these to guide our submarines so, when they were shifted, Papa's submarine hit the rocks and sank. The whole crew died. No air."

"What was the name of your father's submarine?"

"The *Akula*."

I have a swig of beer.

"Why? Have you heard of it?" he asks.

"No. Just curious."

I have, of course. But there's nothing to be gained by explaining to him that it was the British, not the Americans, who were responsible for the sinking. And that my gym buddy Tim was the principal culprit. The last thing the world needs is another Russian-English vendetta.

"It would be a big surprise if you did know," he continues. "It was all very secret. *Very* secret. We only found out the details from a friend of the family who was senior in the Navy. Even then, we could not talk about it in public. You see, Braddock, we Russians do not like to admit our defeats."

"Hmmn."

"Fucking Americans," he adds, and orders another vodka.

"How is your mother coping?"

"Not good. That is why I stay away so long."

He shakes his head.

"I speak to Mr. Orlov. He says he will give me a job in Moscow so I can be close to Mama. I teach another Russian for six weeks to take over the club on Samui, then I go home."

"Six weeks? You're only here for another six weeks?"

"Yes. I will miss it. But family must come first, yes?"

I'd better get to the point. The clock is ticking. I light a Marlboro and wade in.

"Vlad, I want you to fix up a meeting for me with Mr. Orlov."

The big Russian studies me for a few seconds.

"Why?"

"It's about Grigory Polzin."

"What about him?"

"If I've been correctly informed, your boss hates him."

"That's correct. But what does that have to do with you? Mr. Orlov is a busy man. He doesn't usually meet just *anyone*."

"It was Polzin who ordered the murder of my daughter."

Vlad frowns.

"Yes. I thought that might be the reason. I had heard – something."

He doesn't elaborate, but studies his empty vodka glass awhile. Eventually, he looks up.

"Very well, Braddock. I will speak to Mr. Orlov. But I cannot promise anything."

"Understood. Tell him I am happy to travel anywhere he chooses. On any conditions he wants."

"What if he does not agree to see you?"

"In that case, I shall have to find a way to kill Polzin without his help."

I don't sleep well.

I wake several times in the night with a pain down my left side, and what feel like ants in my toes and fingers. My temperature is running high, and I might be slightly delirious. Each time I open my eyes, Claire is in the room. She doesn't say anything, but simply stares at me, a worried expression painted on her face.

I can't fall ill now. Not when my revenge might be drawing closer.

To make matters worse, I experience a vivid nightmare – presumably instigated by Vlad's tale of his father's death – in which Katie and Claire are together sealed in some coffin-like box, and gasping for air. Slow suffocation: a nasty way to go.

Oh, Katie.

I hope your end was quick.

13

"I like work: it fascinates me. I can sit and look at it for hours."

Jerome K. Jerome

Someone is shaking me awake.

"Claire?"

"It's Wayan, Mr. David."

The blurry image leaning over me resolves itself into the face of my housekeeper.

She places a hand on my brow.

"You are hot. You may have a fever."

"What time is it?"

"Eight-thirty."

"I must get up. I have to be in the office to open up this morning."

She inspects me, doubtfully. "I don't think you can go to work today, Mr. David."

I heave myself into a sitting position. The pain down my left side immediately returns, though it is duller. Multiple members of the family *Formidicae* are still tickling at my extremities, but less frantically than they were in the night. My fingers are cold while the rest of my body is aflame.

"I'll be OK after a cold shower. Da's travelling back from Bangkok and won't be at the *Agency* until after lunch. I can't leave Pimpim on her own."

Wayan hands me a glass of water, and I become aware of how dry my mouth is.

"Do you want breakfast?"

"I can't say I'm hungry, but I guess I'd better eat something. Let me sort myself out first."

I stand under the shower head and wait for the tepid water to cool my body. My legs are rubbery and I don't entirely trust them to keep me upright.

Whatever it is that's messing with me, it's not alcohol.

Perhaps I have mild dengue fever, or I've contracted some other delightful tropical infection.

Or maybe I've had a mild heart attack.

Shit. That would *not* be good.

Pull yourself together, Braddock, for heaven's sake.

There is nothing wrong with you except over-tiredness and chronic hypochondriasis. So you've had a bad night? Well, boo-hoo. It's not a big deal. Everybody has one now and again. Turn off the self-pity tap.

I do, however, leave the shower running over me for another ten minutes while I wiggle my fingers and toes to get the circulation going.

I towel myself dry and examine my face in the bathroom mirror.

Bells palsy? A minor stroke?

Surely not. My mug is no more asymmetrical than usual. Nothing's drooping or frozen.

Is this how it started for my father?

I carry out the rest of my ablutions and dress.

Despite my self-reassurances, the pain in my upper body refuses to go away. I perform some light twisting and bending exercises, but they make no difference.

Perhaps a cigarette will work more effectively.

I make my way carefully through the lounge and out onto the balcony, ignoring the little squirts of pain in my chest. I try to breathe normally as I am aware Wayan is watching me and I don't wish to alarm her.

Once I've sat down, I chance a deep breath. It's OK. I have another one. The pain is no worse.

I light up.

"Should you be smoking, Mr. David?" asks Wayan, depositing a tray in front of me. She puts a palm on my forehead again.

"Well?"

"You're cooler," she admits grudgingly.

"I'm fine now."

I survey the tray before me. It is groaning with healthy foodstuffs. No sign of any greasy bacon or eggs.

My chest is easing. Before I attack the fruit and muesli, I resolve to smoke my fag down to its filter.

Inhale. And. Exhale.

Repeat.

The tightness is much less pronounced. The flecks of discomfort have departed, as have the ants. I'll live. For now, at least.

Ah, the magical qualities of the Marlboro!

Medical science has things arse about face so far as tobacco is concerned. So much for the objectivity of laboratory tests!

But don't try this at home, kids. To smoke like I do, you need to be a professional.

A professional idiot, that is.

Just say, *No*.

Arriving at the *Agency*, David Braddock Esq. is in good cheer. Pimpim is already installed behind the reception desk.

I fling my Panama at the hat rack, and miss. Undiscouraged, I try again. And miss again.

Pimpim decides that this farce might go on for some time, so she helpfully ends it by hanging up my hat for me.

"Coffee, *Khun* David?"

"Why not indeed? Yes, let's push the boat out."

She gives me a puzzled look, so I add, "Black, please."

As I position my backside on my office chair, the reception phone rings, and Pimpim answers it smartly. She says *yes* several times and makes some notes on her pad.

She then sets a steaming coffee in front of me.

"Who was that?"

"A new client. A lady called Monica Young. She says she knows you, *Khun* David."

"The name doesn't ring a bell. What does she want?"

"She says she wants you to meet her at her hotel in Choeng Mon at two o'clock."

"Does she, now? And why can't she come into the office like everyone else?"

"She said she couldn't leave her hotel. But she did ask specifically for you. Doesn't want to see anyone else."

"Huh."

"I've written down the details. She's at the *Ratchapruek Hotel* in room twenty-four. Says you should go straight up. She'll be waiting."

"Will she now? You should have told her we don't do outcalls."

"Ah, sorry. She was – insistent."

"It's OK. Did she leave a cell phone number?"

"No."

"Well, we'll see about this later. Thanks, Pimpim."

Thus reassured, our receptionist returns to her work station, closing my door on her way out.

I rack my brains.

Monica Young.

Have I ever slept with someone called Monica Young? I don't think so. And if I have, it can't have been a particularly memorable experience. That may not even be her real name. Anyway, whoever she is, she's got a cheek. Deva-ish, entitled behaviour. Possibly American. Definitely white. I should have asked Pimpim about her accent.

Maybe I'll ring the hotel later and tell them to put me through to her room. Or – better idea – I'll get Da to go in my place. That'll take her mind off her troubles. Lift her back in the saddle straightaway, so to speak.

I am not going to do a damned thing today. I'm sensing an allergy to work coming on. Plus, I'm not going to stress myself out over Vlad's upcoming conversation with Orlov.

Stress.

Wait.

Perhaps that's all that is wrong with me. Stress. Yes! Or anxiety attacks, or some such nonsense. And that will soon dissipate once I've made Grigory Polzin eat a bullet or two. Then I'll be as right as rain.

A little Bells goes into my coffee.

I open the newspaper.

No, it's not stress.

I've had a relaxing few hours at the office, but I'm back to feeling the way I did when Wayan woke me this morning.

However, I have a new and compelling hypothesis.

It's too much coffee.

As lunchtime approaches, I note that I have been consuming a lot of caffeine. Four cups so far today. It would also explain why my shaking hands are back.

Google informs me that, while coffee enhances alertness, the drug can cause restlessness, irritability, a raised heartbeat, and even tremors in the muscles. All the symptoms I've been displaying. Well, *most* of them.

So, I've been diluting down Pimpim's poison with whisky to minimise its effects. I've also been through half a packet of Marlboros.

These palliatives, sadly, are not proving to be effective.

I'm sweating, headachy, and have what seems like cramp in my side.

By the time Da shows up, I've managed to force down a lunchtime baguette and some water, but I'm not at my best. Da too appears deflated. Her brisk stride has gone, there are dark circles under her eyes, and some heavy invisible weight is pressing down on her. We look at each other.

"You look terrible," we say in unison.

Our laughter serves to break the tension.

"You should take the afternoon off," I tell her. "Put your feet up."

I can't ask Da to meet Monica Young. It was selfish of me even to consider it after what she's been through. I can handle it. I only require another whisky.

"Don't we have any clients this afternoon?"

"No. Apart from one new client. I'm seeing her at two o'clock at the *Ratchapruek Hotel*. So, Pimpim can man the office while I'm out. You don't need to be here."

"Since when do we meet clients at a hotel?"

"Special request," I reply. "It's a one-off."

She doesn't pursue the matter, but continues, "Well, in that case I'll call Prem in so I can debrief him on his surveillance. We should get a report – even a provisional one – to Mr. Moretti. I'll do that."

"Are you sure?"

"To tell you the truth, David, I'd welcome some normality. Yesterday was – harrowing. And the flight back with Tong's parents this morning wasn't much better."

"Do you want to talk about it?"

"No. Thanks, but no. I want to do something routine and trivial for an hour or two. Relax my brain. After that, I promise I'll head home, OK?"

"OK."

I leave Da and Pimpim in peace and drive to Monica Young's hotel.

Despite what I said to Da, I haven't yet decided whether I'm actually going to meet our mysterious client. Part of me says *screw her* while another part of me wonders whether I have already screwed her. I figure I'll have a couple of drinks and a few Marlboros in the *Ratchapruek*'s bar while I make my mind up. That way, I can see what condition I'm in at two o'clock, and whether I'm in any fit state to speak to anyone. If this pain in my chest hasn't abated, then the only person I should be talking to is a doctor.

And I *hate* doctors.

My watch tells me it's two.

I haven't budged from my bar stool for the last hour. My cerebrum is abuzz with concern for Da. I've never before seen her so defeated. She's always been a rock. My rock, in effect. Dependable. Unflappable. Indestructible.

But every person has their breaking point. And she is awfully close to hers.

So, despite the fact that I'm burning up, and still in some pain, I tell myself not to be such a baby. Having listened to Vlad's litany of family woes, and witnessed Da's distress first-hand, my own problem of a lost daughter is almost trivial by comparison.

Katie is much in my head, though, as I climb the hotel stairs and knock on the door of room twenty-four. She must be. And I must be a little delirious too, because the young woman who opens the door bears a passing resemblance to Katie. Except that this female has cropped black hair, Goth makeup, and wears glasses. Yet there is something familiar about her that ...

"Hello, Dad," says the apparition.

Interlude Number One

Let's interrupt this narrative for a short while, shall we?

David Braddock. *Ugh.*

I can only talk about myself in that life for so long before the accumulated evidence of my bad choices and patent stupidity begins to make me queasy.

Besides, it's time to remind you that this little tête-à-tête you're having is a conversation with someone located Beyond the Veil. And if I can drag you away momentarily from the story of David Braddock's limping progress in pursuing his Russian vendetta, we can perhaps have a quick session on the hereafter.

The Afterlife is a big subject, so I thought – taking a leaf from best website practices – I'd jot down an initial batch of FAQs ('Frequently Asked Questions') to kick us off.

By the way, if you are one of those rare types who is not interested in what happens after you're dead, you can skip this section. Have a cup of tea, or something.

For the rest of you, let's start with a spot of debunking.

"Life and death are one, even as the river and the sea are one," according to Kahlil Gibran.

Bollocks are they.

Although they do have certain things in common, which I'll come to in a minute.

First, though, I should tell you that nothing is eternal. You won't be forever thirty-three in the next life. There are no gold mansions. You're going to get wrinkles and arthritis. *Again.* Also, you're going to die in the next life too. Everything and everyone do. So, the believers in rebirth –

Buddhists, Hindus, *et al* – got that part right. Given this state of affairs, it's only the fact that you don't remember all your previous lives that stops you going completely potty.

You think you want to live forever?

Really?

You don't, honestly.

Some Returners, like myself, do remember a previous life or two, and that's bearable. But imagine having your mental attic stuffed with others' memories. You'd barely have enough brain function left to carry you through the day. (By the way, *Returner* is not an accurate term, since it's not really *you* who returns, but let's park that for now.)

Is there a white light at the start? Yes. And it's especially bright. Trust me, you don't want to die with a hangover.

Are you going to meet God in the Afterlife? No. His address and phone number are unlisted, so good luck with that. I suspect that, *if* He exists, He's a bit of a hermit. I would be too, if I were Him. Imagine all the ass-kissing He'd have to put up with. Personally, I'm inclined to believe He doesn't exist, and that the Universe is simply a set of rules that subsist for a period – admittedly a long period – then wink out like a blown light bulb. Indeed, if pressed on the subject, I'd wax lyrical about *many* Universes, each existing in their own way with their own physical laws, some of which would permit life to develop, some of which wouldn't.

But I'm not going to get too metaphysical here or you'll start skim-reading, and that's a bad habit to acquire – unless you're wading through a particularly tedious business report, in which case it's an essential skill for protecting your mental health.

Anyway, eventually they all end and/or begin, but don't ask me how that works. We dead are not all-knowing.

I understand that must come as a disappointment.

In fact, *disappointment* is something you'd better get used to. Because your next life, if you have one, is probably not going to be that much different from your current one.

Different, in some ways completely, yes. And the same.

You'll still be living on a small blue planet spinning its way through space. You'll still get tired and sick and happy and depressed. On the upside, you'll still be able to buy cigarettes, watch TV, and make the Beast with Two Backs. On the downside, though, you'll continue to be susceptible to piles and herpes and yeast infections and mosquito bites. Also, if you're a boring so-and-so now, the chances are you'll be a boring so-and-so next time around too.

You won't necessarily meet your loved ones again, or if you do, you won't automatically recognise them nor they you. I haven't seen Claire since I passed over. I have seen my mother-in-law, though. A mixed blessing, that.

What else?

Oh, yes.

You will have to earn a living, find somewhere to live and someone to love. Eat. Sleep. Do your laundry. Go to the dentist. Get your car serviced. Worry about money. Stop your neighbour's dog crapping on your lawn. Fill in your tax return. Spend time with people you don't like.

Yeah, that's right. It just goes on. And on. And on.

So, are life and death one?

No.

And yes.

And maybe.

Sometimes.

14

"If you asked me now who I am, the only answer I could give with any certainty would be my name. For the rest: my loves, my hates, down even to my deepest desires, I can no longer say whether these emotions are my own, or stolen from those I once so desperately wished to be."

Evelyn Waugh, Brideshead Revisited

A sleepwalking David Braddock steps into room twenty-four of the *Ratchapruek Hotel.*

I want to ask the ghost of Katie why I am hallucinating her now as the afternoon sun blazes through the window in a cruel imitation of normality. And why isn't her mother with her to explain this to me? I am accustomed to Claire's night-time hauntings, but this vision has so stunned me that all my physical pain has evaporated, displaced by shock. My body is numb, and the ability to speak has deserted me. I fear my legs will give way, so I sit down on the edge of the bed. My eyes remain fastened to the phantom.

She closes the door quietly, removes her glasses, and turns to kneel in front of me. Her fingers touch my leg, and a pilomotor reflex kicks in – what the Germans term *the holy shiver*. The hairs are standing up on the back of my hands.

"It's all right, Dad," she says. "It's me. It's *me*."

Still no words come. I can't trust myself to open my mouth. An abyss of hope opens up as the young woman grasps my tightened fists.

She's real. Whoever or whatever she is, she's real.

The doppelgänger throws her arms around my neck and pulls me forward against her. We hold each other for a few seconds, and I stroke her hair, tentatively at first, then with increasing conviction. Her shoulders heave: she is crying. She breaks from me and eases herself up onto the bed, wiping away her tears.

"Say something, Dad. *Anything*."

"Jesus Christ, Katie."

It *is* her. I am not made mad with grief. Eurydice has indeed returned from the Underworld.

My daughter is *alive*.

My own tears come. Katie takes my face in her palms, smoothing away the wetness.

Now words tumble out from me. Garbled, incoherent, uncomprehending.

"But, *how*? Your abandoned flat? Buchanan and Polzin? Why didn't he –"

Before she can respond, my confusion is supplanted by anger.

"It's been *three months*, Katie. Three months since you disappeared. I've spent all that time thinking you were dead. Have you any idea what I've been going through? Why didn't you contact me? Why didn't you let me know you were all right? Just *one* call."

Her lip trembles, and she starts to sob again.

"Dad, I –"

"Shhhh. Shhhh. I'm sorry. I'm sorry Katie," I say, appalled at my outburst. I hug her tightly. "Explanations can wait. You're safe. That's all that matters."

"No." She controls herself, and pushes me away. "Explanations can't wait. I owe you that." As she exhales, there is a shudder in her breath. "I have wondered many times over the last few weeks what I would say to you when we were finally together again. But I still don't know where to start."

"It was Buchanan who took you, wasn't it?"

"Yes."

I swallow. "Forcibly?"

"No."

"And Polzin was behind it?"

"He was."

"Yet Buchanan is a paid assassin. A gun for hire. Presumably, therefore, a man who can't afford to have a conscience. Why didn't he follow through? I'm well aware that you can be persuasive, Katie, but I can't believe you talked him out of it. Did you offer him money?"

"No."

"Then – what?"

"Wayan."

"Wayan?"

"He couldn't kill me because he loves her. And because of her link to me. He's had enough of the killing game. He's done."

I snort.

"Is that what Buchanan told you? That he wants to settle down with Wayan in a little white cottage with honeysuckle and roses in the garden? There must be some other reason."

"There isn't."

God, I need a cigarette. Unfortunately, Katie's room has no balcony. A discussion of Buchanan's feelings for Wayan – *my* Wayan – is not something I can stomach at present. I change tack.

"Where have you been since you left your London flat?"

"Various places." She gestures vaguely. "Birmingham. Hamburg. Marseilles. Amsterdam. Anonymous places. Staying on the move, keeping under the radar.

"My punky disguise was Robert's idea. He organised the fake papers. Plus, he persuaded me that I shouldn't contact anyone. You see, for Grigory to be convinced I was dead, everybody else had to believe it too. Even you, Dad. If you and the rest of my family and friends were grieving for me, he'd have to accept that Robert had done his job and made my body disappear."

I keep my mouth shut with difficulty as she continues.

"And, there isn't only danger for you and me, but for Robert as well. He told Grigory that I was dead, and that I am buried in an unmarked grave. In not carrying out the assassination and in protecting me, his life is on the line too. If his employer were to discover what he's done, my ex-father-in-law would be certain to put a price on his head.

"So, yes, I went along with whatever Robert suggested: the disguise, the travelling, and the radio silence – even though that was the hardest thing of all. He is an expert on living invisibly, after all. He's been doing it successfully for many years.

"I grew to trust him, Dad. And I was right to."

"Buchanan has been with you all this time? You and him – together?"

"Yes. And before you ask, *no*, Robert didn't try anything on with me."

I wish she'd stop calling him *Robert*. My daughter is displaying too high a regard for this asshole assassin. Way too high. Perhaps she's succumbed to Stockholm Syndrome – identifying with her kidnapper. Except that she wasn't kidnapped. If I take her words at face value, she entered into this barely-credible arrangement voluntarily.

I get out my Marlboros.

"Dad, this is a non-smoking room."

"I couldn't care less. I'll pay to have the room fumigated if that's what the hotel wants. I need a fag."

Katie finds a plastic cup to serve as a makeshift ashtray, and pours me some water. She opens a window. With a Marlboro in one hand and a glass in the other – Bells would have been preferable, but never mind – I am less manic. The surreal nature of the situation recedes a little. I suck deep on the smoke. My daughter places a palm on my leg, and gives me a moment to process. I put down the water, and lock my fingers in hers.

An unwelcome thought hits me.

"Wait. Is he here? Did Buchanan come with you to Samui?"

"Yes. He's here."

"To see Wayan?"

Katie nods.

"Does he think Wayan will throw herself into his arms on account of his one good deed? It changes nothing. He's still a killer, and he's hurt her badly. Twice. He must be deluded if he expects to rebuild that bridge."

Katie rides my annoyance before responding.

"Robert loves her, Dad." Fucking *Robert* again. She continues, "If I've learned nothing else about him these past months, I've understood that. I doubt he *expects* Wayan to forgive him. But he has to try. You would try if it was Mum, wouldn't you? Whatever you'd done?"

"Where is he? Is he in this hotel? I want to talk to him."

"He's not staying here. He's in a different hotel."

"But –"

"You must meet, of course. But *tomorrow*, OK? *Tomorrow*. Today is for us. For you and me. You need time to absorb all this and to calm down. We'll talk first. You're going to have lots of questions – detailed ones – and I want to answer them properly."

"Was that Buchanan's idea too?"

"No, mine."

"Huh."

Katie squeezes my fingers. "Is that all right?"

"It seems like I have no say in the matter. Isn't he worried I might turn him in? You're aware that Interpol is after him."

"You won't turn him in, Dad," she says firmly. "He saved my life. He could have told Grigory that he wouldn't do the job and Grigory would have sent someone else to do it. I'd be dead now if it wasn't for Robert."

"*Robert!* Ugh! Is that even his real name?"

"I don't know what his real name is. And I don't need to."

I resist the urge to trash the 'trusting' nature of their relationship, and instead put an arm around my daughter. She looks into my eyes.

"Did you speak to Leona after I vanished?" she asks.

"Yes. I know everything about the genuine circumstances of your husband's death. And the court fiasco."

"Good, I'm glad she told you. She promised me she would. So, you're informed about the plan we'd hatched concerning Alexander?"

I stay silent, and stub out my cigarette.

"Does that change how you feel about me, Dad? That your little girl is a scheming killer? That I planned to murder my husband? That I am the sort of person who is happy to pervert the course of justice?"

I tighten my arm around her in reassurance.

"You're no cold-blooded assassin, Katie, simply a woman who was being abused."

"I deceived you too."

I shrug.

"Yes, you did. But you had your reasons. Even if I don't agree with them."

"I'm sorry. I didn't want you to be involved in all that – mess."

"At this point, I would forgive anything, to have you back. You've got some balls, though, I must say. More than any surviving male member of the Braddock family."

I release her from my embrace and light another Marlboro.

"So, daughter of mine. What happens next? I'll bet Buchanan has a view on that. He is the type who plans ahead, is he not? What is next envisaged for Katie Braddock?"

"First, it's Monica Young. Katie Braddock is dead and gone. I can't go back."

(It's difficult to argue with this. When Euridice glanced back over her shoulder, she was returned to the Underworld. And we don't want *that*.)

"Does that mean you have to keep that godawful hair and Goth makeup? I can't say it suits you. Do you have to continue to look like someone who's just risen from the tomb?"

"Even though, in one sense, I have?" She laughs. "No. Now that I'm in Thailand, I can go back to having my hair its natural colour and usual length. I'll dye it strawberry blonde once it's a bit longer."

"Thank God for that. And you'll stay with me?"

"No, not right away."

"But –"

"Let me finish, Dad. Robert and I have discussed this, and we concluded that it's best I stay on Koh Phangan, and that you and I see each other at weekends. When you're not working."

I don't like the sound of this.

"Why?"

"Just in case."

"Just in case of what?"

"In case Grigory Polzin has sent someone to watch you."

"Even assuming he did that originally, why would he still be doing it? After three months?"

"Do you want to take that risk? After we've been so careful?"

I consider the question.

"Maybe not. But how long does this arrangement continue with you living on Koh Phangan? And what are you going to *do* there?"

"One thing at a time, Dad. Plus, we need to come up with a cover story."

"For whose consumption?"

"For the people at your office and for your friends, for a start. They will wonder, *Who is this Monica Young and why are you spending your weekends on Koh Phangan with her?*"

"Well, we can't say you're my girlfriend from England. That would be a Freudian nightmare."

"I thought – your goddaughter. The offspring of an old friend of yours who is now deceased. I've come into Daddy's money and have taken a year off work to travel Asia. You're keeping an eye on me to make sure I don't get into any trouble. *In loco parentis*, as it were."

"I'm not sure what Da will make of that. She doesn't see me as the philanthropic, considerate-godfather type. But she has her own problems at the moment, so she's not her usual inquisitive self. It might fly with her."

"What's wrong with Da?"

"That's a long story. I'll tell you about it this evening over dinner. A discreet table for two somewhere out-of-town?"

"I'd like that."

"And what about your grandmothers? Natalie and Nang?"

"They can't know about my being alive, Dad. Not yet. Only you, me, Robert and Wayan. We will tell them, in time. But not yet."

"Hmmn. This is a lot to assimilate, Katie."

"Yes."

My heartbeat and breathing are almost back to normal. Katie's room has stopped wobbling. It no longer resembles a *Twilight Zone* set. The bright sun is simply that of a regular Samui afternoon, and not the white light of death or the glare of delirium. The pattern on the bedspread is unmoving. This is not a dream. It's an ordinary day at the *Ratchapruek Hotel*.

The *Ratchapruek Hotel*. Ha. The last time I was here was some years back. I brought Wayan to an ill-fated magic show where a living person was turned into a corpse. On this occasion, a corpse has been turned into a living person.

That's *real* magic.

"What will I say to Wayan?"

"Tell her the truth."

"That Robert Buchanan is here?"

"Yes. That he saved my life and that he wants to see her."

"She won't see him," I say definitively.

"Perhaps not at first. But it's our job to persuade her otherwise. To hear him out, at least."

I cough out a lungful of smoke.

"*Our job?* When did that become *our* job?"

"Don't say anything damning about Robert, will you? Say that I'm only breathing because of him, and that he wants to meet her tomorrow or the next day to explain. Ask her to give him a fair hearing, that's all."

I recover my jaw from the floor before I respond.

"You expect a lot from me, the two of you. Too much, maybe. It is no part of *my* job description to act as an advocate for Robert Bumhole Buchanan. Besides, Wayan has heard his bullshit explanations before –"

"Dad." Katie does a passable impersonation of Buddha *calming the waters.* "Give him a chance. Give Wayan a chance too. Let them work it out without interference, if they can."

"Pah! That's all well and good, but I'm extremely fond of Wayan. She's a dear friend, as well as my housekeeper. I don't want her hooking up with some psycho killer."

"Are you sure it's not because you don't want her hooking up with *anyone*?"

"That's ridiculous. If Wayan decides to hand in her notice, I'm sure I can find another housekeeper."

"That's not what I meant, Dad. And you know it."

Resistance appears to be useless. I assume a martyred expression.

"All right. I'm not promising anything, but I'll *try* to be objective."

"Try hard."

EVERYONE DIES

My daughter and I spent a further half-hour together in a less combative vein. By the time I left the hotel to face Da, relief at Katie's return had replaced my confusion, shock and anger. In a few short hours, *everything* has changed. The world is upside-down again. Or perhaps it's the right way up. Hard to tell.

I now have Katie's Thailand cell number.

"I didn't call your mobile, Dad," she expounded, "because I couldn't be sure who you'd be with or what you'd be doing. Plus, I thought if we met in my room it would be less messy if you fainted at the sight of me. Hence, I phoned your office to set up the mystery meeting here."

My ever-practical daughter. And after all she's been through.

I wonder who she gets it from.

So now I'm back at the *Agency*, and knocking on Da's office door.

Lie convincingly, Braddock. There's a lot at stake.

"I've done the report for Mr. Moretti and emailed it to you, David. If you're happy with it, I'll send it out."

"Right."

"How did it go with Monica Young?"

"Well ... interesting. It turns out we did know each other. I didn't twig with the name as I knew her as Monica Jenkins. She's married and divorced since I last saw her. She's my goddaughter."

"Someone trusted *you* to be a godfather?"

"Yes. An old friend from my schooldays. Now deceased. I haven't laid eyes on Monica for years."

"I see. So, what's she doing on Koh Samui?"

"She's taken a year off work to tour Asia on her own. She'll be, maybe, spending a couple of months on Koh Phangan."

"Huh. It must be nice to be in a position to take a year off work. What does she do for a living?"

"She's an actress."

"You mean one of those people who spend their time pretending to be someone they're not?"

"Er. I guess so. Though she's not a very successful actress, I gather. Her inheritance is paying for the trip."

For a second, I panic that Da is about to accuse me of outright lying, but I can detect no censorious glower in her eyes. Indeed, there is no sparkle at all. She looks tired, done in. The acidity in her words is nothing more than the echo of customary routine. I remind myself that her husband has died. Why would she care about any of this? I'm over-thinking.

Da does have one further question, however.

"How old is she?"

I shrug.

"Twenty-seven? Twenty-eight? Something like that. She's a Goth. Definitely not my type, if that's the inference behind your query."

She shrugs. All energy has left her and she's lost interest in the conversation.

"Well, I'll be off home. I need to collect Pratcha. I'll see you tomorrow."

"As to that," I say, "would you mind if I took the next couple of days off? I want to help Monica get settled and sorted out with somewhere decent to stay on Koh Phangan."

"That's fine, David. Business is quiet, and I can hardly complain as I'll be taking leave for Tong's funeral."

"But, if you need someone to talk to, Da, then obviously I'll –"

"No. It's all right. I'll see you later in the week."

"I'll send off the Moretti report today after I've been through it."

"As you like."

She leaves.

Well. That went better than expected. Even if Da is suspicious about my account, she's never going to guess what is really going on. First, my relationship antics are understandably low on her priority list of things to monitor. And second, the truth is too damn incredible.

Wayan's reaction to the candid recounting of today's events is more emotional. I am glad I told her to sit down before we talked. And that I had a bottle of Bells to hand to steady my own nerves while I watch her on the rack.

It is painful for me to describe.

Shock. Disbelief. Anguish. Inner turmoil. All made worse by her desire not to upset *me* with her responses. Her desire to empathise, and to be happy for me at the miraculous reappearance of my daughter, has to slug it out with her confusion over the return of Robert Buchanan and what that might mean. This is one of those times I wish Wayan were less solicitous of others' emotions. By rights, she should be throwing plates around and tearing her clothes. Perhaps that will come later, when I go out to meet Katie.

"Robert wants to see me?" she asks, her voice hoarse.

"Yes. But nobody is going to force you to see him."

"Do *you* think I should, Mr. David?"

An instant of reckoning.

If I answer *no*, she will not see Buchanan. Of this I am certain. Every atom in my body tells me so. Wayan is in such profound anguish that any thread will lead her. She trusts me, values my advice, understands I will never cause her harm. Whatever I counsel, she will accept.

I want to tell her not to see him, to instruct her to send him away forever, to offer him no hope of a reconciliation.

But I cannot.

Aside from my promise to Katie, there is something else that stops me. It is the stirring of hope in her eyes. A hope I want to see dashed – but not by me.

I hear myself say, "I think you should give yourself a day or two to weigh things up, Wayan. There is no hurry. None. There is no pressure on you, even though you may feel there is. We can discuss it. You and me. As many times as you like. You can use me as a sounding-board."

"Aren't you angry with him?"

"Very."

"Won't you be angry with me if I meet him?"

"No. I won't. I could never be angry with you."

She looks at me for a moment.

"I want to tell you something," she says.

"Then, tell me."

"I never fully appreciated until now what a good man you are, Mr. David Braddock."

To cover my embarrassment, I become pragmatic.

"Be that as it may," I mumble, "for the time being you cannot share with anyone what I have told you today. Especially not Da. She can't know about Buchanan being here. And she believes Monica Young – Katie – is my goddaughter on a visit to Asia. I need you to be clear on this. Katie's life might depend on it."

"Then I will be clear, Mr. David."

The way Wayan looks at me now! How many times have I wished for this!

But I must be composed. I must ignore the pain in my chest. Even though it is a good pain.

I take another mouthful of whisky and light a Marlboro.

To business.

"Let's get our stories straight, and we'll discuss what happens next."

Katie and I are at a quiet table at *Valentino's*.

We have the same waiter who served at table when I was here with Da. He's probably wondering how many more women I'm going to bring along.

"So, Katie, when do I meet Buchanan?"

"Tomorrow morning. My room at the hotel. Nine o'clock."

"Good."

"And I will be there too."

I consider this.

"That's also good."

"By the way, I need to cadge some money from you. Ever since we went on the run, Robert has had to pay for everything."

"It's OK. I've brought ten thousand Baht cash for you for starters. And I'll repay Buchanan every penny he's spent."

"I doubt he'll accept it."

I fight the urge to grind my teeth.

"We'll see."

"Anyway, it's only until you inherit from my estate."

"Let's not go into all that now. Your vulture-lawyer Thor has already been in contact with me about probate. I told him to do nothing for the time being, and to take your apartment off the market."

The waiter fills our wine glasses and flashes me a knowing grin before moving off.

"How did it go with Da and Wayan?"

"I've told Da the lie and Wayan the truth. Da didn't react much."

"And Wayan?"

"That was a more difficult conversation."

"Was she upset?"

"Have a wild guess."

Katie drinks some wine and waits for me to elaborate. When I don't, she says, "What did you say about her meeting Robert?"

"Don't worry. I was even-handed. More even-handed than that fuckwit Buchanan deserves."

"Define 'even-handed'."

"I told her to think it over, and to take her time. She asked my opinion as to whether they should meet, and I said it was her decision, but that whatever she decided, it was fine by me."

"I'm proud of you, Dad."

"Yes. Well."

"I am."

"Enough about Wayan. I have a million questions for you."

"I'm sure you have. Fire away."

"Let's order first. I can restrain my curiosity for a few minutes."

"Not to mention your outrage."

"Yes, let's *not* mention my outrage. It's lucky that I love you. What do you want to eat?"

Over dinner, as I interrogate and Katie supplies the details of her adventures since her disappearance, I become aware that she is inspecting me.

"You've lost a lot of weight."

"Uh-hu."

"Actually, Dad, you don't look well. I've noticed, despite your best efforts at concealment, that there is a quivering in your hands. An involuntary tremor, I'd say. Also, your eyes are bloodshot – and it's not just from your crying earlier, is it?"

I attempt to make light of this.

"I've been having one or two issues lately, nothing serious."

"Health issues?"

"Some aches and pains. But, like I say, nothing serious."

"Have you seen a doctor?"

"No."

"You should. I don't want to lose you. Not after – everything. And you smell of whisky."

"That's not altogether surprising, is it? Given the circumstances."

"See a doctor."

This morning I would have baulked at the idea, but now, on the whole, it seems like a sensible course of action.

"OK. I will."

"That ache in your side's back, isn't it?" says Claire.

I finish undressing and slide into bed.

"Only a bit."

"Liar."

"Did you know Katie was alive?"

"That's a stupid question, David, even for you."

"It's been a weird day."

"It's not going to get any less weird so long as you insist on talking to me."

"I guess."

"Perhaps, now that you have a living daughter again, you should consider putting an end to your conversations with your dead wife."

"Should I?"

"Yes."

"Would *you* like that?"

Claire doesn't answer.

15

"Death doesn't all of a sudden make life noble."

Amy Yamada, Trash

I open my eyes and stare at the bedroom ceiling.

I'm not in a straightjacket.

That means yesterday did happen, and my mind has not undergone a complete collapse.

I *did* meet my daughter and have dinner with her. She *is* alive.

I also had a discussion with Claire, who is *not* alive. But let's park that for now.

I'm sufficiently sane to function and, at this point, that's enough.

For once, the vagaries of fate are favouring David Braddock. I'll take it.

Over breakfast, my housekeeper is still in a state of bewilderment at the turn of events, and remains unsure as to whether or not she should meet with Buchanan. She tells me she hardly slept, her senses reeling at all the ramifications of the new reality that were coursing through her head.

"There is no rush, Wayan," I say. "Buchanan isn't going anywhere, and he has no right to a quick decision from you."

"Mr. David, do you think I could talk to Katie?" she asks. Her tone is nervous, her words tentative.

"I'm sure she will be happy to come and see you later today if it helps."

"It might. She has spent a lot of time with Robert."

Yeah, too much.

I don't voice this.

"I'll speak to her this morning."

"You're seeing Robert?"

"Yes. Nine o'clock at Katie's hotel."

"Ah."

I give her the low-down on my dinner with Katie, and she listens attentively in case I decide to mention Buchanan.

I don't.

I arrive at Katie's room a few minutes early.

Buchanan is already there, as is my anxious-looking daughter.

With difficulty, I restrain the impulse to pick up something heavy and blunt, and to smash him on the head with it.

We don't shake hands, and he remains seated. Katie has arranged three chairs to face each other. I can almost hear the music from the scene in the film *The Good, The Bad and The Ugly* where the trio of gunfighters square off.

I sit. Introductions are unnecessary, and Buchanan speaks first.

"I'm sure you have a lot of questions, Mr. Braddock. And probably quite a few things you want to say to me too."

His words are uttered calmly, and I can detect no sarcasm in the *Mr.* with which he addresses me. He must realise I am on a hair-trigger.

"You bet I have."

"Dad," Katie throws me a warning glance.

I light a Marlboro and hope that the quivering in my hands is not too evident. The female in the room risks leaving her chair to open a window. When I don't throw myself at Buchanan and put my hands around his throat, she exhales a sigh of relief, and passes me a cup for my cigarette ash.

"I suppose you expect me to be grateful, do you, Buchanan? For not murdering my daughter."

"No."

I take a long draw on the Marlboro to slow my breathing.

"Good. Because I'm not grateful."

He doesn't rise to the bait, but continues to watch me.

"And I'm not intimidated by the fact that you're a paid killer," I add.

"From what your daughter has told me about you, I didn't imagine you would be."

Is there a slight trace of a North-East accent there? Scottish, maybe? Some small tell-tale sign of his origins?

"How can I be sure that this *change of heart* of yours is real? That you're not still working for Polzin, and this is not some twisted scheme of his to lull us into a false sense of security so that you can kill us both together?"

A signal of weariness from the other man.

"I guess you can't. Though, I've spent three months with Katie, and that's a long time to keep up a pretense of sincerity. She's likely to have suspected something if that were the case, don't you think? Perhaps you should ask her."

"I'm asking *you.*"

He raises a hand.

"All right. First off, why would Grigory Polzin want *you* dead? No offense, but you don't represent any kind of a threat to him, and you weren't involved in his son's death. So, why would he want me to kill you? And as for Katie, I could have shot her any time. In her apartment, for instance. Your reasoning doesn't make any logical sense."

"Yeah, well, I'm not big on logic at present."

"I can understand that."

I want him to sound smug so that I can smack him one. But he's being careful and measured. I blow some smoke in his direction and am disappointed that he doesn't cough.

"Why didn't you let Katie contact me? I've been off my head with worry since she disappeared."

"I've never stopped her from contacting you. She's had a phone."

"Maybe not exactly *stopped* her, then, but you *advised* her not to."

"Yes, I did."

"Why?"

"Because that maximised our chances of staying alive. There was no body to prove Katie's death. Polzin might have had you watched. He might have been suspicious of my intentions: he's not the trusting type. You might be a lousy actor. Any number of reasons.

"So, yes, you had unnecessary grief. But Katie and I are still breathing. And now you can put your grief behind you and move on."

"Just like that?"

"Just like that."

There is a momentary break in the jousting while I crush out my cigarette and light a fresh one. Katie uses the opportunity to offer the two combatants some water. We both say yes. My daughter is being surprisingly quiet. She is following a strategy – I presume – of allowing me to let off steam, while hoping her presence will inhibit me from violence.

"So, Buchanan," I say, taking up my cudgel again, "how many people have you murdered for money?"

"That's not relevant."

"*Really?* I think it is. If you expect me to trust you, I need to know what sort of a man I'm dealing with. For instance, are you the 'Captain Nemo' that Interpol is looking for?"

"I know nothing about anyone called 'Captain Nemo'. I'm not party to the investigations of Interpol. And I'm not going to discuss this. If that's the price of your trust, then you'd better not trust me."

"So, I'm to take it at face value that you didn't follow through on your assignment with Katie because you love Wayan?"

I spit out the end of this sentence.

"What other reasonable explanation is there?"

"I'm not sure that's a *reasonable* explanation at all. That's my point. If you are so enamoured of Wayan, then how come you've already abandoned her twice?"

"Circumstances," he replies.

I am gratified to see that he is squirming slightly in his chair.

"Circumstances," I echo. "Is your name even Robert Buchanan?"

"No."

"I thought not."

"Listen," Buchanan says. Then he dries up.

"I'm listening."

"This is not easy."

"My heart bleeds for you."

Katie places a restraining hand on my arm, and I sit back.

The assassin fiddles with the cuffs of his shirt before he speaks again.

"I'm not proud of many of the things I've done in my life. I've made a lot of money from actions that most people would view as abhorrent. But I am proud of this: that I met Wayan and that she had feelings for me. She is the one bright point in my existence. I recognised that when I met her in London. And all that has happened since then has been because of her."

He's either a bloody good actor, or he is sincere. But he's not wriggling off the hook that easily.

"I get it. You've had a miraculous conversion on the road to Damascus, and it's turned you from a cold killer into a tender-hearted lover. It's enormously moving."

"I understand your cynicism. I do." A sad smile plays around his lips.

"Therefore, following this wondrous change of character, you anticipate that Wayan will welcome you back with open arms, and that Katie and I will stand behind you all the way."

"I anticipate nothing, Mr. Braddock. I consider it likely that Wayan will turn me away and say she never wants to see me again. I could hardly blame her if she took that line, could I?"

"No, you couldn't."

"And if that is her decision, I will respect it. I will disappear from her life permanently."

"What would you do, Robert?" This is from Katie.

"I dunno," he says. "But I will not be going back to my previous ways. Of that, I am certain."

"Touching," I interject into the *schmaltz*. "But I have another question."

"Then, ask it."

"This nonsense about Katie living on Koh Phangan, and me visiting her at weekends. That wouldn't be so that you have two whole days out of seven with Wayan without my being around, would it?"

"Dad, I've told you –"

"No, that's not it at all. It's simply about our remaining careful in the short term. Obviously, Katie won't want to stay on Koh Phangan indefinitely."

"So, for how long."

Buchanan's features arrange themselves into a *who-can-say?* expression.

"But *you* will be remaining on Samui? So that you can hang around Wayan."

"Would you prefer it if I went to Koh Phangan too, and hung around Katie?"

"Yes. No. I don't know. I'd like it best if you just pissed off back to wherever you came from, if I'm being honest."

"What will you do while you're here, Robert?" asks Katie.

He rubs a hand across his eyes.

"Before you answer that, let's have a show of your good faith," I say.

Buchanan's eyebrows crease in puzzlement.

"What do you mean?"

"Give me your cell number and the name of the hotel where you're staying. Also, the name you're travelling under."

He glances at my daughter for guidance. She gives a small nod.

"I'm staying at Lotus Blossom Villas, and my passport says I'm Howard Grealish, a citizen of the United Kingdom."

I pull out a notebook and write this down.

"Show me the passport."

He pulls it from his pocket and holds it out to me for inspection.

"And your cell number?"

Katie interjects.

"I have Robert's number, Dad. I can pass that to you later."

I grunt an acknowledgement.

"So, what *will* you do here, Robert?"

This easy familiarity between the two of them renders me nauseous. I light another Marlboro.

"Wait. Sit on a beach and wander around the markets, I suppose. Until Wayan decides, I'll wait. What else can I do?"

"Well, you could *run away*," I remark. "What makes you think I won't turn you in to the police? After all, I do have cause." I tap my notebook. "And, now that you have kindly supplied me with your whereabouts and travel document details, it should be easy enough for the local plods to pick you up - or at least make it difficult for you to get out of the country."

"I'm through with running. Besides, I don't believe you'll turn me in to the police."

"Oh? Why not?"

"Because of the risk that would pose to Katie's continued anonymity."

"Is that a threat, Buchanan?"

"No. Merely an observation. If I were to be arrested, who knows what might follow? My detention in Thailand would be newsworthy, no doubt. And it could create a trail that might lead a suspicious Grigory Polzin to Katie."

He cracks his knuckles.

"Listen, Braddock," he says, dropping the deferential *Mr.* for the first time, "I don't want anything to happen to Katie any more than you do. If Polzin does track her to Thailand, it will not be because of anything I do or say. And you can take *that* to the bank."

"Hmph."

"Also, you don't strike me as the sort of man who would shop me to the police. Otherwise, I wouldn't have given you that information."

"You have no idea what sort of man I am."

"Dad won't talk to the authorities, Robert. There's no need for you to worry."

"Don't be so sure, Katie," I respond brusquely. I point a finger at the assassin. "This is one dangerous man. A lot of lives might be saved if he were off the streets."

Buchanan leans back in his chair and spreads his arms in a gesture of submission.

"Whatever the truth of the matter," he says, "I am in your hands, David Braddock."

I'm not convinced about Buchanan.

Katie might be sold on him. But I'm not.

For sure, he played the scene well. However, that only carries me so far down the road. My skepticism towards members of my species – and their murky motives – has been the mainstay that has kept me going these last years, and I am not about to surrender it so readily.

At Katie's request, we travel separately to my apartment.

My daughter and Wayan greet each other warmly, with tears and hugs. It has been some time since they last met, but their fondness for each other is evident. They sit on the sofa and wait for me to leave, while trying not to make it too apparent that my presence is superfluous.

"Well, while you ladies chat, I'm off to the hospital to book myself in for a check-up."

"That's an excellent idea, Dad. And don't hurry back. Wayan and I have a lot of catching-up to do. Give us a few hours, OK?"

"Right."

I fortify myself with a couple of whiskies at the Irish Pub before proceeding on to the international hospital, where an officious female informs me that, owing to a cancellation, they can fit me in for the full works tomorrow morning: cardio tests, blood, urine, blah blah blah. I am instructed not to eat or drink anything, except water, from six o'clock today – at which point I am wishing I'd had a few more fortifiers at the pub.

Happily, no restriction on smoking was mentioned.

My nicotine intake for the hours up to my appointment will be accordingly unrestricted. And, doubtless, more excessive than usual.

In a rare surge of empathy, I ring Da to see how she is.

"If you ever need to talk," I say, "you only have to –"

"Thank you, David. I appreciate that."

"We could meet for breakfast or –"

"I'll bear that in mind. Not for the next few days, though. I'm sure you have other things to do."

"I'm scheduled for a medical tomorrow, as it happens."

"I'm glad to hear it. That's well overdue. Anyway, I have to go. Bye for now. See you on Friday."

It seems nobody wants to talk to me today.

When I eventually arrive home, Katie and Wayan are drinking tea. I pretend not to notice that they both have red eyes.

Under cover of darkness, Katie lets me drive her back to the *Ratchapruek Hotel.*

"Well?" I say. "How did it go? What's happening?"

"Wayan has agreed to see Robert tomorrow morning at Lotus Blossom Villas. I'll be going along too."

"*Tomorrow?* Bloody hell, you must have been persuasive. What time?"

"Ten o'clock."

"Ten? Then I'd better change the time of my medical."

"That's not necessary, Dad."

"Why?"

"You're not invited."

"Does Wayan need a lift? Because –"

"Already organised. And don't try to talk Wayan out of it."

"I know better than to argue with a woman who's already made up her mind."

"Good. You're learning." She pats my arm. "There's hope for you yet."

16

"Don't worry about your heart, it will last you as long as you live."

W. C. Fields

In lieu of breakfast, I have three Marlboros.

Wayan joins me on my apartment balcony. She has decided to forgo food this morning to show solidarity. I tell her that is unnecessary, but she says if I have to fast then she will too.

"Your daughter is a wonderful person, Mr. David," she says. "Katie is kind and selfless, as well as brave."

There is a lot I could add on this topic, but I remain silent as Wayan continues.

"I hope you are not offended at not being asked to see Robert with me this morning."

"Not at all."

"I want Katie to be there, though. For support. She knows Robert and, well, I might need her if things become - difficult."

"I understand. You trust her."

"It's not that I don't trust you, but -"

"It's best if I'm not around, Wayan. I'd say something stupid, or get annoyed - and that wouldn't be helpful. My emotions about Katie would interfere. And this is about you, it's not about me or my daughter. This is a difficult situation for you, and whichever way you want to handle it is fine by me."

She twists her fingers.

"I don't know what to think or how I feel, you see. I want to hear what he has to say. But I will want to talk to you afterwards, Mr. David, for your advice. When I understand more. If that's all right?"

"Of course. Whatever you want."

Thus reassured, she asks about my medical appointment, and I tell her it's routine, and nothing to worry about. Which, considering recent events, is true. Compared with Katie's return from the grave, there is nothing any doctor can tell me that will be half as shocking.

Unless it's that I'm healthy.

I park the jeep in the car park of the international hospital. I'm early, and I have no desire to hang around inside this place any longer than necessary. So, I sit in my vehicle and smoke a couple of cigarettes while watching the comings and goings. Folks on crutches – bike and car accident victims for the most part, I expect – swing themselves around while friends and family fuss at their side. Individuals with their arms in slings, people in wheelchairs, elderly patients with Zimmer frames, slink or squeak their way into and out of the main entrance. Two bored ambulance drivers are squatting in the manicured grounds under the shade of a large tree. They are smoking, contrary to regulations. They look cheerful.

I hate hospitals.

They have an atmosphere about them. I'm not only referring to the antiseptic smell, the bright, soulless lighting, the bland, endless corridors, the squeaking gurneys, and the blank-faced auxiliaries. I'm referring to that pervasive, ill-defined fear, simmering below the surface. The same apprehension one experiences in a dentist's waiting-room, but magnified tenfold. Here, worse things than root canal treatments occur. Even the signage carries a threat, however sanitized the wording. Nobody speaks loudly. The expressions of the reception staff are tranquil and focused, perhaps carrying a slight hint of embarrassment that their livelihood comes from others' suffering. We help you, not from altruism, but for money. The doctors, surgeons and nurses, on the other hand, are less squeamish about this: *we are professional carers, and therefore worth our pay.*

And whenever I set foot in one of these cathedrals of medicine, I am reminded of Claire. Of her pain at the end, of the useless, bleeping machines to which she was connected, of the futility of her struggle. The rain on the window of her private room. The branches scratching against the glass.

Happy days.

But I am not here to go under the scalpel, I tell myself. I am not dying. This is only a check-up. Tests. Nothing more.

Don't be such a baby, Braddock.

I announce my presence, hand over a credit card, and it begins.

It takes an age. I can't even have a Marlboro.

I am passed from one department to the other. I contemplate ringing Da during one extended wait, but conclude that might increase my general glumness.

Blood pressure. Poking, prodding, weighing, measuring. A few general questions, answered reasonably truthfully, and duly recorded. Blood sample. Urine sample. Stool sample. Treadmill: suckers attached to my bare chest. Blowing in a tube. Chest X-ray. Prostate-stroking. It goes on.

Eventually, a fresh-faced nurse announces that I will be emailed as soon as my results are ready, and an appointment arranged with the doctor. I thank her as gracefully as my wounded dignity will allow, smoke a Marlboro in the car park, then drive to a beach bar where I down beer, whiskies and chicken rice.

My phone rings. It's Da.

"Have you finished at the hospital?"

"Yup."

"How do you feel?"

"Sore."

"And a little violated?"

"For sure."

She snorts.

"You should try being a woman."

"One of these days I might. There are places in Bangkok could sort that out for me. How's it going with you?"

"It's quiet at the *Agency*."

"That's not what I meant. How are *you?*"

"Oh, I'm all right. One day at a time."

"And Pratcha?"

"Subdued. It hasn't sunk in yet about his dad."

"Do you want me to come into the office?"

"No. Not necessary."

I call Katie. She's at her hotel, and Wayan is back at the apartment.

"Is it safe for me to go home now?"

"Yes. And I'm taking a late afternoon ferry to Koh Phangan."

"You're leaving so soon?"

"Yes. Let's not argue about it."

I toy with arguing, but don't.

"I'll give you a lift to the ferry port, then. But I'll go and see Wayan first. Is she OK?"

"She's OK, Dad."

Wayan presents me with a cup of tea: that nectar of the gods that makes everything better.

She is both enhanced and diminished at the same time. It's a difficult thing to read. Something inside her has shifted. Her eyes are those of a woman, not those of a girl. But maybe they have always been like that, and I haven't noticed.

"Do you believe people can change, Mr. David?"

"I believe *some* people can change," I say judiciously. "It depends on the person."

"Robert has done some terrible things," she announces.

"Like what?"

"He told me that he has killed people for money. That is what he was doing on Bali when I first met him."

"Yes."

"He has worked for people who smuggle drugs. And he has many names."

"Robert Buchanan is not his real name, right?"

I want to ask her what it is, but I don't. Because this is about *Wayan*, and I have to restrain my prurient curiosity. Besides, if things go pear-shaped, I can always winkle his name out from her later. Plus, Katie would have heard it too. Unless ...

"Was Katie with you the whole time?"

"Yes."

That's a relief. For all sorts of reasons.

"She was wonderful, Mr. David. She helped us to talk when it was difficult."

"Which I guess was most of the time, eh?"

Wayan lowers her eyes.

"We spoke a lot. Well, Robert did most of the talking. It wasn't easy for him."

This rankles, so I say, "Harder for you, though."

There is a long silence.

"Would it bother you if I have a cigarette?"

"You don't have to ask, Mr. David. This is your apartment."

I light a Marlboro.

Eventually, she continues.

"I fell in love with a man who shoots people. That's hard to come to terms with."

"I imagine it is."

"Robert was candid with me. He didn't hold anything back."

"Did he tell you how many people he had killed, and their names?"

She shakes her head decisively.

"No. And I don't want him to tell me. But, several. It's enough to know that he has done it. I don't need the details."

"I understand. So, what happens next?"

"He asked if I would see him again. Just the two of us this time."

"What did you say?"

"That I would have to think about it."

Anguish flows into her face.

"But should I even be considering it, Mr. David? Bearing in mind what he has done. What sort of a person am I not to refuse him straightaway? What does it say about me?"

I reach over and take her hand.

"You are the kindest, gentlest person I have ever met, Wayan Lastri. What it says is that you believe in giving second chances, in trying to understand. That you don't condemn people without hearing them out."

The following words almost choke me, but I sense they are required.

"Robert *did* save my daughter, whatever else he has done. And Katie believes his feelings for you are genuine."

"Yes, she said so. But do *you* think I should see him again? Give him more time to explain?"

"I think you've probably already made up your mind on that, Wayan. Haven't you?"

A tear makes its way down her cheek, and I wipe it away.

I try as best I can not to flinch at the pain in my chest as I help Katie to the jeep with her luggage. Although I had hoped she would stay longer on Samui before decamping to Koh Phangan, I am reconciled to her removal since I will be seeing her again on Saturday. Then we can spend the whole weekend together - and without Buchanan hanging around. I suppose I should be comforted that my daughter is taking her security seriously, though I believe we are being over-cautious. In the Thailand sunshine, the machinations of Grigory Polzin seem like the stuff of fantasy.

During the short drive to the ferry at Ban Rak, we discuss Wayan and her dilemma, though I don't express my views on the subject too forcibly. Best to keep it light. There has been quite enough drama going on without my adding to it.

Katie waves to me from the deck of the boat as it slides away from the pier. Yet another goodbye. But I won't let sadness overtake me. This is only a temporary parting.

I stroll back to the jeep with my trembling hands stuffed into my trouser pockets so that I don't have to look at them. For the first time in ages, trepidation about my own health creeps unbidden into my consciousness. My trip to the hospital this morning has unnerved me, that's for sure. It has let loose a gaggle of honking questions that until recently wouldn't have disturbed the Braddock psyche one iota.

Supposing something chronic were to befall me now? Suddenly, my own well-being has taken on relevance. The cavalier attitude that I have exhibited towards my physical and mental condition in recent months shows itself as irresponsible and childish.

A motorbike roars past, stirring me from reverie. I kick at the dust by the side of the road while I find my car keys. I climb into the jeep and light a Marlboro. But it's hard to stop thinking. By rights, my brain should have exploded already. Perhaps some of it has. That might account for my unruffled acceptance of this latest distorted version of reality.

The soup is hot. The soup is cold.

Katie is alive. Katie is dead.

The soup is hot again.

Katie is resurrected.

And, meanwhile, the world continues as if nothing remarkable has happened. The island traffic remains awful. The *soi* dogs are still sniffing each other's butts.

I have left my sunglasses at the apartment, and the red orb now lowering itself towards the sea throbs in my eyes. Another hour or so and the ocean will swallow the sun.

The beginning of every night is also an ending. The day passes away as the night is born. But tomorrow it will live again and, for a time, it will be the turn of the darkness to hide.

I need a drink.

Several drinks.

I hear my phone ring. The display informs me that it's the number of Katie's rescuer.

"Yes? What do you want, Buchanan?"

"Can you talk?"

"I *can* talk. Though I'm not sure whether I *want* to talk to you."

He doesn't have a comeback.

"Go on, then," I say. "To what do I owe the pleasure of this call?"

"I want to run something past you."

"What?"

"I want to take Wayan to dinner."

"You're asking my permission?"

"Yes. She wanted me to talk to you about it."

"Did she? And what if I say no?"

"I dunno what happens then, to be truthful. I'm in uncharted territory."

You and me both.

"When do you want to take her out to dinner?"

He hesitates.

"I thought – Saturday evening. To give her a couple of days to reflect. But then I remembered you'll be on Koh Phangan this weekend with Katie, and I don't want you being suspicious that I was waiting until you were off the island to –"

"When?"

I hear him take a deep breath.

"Tomorrow evening. Friday. That way, you can be sure she's home safe and sound before you catch the ferry on Saturday morning."

"That's considerate of you. And you'll leave her alone until I'm back on Sunday evening?"

"Yes."

I'm in a bind here. I'm not Wayan's father or guardian, for God's sake. What if I refuse and she sees him anyway? What if –?

Sod it. It's her call, not mine. It's her life, not mine.

"Where do you want to take her?"

"Wayan wanted you to recommend a suitable restaurant."

"Are you fucking kidding me, Buchanan?"

"No."

I try to remember what is the noisiest, dirtiest and least-suitable place on the island for a romantic tryst, then stop myself.

"*Valentino's,*" I say with a sigh.

"Does Wayan know where that is?"

"No, she's never been. It's the sort of spot where you go with a date. And Wayan and I don't date."

"Where is it? Do you have the number?"

"What am I, your bloody personal assistant? Google it. There's only one *Valentino's* on the island."

"OK. I'll pick her up at seven-thirty from your apartment."

"You can tell her that yourself."

"Right."

"And one more thing, Buchanan. Don't think for a moment that this chummy call changes anything. If you *ever* hurt Wayan again, I will make you wish you had never been born, assassin or not. Are we clear?"

"As crystal. But I will never –"

I've heard enough. I cut the line.

The stripping away of delusion is a brutal exercise.

Claire has gone. My wife has departed, without even a farewell. And she isn't coming back.

Not this time: it's irrevocable. She and Katie have exchanged places.

The only person in my bedroom from now on will be me.

I'm stuck with being sane.

It sucks.

17

"I'm killing time while I wait for life to shower me with meaning and happiness."
Bill Watterson

It's Wednesday – hump day – and I'm at the hospital waiting nervously to see the doctor.

The last few days have passed as if in a dream.

The atmosphere on Friday at the *Agency* was stilted and uncomfortable. I repeated my offer to Da of our having a heart-to-heart chat over breakfast, and she once again took a rain check. I vacillated over proposing we have dinner, but our last *tête-à-tête* at *Valentino's* is still too fresh in the memory, and a second visit to that venue smacks a little of romantic assignation – a notion, I am sure, neither of us wishes to contemplate. Plus, I don't want that smarmy waiter making absurd assumptions.

That evening, to my great disappointment, Wayan and Buchanan occupied a table at that restaurant for over two hours. I'm ashamed to relate that I considered planting a listening device in Wayan's handbag, but prevented myself at the last minute. She dressed modestly for the occasion, but still looked pretty hot, I must say – and, despite her misgivings and obvious nervousness, she honoured the appointment.

I stayed in, stewing and fighting the urge to consume copious measures of Bells, while burning my way through a packet of Marlboros. Concentrating on my laptop proved impossible, so I watched a film about an English army butchering a load of Scottish rebels, an experience I found uplifting for some reason.

Given Buchanan's concern about Polzin tracing Katie through contact with me, why is it OK for him to turn up at my apartment to collect Wayan?

Surely that's just as reckless? I mused on this during a part of the movie where no Scots were being slaughtered.

Double standards. I'll have to have a word with him about it.

I then proceeded to sit up like the anxious father of a teenage girl, fretting about what time Wayan would be home. That turned out to be a quarter past ten.

"How did it go?" I asked.

"It was difficult, Mr. David."

She didn't elaborate.

"Will you see him again?"

"I haven't decided. But not this weekend while you are away."

"Ah."

"Do you need anything?"

"No. Thank you."

That was all. I didn't push it.

Wayan needs time to see Buchanan for what he is, and I'm trying not to interfere. Although, the temptation to drip some poison in her ear about the smooth-tongued killer is almost overwhelming. I wish she didn't instinctively see the good in everyone.

Steady, Braddock.

My weekend on Koh Phangan was an altogether happier affair.

Katie has rented a one-bed beach hut at Haad Salad on the north-west coast for her first week on the island while she looks around for something more comfortable. At least, I'm hoping she'll plump for somewhere more upmarket and less Robinson Crusoe. A modern two-bed villa, for instance, where I can stay without becoming mosquito feed. I'm too old for all that New Age stuff, and consequently for my visit I'd pre-booked myself into a civilised hotel with proper air con a hundred metres down the beach from Katie's shack.

Saturday morning, I was up bright and early. Forgoing the slower vehicle ferry from Nathon, I left my jeep in the car park at Mae Nam pier, and caught the early Lomprayah Catamaran to Thongsala where I jumped in a *songthaew*.

It had been some time since I'd last set foot on Samui's smaller sister, and I'd forgotten how much more relaxed it is on Koh Phangan. Commercial development has yet to run riot, and therefore time does not so much run as walk here. This sleepy lump of palm-and-coconut-covered rock accordingly continues to act as a magnet for hippies, stoners, criminals on-the-run, and yoga hags – not to mention the pleasure-seeking youth high on drugs and liquor who attend the regular Bacchanalian parties at Haad Rin on the other end of the island.

Katie and I spent most of our time together strolling along the small, sheltered bay, grazing on Thai food, and drinking moderately. Once the sun was down, we smoked a couple of joints.

We talked a lot. And we had a lot to talk about.

We agreed tacitly, however, that we would not talk about the future. Not *yet*. We wondered out loud what would happen with Wayan and Buchanan, and neither of us was confident enough to lay a bet on the outcome.

"Wayan wouldn't tell me Buchanan's real name. I find that odd." I slipped this in casually.

"Well, why would she need to?"

"Of course, you know it as well, don't you? You must do, Katie. You were there."

"Nice try, Dad."

"But I don't see why –"

She handed me the spliff.

"Have another puff on this and forget about it."

"Keeping secrets is a bad idea. You should have realised that by now."

"You're just nosy. And maybe a little teeny bit jealous."

She put her arms around me.

"Aw, sod it then," I said, and took a long pull on the doobie.

"Attaboy. And, by the way, we're not spending any time tomorrow searching for accommodation for me. I've got my hired bike. I can do that in the week."

"But –"

"So, I'll choose somewhere that suits me, father-of-mine. But, don't worry, there'll be a bedroom for you too."

"As long as you make sure you're not surrounded by man-hating yogis who'll disapprove when they see me smoking."

"Trust me."

"All right. But pass me that mozzie spray."

Monday was fairly busy at the office. Which was a pain as only myself and Pimpim were around, Da being occupied with Tong's funeral arrangements for the following day.

In the afternoon, head-shrinker Braun dropped by the *Agency* to thank me for the referral of my alcoholic client. He stared at Pimpim appraisingly, and asked whether I'd ever thought of selling up.

"Not really," I said. "Why?"

"Well, it strikes me that if a private investigator can become a therapist, then perhaps it could work the other way around too."

"You'd like to be a PI? Do you have some long-held secret desire to stalk brown-skinned women while wielding a camera?"

"It might make a change. Help to keep me young. If you do ever have leanings in that direction – of quitting the business – let me know, will you?"

"You'll be the first name on my list."

The dirty old bugger.

Tong's funeral was a sombre, dignified affair. I was the only *farang* attending. Wayan accompanied me. I counted fifty mourners, but many of them seemed to be friends and family of Da. Tong's parents were dreadfully quiet, grief-stricken still.

The occasion had been preceded by a night vigil of monks, and all religious practices were rigidly observed over the course of the day.

Da was both sad and sensational. I only spoke a few words with her, though she and Wayan went into a long huddle at one point.

My joy at Wayan's not seeing Buchanan over the last four days was tempered by the news that she is meeting him again tonight. I made no comment when she told me, and did my best to appear neutral.

Last night I called Nang and Natalie to report that there was nothing to report. To say that it felt weird would be an understatement. I was racked with guilt at not informing them of Katie's resurrection, even though it's probably for the best. *For now.* Natalie didn't have much to say and didn't offer any explanation as to why it's been so difficult to get hold of her. Nang was her usual right-wing self, but relieved that I was sober.

There was a missed call from Hitomi, which I have not returned. I can't talk to her now. Not with everything that's going on. Even though I'm curious as to whether Sam Trask has been in touch with her.

My reverie is interrupted by a nurse waving at me. It's my turn to face the doctor.

I haven't had a drink in three days.

Maybe that will earn me some bonus points.

Dr. Soo is of Chinese descent. She has a businesslike manner and absolutely no sense of humour. She peers at my report disapprovingly.

"Can we split this into good news and bad news sections?" I ask.

"Which do you want first?"

"The good news."

"Well." She strokes her chin. "You're still alive."

"It that it?"

"Very nearly."

"Ah."

"It says on your questionnaire that you smoke a lot of cigarettes. How many is that per day exactly?"

"I couldn't say *exactly*."

"Then, how many *approximately*?"

"Say, two packets."

"Forty? That would be about two-to-three cigarettes per hour on average. Does that sound right?"

"Maybe two-and-a-half packets."

"Any trouble breathing?"

"No. It happens automatically."

"Chest pains?"

"Sometimes." *Like now.*

She makes a note.

"Your alcohol intake is alarmingly high."

"For the last three days, I haven't had a drink."

"How long have you had that tremor in your hands?"

"Four months. Since my daughter disappeared, presumed murdered."

The sympathy plea goes unacknowledged.

"How strong, would you say, is your craving for alcohol?"

"No worse than any other heavy drinker."

"So, you see yourself as a heavy drinker rather than an alcoholic."

"Yes."

"What's the difference?"

"An alcoholic goes to meetings."

Not a flicker of a laugh.

"Have you tried giving up drinking before and gone back to it? Does it cause issues with work and family?"

"Yes, and yes."

"Do you have trouble sleeping? Restlessness? Nausea? A racing heart? Seeing, hearing or feeling things that aren't there?"

"Yes."

"Which?"

"All of the above."

She stops writing.

"You suffer from hallucinations?"

I nod.

"What form do they take?"

"I see my dead wife and have conversations with her. Though, in fairness, I used to do that before the drinking."

"Have you seen a mental health specialist?"

"No. Only my dead wife."

"This is not a joking matter, Mr. Braddock."

"No. Sorry."

"Have you lost a lot of weight recently? You appear rather gaunt."

"Yes."

She consults my paperwork again.

"Your tests show you are still carrying a lot of visceral fat. Fortunately, you say there is no history of heart disease in your family. Though your father died of a stroke. I don't suppose you are exercising?"

"No."

She sighs.

"Your renal and liver functions are only just within the tolerable range. Your cholesterol is high, as is your blood pressure. Sugar slightly concerning. Blood and urine are OK otherwise. No sign of sexually transmitted infections. Slightly enlarged prostate, but no lumps. Chest X-ray clear. Some suggestion of arrythmia during your time on the treadmill. I understand we had to terminate the exercise early?"

"Uh. Yes."

"Is there anything else you need to tell me? Your completion of your questionnaire was, I suspect, not entirely forthcoming."

I decide to own up.

"Sometimes, I have a pain down my left side, and a tingling in my fingers and toes."

"Your arteries are doubtless choked up with deposits from all the smoking. You're a prime candidate for a heart attack, Mr. Braddock, your family history notwithstanding. If your vessels are too blocked, you could end up having a limb amputated."

I take a deep breath.

"What do I need to do?"

"That depends on how long you want to live. If you continue with your current lifestyle there is no point in your planning too far ahead. I shouldn't book any holidays at Christmas, for instance."

"I see."

"There are things I can prescribe for you, but frankly, unless you stop smoking and drinking, and start to eat properly and take care of yourself, that's probably a waste of my time and your money."

"You have an interesting bedside manner, Dr. Soo."

"Sort yourself out, Mr. Braddock." She hands me some leaflets. "Read these, and follow the advice. To the letter. If you're still alive in a month, come back and see me. Then we'll talk again."

"Right."

"And here's a copy of your test results. You might want to have them framed and hung on the wall. Or as a gift to your beneficiaries."

I phone Katie and tell her I'm not dying: I simply have to cut down on the booze and cigarettes. She sounds relieved.

I have a couple of Marlboros before driving to the office to give Da the same story. She's relieved too.

I suspect you have noticed that it's been some time since I last mentioned killing Grigory Polzin.

The fact is that, with Katie's reappearance, the Polzin affair has taken a twist. It is no longer so black and white. The Russian's plan to murder my daughter has failed. More to the point, *he is not aware that it's failed.* Only yours truly, Wayan, Buchanan, and Katie herself know that she is alive. How much danger is there still for Katie? She and Buchanan have been crafty, vigilant and meticulous in concealing their tracks. My earlier view about Katie's going to Koh Phangan being overly-cautious has given way to my admitting the good sense of such measure.

Don't misunderstand me. Every visceral instinct in my body screams at me to murder Grigory Polzin for ordering the hit on Katie. But, am I thinking straight? While I believed my daughter to be no more, the idea that my attempt on Polzin's life might turn out to be a suicide mission was not especially off-putting. But now, it's different. I would be risking my continued existence for what? The rule of retribution? The satisfaction of seeing that bastard dead? The punishment of an affront to the manly pride of the Braddocks? The removal of a ruthless oligarch for the greater good?

How would it benefit Katie if her nemesis dies but her father also perishes? Does one outweigh the other?

I am *not* getting cold feet.

I am attempting to introduce some rationality into my emotion-soaked ponderings.

Is shooting Polzin still a good idea?

Or would it be better if I shot Buchanan instead?

How about both of them?

Men must either be caressed or else destroyed.

One thing is for sure: I'd better go back to the gun range, and practice, practice, practice. Then, whichever way it goes, I'll be ready.

A call from Vlad serves to remind me that, my current deliberations notwithstanding, the wheels of Polzin's destruction have already been set in motion.

"Let's meet," he says.

"When and where?"

"Tonight. Around nine. At the club."

Excellent. If nothing else, it will stop me fixating on Wayan's assignation with Buchanan this evening. With any luck, this will be the day she gives him the heave-ho.

Vlad's office is small and cramped, and his air-con unit needs servicing. The room smells of intimidation and stale sweat.

The man himself is sporting an impressive black eye – I would hazard a guess as the result of a recent Muay Thai match.

He catches me staring at his shiner, and in the voice of affronted manhood announces, "I won."

"I'm sure you did."

"He was a Frenchman."

"It just gets better."

His brief smile is replaced with a more earnest expression.

"Well," I say. "Do you have some news for me?"

"Mr. Orlov has agreed to see you."

"Any preconditions?"

"Only that he chooses the time and place. And you won't receive much notice, for security reasons. But you won't have to fly to Moscow, so you don't have to worry about a Russian visa."

"So, the meeting will happen somewhere in Asia?"

"He didn't share that with me, but I guess it will."

"And – soon?"

"Knowing Mr. Orlov, yes. Now, shall we have a vodka?"

"Only a Coke for me."

He glares at me disapprovingly, as though I've said I want to sleep with his mother.

18

"Eat right, exercise regularly, die anyway."

Anonymous

The strange has become the normal during the two-and-a-half weeks that have jogged by since my consultation with the po-faced Dr. Soo.

In this time, I have twice visited Koh Phangan, and my daughter's revivification no longer seems miraculous. How quickly the human mind can adjust to changed circumstances!

If further proof of this were needed, Da's and my civility towards each other, which would have been inconceivable a little while ago, continues unabated. I struggle to recall any recent trenchant remarks or sarcastic exchanges at the office. However, I must remember that she is recently widowed, and it may be that her sharp tongue will return once she has worked her way through the sensations of grief, guilt, and concern for Pratcha that must be camping out in her head. The ease between us - or *truce*, as my cynicism asserts - has doubtless been assisted by the sudden influx of work into the *Agency*. As well as the usual infidelity patrols, we have also been called upon to look into collecting evidence on matters of business rivalry, administrative obfuscations at various local government departments, and the theft of a laptop on which were saved important confidential documents relating to a dodgy land deal. The perpetrator of this last instance of larceny turned out to be our very own employee Prem. I shan't weary you with the details, but suffice to say the missing item was returned anonymously to its grateful owner, and Prem received a hard kick up the backside from me, plus a telling-off from Da which reduced him to tears.

Better him than me.

My phone calls to DI Zachary in London go on for the sake of form, but I have been careful to introduce a note of resignation into my voice, as if hope of a positive outcome is fading. The good DI, while maintaining a sympathetic tone, is unable to conceal entirely her delight that she might only have to suffer further communication with me for a limited time – though she remains steadfast that she wishes to talk to me about Monique Fosse the next time I am back in the UK. Still, a chat about Monique Fosse is infinitely preferable to one about Monica Young.

Nang and Natalie also remain in blissful ignorance of Monica Young's existence. Tricky calls, those. If Hollywood were aware of my lying/acting talents, I cannot help but think that a morally-reprehensible Oscar might be in the offing. Is *Best Supporting Actor in a Foreign Farce* an official category?

But by far the most depressing aspect of my new reality is Wayan's carrying on seeing Robert Buchanan. I started out confident that she would tell him to sling his hook once it dawned on her what a first-rate shit he is, and what a long history of first-rate-shittiness he has behind him. Such initial optimism on my part has given way to an insidious pessimism that the bastard might actually succeed in worming his way back into her good graces. On such topic, I still bite my tongue in front of my housekeeper, but I am not sure for how long I will be able to do this. Buchanan and I have not exchanged a single word since his phone call requesting my consent to take Wayan to dinner.

This unfortunate fact was what inspired Katie to suggest that Buchanan and I should make an effort to get to know one another better.

"You are joking," I said.

But she wasn't.

"I've spoken to Wayan about it, and she agrees the four of us should spend next weekend together here on Koh Phangan."

"Like one big happy family, eh? The assassin, the private detective, the woman who doesn't exist, and a Balinese housekeeper-turned-gangster's-moll. Maybe we should all wear matching shirts too."

"I'm serious, Dad."

"That's what worries me. But Wayan hasn't mentioned anything about this."

"You can hardly expect her to, can you? Since you've stopped drinking, you're like a bull with a sore head."

So here we all are on Koh Phangan, checked into one of the more discreet boutique hotels. The only saving grace about this place is that they don't have a spa, so there are no yoga hags around *Ohm*-ing and eating quinoa salads. I am also pleased to report that Buchanan and Wayan have separate rooms. I will make a point of patrolling the hallway later to make sure they are not tempted to bunk up together. I'm hardly temperamentally suited to the role of chaperone, but needs must. These are strange times indeed.

No alcohol has passed my lips for twenty days, and I have made a serious effort to cut down on cigarettes. Consequently, my breathing doesn't feel so constricted, and my chest pains are less frequent. Also, during my recent trips to the gun range my hands are not as shaky – though that may be because I've been imagining Robert Buchanan as the target. I can't claim to be in the best of health, and I doubt that Dr. Soo would be massively impressed with my attempt at personal improvement, but it's a start.

Ah, Koh Phangan.

White butterflies flutter above the sun-dappled greenery. Arching honeysuckle twirl alongside phosphorescent, drooping leaves and coarse tropical trunks. Yellow and purple flowers catch the light like small, slow-motion explosions. Browning coconut husks lie scattered, neglected in the long grass. The sound of cawing floats on the heated air.

It's only the people that spoil it.

The sun is slipping gingerly towards the horizon and the sky is lit pink, as Katie and I nurse sundowners on the hotel deck while watching Wayan and Buchanan walking slowly away from us along the quiet beach. They aren't holding hands, but their shoulders brush as the water laps over their bare feet.

"What are you thinking about, Dad?" my daughter asks.

I remove my Panama hat and set it on the table. I have been wearing this gift from Wayan so frequently these last months that it has become something of a trademark. If I go out on surveillance, I have to leave it at home – it makes me too recognisable: the galericulate detective, ineffectually concealed beneath a hat.

"I'm thinking about you, Katie. And what you are going to do."

She crooks an eyebrow.

"I've told you. I'm going to be a yoga teacher as soon as my training is finished."

"That's not a permanent solution. You can't hide out indefinitely on these islands. We both know it."

"I don't see why not. I'm happy here. Besides, what's the alternative? Go back to London and get my head blown off?"

My daughter reaches across the table and takes my hand.

"Dad, you're not considering doing anything stupid, are you?"

"Like what?"

"Like going after Grigory Polzin, for instance. Tell me I shouldn't worry about that."

"You shouldn't worry about that."

"Do you promise?"

"Yes, I promise. Though I can't say the thought hasn't occurred to me. But murder's not my thing, however much I want that bastard dead."

Katie relaxes a little before adding, "And you're not going to employ anyone else to kill him?"

"Someone like Buchanan, you mean?"

"Robert won't do it. He's quit that game."

"Do you believe that?"

"Yes, I do."

"Doesn't it worry you that, if things don't work out for him with Wayan, he might tell Polzin you're still alive? Or perhaps that he might go through with his original assignment, albeit late?"

"No."

"You sound sure."

"I am. You might not trust him, but I do."

"You trusted Alexander too. That didn't turn out well."

"Thanks for the memory."

I squeeze her hand. "Sorry. That was unnecessary, and unkind of me."

"Yes, it was."

"Let's talk about something else."

Before dinner, I stroll up the road away from the beach, and treat myself to a Marlboro while I amble along. I've earned it.

I don't like lying to Katie but the last thing she needs is to be worrying that her father is going to get himself killed in some half-baked assassination attempt. I console myself with the thought that, as yet, Vlad has not come through with a date when I can meet Orlov. So, technically, as of today I have no fixed *plan* to dispatch Polzin.

I wonder how transparent I appear to Katie. Is it credible to her that I have become a cowering wimp who will stand idly by while she passes the rest of her life in miserable exile as a yoga bum taking in stray cats? And is it credible for me to believe that *she* will do nothing to Polzin?

This notion pulls me up short.

Bollocks.

Much as I love Katie, I have to remind myself that this is a woman who planned Alexander's death. She too has the Braddock streak of ruthlessness running through her.

I need to chase Vlad again. Soon.

I light a second Marlboro, turn back and make my way down the slope towards the hotel. Lights twinkle through the trees.

In the car park, I notice a small white car on the back window of which are stenciled the words *IF YOU CAN READ THIS YOU IS TOO CLOSE*. Something registers. With the return of sobriety, my grey cells appear to have started working again. I swear I've seen this car before during my visits to Koh Phangan. The vehicle has blacked-out windows – not uncommon in Thailand – but is otherwise unremarkable. There is no-one inside. I look around and, as there is nobody else in the area, I try the door handle. Unsurprisingly, it's locked. I am probably being paranoid, but I make a note of the registration number. I'll have it checked out. Just in case.

Wayan and Katie are slumped on comfortable sofas at an outside area of the hotel. They are chatting contentedly, and drinking what appear to be sodas.

"Where's Robert?" I ask, hopeful of the response *In Intensive Care.*

"Taking the night air before dinner," replies Katie, pointing off to her right.

Buchanan is standing about fifty yards away on a rocky bluff overlooking the cove. He seems preoccupied, staring across the bay. I tread carefully across the stones and grass to join him. He makes no acknowledgement of my presence, but remains rooted to the spot as if hypnotised. I follow his gaze which is fixed on the tree-line, softly backlit in the darkness by the lights of a hotel in the next bay. A light wind rises up from the sea, ruffling the trees. Buchanan watches them sway, transfixed by their slow, easy movement.

"Communing with Nature?" I say.

"Not exactly."

"Then, what?"

He turns slowly to face me.

"I have a phobia about trees."

"Trees?"

"Yes. Hylophobia."

"How does that work?"

"Not all trees. In fact, only European forests. Palm trees and coconut trees don't bother me. That's why I don't generally feel anxious when I'm in this part of Asia. But beech, oak, birch ... trees with low spreading branches, I guess."

Maybe he's taking the piss, but I doubt it. Who would make up a story like that? I suppose all the years of doing what he's been doing would mess up most people. You can only dissociate for so long. Behind Buchanan's mask of calm, I imagine a veritable army of caged-up demons must slither over each other, searching for a way out. He's more vulnerable than he appears, this man my housekeeper loves. I might be able to use that.

"What the hell do you think they're going to do? It's not like they're able to pull up their roots and chase after you."

Buchanan bites his lip.

"Beats me. I've never been able to work it out. Ridiculous, really. A grown man terrified of bark, leaves and shadows. Something indescribably oppressive that I can't –" He shakes his head. "But then, a phobia is not a rational fear, is it? You've trained as a therapist, Braddock. You should understand these things."

"Oh, I do."

"Then, what's your read on it?"

"I'd say you're a ruddy nutter. Borderline certifiable, if you want my expert opinion."

A frown from the assassin.

"That doesn't sound like a terribly professional analysis. I thought you head-shrinker types weren't supposed to use words like 'nutter' and 'crazy'."

"I'm more of a post-modern practitioner of psychoanalysis. I believe in calling a spade a spade. Or, in your case, a bloody shovel."

My sarcasm makes no impact on him. He's back to staring at the distant palms, too troubled by his obsession to rise to my bait. Perhaps I should wave a twig and see if he runs away.

"They talk to each other. Maybe you're not aware of that."

"Talk?"

"Trees. They talk. They're social beings. They communicate through their root systems or via mycelium: different types of fungi depending on the tree. Acacia trees give off a type of gas to warn their neighbours of the presence of herbivorous predators, so they can all send toxins into their leaves. Other trees make use of their underground interconnections to send chemical signals to each other."

"Fascinating." I yawn. "And is this how you occupy your mind while you're waiting to shoot someone? Worrying about whether the nearby shrubs are saying to each other, 'Here comes Robert Buchanan. Let's gang up and do the bastard.' *Sweet.*"

He gives up on the conversation. But I have the urge to poke this weak spot a bit more.

"Anyway," I say with calculated malice, "if you're frightened of oak trees, then you should be terrified of me."

"Why is that?"

"Because my surname 'Braddock' is derived from the Old English words for 'broad' and 'oak'. My proximity might prove fatal to you. Perhaps, Buchanan, I am destined to be your nemesis."

He studies me for a few seconds before replying.

"That might be so. Someone is going to kill me one day. Only, I don't know who or when. It might be you. Who can say?"

I snort.

"Do you expect me to feel sorry for you?"

"No. Not at all." He turns once again to the horizon before adding, "Do you think you *could* kill me?"

"If necessary. Not in a fair fight, though. I'd have to be sneaky about it."

"Yes. Well, I'm not yet ready to die. Not now that I have something to live for."

"How many people do you reckon you've murdered? Others who had something to live for? A couple of dozen? More?"

No reply.

"Did you take a contract to assassinate Akira Tanaka last year? A Japanese-American who was film-making in Dubai?"

A sigh escapes Robert Buchanan.

"We should rejoin the ladies," he says. "We've done enough bonding for one evening. Don't you agree?"

Am I sitting down to dinner with the man who killed Hitomi's husband?

When I asked the question, it would have been easy for him to deny it. A simple *no* would have sufficed. Yet he said nothing. That may be because he didn't want to get drawn into an endless succession of enquiries into his wrongdoings over the years. Better for him to clam up and discourage further discussion. Or maybe he didn't think I would believe him. Or ...

Who can tell what goes on in Buchanan's head? If he ever stops to consider fully the implications of his time spent in that most lethal profession, surely it would fill his consciousness with a nightmarish present. It would hollow out someone with any trace of humanity in them. Any *normal* person, that is. But then, any normal person would never have embarked on Buchanan's path in the first place.

"Shall we order?" says Katie.

For the sake of the two females in our party, the two males have an understanding that there will be no strained atmosphere during the meal. We both say yes, and express our desire for Thai cuisine.

"You boys were gone some time. What have you been talking about?" asks my daughter.

"Wood mostly," I say.

The relentlessly cheerful meal has finished and we have all retired to our respective rooms for the night. The white car, I noticed, was no longer in the car park.

Something and nothing, in all likelihood.

Following Buchanan's ramblings about matters arboreal, I have been unable to resist scouring the Internet for a crash-course on oak trees to discover what my bark-clad relatives get up to. Bradd*oaks* (I learn) carry toxic tannins to kill or discourage chewing insects – though this information is not particularly useful should I decide to do away with Wayan's paramour. It's not as if he's likely to bite me.

Why did he mention his tree phobia to me? One would expect that a man like him would never wish to disclose any weakness, lest it prove his undoing. Especially not to *me*.

Then it hits me that there are probably only three people on the planet with whom Buchanan can have any sort of conversation about his life: Wayan, Katie, and me. We are the only ones who know something of his history. How lonely and isolated his existence must be for him to want to share information on his debility with a likely enemy.

On this gratifying note, I slide open the glass doors to my balcony and light a Marlboro. Were I not determined to stay dry, I would down a couple of celebratory whiskies: a toast to Robert Buchanan's vulnerability.

I take a deep draw on my cigarette.

Did he kill Hitomi's husband?

I reflect that, had the man answered my provocative query in the affirmative, I would have been presented with a dilemma: whether or not to disclose this information to Mrs. Tanaka. I am spared that quandary: I have plausible deniability on my side.

Oh, Hitomi.

A pox on my moral cowardice.

19

"One of the painful things about our time is that those who feel certainty are stupid, and those with any imagination and understanding are filled with doubt and indecision."

Bertrand Russell

Sleeping in my own bed last night didn't give me much rest.

I dreamed a giant goose was chasing me through a wharf district of Victorian London. At first, I was confident I could outrun the honking white bird, but then I became aware of a chain dragging on my left leg; that each time I turned a corner further links had been added to the chain; and that my pursuer was gaining on me. Fortunately, I woke up before the surreal chase reached a conclusion.

What this signified, I have no idea. *Man Intimidated by Waterfowl* is not usually the stuff of nightmares. It may be a reflection on how absurd my existence has become, that my fears are laughable ones, that life is through with laying golden eggs, or that I ate a dodgy prawn yesterday evening. As I've said, I'm not big on portents and foreshadowing.

However, what was apparent from the moment I opened my eyes was that my chest pain had returned, and I had to lie still for a good ten-to-fifteen minutes before it slackened. So much for temperance leading to health improvement. *Humbug.*

Wayan joins me for breakfast. She has something on her mind, and it doesn't require a genius to work out what it is.

"Mr. David, can I talk to you about Robert?"

"Of course. Robert. Or whatever his real name is."

This is a cheap trick on my part, but she lets it go.

"Thank you for being so kind as to come to Koh Phangan at the weekend. I know you didn't really want to. But Katie and I thought if you and Robert –"

"It's all right, Wayan," I interrupt gently. "I understand that in some bizarre female way, you and Katie are looking for approval from me for Buchanan. In Katie's case, she wants me to recognise that what he has done for her was done for noble motives. In your case, well, you can speak for yourself."

Wayan twists her fingers before making a brave attempt to achieve eye contact with me.

"A lot has happened in recent months, Mr. David."

"Indeed, it has."

"When you lose someone – you believe forever – and then they come back, it's hard to accept that it's real. You question everything. You must understand that because you have been through it with Katie."

"Yes."

Wayan swallows hard before continuing.

"At first, I wasn't sure I wanted to let Robert back into my life. He treated me badly before. I wasn't willing to trust his intentions. I was afraid that he might hurt me again; that he might disappear again."

I pat her hand. "Take your time. It's OK."

"He has been open with me about ... Well, I know how he has been living, what he has been doing. At the beginning, he started to give me details ... but I said I didn't need to know – didn't want to know – all the specifics. It is bad enough that he has killed people. Hearing their names might make me ..."

She falters.

"Complicit? An accomplice to his crimes? No. You are not. What he did, he did without regard for you. You were never involved, Wayan. All this is on his shoulders."

She looks down at her hands.

"I suppose that is true. But nonetheless, if I accept him now, it means that in a way I accept his deeds."

"That depends on whether you believe that he has changed, that he is capable of change. That he is no longer the man he was."

Wayan raises her head.

"What sort of a man do *you* think he is, Mr. David?"

"Does it matter?"

"It does to me."

"Do you still love him?"

A beat.

"Yes."

"Despite everything?"

"Despite everything."

There is much I could say. I could ask her whether she believes Buchanan should be punished for his crimes; whether she is prepared to live with him as a fugitive from justice for the rest of her life; how she would cope if he absconded again or reverted to his previous self; whether he is too damaged a person to make her happy. I could counsel her that he is still dangerous and, if cornered, could hurt her physically. I could tell her that I fear for her safety.

All this I could do, and more. But she is an intelligent woman, and she will already have worked these things through. There is something more fundamental she needs to hear.

"I love you, Wayan. You are family to me. Over these last years, there have been times when you were my only family.

"I have observed you and Robert these last two days. Given who I am and who he is – or was – it would be easy for me to be cynical about his intentions, but …"

I recall him straightening a shawl across her shoulders, her brushing a fallen leaf from his leg, their quiet chuckles, the comfortable gestures of familiarity, the proximity of their bodies, and the ease between them.

Despite everything.

Without someone to share your life, what else is there? If you are fortunate enough to find your soul mate – however imperfect that person might be – would you not forever regret it if you passed up the possibility of happiness with them?

The accumulation of years may not have brought me wisdom, but it has brought a recognition of how little I know of the world and of the intimate workings of the human heart. The more we learn, the less we understand. And Buchanan may not be so different from me, after all. If I might once again hold Claire in my arms, I would pay any price. I would, without a second thought, annihilate the planet to bring her back.

Not so very different.

We are all potential destroyers. All we need is the appropriate motivation.

A tear spills down Wayan's cheek as she waits for me to resume. She is holding her breath.

"I don't consider Robert to be a good man. I can't say that, no matter how much you might want me to say it. His past sins outweigh his recent worthy deeds, in my book. But I am not the oracle. I am not qualified to give any final judgement. And I *do* think that with you at his side, he might become a better man. You see, you have that effect on people, Wayan Lastri. You have had that effect on me."

She rises and puts her arms around me and, for now, there is nothing more to say.

We are curious creatures. Inexplicable, inconsistent, unpredictable.

Needing.

And the reason for my drinking comes sharply into focus. It has not been not the product of mental or physical disease, but rather the result of existential angst: the sensation that my life following Katie's 'death' has had no positive meaning. For sure, devoting myself to the extermination of Grigory Polzin has given me a goal – a reason to continue breathing – but an existence geared solely towards revenge can hardly be characterised as 'positive'. My confused state of mind since my daughter's return has been brought about by trying to establish, now that a *constructive* meaning is once again possible, *what* that meaning should be. That is why killing Polzin is no longer a straightforward matter.

And I can't help but ponder on whether the ache in my chest may be not so much from the presence of a biological cause as from an absence: the lack of someone tender to touch the core of me.

Back to the reality of the *David Braddock Agency.*

I can't face Da while I am blubbery and sentimental. So, having opened up my heart, I now have to close it again. Be that stiff-backed, stubborn Englishman that she has become accustomed to.

This morning's discussion with Wayan has clarified one thing, though. I will not be turning in Buchanan to the authorities, and any lingering notion I may have had about killing him has been dispelled. That boat has sailed. My concerns for my housekeeper remain but, I remind myself, she has other options. It is not yet certain that she *will* ride off into the sunset with her lover – though at this juncture I wouldn't bet against it – but if she does, and it doesn't work out, she has the resources to return to Bali. Or to me. If I'm still around.

I ascend the stairs to the *Agency*, wish Pimpim a good morning, throw my Panama at the hat stand, and miss. While our receptionist diligently retrieves it, I knock on the door of Da's office and go in.

Sitting at her desk, Da exudes glumness. Her expression as she raises her eyes to me says, *Now what?*

"Did you have a good weekend?"

"The usual," she says. "How was your trip to Koh Phangan? Is your goddaughter still enjoying herself?"

"I didn't see much of her," I reply, wishing to discourage a discussion which could go rapidly downhill if Da gets too probing. "But there was something happened while I was away that I'd like you to look into for me."

"Oh? What's that?"

"I keep spotting the same white car on the island. It was there at the weekend, and I'm sure I've seen it a couple of other times."

"A white car? There must be lots of white cars around, David."

"This one has black-tinted windows."

"So? That's hardly unusual."

"And a distinctive message on the back. I'm certain it's the same vehicle."

"Did you have sight of the driver?"

"No."

"Do you think you're being followed?"

"Perhaps."

Her eyes narrow.

"Why would anyone be following you on Koh Phangan, David?

"I have no idea."

"Why would you *think* someone is following you? Have you started drinking again?"

"No. Absolutely not. Want to smell my breath?"

"That's not necessary," she says, wrinkling her nose.

I tear the page from my notebook containing the vehicle's details and hand it to her.

"Check it out for me, would you? See what you can find out. *Discreetly*. Use one of your police contacts. I'd do it myself, but my credit is low with local law enforcement at present."

Da holds the paper as if I've passed her a piece of used toilet roll.

"How urgent is this?"

"Your boss gives you an assignment and you ask how urgent it is?"

"It's just that I'll need to leave the office for a few hours to deal with it, and I have a client coming in to see me at one o'clock to go through his final surveillance report."

"No problem. I'll handle him. Give me his file. I have no fixed appointments today anyway."

No reply. Da stares sightlessly at the vehicle details, her mind elsewhere.

"Da?"

She pulls herself back, and attempts a smile. It's a sad smile.

"Are you all right?"

"Yes. I'm fine."

"No, you're not fine. What's wrong? Is it to do with Tong?"

She smiles again, but this time it's more convincing.

"You're improving."

"In what way?"

"Not so long ago, if you thought I was in a strange mood, you'd have asked me if I was on my period."

"I'd never have said anything so crass."

She throws me an old-fashioned look but says nothing.

"*Are* you on your period?"

She laughs. It's so rare that I amuse her, that her reaction takes me by surprise.

"Seriously, Da, if you do need to have some time off –"

"No," she says firmly. "I prefer to keep busy. And, yes," she sighs, "sometimes Tong's death catches me unawares. I had so many things to sort out up until his funeral, that I didn't really have the opportunity to dwell on what had happened. But, since ... well ... it's the *what ifs* that get to you. Not all the time. It's only on occasion that things pop into my head."

Da straightens her paperwork and metamorphoses back into her professional, well-organised self.

"Anyway, David, we can't have me going crazy. We already have one lunatic in the office." She waves the paper with the vehicle details. "I'll start on this right away. Pimpim has the client file for this afternoon."

"Listen, if you ever want to talk –"

I reach for her hand, but she withdraws it.

"Yes, thank you. But I don't feel like talking. Not yet, anyway."

"I am truly sorry, Da. About Tong, I mean."

"Yes, David. I know you are," she says.

She rises and leaves the room without another word.

When we close the *Agency* for the day, Da has not returned. I read this as a positive sign, that she has been making progress on tracking down details of the white car. I am tempted to ring her, but decide it can wait until tomorrow, so I call Nang instead for a chat and a lecture on how the Tory Party must not underestimate the duplicitous Labour Party devils. Then I try

Natalie but there is no answer: she appears to have reverted to her previous position of avoiding contact with me unless it is strictly necessary. Ah, well.

Wayan is out with the Penitent Assassin this evening, so I settle down for a few hours of coma-inducing American TV.

Halfway through some unmemorable tripe about a terrorist plot to nuke New York, my cell phone trills. The display tells me it's Vlad.

"Braddock?"

"Yes."

"The meeting with Mr. Orlov is arranged. Thursday, this week."

"Excellent. Where?"

"I will see you at Samui airport at ten in the morning."

"Are we flying to Bangkok? If so, shall I book a ticket?"

"I will arrange flights. Just be at check-in at ten, and bring your passport."

"Isn't he in Bangkok, then? Otherwise, why do I need my passport?"

"I can't discuss where he is. Security reasons."

"That's rather paranoid, isn't it, Vlad?"

"It's how he does things."

"All right. Whatever you say. I'll be there."

He rings off.

The passport requirement could be a red herring. They love their spy games, these Russians. But there are direct flights or easy connections from Samui to any likely destination, so I'd better play along. No cock-ups on my side.

So, it's *on*. I take out a Marlboro.

Starting Thursday – all being well – I commence my new vocation for real.

David Braddock: apprentice assassin.

20

"Someday this pain will be useful to you."

Ovid

Morning has broken.

Tuesday.

I'm jittery.

Now that the idea of Polzin's death is assuming a concrete shape, it is as if all the nerve endings in my body are popping like corn in a microwave: little explosions of excitement mingled with sensations of fear at the prospect of facing the Russian with a gun in my hand. My slightly trembling hand.

Suddenly, all the weeks of waiting, of researching, of racking my brain, have become compressed into a fast-paced countdown to Thursday's rendezvous with Orlov. That will be when I finally commit; when I potentially offer up my life in exchange for the possibility of Katie being able to restart hers. Motive: a slippery animal, and not one that warrants too close attention. Am I really contemplating putting an end to Polzin so that my daughter can end her existence as a fugitive, or is it for the less-laudable reason of hurt pride; that someone has dared to affront the Braddock name by attempting to murder one of my own?

How helpful it would be at this point if I believed in God. That way I could pray for a sign – *any* sign – as to what I should do. To shift the burden of resolution onto broader shoulders: how appealing a prospect. Right now, I am so skittish that the merest thread would lead me.

But it isn't going to happen. It's on me.

So, screw all that. Let's concentrate on getting through today. Deep breaths. Practical matters. Mortal contemplations later or – preferably – not at all.

Pull yourself together, Braddock.

Da's door at the *Agency* is open, so I walk straight in.

"There's someone to see you," she says. "I've left him in your office."

"Whoever it is can wait. I want to know what you've discovered about that vehicle on Koh Phangan."

"But –"

"Now would be a *really* convenient time for you to tell me."

"You're going to be disappointed."

"I'm usually disappointed. Go on."

"The car is owned by a guy on Samui. A local. He has two cars that he rents out to tourists 'unofficially'. Which is to say, that all his business is done in cash, nothing traceable. The car was returned yesterday. It had been hired for three weeks by a young Danish man and his girlfriend, whom I gather flew home last night."

"Names?"

"No names."

An exasperated sigh breaks from her. I can sympathise. It can't be easy working with an idiot. And a secretive idiot, at that.

"Look," she continues, "this is an unregistered business, David. It was difficult enough to obtain those details. But there is nothing sinister to report. Did you expect there would be? Are you being pursued by international spies? If so, maybe we should purchase some rocket launchers and start communicating in code."

"All right."

"And you're not going to tell me what this is about, are you?"

"No."

"Fine."

Da folds her arms.

"Did you have to lay out any cash for this information?"

"No. I called in some favours."

"Then, I owe you a favour."

"Go and see your visitor. He's been waiting ten minutes already."

"Thanks, Da."

"Whatever. I wasted a whole afternoon, and now I have work to do."

I am dismissed. The white car mystery is put to bed. My paranoia creeps down a notch.

A wizened old Thai man with a bald head is sitting in my visitor's chair. He is dressed in peasant garb and wears thick spectacles. There is something familiar about him and yet ...

"Do you not recognise me, Braddock?"

"Er –"

"Perhaps the absence of orange robes is confusing you. Though you were always easily confused, as I remember."

"*Ananda?* Is that really you?"

The Old Monk inclines his head.

"Nothing is *really* anything. Do you recollect so little of your lessons with me, White Tathagata? How discouraging."

"What happened to your robes?"

"I am no longer a monk. Simply a farmer, living quietly with his wife."

"I am so happy to see you."

"Please sit down at your desk, Braddock. I am worried you might attempt to hug me, and that would be disagreeable."

I drop into my chair and stare at the old buzzard. He is more shrunken, but the light in his eyes burns with the same intensity. He picks something from his teeth and gazes disapprovingly around my office.

"What are you doing on Samui?"

"Although I am no longer with the *sangha*, I remain in contact with several of the members of the Supreme Council. There have been reports that *Wat San* has fallen into disrepair and that the monks there are not fully carrying out their duties. Accordingly, I have been asked to pay an unannounced visit to see if that is the case."

"It *is* the case. The old temple has gone downhill since your time. Well, it's good of you to drop by the *Agency* while you're here. I'm flattered."

"As you should be."

I pull out my packet of Marlboros.

"Do you want a smoke?"

The Old Monk holds up a defensive hand.

"I no longer smoke. My wife dislikes the smell of tobacco."

"Oh, I see."

He takes a cigarette and lights up. I join him and we sit in silence.

"I hear you have troubles, Braddock," he says eventually.

"Who told you that?"

He shrugs.

"You did. Just now."

"Ah."

"Are you meditating? You look a long way from the Path to me."

"No, I'm not meditating."

He tuts.

"That is bad."

I flick some ash at the ashtray in what I hope is a nonchalant fashion. I make a vague affirmative noise.

To switch subjects, I say, "Is your wife travelling with you?"

"She is here, yes."

"Visiting your son?"

He gives a grunt.

"I'd like to meet her. I've never experienced a living saint before."

"I don't think you should meet. You would not be a good influence on her."

"Right."

"Following the Way is important. But, for those who are not monks, family is also important. If you are not doing anything else, I hope you are giving your family attention."

Eerie. Am I so easily readable? Does the old bugger have a hotline to the Buddha? If so, I wish he'd give me the number. Next, he will be instructing me to read my father's manuscript. Except he can't do that: he doesn't know it exists.

The cigarette smoulders in his fingers. He tilts his head to the side and his stare drills so far into me that I squirm.

"Are you?"

Maybe I should reply that I am paying my daughter so much attention that I'm planning to kill for her. Not a response he would be expecting, however good his cold-reading skills.

Probably not advisable. *I do my best,* is a safer response.

"I do my best."

But he hasn't finished.

"That heavy black cinder is still lodged in your heart, Braddock. Perhaps even more firmly entrenched than when we were last together. Are you even aware it is there?"

"I –"

"You should be more heedful, White Tathagata. More honest with yourself. Otherwise, this cinder will kill you. You appear quiet, but some hatred shouts from within you. I can hear it."

"That's the sound of one cinder clapping."

The old Monk curls his lip.

"Always joking, but never funny. Life is not a joke."

An enigmatic Zen dressing-down. That's what this is. What a way to start a Tuesday. Weaponised spirituality.

How I've missed this.

"Be careful, Braddock," he says, stubbing out his cigarette. "When you get into trouble, I won't be there to save you next time."

He rises. The conversation is over. He has said what he wanted to say, and turns to leave.

"Will we meet again?" I ask.

A moment of hesitation.

"In another life, perhaps."

I see him out. He descends the stairs without looking back.

When I return to my office, I notice that my pack of Marlboros has disappeared.

"That was that Ananda, the monk, wasn't it?" says Da.

"It was."

"Is he coming back?"

"No. He's gone. Gone beyond. Gone beyond beyond."

"What did he want?"

"He didn't want anything, Da. That's the point."

Well, I did say I'd appreciate a sign.

With Ananda's brief appearance, the vacillations of my overthinking brain have been stilled.

How ironic that it has taken a holy man to seal Grigory Polzin's fate.

Even as the Old Monk was advocating taking care of family, he was unknowingly advocating murder.

The fewer the words, the greater the meaning.

It only took the cunning bastard a few minutes to stir me up. It was just like old times, with me on the receiving end, as always.

For great belief, there must first be great doubt.

Great. Doubt.

A cinder in my heart, he said. Still lodged.

Beware the anger of the quiet man. Me.

And at long last I can admit to myself what I have denied, what my dark jesting was meant to keep at bay, the truth I have suppressed for so long. That within me there is a deep well of anger, a resentment that has festered for years, a hatred towards the world for all that it has stolen from me: Claire, my former existence, my self-respect, my peace of mind. Poisonous. And I recoil at the idea that, while Katie has been spared, she might yet be snatched from me too.

For no matter that we might consider ourselves rational and civilised, it is all surface. We can choke down our indignation at the uncaring randomness of life's atrocities – but we cannot do so indefinitely. Within every human – no matter how enlightened he believes himself to be – lurk the blind, furious urges of a beast. Yes, for a time we can cage our violent instincts, but the bars had better be strong. And even the sturdiest bars will bend if the rage attains its full power. Then the animal will emerge to do what must be done, that which cannot be resisted.

This is what I am.

My way is clear. Softer matters can wait. The cinder has to be dislodged.

No more distractions.

I shall roll up my accumulated bitterness into a ball, and hurl it with all my strength at a single loathsome target, one worthy of my spite: Grigory Polzin.

Then, finally, I shall be cleansed.

And Katie will be safe.

After the *Agency* has closed for the day, I go to the shooting range.

There is not the slightest tremor in my hand, nor any pain in my chest. I don't even want a stiff drink.

I don't kid myself that everything is fine with me, but the respite is welcome. Maybe, now that I am firm on my priorities, I am like that surgeon I read about who suffered from Tourette syndrome, but who was able to set aside all involuntary movements and vocalisations when focused on his work. After all, I should, one assumes, be more capable of controlling my impulses than him – it's not like I'm shouting obscenities and barking. If I were unwittingly doing so, I'm sure I could rely on Da to point it out. With relish.

She asked today if we might have our previously-deferred breakfast tomorrow at the Belgian bakery. It smells like a trap, but I said yes anyway. Unlike Buchanan with his trees, I'm not afraid of croissants.

At the range, my aim is shit-hot. I could shoot anyone today. Hope I can keep *that* up.

A day-and-a-half to go before I meet Orlov. The minutes keep ticking away.

In the spirit of eliminating those items which might distract me from my homicidal purpose, I am determined this evening to phone Hitomi and sever all contact. I have likewise resolved to banish all thoughts of reading my father's manuscript until after Polzin is dead – though, in fairness, this was an easy decision. As for Wayan and Buchanan, they can sort themselves out without further interference from me.

I wonder if I'm less annoying to be around when I'm not dithering. I must remember to ask Da about this at breakfast tomorrow. She'll give it to me straight.

Time to call Hitomi and get this over with.

She answers after a few rings.

"Hi, Hitomi. Are you OK to talk?"

"David, yes. Funny, I was thinking about you."

"Ah."

"I've been consulting my horoscope, and it said I should expect to be contacted by someone from my past. I wondered if it might be you."

Either me or Sam Trask, my dear. But although I'm curious about the ex-soldier, I'm not about to enter into a discussion about him. That's … irrelevant now.

"You've never struck me as someone who would be into astrology."

She laughs.

"Too unscientific for a modern educated woman, you mean? Well, we're all prone to want our wishes to be granted and our biases to be confirmed. Besides, we of Oriental descent find it hard to cast off old patterns and superstitions. It's in the blood, even though we know it's all nonsense."

"I see."

"I detect from your tone that this is not going to be a chatty call."

"You're very perceptive."

"No. Just well-practiced at recognising when someone is leading up to bad news. I've had a lot of that in the last couple of years. What is it, David?"

I tell her I've met someone, that I've decided to move on with my life, start again. I burble on for a couple of minutes before she interrupts.

"So, you've called to say that you don't think it appropriate now for us to talk to each other. Is that it?"

"Yes. Sorry, but I –"

"It's perfectly all right, David. I do understand. And it's not as if we've been lovers, and had some deep and meaningful relationship."

"No, I guess not."

She is silent awhile. I am about to make some facile, homely remark, when she says, "I appreciate what you have done for me, David. You have been a good friend to me since Akira's disappearance. But I do get it."

"Thank you for making this easy. I don't want to hurt you –"

"I'm not hurt. A little sad, perhaps, but that's all."

"Yes."

"So, I guess this is goodbye." The line crackles before she adds, "Be happy, David Braddock. I shall miss you."

"I'll miss you too, Hitomi," I say, but she has already ended the call.

Wayan is out and I don't expect her back for at least another hour. I'm alone in the apartment: alone with my resolution and my reflections on today's visit from the Old Monk. A soda sits at my elbow. I couldn't swallow a whisky now even if I wanted to. To meditate would be good, but my concentration is too scattered for that.

I smoke a cigarette on the balcony and gaze up at a night sky punctured by the distant light of innumerable suns. It is warm: not a breath of wind disturbs the trees. For want of anything better to do – and to keep more tenebrous thoughts at bay – I turn over in my mind my last conversation with Hitomi Tanaka, and contemplate the notion of horoscopes. Hmmn. I can only wonder at the credulity of astrology's disciples.

Astra inclinant sed non obligant - the stars incline us but they do not bind us. Except that, I doubt they even *incline* us. Destiny is not to be found in the heavens, if it is to be found at all. The future is not fixed: free will exerts a greater force than astrological determinism. To believe otherwise is to abdicate responsibility for our actions.

Our fate, like our faults, lies not in the stars, but in ourselves that we are assholes.

21

"This very heart which is mine will forever remain indefinable to me. Between the certainty I have of my existence and the content I try to give to that assurance, the gap will never be filled. Forever I shall be a stranger to myself."
Albert Camus, The Myth of Sisyphus and Other Essays

It's dull weather-wise when I park outside the Belgian bakery, but that's fine by me. After all the recent excitement, I am glad of some dullness.

Da is already sitting at one of the outside tables and she has Pratcha with her.

"I hope you don't mind my bringing my son along," she says. "He has no school today."

"Not at all."

She is not dressed for the office, but is smart nonetheless. Her hair is loose, and she has eschewed her 'business' spectacles. The makeup is subtle but becoming.

"You look nice," I tell her.

"Thank you. I hadn't expected to be receiving compliments this morning."

"That's all right. I hadn't expected to be giving them."

I pick up a menu.

"Is Pratcha OK with non-Thai food?"

"Yes. I want to expose him to some European ways. I figured this was an easy way to start him off. He needs to learn about *farangs* for his later career."

The four-year old is more interested in picking his nose than fine cuisine. He manages to corner a booger, and Da says something stern to him before wiping his fingers with a tissue. He glances at me for male support and I wink at him. Thus reassured, he wanders off to inspect a nearby fighting cock strutting around its wicker cage.

Malee totters out on a pair of high heels to take our order. Her vivid lipstick, eye shadow, and lace mini-dress are in stark contrast to Da's understated look. I request three croissants and fruit juices. As Malee returns to the kitchen, I become aware that Da is scrutinising me closely.

"What?" I say.

"Nothing."

"There is *something*. I know that expression of old."

"Let's say I was curious," she replies coyly.

"About what?"

"Well, after you let it slip that the last occasion you'd slept with someone, it was with Malee at Christmas."

"I didn't *let it slip*. I confided that to you in confidence," I grumble.

"Yes. Right."

"So, you thought you'd like to see her and me together to see if some of the magic was still there, and whether we'd be able to stop ourselves from sticking our tongues down each other's throats?"

"Something along those lines."

I scratch my chin.

"And I suppose this is also part of Pratcha's education on matters *farang*? To show him how depraved we Europeans are; how we are addicted to despoiling the young, innocent maidens of Thailand?"

"Now you're overreacting."

"You are staggeringly nosey."

"Anyway, that's not the only reason I wanted to have breakfast with you."

"Oh, there's more? Some bomb you want to drop?"

"No bomb. I felt it was time to accept your offer of breakfast, that's all. In the interest of our maintaining a smooth working relationship."

Her innocent expression immediately raises my suspicions, but before I can come up with some cutting remark, Malee reappears and sets out our plates, cutlery and glasses. I make a point of not acknowledging her, and she moves off to another table while conducting some muttered dialogue with herself. Da calls Pratcha back to the table.

"So, did I pass the test?"

"There is no test," she says, settling her son on his chair. "But, if you are asking whether I believe you and the waitress have been continuing your liaison, I'd be inclined to say *no*. At least not on this morning's showing."

"We could be pretending not to be interested in each other."

"I doubt she's bright enough for that, and you're a terrible actor."

"Huh."

"So, you haven't had sex for over three months. How's that working out for you?"

"Can we discuss this some other time? Preferably not in front of a four-year-old. In fact, preferably not for a few hundred years."

She grins.

Pratcha is holding a knife and staring at his croissant dubiously.

"Here, I'll show you," I say to him. "You don't cut the croissant, Pratcha, you break it with your fingers. Like this." I demonstrate, and he gets it. "Now use your knife to spread some butter on it. And jam, if you like. OK?"

He says nothing, but sets about his breakfast. I squeeze his shoulder.

"Attaboy."

Da tastes her fruit juice.

"Do you miss it, David?" she asks.

"Miss what?"

"Family life."

"God, you never stop, do you?"

"I'm just asking."

Her tone is soft, and I am a little disarmed.

"Sometimes. Yes, I do. But those days are long gone, never to return, sucked under by the sludge of time. One has to move on. You can't hold onto the past. It slips through your fingers."

She nibbles at her croissant.

"I imagine you were a good father to Katie when she was little."

"I guess no worse than any other repressed, middle class Englishman who is incapable of properly expressing his feelings."

"Hmmn."

"Anyway, shouldn't we be talking about you? You've had more to cope with than I have in recent weeks."

"I'm not ready to go into all that now, David. I'm still processing it. But I am starting to think about my future, and what I should do."

"Oh?"

"Well, the *Agency* is up-and-down. You have to keep pumping money into it. You can't go on doing that indefinitely. At some point, you'll sell up, perhaps go back to England. It's simply a question of when."

"In the spirit of full disclosure, Da, I should tell you that the psychiatrist Braun – whom you may remember – called by the office while you were on leave, and said he was interested in buying the business. I haven't mentioned it before because I told him it wasn't for sale."

"I see."

She lowers her head.

"But if we ever do sell, I've decided you will have all the proceeds and I'll try to negotiate a position for you with the new owner. Meanwhile, if something were to happen to me, you should know I've made a will leaving the *Agency* to you, along with a lump sum in cash."

Da stares at me.

"Why would you do that?" Her voice takes on an edge. "I told you, I don't need any charity –"

"This has nothing to do with charity, Da."

"Then what has it to do with?"

"It's about you receiving what you deserve. You may not have put any money into the *Agency*, but you've put in your heart and soul. More so than me, if the truth were told. Now, eat your breakfast. Pratcha has already finished his."

In the office today, the atmosphere has been positively serene. I attribute this in no small part to the conversation over breakfast. It was like a breath of domesticity, a short but welcome respite from the contemplation of my more lethal primary purpose.

So, here I am sitting at my desk with a cup of coffee reflecting that, despite all the emotional wrenches, the excessive drinking, and the cartwheels that my mind has been performing over recent months, I have still managed to get a few things done. Somehow, in the midst of my constant flip-flopping, the dialogues with my dead wife, my health issues, and the stilted long-distance phone calls to Nang, Natalie and Hitomi, I have been inching nevertheless towards a final tidying-up of my affairs. My dispositions are a case in point.

The Last Will and Testament of David Braddock was signed and witnessed in London in December. In it, I leave the *Agency* and some cash to Da, and a larger monetary amount to Wayan. The residue – and by far the largest part – of my estate is bequeathed to Katie provided 'proof of life' can be shown within twelve months, otherwise it all goes to my niece Jenny. The document was drawn up at a time when I believed my daughter was dead, but I was still inclined to play the *what if* game. A triumph of hope over common sense, as it turned out.

A Thai will, executed on my return to Samui, mirrors the provisions of my English one so far as my Thailand assets are concerned.

My affairs are therefore, so far as it is possible, in order. In the event of my untimely demise, nobody close to me will have to go scrambling around for paperwork or suffer any anxiety on the financial front. Everyone has been taken care of.

No further documents remain to be executed.

Only one execution now remains to be carried out. And that involves bullets, not paper.

Bullets. *Yes.*

I finish my coffee and ring Wayan to tell her I'll be home late after work as I'm going to the shooting range.

Round after round, the bullets rip through the target sheets. I am like a machine. I reload the pistol with ease, like a seasoned gunman. My earlier tentative fumblings with the weapon seem consigned to the trash bin of history, to a less resolute time.

After I've fired off about four dozen shots, I experience a sensation of being watched. When I turn around, I see Robert Buchanan perched on a low wall. I discharge the rest of my ammunition clip, and return the gun to the service window.

Buchanan is wearing island attire and a Panama hat not dissimilar to mine. Perhaps Wayan likes her men to dress the same, and she bought it for him. Or maybe he's trying to look more like me. *Ha.*

"Wayan said I would find you here," he remarks as he removes his sunglasses.

"Have you come to give me some tips?"

"I wondered if you might let me buy you a coffee."

He has the air of a man who has something to say.

"Sure. Why not?"

We order drinks at the counter of the range's small café, and sit at a corner table.

"You and Wayan appear to be getting along well. Fantastically well, considering."

I make an effort to keep the resentment out of my voice.

"Yes."

"Do you speak every day?"

"Every day on the phone. And we meet regularly, as you are aware."

"I don't know how you manage to fill the rest of your time. I'd be bored hanging around the island with nothing else to do but wait until Wayan is available to see me. It seems somewhat emasculating after the life you've been leading."

"I enjoy having nothing to do. It's restful."

Two cappuccinos are set in front of us. Buchanan stirs his coffee slowly, then sucks the froth from the spoon.

"In my experience," he says, "there are only seven reasons why a man goes to a shooting range. One, he used to be with the armed forces and likes to keep his hand in. Two, he's a committed shooting sportsman. Three, he's a North American staying in practice for the hunting season. Four, he's a professional assassin and needs to remain sharp. Five, it's a social thing – he goes to the range with his buddies. We can discount these first five items on the list so far as you are concerned."

"Go on."

"Six, he has reason to be worried about his personal safety or that of his family. And, seven, he's decided to kill somebody."

"Or – eight – he's trying some new pastime for a change."

"The fact that you've been coming here for weeks probably rules that out."

"I'm sure there are other reasons. You just haven't come across them."

"Perhaps. So, what is yours?"

I drink some of the cappuccino. It's bitter as hell.

"You're the expert on the subject, apparently, so what are your thoughts?"

He pulls at an ear.

"You *could* be taking precautions in the event that Polzin discovers Katie is alive and comes after her. But you don't strike me as the sort of man to sit on his hands and wait on the acts of others. That would be altogether too passive for you. You're more likely to take a proactive role in events."

He pauses.

"Spit it out, then."

"On balance, I'd say that you're planning to kill Grigory Polzin so that Katie can return from the dead in safety. So that she won't have to spend the rest of her life as an anonymous fugitive."

"On the other hand, I might be planning to kill *you*."

"You wouldn't do that," he replies with a trace of smugness.

"Oh, and why not?"

"Because of your relationship with Katie and Wayan. No, if you were going to do anything to me, it would be to turn me in to the authorities. And if you were going to do *that*, you'd already have done it by now."

I chance another mouthful of cappuccino. It's still bitter.

"Supposing I am thinking of killing Polzin, what does it have to do with you?"

He drains his coffee.

"Is there anywhere around here where we can get a real drink?" he says. Then, he adds, "That is, if you're OK with alcohol. I hear you're on the wagon."

"The occasional beer doesn't count," I respond through gritted teeth. "I am *not* an alcoholic. I'm staying off spirits for the time being that's all."

"Whatever. That's your business."

"Yes, it is."

The owner of the Thai hostelry notices his only two customers have become dark shadows in the gathering dusk, and switches on the overhead strip-lights. It's unsubtle, but at least we can see our bottles of Chang now. In anticipation of further business, the owner's wife stirs stainless steel pans full of indeterminate vegetables and noodles, and the smell of charcoaled chicken wafts our way. A dog lies on the concrete floor hoping for scraps. It's a dump, and you'd only eat here if you had a death wish, but the beer's cold and you can smoke.

I light a Marlboro.

"So, Buchanan," I say. "What is it you want to get off your chest? I doubt you're here for the pleasure of my company."

"Speaking hypothetically, if you were to decide to kill Grigory Polzin, how would you rate your chances of success?"

"Assessing those odds is more in your line of work than mine. What would you say?"

"If you were working alone, not high. You can carry out Internet research on the man, and learn how to fire a gun easily enough, but those won't carry you far. Of course, you might have some personal knowledge of his habits through Katie's association. That might help a bit, but ... not enough."

"What else would I need?" I add, "Speaking hypothetically, that is."

"Access to a weapon and ammunition, for a start. Unless you were lucky enough to catch him in Thailand, I guess, which seems unlikely. You can't put a gun and bullets in your luggage and expect it won't be picked up. Airports are rather strict about that sort of thing. You'd need someone who could supply you in-country with the requisite hardware."

"I'm sure there are guns to be bought on the street in Russia. It's a gangster society."

Buchanan throws me a dubious look.

"You think it's so simple? That you can wander down the back-streets of Moscow until you find someone with a suitcase full of pistols?"

"I might have a contact in Moscow who can source my hardware."

He studies me.

"A *reliable* contact?"

"*Hypothetically*, a reliable contact."

Buchanan has a swig of Chang.

"Even assuming that to be the case, you'd still wind up dead. And Polzin would still be alive."

"Why?"

"You'd never get near enough to him. I've met him, remember. Moscow is his home turf. His buildings and private houses are crawling with security. He is accompanied everywhere by armed bodyguards. No. In my view, you'd have to assassinate him while he was travelling abroad. He'd still have goons with guns around him – that goes without saying – and the probability of your own survival would be close to zero, but you might pull it off."

"Thanks for the vote of confidence."

"*Provided*," he continues, "you had information about his travel plans in advance. Which you won't have. Polzin plays his movements close to his chest. He has enemies other than you who might want him dead."

I stub out my cigarette and light another.

"You appear to have given this a lot of consideration."

"I have. It's my business - *was* my business - to think such things through."

"Was?"

He ignores this, and continues.

"But even if you *could* kill him and escape without being captured or recognised, that wouldn't achieve your objective of keeping Katie safe."

This makes me concentrate.

"Why not?"

"Are you so naïve as to believe that Polzin's surviving son Mikhail wouldn't want to track down his father's murderer? For sure, there would be several possible candidates to investigate, but you're going to be close to the top of the list. And you're not exactly hard to find, Braddock, are you? He might order a hit on you to play safe. A scattergun approach, shall we say?"

Shit, that's true.

"And, if Mikhail comes for *you*, what is the likelihood of his finding Katie too? And perhaps me. And Wayan. It wouldn't take much for all the dominoes to fall, would it? For all we know, the Polzins may still be keeping tabs on you now. That's why I was so keen for Katie to stay off Samui for an extended period."

I remember the white car on Koh Phangan. But Da has already explained that. It was innocent. *Wasn't it?*

I order us two more beers while I mull this over.

Eventually, I say, "Well, it would probably be advisable for me to bump off Mikhail too."

"Just like that?" he replies with scorn.

"Why not?" I say blandly.

"Because as soon as something happens to his father, Mikhail's security will quadruple. It would be nigh-impossible to get to him."

"So, I'd need to assassinate Polzin and his son when they're travelling together. Problem solved."

"Problem *not* solved. The two of them don't travel together for that very reason. And, incidentally, you are in the realm of fantasy if you suppose you could manage two murders and escape alive and unidentified."

"Well then, the best thing would be for me to kill Grigory Polzin and make sure I'm shot at the same time, so that his son doesn't have to come looking for anybody."

"For a supposedly intelligent man, you say some stupid things, Braddock."

"That observation has been made before."

"Do you really hold your life to be so worthless that you'd contemplate a pointless death?"

Buchanan's logic runs through me like a jet of freezing water. He understands this game. I don't. I'm playing at it, making it up as I go along. Even with Orlov's help, is it realistic to suppose I can bring about the demise of Grigory Polzin without there being consequences?

"*Un*-hypothetically speaking, then," I say after a pause, "you think I should give up on any idea of revenge, and of Katie being able to enjoy a normal existence?"

"No."

"Then, what?"

He looks me in the eye.

"I think you and I should separately carry out simultaneous assassinations of Grigory and Mikhail Polzin."

"You and I –?"

"Yes."

"You must be joking, Buchanan."

"No, I'm perfectly serious."

He interlocks his fingers around his bottle of beer.

"I've had plenty of time to mull this over during the last weeks and months.

"So long as Katie is alive, there is always the potential for her being discovered. She is not out of danger, and she can't spend the next fifty years hiding on Koh Phangan. We both know this.

"If the Polzins learn Katie is not dead, they will come after her, and they will come after me too. In the past, that wouldn't have worried me: I'm experienced in staying invisible. But now, it's different. I have Wayan, and it will be much harder for me to stay under the radar – at least the underworld radar – when we are together as a couple. And we *will* be together as a couple, have no doubt of that. I will do *anything*, Braddock, to make sure nothing bad happens to Wayan, even if that means temporarily taking up my old profession again. I should add that I don't want Katie endangered either. You might not appreciate it, but I've grown fond of her. She's taken risks for me."

"You're becoming sentimental in your old age."

"No, sensible."

"Ah, that."

Buchanan's face is a mask of determination.

"Grigory Polzin must die for all of our sakes. And his son too. Only then can we get on with our lives."

"How can I trust you?"

"You don't have to trust me. You can rely on my self-interest, if nothing else."

My Marlboro has burned out but, puzzlingly, I don't feel like lighting another one.

Everything Buchanan has said makes sense, dammit.

But charting what to do in a profound dilemma like this is not so straightforward as making a list of pros and cons, and ticking my way through them. That will not produce a conclusion. No. The working of the mind of *logos* is much more subtle and complex than that. And any carefully-considered weightings I might assign to my inventory of positives and negatives will be a sham, since concealed bias predetermines the result.

For it is not reason that drives our most serious actions, but emotion. What we term logic may be nothing more than a later rationalisation of a decision already taken by that part of us that is hidden from our conscious self. Therefore, I'll listen to my gut.

And my gut tells me I should go with Buchanan. I *do* need help, that is evident, and he has the motivation and experience.

But let's see what Orlov has to say first before I commit to anything. I could propose that the assassin accompany me to see the Russian, but I don't want to spook the oligarch and risk his cancelling the meeting.

"Braddock?"

My drinking companion is peering at me anxiously, awaiting a response.

"I'm mulling it over."

"I thought you'd zoned out on me."

I finish my second Chang.

"Can you source weapons for us?"

"Yes. Moreover, with my international contacts, I can have them delivered pretty much anywhere at short notice."

"Fake IDs, if needed?"

"The same. All at a price, naturally."

"Naturally."

Two young Thai men have pulled up on motorbikes, and are buying food. The dog stirs, but it doesn't seem his luck is in tonight.

"What about inside information on the Polzins' movements?"

Buchanan scratches the back of his neck.

"That will not be so easy."

"No matter. I have someone who can help there, if he's willing to play ball."

For the first time, he looks surprised. Maybe even a little impressed.

"Really? Who?"

"I'd prefer to keep that to myself, for the moment."

"Can he be trusted?"

"Don't worry. At this stage, I won't be mentioning you."

"Right."

"There is one thing I want to clarify for you, though."

"What's that?"

"If we partner together for this enterprise – and that is still a big *if* – it will be on the basis that I kill Grigory Polzin and you kill Mikhail."

Buchanan shakes his head dismissively.

"That's a bad idea. Grigory always has *at least* two bodyguards with him, whereas Mikhail only travels with one. Mikhail is therefore the easier mark. You should take him, and I'll take the father."

"Be that as it may, this is not negotiable."

"I can understand that you would want the satisfaction of pulling the trigger on Grigory since he was the one who ordered the hit on Katie. But what does it matter? He'll be just as dead anyway. And through the telescopic sight of a sniper rifle, he's only a distant target."

"I won't be shooting him from a distance. I'll be taking him out with a hand-gun at close range."

"That's an insane idea. You'd be signing up for a suicide mission. Why on earth would you want to do *that*?"

"Because I want to see the whites of his eyes before he dies. I want him to know it's *me* that's dispatching him."

"Even at the cost of your own life? Listen –"

"*It's not negotiable.* So, if you want to withdraw your offer and walk away, do it now."

He stares miserably at his hands.

"You're a reckless idiot," he says.

"It's a Braddock family trait. Call it an *oak* thing. You're all clued up on oaks, aren't you, Buchanan? Genus *Quercus*: murderous psychopaths the lot of us, right to the tips of our spirally-arranged leaves."

"Huh."

"So, are you 'in' or 'out'?"

He finishes his beer and places the bottle on the table.

"I'm 'in'."

"I hope you didn't mind me telling Robert you were at the shooting range, Mr. David," Wayan says warily after I'm back at the apartment.

"Not at all. We had a good talk, as a matter of fact."

"*Really?*" She is suitably astounded. "You didn't argue?"

"No. We've both decided we should make a bigger effort to get along. So, that's what we're doing."

"Oh."

"And there's no need to cook me anything. I'm on surveillance duty this evening, so I'll have something to eat while I'm out."

"What if I make you a sandwich to take with you?"

"That would work too."

She hesitates before going to the kitchen.

"So, you and Robert are all right?"

"Couldn't be better. In fact, we may start spending more time together. It seems we have a lot more in common than we first thought."

Surveillance duty: as boring as hell.

I'm in my jeep munching Wayan's sandwich, drinking water, and keeping a practiced eye on the happenings at *GoGo's*.

To relieve the monotony, I phone Natalie who forces herself to have a brief, impatient talk with me before making her excuses and ringing off. Apparently, she's meeting her friend Laurette for afternoon tea, and that has priority.

I also call Katie several times, but she's not picking up. Eventually, I decide it's nothing to be worked up about – she's probably having an early night.

That's the trouble with doing surveillance: I have too much time to think, and it's usually about gloomy stuff. Now, for instance, I'm musing on the accounts of people who have had a near-death experience and report seeing a white light, which they accept as proof of the existence of God. Though the more scientifically-inclined assert that this is a neurological feature of the brain *in extremis* as it approaches its final threshold.

The White Light. What next, for goodness' sake?

I suppose it's not surprising, given the day I've had, that my mind is exploring its junkyard on the topic of mortality.

But enough is enough.

I switch on the radio.

It's playing Bob Dylan's *Knockin' on Heaven's Door*.

Fuck the universe.

22

"Never do an enemy a small injury."

Niccolò Machiavelli

The cover story for my trip to Bangkok today is that I have some unexpected legal matters to resolve with my former business partner Asda Nueng following last year's sale of my share of our antiques business. Given the labyrinthine nature of Thai bureaucracy, this won't raise any suspicions. Plus, nobody on Samui knows Asda, so the chances of my fib being discovered are miniscule.

However, my first job of the day is to get hold of Katie on the phone. I had a troubled night worrying that I may have taken her unavailability yesterday evening too lightly.

I ring her mobile at eight o'clock: no response.

After forcing down some breakfast, I try again at eight-thirty: still she isn't picking up.

As the hands on my watch sweep round towards nine o'clock, I am moving into panic mode and starting to wonder whether I should call off the meeting with Orlov and catch a ferry to Koh Phangan instead.

Then my cell phone trills and Katie's number comes up on the display.

I answer as calmly as I can.

"I have lots of missed calls from you, Dad," she says sheepishly. "What's up?"

"Is it surprising that I'm anxious when you don't answer your damn phone, all things considered?"

"Ah, yes. Sorry. I was, um, otherwise engaged."

"I'm going to need more than that, Katie."

There is an embarrassed cough.

"I went over to Haad Rin yesterday evening and met this nice guy in a bar. I smoked a joint and had a few drinks and, er ..."

"I'm waiting."

"Well, one thing led to another and I ended up going back with him to his hotel."

"For the night?"

"Yes."

"I see."

She responds to my cold tone with indignity.

"Do you know how long it is since I last had sex?"

"Strangely enough, no I don't. It's not something I want to think about."

"Well. It's been a while."

"Uh-huh."

Katie realises this line of argument isn't going to cut much ice with me, so she decides to run up the white flag.

"But, you're right. It was irresponsible of me not to at least send you a message. I should have understood that you'd be worried. I guess I just got a little ... carried away in the moment."

"So, who is this guy?"

"A tourist. And a rather dishy one, actually. From Denmark."

"He's *Danish*?"

"Yes. Why? Do you have something against Danes?"

Only ones that drive white hire cars. But I'm being paranoid, surely. Da explained that. It's a coincidence, nothing more.

"No," I reply breezily. "We don't get many Danish folks on the islands, that's all."

"Hmmn."

"Are you seeing him again?"

"I don't think so. It was a one-off thing. Plus, there are better-looking men around if I need the company," she adds mischievously.

I clear my throat to indicate this discussion is at an end.

"Right. Well, I'm off to Bangkok today to see Asda. We may or may not speak again later."

"I'll call you tomorrow morning, Dad, I promise. Enjoy Bangkok. Don't do anything I wouldn't do."

"Whatever I do in Bangkok, it won't be with someone from Denmark."

I arrive at Samui International Airport a few minutes before ten.

Vlad is by the check-in area hopping agitatedly from foot to foot.

"Do you have the tickets?"

"We're not going to Bangkok," he says.

"We aren't? Has Orlov called off the meeting? Because if so –"

"No. It's happening here on Samui."

"Where?"

"Follow me in your jeep. You'll see when we get there."

"Don't you think all this secrecy is a dash over-the-top, Vlad? This is not the Cold War."

"Mr. Orlov's orders. He's a careful man."

"All right," I say huffily. "Take me to your leader."

I stay close behind Vlad's monster-sized truck as we leave the airport. We drive through Bang Rak, Mae Nam and Nathon, and continue down the west coast of Samui, until the Russian turns into the driveway of the five-star *Chakri Throne* hotel.

Vlad insists on frisking me in the car park for concealed weapons, which doesn't improve my mood.

"Sorry about this, Braddock."

"Whatever."

Orlov is in one of the suites overlooking the ocean. He is tanned and fit. His dark suit jacket – which has been tailored to within an inch of its life – is draped over a chair, and he greets me warmly in shirt-sleeves, apologising profusely for the last-minute change of arrangements. Too profusely. The smile doesn't reach his eyes. I guess he's sizing me up.

"I'm afraid that in recent years I have developed something of an obsession about my personal security, Mr. Braddock," he explains, ushering me out onto the balcony. "I flew down here from Bangkok on an early flight this morning, using the passport of one of my bodyguards. So, everyone – or at least anyone taking note of my movements – will think I'm still in the capital. Fortunately, my bodyguard bears a passing resemblance to me. It's proved useful in the past."

I make no comment.

"Is it too early for you to have some champagne?"

"No."

He nods to Vlad who pops the cork off an expensive bottle of bubbly.

"Have one yourself, Vlad," he says, while we settle ourselves into deep-cushioned wicker chairs.

When the three flutes are full, Orlov proposes a toast to cooperation.

We chink glasses and drink.

Orlov pats his companion's thigh fondly.

"This is a good man, Mr. Braddock. Vladimir's father and my father were in the Russian Navy together. I trust him with my life. And I trust his judgement. It is because of him that we are meeting today."

Vlad bows his head modestly.

"I appreciate you are a busy man, Mr. Orlov," I begin. "So, I will skip the small-talk about the state of the Russian economy, and cut to the chase."

Orlov raises his eyebrows.

"The Great Recession in my country is hardly a small matter. All of us are suffering."

"But some more than others, eh?"

He holds up his palms.

"As you say."

"Then, let me get to the point."

"Please do."

"Grigory Polzin ordered the killing of my daughter."

"So I have heard. Unfortunately, Mr. Polzin has a reputation for ruthlessness. Especially in family matters. My condolences for your loss."

Of course, I haven't truly *had* a loss, and I experience a twinge of disquiet before I plough on.

"I intend to kill him."

Not a flicker from Orlov, though Vlad shuffles his feet.

"That's a serious matter."

"I want to know if you will help."

"And why would I want to do that, Mr. Braddock?"

"Because, according to what I have picked up, you hate him almost as much as I do. And, as you apparently already know the story of my daughter Katie, your presence here today signals to me that you are interested in having Polzin taken out of the picture. Otherwise, why would you have come?"

"I may have had something less drastic in mind."

"I doubt that."

Orlov raises his glass to his lips. His expression becomes thoughtful.

"You may not be aware that there is an understanding in my country that we oligarchs do not murder each other. My government deems it detrimental to the business environment, and tends to discourage it. Indeed, were that not the case, I suspect the streets of Moscow would constantly run with blood. We Russians can be rather over-competitive at times, you see. We require checks and balances."

He pauses before going on.

"Tell me, do you have any experience of carrying out an assassination, Mr. Braddock?"

"No, but I can fire a gun. I only need to get close enough to Polzin to do it."

"You sound like a man neglectful of his own safety, if I might say so. Enthusiastic in his intention, but rather ill-prepared. The idea of revenge can make one fevered and unrealistic."

"I'm sure it can. But it can also provide focus."

"Yes." He peers at me. "You do appear focused. And your anger is cold. That's good. But I am sure you will appreciate that, were I to agree to become involved in your 'project', it would present certain risks for me personally."

"I don't require you to supply me with weapons, only information. There is no record of our meeting. As you said, you are 'officially' in Bangkok today. Only Vlad here knows we have even spoken, and he won't be telling anyone. There will be no trail back to you. You are an intelligent man, or you wouldn't be where you are. I am sure you have considered all of this."

"And here I am," he says with a chuckle.

"Indeed. Here you are."

Orlov pushes back his chair and stands, staring out at the sea. For a couple of minutes, he doesn't speak. This is a person who grasps the power of quiet: let others chatter away, unable to endure the weighty silence. He must be a formidable presence at the negotiating table.

But I've read that book too. I keep my mouth closed. Vlad twitches slightly and stares at his feet. Eventually, Orlov comprehends that I will wait as long as necessary.

He says over his shoulder, "A magnificent view. I regret I have not been able to make fuller use of my villa here over the years. And the clouds are dispersing. It looks like it's going to be a delightful afternoon."

"That rather depends on how you respond to my request."

I place a Marlboro between my lips, and Orlov watches me light it.

At a sign from his boss, Vlad refills our glasses. After a few more seconds, Orlov sits down again.

"What information do you need?"

"Grigory Polzin's travel plans. It will be too hard to get to him in Moscow, so I have to do the deed while he is abroad. I should add that his son Mikhail will also have to be eliminated, so I will also require his travel schedule. *For security reasons*," I add grimly.

Puzzlement crosses Orlov's features.

"Mikhail too? But they never travel together. And as soon as something happens to Grigory –"

"They will go to see the angels together."

"You can't be in two places at one time, Mr. Braddock."

"I have an associate to carry out the second killing."

"Do you indeed? And who is that?"

"Someone like myself who has a strong reason to want to put an end to the Polzin clan. He *is* experienced in the art of assassination. But, don't worry, he has no knowledge of our meeting, and will not be party to where the information on the Polzins comes from. I have never, and will never, mention your name to him. You have my solemn word on that."

"Grigory *and* Mikhail, eh? No-one can deny your ambition, Mr. Braddock."

"So, *can* you assist with the info I need?" I press him.

"As it happens, I *do* have someone on the inside of Grigory's organisation who has been useful in alerting me to certain issues from time to time. But, as you will understand, he does this at great personal risk, and therefore I do not consult him unless I deem it important. I do not put his well-being in jeopardy lightly. I only use him when I need to."

"Though I'm sure his aid comes with a price attached."

"Nobody does anything for free." He adds, "But, I would cover that on this occasion. In the interests of goodwill."

"Appreciated. And this person has access to details of the Polzins' travel plans?"

"He can have. But you should be aware that such arrangements are inevitably made at short notice. You and your associate will have to be prepared to act quickly."

"We'll be ready."

At this point, Vlad pipes up.

"Perhaps I could do something too."

"Like what?" asks Orlov. "Take part in one of the assassinations, you mean?"

"Yes."

Orlov gives a firm shake of the head.

"No, Vladimir. I'm not willing to let you be involved in any killings. I owe it to your family to keep you out of all that."

Vlad is about to object, when I say, "But you might be useful in providing me with an alibi for when the Polzins go down. I am going to need an alibi."

"He can't be implicated in this in any way," says Orlov sternly. "Quite apart from anything else, we don't know how wide-ranging any official investigations will be if you and your associate are successful. Assuming you aren't killed yourselves, that is.

"*No.* I don't want Vladimir entangled. He is my employee. There can't be any suspicion of a trail leading back to me. If he has to give evidence to the police as to your innocence, Mr. Braddock, it would inevitably come out who it is that he works for. I may then be implicated in the Polzin deaths, and that is *not* going to happen."

Vlad looks crestfallen.

"However," Orlov adds, his voice less harsh, "I would have no objection to Vladimir *arranging* an alibi for you, provided he himself is not part of it."

"That works for me," I say.

"Well, it's *something*, Mr. Orlov," retorts a morose but respectful Vlad.

"Are you familiar with the Dark Web, Mr. Braddock?"

"Somewhat."

"Vlad will instruct you on its use. We will proceed like this: you will receive one message - and one message only - setting out the Polzins' schedule. So far as possible, flight times and destinations and hotel particulars will be included. There is no guarantee, of course, that both Grigory and Mikhail will be travelling. One of them may remain in Moscow. I have no control over that."

"Understood."

"In any event, it will then be up to you. I will disavow all knowledge of this project, and there will be no repeat supply of information. You will have one shot, if you will pardon the expression. Are we clear?"

"We are. And, for my part, I anticipate that I will receive this message soon, and that the Polzins' destinations will be in South East Asia. Maybe Hong Kong, Macau, Bangkok, Singapore, and/or Phnom Penh."

"Why would you assume those things?"

"Because I suspect that your presence now in the region is to stir up things on the Asian casino deals; that you expect Polzin to react fast to this affront on your part; and that he will be on the ground here in a matter of weeks if not days – because he is not the sort of man to let the grass grow under his feet."

Orlov permits himself a tight smile.

"You read me unnervingly well, Mr. Braddock. Your powers of deduction are impressive."

"Oh, they're more impressive than that, Mr. Orlov. For instance, given all the circumstances and the fact that you are on Samui laying a false trail for yourself, I also deduce that you had *already* decided to assist me before you ever got on a plane in Moscow. And, therefore, it follows that your messing with me this morning was simply for your own amusement, and to impress on me your status as top dog. How am I doing?"

"Not bad. But you are not entirely correct when you say I had already made up my mind before I flew here. I wanted to hear your viewpoint in person and see for myself how determined you were before I finally committed."

"And you have no qualms that I might be part of some devious Polzin plot against *you*?"

A dismissive gesture from the oligarch.

"No qualms at all. I know for certain that Grigory Polzin ordered your daughter killed. I can't imagine any father striking a deal with him after that, unless it was out of fear. And you have no fear."

"Don't I?"

"No. Otherwise you wouldn't be volunteering for what is – let's face it – a suicide mission."

In the hotel car park, I call Buchanan.

"Are you busy?"

"No."

"Have you been to *Wilbur's Restaurant* at Taling Ngam, in the south of the island?"

"No, but I'm sure I can find it."

"Meet me there."

"You want me to come now?"

"There's no time like the present. *Chop chop.*"

Wilbur's is almost empty, so I select a table with a view of the Five Islands which shimmer in the distance. The sun has come out and it sparkles on the sea like shoals of flying fish.

The two glasses of champagne I had with Orlov haven't dulled my senses, and I'm tempted to have a whisky while I'm waiting for Buchanan. But, as I've been doing so well in staying off spirits, I make do with a beer. It's rather warm, so I ask the barman for ice. He brings me a tumbler with big chunks of the frozen stuff in it and, by way of apology, a bowl of nuts.

My assassin colleague pitches up soon afterwards.

"Are we having lunch?" he asks.

"We may as well. The seafood is good here. The European fare not so much, and the pizza is especially doughy."

We order some grilled seabass and Thai vegetables, and Buchanan tells our server he'll join me in a Chang.

"A cold one," I add.

He bows and withdraws.

"This place is a bit out of the way, isn't it?"

"I've told everyone I'm in Bangkok today, so I'm keeping my head down for a few hours until I can credibly 'return'. It's too exhausting to think up a convincing explanation for why I haven't left the island. It's much easier this way."

"And did your reason for going to Bangkok have anything to do with the talk we had yesterday?"

"It did. But I managed to sort out matters here on Samui."

Buchanan's drink arrives and the waiter hovers anxiously while the temperature is tested. My companion gives a thumbs-up, and the Thai moves off.

"Would you care to enlighten me on what these 'matters' are?"

"The contact I spoke to today believes he can supply me with the Polzins' travel schedule."

"And who is this contact?"

"You don't get to know that. I promised him his name would never be disclosed to anyone. That includes you. And, from my side, I told him that I had a partner in this project, but I wouldn't give him your name."

"You don't know my name," he responds evenly.

"Fair comment."

"Are you sure this contact of yours is reliable, that he won't betray us to Polzin?"

This annoys me, and I lean forward and prod his chest.

"Listen," I say, "I don't question you about the dependability and loyalty of your suppliers of weapons and fake documents, or ask you who they are, do I? Let's have a little respect here."

"Fair comment."

This is delivered without a hint of irony.

He's rather deadpan, our Mr. Buchanan. Though, that's not altogether astounding. And, anyway, it's not his *bonhomie* that I need. I can find that anywhere. What I can't find just anywhere is guns and someone with a willingness to blow someone else away.

"So, it's on. What shall we toast?" He raises his glass.

"How about the Devil? We're going to need his luck."

"Yes, we are. What details *can* you share with me, then?"

"Let's eat first. I never discuss assassinations on an empty stomach."

"How English."

"Yeah, I forgot you Scots have a deep resentment of the English."

He rolls his eyes.

"You never stop probing, do you, Braddock?"

"I'm a private detective. It's what I do."

We consume our grilled fish in near-silence, then request coffee.

I light a Marlboro.

"OK, here's the deal," I say. "My contact will send us the lowdown on the Polzins' movements via the Dark Web. I assume you are familiar with that?"

He signals assent.

"One of Grigory Polzin's competitors is trying to muscle in on a couple of his casino deals here in South East Asia. Polzin is pissed about it, and it's likely that he will be flying out soon to this part of the world – perhaps in a matter of weeks or even days – to sort things out. We will not receive much notice of his schedule, so you'd better get cracking organising papers and weaponry for us."

"To be delivered where?"

"For the guns, it could be Cambodia, Thailand, Singapore, or China. We won't know until we receive the schedule. The fake IDs – well, let's talk about that later. I've got a few ideas there. But if it's Hong Kong or Macau, we might also need fake visas, maybe."

"As you say, let's have a separate discussion about those. Also, I'm going to want passport photographs of you for my man."

"You'll have those today."

"What else?"

I choose my words with care.

"There is no guarantee that both Grigory *and* Mikhail will fly to Asia. If they do, they will, as we are aware, travel separately and likely to different destinations and different meetings. But there is always the possibility that only one of them will come here, and the other will remain in Moscow."

"If only one of them travels, it's likely to be Grigory. If he's wound up about these deals, he'll want to throw his weight around in person. But we can't be sure he wouldn't send Mikhail."

"No, we can't."

"So, to the list of documents, I have to add Russian visas for both of us, just in case."

"Yes."

"And a gun may need to be delivered to one of us in Moscow."

"Correct."

He puffs out his cheeks.

"You know, Braddock, given all the uncertainties, this has all the makings of a right royal clusterfuck."

"Ah-ha."

"If I have to assassinate Mikhail in *Moscow* ... well. Perhaps I'll have drawn the short straw after all. Your job in Asia with Grigory might actually turn out to be easier."

"There you go."

He sucks the froth off his coffee spoon. That is a *really* annoying habit.

Then, he says, "There are a lot of factors and practicalities to be considered. We should spend some serious time together, Braddock. Otherwise we will have a disaster on our hands."

"I thought you'd never ask."

"I've been reflecting on this."

"Go on."

"On Tuesday, I'm going to Manila for a couple of days."

"Why?"

"Let me tell you, living the way that I have to do is not straightforward. I need to visit a bank there to make some transfer arrangements, and I have organised a lawyer to fly in from Europe. So, I suggest you come with me. We can extend the trip as necessary, and if word comes in on the Polzins, we can jump on planes and go to wherever we need to. We'll be away from everyone, so we can focus on the assignment, and on nothing else.

"Also, it strikes me that if all our counterfeit documents are delivered to us there, then we have them for whenever we require them."

"And we tell the ladies in our lives that we're spending time together for their sakes – because they don't want any animosity between us. We are *making a sacrifice for them.*"

"Hmmn. I'm a little uneasy about using *that* as an explanation. Plus, do you think they'll buy it?"

"We can but try. It's something they'd *like* to happen, so they might end up convincing themselves that it's not a lie. Anyway, I've already started sowing those seeds."

"What will you say to the people at your office?"

"At the *Agency*? There's only Da to worry about, but she can be tricky. I'll put a story together, and speak to her on Monday. Meanwhile, I'll talk to Katie either over the phone or while I'm on Koh Phangan at the weekend."

"OK. And I'll discuss it with Wayan."

"Remember you and I haven't met today, though. We spoke on the phone this afternoon. I called you."

"Got it."

The mention of Koh Phangan has triggered something in my head.

"Tell me," I say, "does Polzin employ a Danish enforcer? Some Nordic heavy?"

"I have no idea. He employs a lot of people. Why?"

I explain about the white car and Katie's dalliance with a Dane.

Buchanan pulls at his lip while he calculates.

"It's probably nothing, but let's not take any chances. When you tell Katie of our Manila idea, why don't you suggest that – while we're away – she and Wayan go on a shopping trip to Singapore for a few days? Starting on Monday. That gets them both out of harm's way, for a while, at least. I'll raise it with Wayan."

"Perfect. If we can both lie with a straight face, all will be well."

He eyeballs me earnestly.

"But this is the last time *ever* that I will lie to Wayan. About anything."

"OK."

"I mean it."

"Yes. I can see that you do."

23

"Books say: She did this because. Life says: She did this. Books are where things are explained to you; life is where things aren't."
Julian Barnes, Flaubert's Parrot

Another psychedelic episode for me last night, except that in this dream I was the pursuer, not the pursued.

I was following a man who appeared familiar, but I couldn't quite place him. He was dressed in a black coat and carrying a briefcase which sported a faded sticker of the Stars and Stripes. The setting was (again) a clichéd version of Victorian London whose streets were covered in a light dusting of snow: dirty brick buildings, shadowy figures in stove-pipe hats, and shivering, snotty-nosed beggar children.

After many twists and turns through gaslit alleyways, my quarry disappeared through a door, which turned out to be the entrance to an undertaker's. In the display window of this establishment, an enormous cooked goose was on show, supported on two side-by-side coffins bearing respectively the flag of Denmark and a motheaten Union Jack. When I tried the door, it was locked, but as began knocking on it, I became aware of the sound of ringing.

This turned out to be my cell phone bidding me return to the world of the conscious.

As I fumbled on my bedside table for the device, I noted that the time on my clock showed a few minutes after seven. The number on the phone's screen was unfamiliar.

"Hello."

"Mr. Braddock?"

"Yes."

"This is Ivan from *Punchy Joe's Gym*."

"Why are you ringing me at this godforsaken time of the morning?"

"I am sorry, but my friend Vlad is in big trouble. He asked me to call you."

I was now fully awake.

"What's happened?"

"Around three o'clock this morning, Vlad was involved in a road accident."

"Is he all right?"

"Yes, but his truck hit a motorbike, and the man on the bike is dead. Vlad is at Bophut Police Station, so he asked me to contact you to see if you can help him."

"I'm on my way."

While I dressed, I rang my Thai lawyer and got him out of bed. I told him I was going to need the services of a fixer and supplied him with a brief overview of the problem.

"I'll send *Khun* Sud over straightaway. Tell your friend – if the police will let you see him – to be polite to the officers but to say as little as possible."

Unshaven and unshowered, I am now at the police station.

Fortunately, the policeman on the desk doesn't hate me, and when I drop Sud's name, he is inclined to be helpful. Sud – which is the Thai for 'tiger' – is a force to be reckoned with on Samui, and the best in the business for sorting out little difficulties involving *farangs* and the authorities. Like unlawful killings, for instance. Vlad is moved from the cells to an interview room where I am allowed supervised access to him.

The Russian looks awful.

"I am sorry, Braddock," he says. "I didn't know who else to call."

"Is Mr. Orlov still on the island?"

"No. He left yesterday evening for Bangkok. And I don't want him to find out about this," he adds. "He will think I am a stupid idiot."

"You *are* a stupid idiot. What happened?"

"I was driving my truck on the ring road at Chaweng when this guy on a motorbike pulled out of a side street without looking."

"Around three o'clock according to Ivan, right?"

He nods.

"Had you been drinking?"

"Yes," he replies timidly.

"How much?"

"A lot. For about five hours. But, I'm sober now."

"I bet you are. Was the guy you killed a Thai?"

"No."

"Well, that's good news. If he had been a local, you'd be in deep shit. The coppers here are more relaxed about a *farang-on-farang* death. It makes Sud's job easier if it's only about money. Was he European or Asian?"

"He was British. An old man. No helmet, no lights. He was probably drunk too. One of the policemen said his name was Timothy Jennings. In his passport he had a retirement visa. He lives here. *Lived* here."

"Tim Jennings?"

"Yes. You know him?"

"I *knew* him."

"Ah."

Karma takes its own sweet time, doesn't it?

Unwittingly, in one drunken moment, Vlad has avenged his father's death a quarter-of-a-century after the event. The man primarily responsible for the sinking of the submarine *Akula* lies on a mortuary slab, put there by the sailor's son.

Of course, I'm not about to enlighten Vlad on this fact. I owe that much to the memory of Timothy St. John Jennings R.N. (Retired). It's bad enough that I'm assisting his feckless killer to evade justice. But, after all, Vlad is alive, and Tim is beyond caring about the unfairness of the world.

And I need the Russian *not* to be behind bars. So, conscience, get back into your box.

"How fast were you travelling?"

"*Pretty fast.* The road was empty, you see, and he came from nowhere."

"Right."

Vlad has gone pale at the recollection.

"He went under my truck. His head and feet ... It was a horrible mess. They couldn't even find two of his toes."

The door to the interview room opens, and a somber Sud enters. His sleeves are rolled up and his arms are covered in scary tattoos. The policeman more or less stands to attention: a good sign.

"I'd like to speak to my client in private." He addresses the official in Thai. "If that is all right with you."

It *is* all right with him. He leaves, and Sud sits down.

I volunteer the information that the dead man was a retired British ex pat with no family on Samui.

"No Thai wife?"

"No."

"Can you lay your hands on some cash quickly?" he asks Vlad, cutting to the chase.

"Er –"

"*I* can," I say, "as soon as the banks are open."

"Good. Then tell me the details and let me speak to some people."

"How long will that take?"

Sud glances at his watch.

"We should have you out of here in a few hours, *Khun* Vladimir, if Buddha is willing. There will be more paperwork to complete later - and more negotiations - but we can do that without you being locked up in a cell."

"I'll pay you back, Braddock," gushes a relieved Vlad.

"You certainly will," I respond, before turning to Sud. "Do you need me to stick around? I'd like to inform the man's friends of his demise before I go to the bank."

Sud nods his head.

"How much money do you require?"

He jots down an amount on a piece of paper and hands it to me.

"That seems reasonable," I say.

"That's only the first instalment," he replies, "but, I'll do my best to haggle down the total."

I phone Da to explain I'll be late getting to the *Agency*, then drive to *Rhino's*, hoping to catch my surviving gym buddies before they go off to do nothing for the day. I'm in luck. Shane and Noah are in the Parlour drinking coffee and watching a couple of lithe Thai girls doing stretching exercises on the floor mats.

"Hey, look who it is," says Noah. "We were beginning to think you were dead."

I lower myself warily onto one of the brittle plastic chairs.

"I'm afraid it's not me that's dead."

They absorb my solemn expression and set down their mugs.

"What's up?" asks Shane.

"It's Tim. He was hit by a truck last night while he was out riding his bike. I've just come from Bophut Police Station."

"Jesus. The careless bastard." Noah strokes his beard. "I assume he was pissed?"

"It seems likely."

"Was the driver a local?"

"No, a Russian."

Shane curses. "So, the Cold War isn't over after all." He tuts sadly. "Poor bugger. He doesn't even have a wife to take care of arrangements. Looks like that will be down to you and me, Noah. Like last time."

"Last time?" I say.

"Oh, yes," replies the big New Zealander. "We members of *Rhino's* have a nasty tradition of getting ourselves killed in traffic accidents. It's like God's waiting room here. Guernsey Ted got squished by a cement truck two years ago and, the year before that, Lee from Liverpool had his head knocked clean off by the grab of a mechanical digger at Chaweng Lake. So much for the notion that exercise prolongs your life, eh?"

I light a cigarette and note the slight agitation in my hand.

"Listen, guys, I have to fly off to the Philippines after the weekend, so I won't be around. But if you need me to chip in to help with the funeral expenses –"

Noah turns one of his eyes on me.

"That's good of you, David. We'll let you know. Meantime, Shane and I will start things rolling. I have the phone number somewhere of Tim's son in Gloucester, so I'll give him a call once it's a respectable time in England. Tim's body will be at the morgue, but we'll go to the police station first and see how the land lies there."

"On the bright side, at least we have something to do today," says Shane.

Noah risks a slurp from his mug and winces.

"There is that."

I take my leave of them.

The Samui ex pat style: lonely life, lonely death. At least I have people to take care of my arrangements in the next few weeks should I find myself, like Tim, pulverised by a Russian juggernaut.

Before I show up at the bank, I make a detour to *Wat Son* on the off chance that I might catch the Old Monk in the process of doing his inspection.

Quite why I do this is unclear to me. Perhaps I'm passing the time until my branch opens, or maybe I'm seeking reassurance about something in the aftermath of yet another untimely demise: proof that life goes on, that there are still immortals walking among us.

Whatever the reason, when I park my jeep at the temple and spot Ananda, I discover that, in the event, I can't face talking to him.

He is trudging through the grounds towards the main entrance where a sturdy old woman waits for him. Presumably, this is Mrs. Old Monk. As he reaches her, his head lowers, and she appears to be giving him a lecture. About what, I can only conjecture, but it's nice to see him on the back foot for a change.

Family is important.

They wander off without noticing me.

Will we meet again? In another life, perhaps.

I put my brain into gear, then do the same to my jeep.

I drive to my bank, withdraw a hundred thousand Baht, stuff it in a canvas bag, and make my way back to Bophut Police Station.

Sud checks the cash and makes a call.

Vlad says to me, "I should give you the Dark Web access details before I do anything else stupid."

I don't disagree.

At the *Agency*, Da is given a redacted version of the morning's events: one which shows me in a positive light. She is suitably disinterested.

"Are you going to Koh Phangan again this weekend?" she asks.

"Yes."

"I'm sure you won't see that white car again. But, if you do, call me."

"OK."

The remainder of the office hours pass without incident. I decide to leave it until Monday before broaching the subject of my Manila trip to Da. That way, I have time to make up a watertight story. Because there will be questions, oh yes.

She's sharp, that one.

I'm home around six-thirty. The apartment is empty. There is a note from Wayan saying she's meeting Buchanan for an early dinner but that she has left a meal for me in the fridge. I'm not hungry, but I eat it anyway and wash it down with a Chang.

I've just finished a Marlboro, and am contemplating a visit to the shooting range when I receive a call from an unknown number.

"Hello."

"Am I speaking to Mr. David Braddock?"

A female voice. Not young. English accent. Slightly nervous.

"You are."

"Hello, Mr. Braddock. My name is Laurette Lang. We haven't met, but I'm a friend and neighbour of Natalie Holland. She might have mentioned me?"

"Yes, I believe she has, Laurette. What can I do for you?"

"I am afraid I have some unwelcome news for you. Natalie passed away about an hour ago. The appropriate authorities will contact you, I am sure, but I thought I should call you straightaway in the circumstances."

I almost drop my cell phone, and I stare at it in shock.

"Mr. Braddock? *Hello?* Are you still there?"

"Yes, I'm ... What happened?"

"Natalie had a minor heart attack two months ago. She was checked over and advised that she needed surgery. She was admitted to the HFA London Hospital yesterday, but I am afraid there were complications and she died on the operating table this morning. I'm sorry."

"Christ, she never told me anything about any heart attack or surgery."

"No." There is a short pause, then she says, "Natalie didn't want anyone to know about her condition. And, she thought, if the surgery was successful, there would be no reason for anyone to be concerned."

I struggle for words.

"That's so *irresponsible.* What about Jenny? God, where *is* Jenny? Where is she now?"

"Don't worry, she's with me. My husband and I are looking after her."

"Is she all right?"

"Well, upset as you might imagine."

"That poor little girl. First, her mother ..."

I choke back a sob.

"Mr. Braddock?"

I can't speak, but manage a strangled sound to indicate I'm still on the line.

"There is more I have to tell you."

With difficulty, I collect myself.

"Go on. I'm listening."

"For the last few years, I have been a close friend of Natalie. She has confided in me about several things that have been worrying her – things she didn't feel she could talk to anyone else about. Private matters. *Family* matters."

"Yes?"

"A month ago, when her surgery was scheduled, she updated her will. Her previous will already left everything to Jenny, and that is the case with her new one. But she wanted to name me as her executor. She had a certain task she specified I should carry out in the event of her death. I'm not yet acting as her official executor – it's too early for that – but unofficially I want to honour her wish directly. Because it matters, and you will understand why."

"What is this 'certain task', Mrs. Lang?"

"Natalie left a sealed letter with me. It is addressed to you. I can courier it to you, if you wish, but it will take a few days to reach Thailand. The alternative is that I email a PDF copy to you now."

A beat.

"I don't need to open the sealed letter, Mr. Braddock, as I already know what it says. She gave me a copy and insisted I read it so that I was fully briefed on the situation. I'm sorry I've been party to personal information that you are not aware of, but this was important to Natalie and I promised her –"

"What does the letter say?"

"I would rather you read it yourself."

"Email it to me, then, Mrs. Lang."

"I will send it as soon as this call is over. I have your email address. Though, I would appreciate it if you would ring me back later. There is a lot to be sorted out."

"Understood. I have your number now on my phone. I'll save it to my contacts."

"Goodbye for now."

"Goodbye. And thank you. Thank you very much."

I switch on my laptop and light a Marlboro while I wait for the email to come through.

All those around me are dying.

Events pile up one on top of the other, unbidden.

The words of the Old Monk return to me.

If you are not doing anything else, I hope you are giving your family attention.

I told him I was. But I wasn't. I was only thinking of *some* of my family, not *all* of my family. I wasn't paying attention to Natalie because I found our discussions uncomfortable. If I'm honest with myself, I was relieved when she didn't answer the phone. I didn't persevere. And all that time she was ill, unable or unwilling to disclose her suffering to me. What must have been going through her head? How concerned she must have been about Jenny, yet even then she couldn't reach out to me. How lonely and abandoned she must have felt.

Conclusion: David Braddock has failed his loved ones once more.

I retrieve my emergency bottle of whisky from a kitchen cupboard and pour myself a large one. But I don't drink it. Not yet.

My hands are steady again, but my brain is all over the place. I take out another cigarette from the pack, then notice that my first one is still burning in the ashtray.

A *ping*.

I open the file attachment to Laurette Lang's message and read it several times.

Notting Hill, London
March 2009

Dear David,

If you are reading this letter, it means that Laurette Lang has been in contact to inform you of my death. Either I have had a second heart attack, or the operation to fix me has been unsuccessful.

You will, I am sure, be feeling angry with me at this moment, that I have not communicated with you about my condition and have proved evasive these last weeks. Perhaps what follows will explain my reluctance to confide in you.

Although we have not openly discussed it, I know you are aware that I have harboured resentment against you for the deaths of my two daughters. In the case of Claire, I recognise that this is an irrational reaction, based on the need to hold someone accountable for what feels like an unfair and senseless loss. But, as regards Anna – dying violently as she did because of your dangerous profession and your inability to protect her – my antipathy has greater justification.

However, in my less bitter moments, I do recognise that my children did not depart this life as a result of any malice or lack of caring on your part. Moreover, during the course of last year when you stood by Katie and supported her so steadfastly, it gave me pause. It forced me to remember what a good father you were to your girl and that, from the time that Claire fell ill, you have had your own pain and grief to deal with. Indeed, since Katie's disappearance, the intensity of your suffering must have increased greatly. I know what that feels like.

This, along with the perilous state of my health, has convinced me to do something that I swore I would never do; to disclose to you a secret that I have hitherto kept locked up for years. So, here goes.

Jenny, whom you thought to be your niece, is actually your daughter.

For reasons of family loyalty, shame, and the desire not to cause further problems for Claire during the fight against her sickness, Anna chose to lie to you that Jenny was the child of her then-deceased husband Max. Her tale to you about Jenny's blood-type was fantasy. Anna made it up to forestall any misgivings you might have had. She wanted to protect you. She wanted to protect everyone concerned.

I know that Anna loved you, David. This is a hard pill for me to swallow given that you were Claire's husband, but it is undeniable.

Before she flew to Thailand to see you that fateful last time, she summoned up the courage to reveal to me the truth of what had happened and her part in it. The reason she was coming to Samui was, at last, to tell that truth to you. She died at the hands of that criminal before she could do so; and, for my part, I decided that Jenny would be safer if you remained oblivious to the real motive for Anna's visit. This is a burden I have carried ever since. Loathe me for it if you wish, but I acted in what I thought were the best interests of my granddaughter.

I can no longer deploy that argument.

In the spirit of full disclosure, I should tell you that I have considered alternative guardianship arrangements for the little girl should something happen to me. Max's parents in Australia are not in the picture. His father is suffering from dementia and his mother is crippled by arthritis. They are not really Jenny's biological grandparents anyway and, had I been able to involve them, it would have been at the cost of perpetuating a great untruth.

So, there is only you to take care of Jenny.

I wanted to tell you this face-to-face. It is not the sort of conversation to be had over a telephone line. When I would have told you, I don't know. But I would have told you soon. Now, unfortunately, the message can only be delivered in a letter from someone who has passed on.

My friend Laurette is aware of the whole story. Besides you, she is the only one who is. She and her husband are good people who will help however they can.

I am sorry for the wrongs I have done you, David. Forgive this foolish old woman, and remember me as I used to be. I know that, at heart, you are a decent man who strives to do the right thing.

So, look after Jenny for me. She needs you. She is the only blood I have left. And she is your blood too.

I am certain you will.

My regards and hopes are with you,

Natalie

Oh, *Anna.*

My sister-in-law, my friend, my lover.

What heartbreak you must have gone through.

And your final words, as you died in my arms, as the blood and the life poured out of you: *"Yours, yours."* They didn't mean that *you* were mine. You were trying to tell me that *Jenny* was mine.

Dear God, Jenny ...

What have I done?

I reach reflexively for my whisky glass, but set it down again without drinking. It's not alcohol I need.

I open the glass doors and step out onto my balcony. Everything is blurred and my heart is thumping like a steam hammer. Sweat rolls down my face, or maybe it's tears – I can't tell. I bellow at the night. It is the cry of a wounded animal, or of something inhuman, that shouts into the darkness.

Then there is silence and stillness. But it is not the quietness of calm, rather a threatening void, a malign nothingness that sucks at my bones. It is karma come for me at last.

With shaking hands, I try to light a Marlboro. It takes several attempts and, when I finally inhale the smoke, it tastes like ancient ashes. I spit, drop the cigarette over the balcony, and watch as the black foliage swallows the small red glow.

I am caught in the maw of time, stripped bare, circled by spirits. My senses fall away, replaced by a trance-like state. A slightly hysterical laugh comes out of me as the meaning of my recent dreams about the gigantic goose presents itself.

The goose is Bob Cratchit's Christmas dinner. And I should change my name to Ebenezer Scrooge since, like the notorious miser, I have been visited by several spirits. It may not be the festive season, but the coldness in my breast is a kind of Victorian winter. However, while Dickens' character was seen by three shades representing past, present and future, the fates have allocated me *five* ghosts. Two from the past: Claire and the Old Monk. Two from the present: Sam Trask and Katie. And one representing a possible future – Natalie – to point me in the right direction. If the universe has any sense of symmetry, then I am still owed another ghost symbolising the future, and who will signpost for me an alternative path to the one revealed by Natalie.

Or perhaps that ghost is already with me. Maybe it is Buchanan, a phantom who offers to assist me along a trail of violence in the yet-to-come.

No.

Wait.

Hold on just one damn minute.

I see this letter for what it is.

It is a *test*: the final test of my resolution to kill Polzin. It is the universe's last dirty trick to deflect me from my purpose.

Forget Polzin. Return to England and play happy families with Jenny.

No. It's not that easy. That route leaves Katie with only half a life, one of miserable exile.

And yet ... the call of my native soil, so long ignored. Thus, it begins as a whisper and grows to a roar.

I have one final revelation, and it is profound.

I can, at last, identify what I've been trying to do these last eight years since I ran away from England; since I fled, traumatised and afraid, from the wreckage of my family life.

I've been striving to find a way back.

To get home again.

This constant reinvention of myself has been nothing more than a diversion, a trick of the light, a way of dissociating from the agony of Claire's death. Her recurring, spectral presence in Thailand, I should have recognised, was the sign showing me this.

Come to an accommodation with your loss, was what she was telling me. *Make peace with it. Don't seek to hide away in a foreign land, for you cannot hide. It doesn't work. Feel the sadness, but live regardless. Cry and rage if you must, but let the tempest blow itself out.*

Your true place is among those whom you understand and who understand you. There is your refuge. In your homeland. In the everyday. In the dreary weather that corrals every discussion. In the inconsequential and the frivolous. In the English rain. In the mist that curls across the rooftops. In the small losses and the petty gains: those trifles that constitute real life. In the end, that's all there is.

Go home.

And I will.

It will be a second chance for me with Katie, the daughter I deserted, and with Jenny, the daughter I did not know I had.

I shall reclaim my family and, in so doing, I shall reclaim myself.

Only one obstacle stands in the way: Grigory Polzin.

And in that single, glorious, and barbaric instant when I remove him from this earth, all debts will be settled, the slate wiped clean.

Then I can return to England.

And, if I'm lucky, it won't be in a box.

Right.

Let's get myself sorted out. Things to do. People to talk to.

First thing, I have to unclutter my head.

I strip off my clothes, step into a freezing shower, and stand there until my entire body is numb with the cold. I towel myself down and pull on a pair of swimming trunks. If Wayan arrives back early, she'll have to put up with the naked Braddock torso. She's made her choice with Buchanan, and if she develops the hots for me now, that's too bad. Next, I pour my glass of whisky down the sink and smoke a cigarette. It tastes ... normal.

I make a list in my head of what to do and what not to do.

Don't tell Katie that Natalie is dead. I need my daughter to go to Singapore, and I don't want her asking awkward questions about why I'm not flying straight off to England to deal with her grandmother's affairs. My next conversation with her will be on Koh Phangan tomorrow, and I must be at my most normal and persuasive.

Call Nang and tell her that Natalie is dead, but don't tell her that Katie is alive.

Then phone Laurette Lang.

Then …

Let's not get too far ahead. I pick up my cell phone and speed-dial my stepmother.

"David, hello."

"Nang. Natalie is dead."

An intake of breath.

"Jesus, David, you need to prepare someone for that sort of news. You don't just blurt it out."

"Well, I've got some more shocks for you, so hold onto your hat."

I go through my conversation with Laurette Lang and summarise Natalie's letter, during the course of which Nang lets slip a couple of uncharacteristic expletives. She checks with me that what she has heard is right. She is so taken aback at this information that she doesn't harangue me for my loose morals and general thoughtlessness.

"This is a lot to absorb, David."

"You don't say."

There are a few sighs, then Nang puts on her sensible voice.

"So, when are you coming back to England? Hopefully, you can catch a flight tomorrow because there's Jenny to consider and –"

"Not tomorrow, Nang, no."

"Then, when?"

"Soon. But I can't say exactly when."

I can hear her outrage growing, and she fires off at me.

"What do you mean, David? This is no time for you to fart around. You need to step up to the mark and show some maturity for once."

"I can't come back straightaway.

"Why not? What's more urgent than *this*?" As I don't reply immediately, she starts running through the possibilities. "Are you sick?"

"No."

"Are you in trouble with the police?"

"No." *Not yet.*

"Is it a gangster problem?"

"No."

"Then, what is it?"

"It's the sort of thing one can't talk about on an unencrypted line, however much one may want to."

"Ah."

I haven't appeased her indignation, but she has picked up on the seriousness of my tone.

"If I could get on a plane tomorrow, Nang, I would. I'm not completely feckless. Plus, I desperately want to see Jenny. You must understand that. I'm not seeking to evade my responsibilities, and I *will* make things right. But there is something I have to do first, and I can't control exactly *when* that thing will happen. Though, I promise you, it will be soon."

"Are we talking days or weeks?"

"More likely days than weeks."

This pacifies her a little, but not entirely.

"Have you any idea of the number of things that have to be arranged following a death, David? Especially as Natalie has no surviving adult family. You are the closest thing she has to a living relative. Who is going to kick off obtaining a death certificate and lodging a copy of it with the relevant authorities? Then there's Jenny to think of, and the funeral to be organised. That's only for starters. You can't expect Mrs. Lang to do it all."

"As to that –"

"Why do I know what's coming?"

We negotiate for the next few minutes. Eventually, she agrees to catch a train to London tomorrow and assist Laurette in holding the fort until I deign to show up.

"You better have a damn good reason for not being here, David Braddock, and I shall expect you to tell me all about it *in detail* the next time I see you."

"I do and I will," I reply, "and I will phone you every day from now on until this thing is concluded. Thanks, Nang, for doing this for me."

"I'm not doing it for *you*," she says icily. "I'm doing it for Jenny. The child needs to be reassured that *someone* loves her."

"I understand," I respond with due humility. "But, thank you anyway."

"So, what do I say to Mrs. Lang about your indefinite absence? She's going to see you as a real deadbeat dad even before she's met you."

"I'll leave that to you to decide. You have a talent for defusing difficult situations."

"Huh. All right, give me this woman's contact information and I'll speak to her."

"OK, but give it twenty minutes before you call. I want to talk to her first to tell her you're coming."

I ring Laurette and give her the gist of my discussion with Nang. Since I don't elaborate on my schedule, I leave Natalie's friend with the impression that I might be in London in a day or two, and place my trust in my stepmother's abilities to come up with a plausible and acceptable reason for any longer delay. I ask whether I can speak to Jenny, but she's resting, so I tell Laurette I'll call again tomorrow.

Now that my Natalie/Jenny conundrum has been progressed as far as it can be, I turn my attention to the matter of bringing the Polzin bloodline to a satisfactory end. I smoke half a Marlboro before picking up my cell phone again.

"Vlad?"

"Hi, Braddock."

"Where are you? You sound like you're at the club. Can you hear me?"

He yells at someone to close a door, and the pumping musical beat becomes muted.

"Is that better?"

"Yes. Listen, can we meet at the Irish Pub on Sunday evening, say around nine o'clock?"

"Sure. Do I need to bring anything?"

"No. Just make sure you're sober and that you don't run over anyone else in the meantime."

"OK."

Finally, I call Sam Trask. I guess it's between nine and ten in the morning in Greensboro, North Carolina, so he should be up and about.

He is. He answers after a few rings.

"David! It's good to hear from you."

"Is this a convenient time for you to talk, Sam?"

"Yeah, it's fine. Funny, I had it in mind to call you, I simply haven't gotten around to it. Since we last spoke, I've met Mr. Reichenbach who offered me some compensation for my troubles. Boy, he is adamant that Jim Fosse is still alive. He even asked me if I would be interested in another trip to Asia to see if I could track him down. I said I wasn't. He was disappointed but not surprised.

"Also, I've hooked up with Hitomi again in New York, and things are going swell there. It's not ideal as I'm working for my sister a few days a week in her Greensboro realty office, and travelling up and down to the Big Apple is a –"

It sounds like he's going to rabbit on for hours, and I have no desire to hear the lowdown on his relationship with Hitomi Tanaka, so I cut in.

"I'm happy for you, Sam. But I don't have a lot of time to chatter now."

"Oh." He sounds crestfallen. "What did you want, then, David?"

"Do you recall that conversation we had about the case I was working on about the abused woman, and how you might be interested in helping me out?"

"I do."

"Are you still interested?"

"I owe you a lot, David," he says cautiously, "but I'd need to understand more about it and what you want me to do."

"There is a man I know of who ordered the murder of a young woman. To be clear, I'm not asking you to do anything violent. All I require is a decoy."

"A decoy?"

"Are you familiar with the Dark Web, Sam? Do you know how to access it?"

"No."

"It's the most secure way for us to talk. If you're agreeable, I'll have someone contact you and tell you how to go about it. He'll give you a code word – *Liberty* – to identify himself as my man."

"This sounds like something from a spy movie, David. Listen, I'd love to help you out, but I'm starting to get my life back together, and I don't want to be involved in anything illegal."

"I'm not asking you to kill anybody, Sam," I say, "but I might be asking you to do something *slightly* illegal."

"Slightly illegal is OK, David. Hell, we all do slightly illegal things every day, don't we?" He laughs.

"We do indeed, Sam."

"What's your man's name? The one who will contact me?"

"He doesn't have a name. You can call him whatever you like. The important thing is that he uses the code word to you."

"*Liberty*."

"That's the one. I recognise that you Americans love liberty."

"We do. So when will I hear from Mr. Nameless?"

"Soon, Sam. Soon."

I have retired to bed, not wishing to face Wayan when she returns from her date. She might detect how disturbed I am, and I am worried that in my current state I could blurt out something that she mustn't know. I can't mention Natalie's death to her either in case it gets back to Katie, so I have to blot it out of my mind along with the truth about Anna and Jenny. For now, anyway.

So much concealment. It's mentally exhausting. Once one embarks on the road of dishonesty, it becomes increasingly difficult to recall what lies you have told to whom, and when.

No, it's much better that I shut my bedroom door so that I can be alone in the dark with my thoughts – of which there are many. Many thoughts and many regrets.

I can no longer even conjure up Claire to listen to my fears and concerns, to advise and to soothe me. She has gone, my lovely ghost. Her message has been delivered and understood. Her purpose is fulfilled. She's done with me.

There is no longer anyone to whom I can talk with candour. All my close confidants have either fallen by the wayside or fallen into shadow.

I close my eyes.

Let me sleep. And let me not dream about a sodding goose.

24

"What part of our history's reinvented and under rug swept?
What part of your memory is selective and tends to forget?"
Alanis Morissette, Hands Clean

My weekend with Katie went as well as could be expected.

Despite her protestations, it was evident that her yoga training was failing to stave off a growing boredom with her *same-same* existence on Koh Phangan. Fortunately, this worked to my advantage inasmuch as she jumped at the idea of spending a few days in Singapore with Wayan.

"I would have needed to do a visa run in the next couple of weeks anyway," she reasoned. "This will kill two birds with one stone."

"Exactly," I replied. "Plus, Robert has to fly to Manila next week to sort out some banking business, and I figured I'd go with him. Change of scenery. So, we'll all be out of the country at the same time, and you'll be company for Wayan while he and I are away."

This raised her suspicions. *Too pat*, Braddock.

"You and Robert are taking a trip to the Philippines together?" She squinted at me. "That's a big about-turn, isn't it, Dad? I'd hardly consider you and him to be best buddies. And when did you stop calling him 'Buchanan' and start referring to him as 'Robert'? Anyway, you don't even like the Philippines. You always told me it was a dangerous place."

I exhaled wearily, hoping it didn't come across as too dramatic.

"Katie, I have to accept that Robert Buchanan is a significant part of Wayan's life, and that you are fond of him too. I don't like the situation and I've never tried to disguise that fact. But I can't change it. So, it's no use my swimming against the tide any longer. Robert and I need to be able to get on with each other, and we both acknowledge it.

"We'll be staying in an upmarket hotel in Manila, so I've no concerns about being mugged. And, by the way, what I *actually* said to you about the Philippines was that there was no sense in my staying at one of their beach resorts as I live on Samui and we have our own great beaches."

She didn't look convinced, so I decided to sprinkle a little truth into my explanation.

"There is something else too."

She folded her arms.

"Here it comes. Go on, then."

I spoke slowly, as if I was having the disclosure dragged out of me.

"Well, the last few times I've been here on the island, I noticed a particular car that always seems to be hanging around."

"What car?"

"A small white Ford. I had it checked out and there is nothing to worry about. It was hired to some Danish tourist, who has now left. But, even so, it set my paranoia off a bit, and it occurred to me that it might not be such a bad thing if you weren't always in the same place. Hence, a short spell in Singapore might be just the thing."

"A *Danish* tourist?"

"Yes."

"That's why you were so weird when I mentioned my one-night stand with a Dane."

"Yes."

Katie closed her eyes and gave a small shake of the head. Then she took my hand.

"We'll never be completely free of Grigory Polzin, will we, Dad? He casts a long shadow over us. Perhaps the best thing to do would be to have him killed. Or to do it ourselves."

"That's enough of that stupid talk," I admonished her. "We'll manage."

"Yeah," she said sadly. "We will. Somehow. Incidentally, I notice you're not smoking as much."

"Is that bad?"

"No. On the contrary, it gives me hope that you're coming alive again."

"I'm not the one who's been dead," I replied. "That would be *you*, Katie Braddock."

Over the course of my weekend on the island, I managed to slip away on each of the days and phone Nang, as I'd promised. She has told Laurette Lang that I have a clot in my leg which is being treated with blood thinners, and I'm not allowed to fly until the doctor gives me the thumbs-up. She also said that the reason I hadn't mentioned this to Laurette myself was because I was embarrassed about having such a 'minor' health issue compared to Natalie's. The old girl is creative, I'll say that for her. Plus, she and Mrs. Lang are hitting it off famously, assisted by the fact that Natalie's friend is a member of the local Conservative Association. I can imagine the political discussions that are going on between navigating the funereal niceties.

I also managed to get Nang to put Jenny on the line. She is shell-shocked, the poor mite, and I doubt the full implications have hit her yet. The conversation wasn't a particularly special occasion for her but, for me, it was the first time I'd spoken to the girl whom I now know to be my own flesh and blood. It was difficult not to become inappropriately emotional. I'm still *Uncle David* to her, of course. That field needs to lie fallow awhile yet.

My meeting with *Vlad The Impaler* at the Irish Pub on Sunday evening was a straightforward affair.

"So, you want me to involve this guy Sam Trask in your alibi for when you're shooting Polzin?" he said.

"Your grasp of detail is, as ever, astonishing," I told him.

He doesn't recognise sarcasm, so he smiled. He didn't even raise any objection to dealing with one of the hated Americans.

I gave him instructions about contacting the ex-soldier, made him repeat the code word several times, and ran through the whole Dark Web scenario twice for good measure.

"OK," he replied.

It's so much easier dealing with international criminal types than with your own family.

There is nothing yet from Orlov who, I gather, is already back in Moscow, and making public noises about his successful business trip to South East Asia. Which crowing, I assume, is carefully calibrated to upset Polzin, and to increase the likelihood of his competitor jumping on a plane and flying east.

While Vlad and I talked, a number of striking females kept fluttering around the big Russian, and had to be waved away. Why is it that women – even my normally sensible housekeeper – are so attracted to bad boys? I ought to take a leaf out of their book and behave much worse. Maybe then, they'd be swarming over me too.

And once I've murdered Polzin I should *really* have some sex appeal.

Monday.

Buchanan has done his job of persuading Wayan to accompany Katie to Singapore. That wouldn't necessarily have been an easy task. My housekeeper is not a great lover of cities or non-essential shopping, and her disastrous jaunt with me to London last year won't have done anything to endear her to those teeming, overpriced, and overpopulated habitats of humanity. However, the opportunity to spend time with Katie that *didn't* have to be totally about shopping, coupled with the planned absence from Samui of Buchanan and myself, clinched the deal.

Accordingly, I have dropped off the two ladies at Samui International Airport in good time for the morning flight to Singapore, and am on my way to the *Agency*.

So far, so good.

I've barely sat down at my desk when Da walks determinedly into my office.

"I have something to say to you," she announces.

"Good, because I have something to say to you too."

She calls over her shoulder to Pimpim, who appears in the doorway awaiting instructions.

"I'd like you to go out," she tells our receptionist. "Don't come back for at least an hour and a half. No, make that two hours. *Khun* David and I have a lot to talk about."

"What shall I do while I'm out, *Khun* Da?" Pimpim asks timidly.

"Go to *Brazilian Blend* and buy yourself a coffee and a muffin, or several coffees. Have your nails done, whatever. Take some money from petty cash, and lock the front door behind you. Oh, and turn our sign to 'closed' before you leave."

A cowed Pimpim duly complies. Da and I listen to her footsteps going down the stairs, then there is the sound of the latch closing.

Mrs. Pintaraporn turns her attention to me.

"Would it bother you if I leave your office door open, David? However much the cleaners try in here, they can't entirely get rid of the smell of your cigarette smoke."

"I'm cutting down," I remark while trying to gauge her mood.

"Good for you."

She lowers herself primly onto my client chair and studies me. The silence goes on for a few seconds, then we both speak at once.

"I'd better go first, if you don't mind," says Da.

I don't mind.

"David, you and I need to have a straight talk to clear the air."

"Does the air need clearing?"

"I have some observations to make, and a confession."

"Go on."

She runs her tongue over her lips before continuing.

"I know about Katie, and about Robert Buchanan too."

I realise my mouth is open, so I close it. Then I open it again to say, "What is it you think you know?"

"I know that Katie is alive and living on Koh Phangan and that you visit her every weekend."

I attempt a poker face. It's a pathetic effort, I expect.

"Come on, David, you didn't seriously believe I'd swallow that story about her being your goddaughter, did you? *You, a godfather!*"

She manufactures a sound that is rather like a snort, but more scornful.

I'm about to speak, but I'm not permitted the opportunity.

"At first, I thought, *he has some European girlfriend and he's embarrassed about her because she's so young*. But you are rarely embarrassed. And it had to be somebody you cared about otherwise you wouldn't be going over to Phangan every weekend. You do tend to become bored of your women quite quickly."

"Thanks."

"I'm a detective too, remember. It did occur to me that she might be some client who was in serious trouble and had gone into hiding. But if it was *Agency* business – even if shady – you wouldn't have had any reason not to tell me about it."

"Assuming I trust you, that is."

"You *do* trust me. That's why what I have to say next is so difficult. By the way, this is where the confession part of this monologue comes in."

I rest my chin on my palms. That way, my mouth won't drop open again.

"Think of me as a priest," I say.

"That's difficult, if not impossible."

"Pray continue."

"Well, I decided to follow you over to Koh Phangan to see for myself what was going on. I took photographs of your mystery woman and checked them against the images and UK reports on Katie's disappearance. She's changed her look, sure, but I could see it was Katie. The family resemblance is obvious. And you and she were very close – in tune – the way a man is with his daughter."

My scalp prickles.

"Stop. The person in the white car was *you*?"

"Yes. Sorry about that." She doesn't sound sorry. "But, when I worked through the implications of your spotting the car, and understood what else is going on, I realised that you must be spooked. So, I made up the story about the Danish tourist and his girlfriend to stop you worrying."

"Plus, you didn't want to tell me it was you," I remark acidly.

"That too."

The main office phone rings. Neither of us moves. We leave it ringing until it stops.

"When you say *you understood what else is going on*, what do you mean, Da?"

"I'm talking about Robert Buchanan's presence here."

"Did Wayan say something to you?"

"No, she's been as tight-lipped as you. But I had the sense that she was avoiding me these last weeks, and whenever we did meet, she came across as evasive. She's usually frank and open with me, so her behaviour was out of character. I asked her if anything was troubling her, but she said not."

"Did you follow her too?"

"No, she's a friend. I wouldn't do that to Wayan."

"You did it to me."

"That's different. Anyway, I saw her with a man at a restaurant entirely by chance one evening when I was out on a surveillance job. It was apparent that they were ... um ... *intimate*."

"And you're nosey, so you snapped some photos of him. And because you'd worked out Katie was here which meant Buchanan hadn't killed her, and Wayan was in love with Buchanan, and this guy showed up about the same time as Katie, then you put two and two together and checked your photos of him against the police identikit of Katie's supposed killer. Correct?"

"Wayan and I are close, we have been for years. If she were dating someone, I'd expect her to tell me about it. And she hadn't even mentioned it. Which meant it was someone she didn't want to – or *couldn't* – tell me about. The identikit picture of Buchanan was poor but I concluded it must be him. Nothing else would make any sense."

"Right."

"Then, when you, Wayan, and the other guy all went off to Koh Phangan –"

"And you followed us."

"Yes."

Da reins in her flow, and waits for me to contradict her hypothesis. When I don't, she speaks again. Now, though, her voice is measured and serious.

"Here's the position, as I see it. Katie is living under an assumed name on an island where it's possible to remain under the radar. But you must still be worried about the man who ordered her death, that he might discover she is still alive somehow, and set out to find her. And, as Buchanan hadn't followed Grigory Polzin's instructions - presumably out of his feelings for Wayan - he'll be worried for his life too. I imagine betraying an oligarch is a dangerous matter."

She takes a breath.

"How am I doing, David?

"Not bad for an amateur."

There is a glint of satisfaction in her eyes at this.

"By the way, I didn't know Katie was alive until she showed up with Buchanan."

"I guessed as much. Your grief over those weeks was too genuine to be an act. It's been a hard time for you, David. I'm sorry."

I process what Da has said, and endeavour to understand why I have not contradicted her or even offered a token defence.

I'm tired. Tired of keeping all this to myself.

"Well, Da, it seems that you're the smarter one in this partnership after all."

"I've been telling you that for years."

"Huh."

I run my hands through my hair in exasperation.

"Jesus, if you can piece all this together so easily, we're right to be worried about Polzin."

Da leans forward and fixes me with a hard stare.

"You and Buchanan are thinking of killing Polzin, aren't you?"

"What makes you say that?"

"Oh, small stuff," she answers casually. "Like you going to the shooting range, these odd trips and meetings. That sort of thing."

My elaborately-prepared explanation about the Philippines is redundant. Surrender is imminent.

"Buchanan and I are flying to Manila tomorrow for a few days."

"Will Polzin be there? Are you going to shoot him there?"

"I haven't said we're going to kill him."

"You haven't said you *aren't*."

Pause. I mentally raise the white flag.

"Manila is a stopover on the road. I honestly don't know where Polzin is going to receive his fair deserts. But it will likely be in South East Asia. I don't know when either. But soon. I have a contact who's trying to get hold of his travel schedule for me."

"Who is this contact?"

"That I can't tell you."

Da stands up and announces, "Let's break for a coffee. I'll make it."

"Have we done?"

"No. Not yet."

She goes off into the main office. While she's out, I make a few decisions. They are likely ill-advised ones. She returns to find me in a contemplative mood.

"Don't you want a cigarette?" she says, putting two steaming mugs on my desk.

"Funnily enough, I don't."

"Good. Now, where were we?"

"I was just about to deny everything."

"We're way past that point, David."

"Yes, we are."

I sense a weight slipping off my shoulders. *No going back.*

"Da, I want you to know that this business with you and the white car doesn't change anything. I still trust you."

She didn't expect this candour and, for the first time today, she is lost for words.

"The fact is, you're one of the few people I can trust. There's nobody I can talk to about any of this except Buchanan. And our discussions are of a, let's say, pragmatic nature."

I am surprised at the bitterness of the laugh that comes out of me.

"I call him Buchanan but I don't even know what his real name is."

"I take it that Katie and Wayan aren't aware of what you're planning for Polzin?"

"They aren't, no."

"Oh, *David*."

"This coffee isn't bad by the way."

"Screw the coffee. Don't try to change the subject."

"OK, OK."

I raise an appeasing hand.

"Then, do you mind if we switch roles for a few minutes? You be the priest and I'll be the person making the confession."

She nods.

I have to tell someone about this.

"Last week, my life became even more complicated than it was already."

"*Really?* How is that even possible?"

"On Friday, I received a phone call from England to say that my mother-in-law had died, and that the child she has been bringing up, and whom I thought was my niece is, in fact, my daughter."

"Oh, wow."

"Indeed. I have rather a lot of skeletons in my cupboard, Da. Are you sure you want to hear about them?"

"I do," she replies resolutely. "Tell me everything."

"*Everything?*"

"Yes."

And I do tell her everything. Much more than I had intended.

Once my castle wall has been breached, my other fortifications and inventions collapse all at once. The words pour out of me like a river. For a man who has compartmentalised his existence, holding it together as I have through force of will, it is a cathartic experience to let go. To tear off the mask of normalcy and respectability. To allow someone to *see* me properly for the first time. To allow me to see myself.

I find myself recounting not only the story of Anna and Jenny, but also the saga of Claire's demise, the memory-numbing sexual indulgences of my early days in Thailand, and my involvement in the world of gangsterism. Some of this material – particularly the Sangukhon-Lamphongchat-Chaldrakun conflicts of the last few years – she knows about already. But now all the isolated events, hitherto scattered like dandruff on a tramp's pillow, coalesce into a coherent pattern of loss, carelessness, and violence.

Da listens patiently and without judgement, only interrupting my unplanned tirade to clarify a point here and there. When she does speak, she does so with softness and without guile.

I lose track of the time, but eventually my unburdening is done, and I slump back in my chair, exhausted. I don't even want a Marlboro to steady me.

Da understands me better now than does any other living person. More so than Nang or Wayan. More so even than Katie. She has become the keeper of my chronicles. Oddly, it doesn't worry me.

"You have been carrying a lot on your shoulders, David," she says.

"I suppose I have."

"It's a miracle that you can function."

For a second, I think she is about to reach out and grasp my hand. But the moment passes. Da is not one given to sentimentality, I remind myself. Her defining characteristic is a steely pragmatism. She is a creature of the intellect first and foremost, not a slave of the heart.

"Even with all that has happened - and is still happening - you are nevertheless determined to kill Grigory Polzin? Even though you have Jenny to raise?"

"I intend to do both."

"You are not an assassin, David. You're not equipped. You'll die."

"I'll be careful."

"You won't be careful, though, that's the point. It's not in your nature."

I can almost see the cogs whirring in her head.

Then she says, "Let me help you."

"*What?*"

"If you're determined to do this, you need someone who has your back."

"I have Buchanan."

"Your alliance with him is only one of convenience. If you do pull off this assassination, what makes you believe he won't shoot you afterwards to cover his own tracks? Do you think his affection for Wayan will protect you?"

"Yes. I believe it will. I *hope* it will. Anyway, I don't want you involved. Don't make me regret telling you all this, Da. I won't have you becoming an accomplice to a murder. No."

"But, I could –"

"*No*. This is not your problem."

"At least let me book your flights and hotels. And perhaps I could be your alibi for when –"

"It's out of the question. Apart from anything else, there's Pratcha to consider. Besides, if you make bookings for me, you'll have to do it by phone or over the Internet, and you would leave a trail that would lead back to you and to me. All transactions have to be handled in cash. Besides, I might not be travelling as David Braddock. After I collect my fake passport in Manila, I'll be Eric Snow."

"*Eric Snow?* You don't look like an Eric."

I don't ask her what an Eric looks like.

"Then, let me *research* flights and hotels for you. That's all. Surely there's no harm in *that*. At least I'd be doing *something*. I can't sit here and do nothing."

"Why not?"

"Give me the names of the cities where you ... Well, give me the names of the cities."

I hesitate.

"*Please*. I'll find appropriate places for you to stay. Discreet, not too big, not too small. It's a job that has to be done anyway, and I'm perfectly capable of doing it. There's no risk to me or to you. No emails, no Internet traceability, nothing. I can do it this afternoon and give you a piece of paper with the information on it. Nothing digital. I'll even wipe the searches on my laptop. You can't object to that, surely? I know it's a small thing, but it would make me feel better."

I give in and tell her the names of the potential cities. She tears a strip off my desk pad and jots them down. I don't tell her that Buchanan and I will be carrying out separate assassinations. It's better that she believes we are conducting a single assignment together. Otherwise, a whole new barrage of questions and objections might start up.

"There is one other thing you can do for me," I say.

"Go on."

"Since Katie's resurrection I have, over the past few weeks, been progressively moving money from England to my private bank account here on Samui. It now has a balance of over seven million Baht, in case Katie needs it. I'd like to transfer six million to your personal account. In the unlikely event that something happens to me, you can make sure it finds its way to Katie. If there is ever any query about the money, you say I was buying out your part of the business or that it was a compensation payment because I'm letting you go."

"You trust me to do that?"

"I do, yes."

The clacking of heels on the stairs announces that Pimpim has returned.

I check my watch. Da and I have been talking for over two hours.

At lunchtime, I go to my bank and move the money to Da's account.

"A business transaction," I inform the cashier, even though she hasn't asked.

Afterwards, I buy a sandwich and smoke what I am shocked to discover is my first cigarette of the day.

Back at the Agency, Da's office door is closed.

"She's with a client," Pimpim says.

Behind my own closed door, I fire up my laptop and check for a message from Orlov. There is nothing.

I make brief calls to Vlad and Buchanan to ensure all is in order, then spend some time searching the Internet for any breaking news on matters Russian. Reportage of Orlov's South East Asian trip pops up on several sites.

Around three o'clock, I phone Nang for an update and expected telling-off. Jenny is at school: the old ladies judge it best that the little girl gets back into a routine swiftly, though they are monitoring her closely.

I have just finished my conversation with Nang, and am contemplating having my second cigarette of the day, when there is a knock on my door.

It's Da. She closes the door behind her, sit down opposite me and slides two pieces of paper across the desk. On them are details of a hotel in each of the cities I'd mentioned to her, and copious notes on flight schedules.

"You *will* use this information, David, won't you? I wouldn't like to think I'd wasted my time."

"Cross my heart," I reply, folding the papers and putting them in my pocket.

"And you will call me every day so that I know what's happening? I don't need anything detailed, don't worry. Just where you are and where you're going. That's all."

"All right. A quick one, though. No lengthy discussions."

With the daily calls I've committed to make to Nang, Katie and now Da, I hope I'll be able to squeeze a murder into my busy schedule once I've factored in time for travelling, sleeping and eating. It would be easier for me to wear an electronic tag.

I tell her the money transfer has been done. She regards me evenly, and an expression of resolution forms on her face.

"I have a proposition for you," she says.

"Oh?"

"But, before I tell you what it is, I want you to promise me that you won't over-react."

"You expect me to make three promises in less than a minute? You're asking a lot."

"Promise me."

"All right. I promise. I won't over-react."

"Good. Now, David, I've given this a lot of consideration, and I think now would be the right time for you and me to hook up."

"*Hook up?* We are 'hooked up'. We're business partners."

"I mean, we should become *partner* partners. Exclusively."

"What?"

She spells it out.

"I want us to move in together, David."

"*What?* Move in together? Have you lost your mind?"

"You said you wouldn't over-react."

"I –"

"Listen, David, it makes perfect sense."

"*Does it?* Run me through your reasoning, please. From the beginning. I must have missed something, or else I've gone back on the whisky and I'm having a nightmare."

"After you've dealt with Polzin, you're going to go back to England, aren't you? You have to, for Jenny's sake. That means the *David Braddock Agency* is finished. You'll give it to me or sell it. Yes, I know you said you'd take care of me financially, but I don't want to be involved in this place if you're not here. It wouldn't be the same."

"Da, I –"

"Besides, you're going to need assistance in bringing up Jenny. I wouldn't try to replace her mother, but I can be a positive and stable female influence in her life. The sort of step-mother that Nang has been to you. And it would be good for Pratcha to have a father. We can raise the two children together, and they will be company for each other."

"But, Da –"

"We don't have to be married straightaway, David, I'm not asking that. We should spend some time getting to know each other on a more intimate basis first. It's key that we put the physical side of our relationship on a proper footing."

"The *physical side*? Can I please –"

"Plus, there are logistics to take into account. I wouldn't be able to come with you straightaway, but to start with I could spend some months of the year with you in England. Then, when the time is right, Pratcha and I will join you and Jenny permanently. I understand this is not the ideal moment to bring this up, but you've only just told me about Jenny, and you're flying to Manila tomorrow. So, I wanted you to think about it while you're away."

Her prepared speech comes to an end and I can finally get a word in.

"Before I make any comments, can I ask how long you've been mulling over this bombshell?"

"A while."

"You haven't come up with all this today?"

"No. Although when I learned this morning about Jenny, everything I'd been musing on finally clicked into place."

"That time we had breakfast at the bakery and you brought Pratcha along –"

"Yes?"

"Was that some kind of a test, a dry run to see how I was with him, and an opportunity for you to assess whether what I'd told you about my not seeing Malee was true?"

"Maybe there was a little of that in it, yes."

I flail around, searching for a clinching argument to bring this discussion to an end. That should be easy: Da's proposition is crazy. But she's caught me unawares, and anyway who could have anticipated *this*? I grasp at a line that pops into my head.

"Da, you can't simply pack up your life on Samui. You have an extended family here: a brother, cousins, nieces, nephews. Pratcha would lose all meaningful contact with his relatives. They'd be half a planet away. And, what about Tong's parents? They wouldn't see their grandson. How would *they* feel about that?"

A long outbreath from Da. When she speaks again, her voice is quiet.

"David, my parents have passed away. My brother is married and living in Bangkok with a family of his own to worry about. My cousin Noona who shares my house is likely to be married soon. My other relatives are carrying on with their lives, and they will continue to do so with or without me.

"Pratcha would obtain a good education in England. He's a bright boy, and career opportunities might open up for him there. As for Tong's parents, I love them but I won't stay here for them, and they wouldn't expect me to."

OK, that didn't work. Let's try something else.

"I appreciate that you might want a companion, and a step-father for Pratcha. It's crucial for a zillion reasons that person is the right man for the job. I'm sure we can at least agree on that. Suitable, reliable. A good man. So, why by all that's holy would you choose *me*?"

I expect at this point that my theory about good women falling for bad boys is to be proved right. Even the *idea* of my shooting Polzin must have unbalanced Da's mental chemistry, and tipped her towards a darker and more exciting fantasy existence.

She doesn't flinch.

"Because you *are* a good man."

"Despite what you found out about me today, you can say that?"

"Yes."

My Bad Boy Model takes a hit.

"You had better define for me what you mean by 'good'."

"Nobody can be good all the time," she explains patiently. "What is important is that you always *try* to do the right thing when it matters. For sure, you mess up sometimes, and you get things wrong. But you always try.

You've cut out your womanising and your drinking because you recognised you had to. You're not a gambler like Tong. You're generous, and kind when someone is down."

"It does sound like I'm pretty irresistible when you put it in those terms, I must admit."

"Don't think it's easy for me to give you these compliments," she says with a harder edge to her voice. "You can also be stubborn and irritating at times."

"Plus, I'm going to murder a man. Does that also fit your formula of someone who tries to do the right thing?"

"If I were in your shoes, and my child was threatened, I may well follow the same course as you."

She tilts her head to the side.

"You really don't get it, do you?"

"Get what?"

"You're so conditioned by your English upbringing that you believe you always have to be strong and tough. But you're wrong, David. It was when you opened up to me today, and I saw your soft side – that's what decided me. This morning, you were open and vulnerable, and I liked it. Male vulnerability is attractive to a woman, don't you understand that?"

"Apparently not."

When I don't add anything further, Da's mood changes and she becomes uneasy. Then, when I still don't speak, she becomes anxious. She has played all her cards, and I'm still not responding.

Eventually, I say, "Da, we're not in love with each other."

"No, that's not why you've gone quiet. Love can come, with work. No, it's something else. It's *me*, isn't it?"

"You?"

"You see me as shameless, that I haven't allowed a sufficient period of mourning for Tong."

"No, it's not that. You and Tong were separated, after all."

"Then, you think I just want a British passport and an easy life for me and my son."

"No, I don't."

"You don't think I'm attractive."

"Stop telling me what I think. You're an exceedingly attractive woman. Gorgeous, if you want my frank opinion."

"You haven't ogled my breasts in years, and you have *never* made a pass at me in all our time together."

"As we're co-workers that would hardly have been appropriate."

"Since when have your relationships here been appropriate, David? That has never stopped you."

I don't have an answer to this. It sounds like a fair observation.

"Oh, I see," she says. "You find me attractive, but not *sexually* attractive. Is that it? You can't imagine yourself in bed with me."

"Listen Da," I say reasonably, "getting together with someone in a romantic relationship is not like a business deal. It's not about pros and cons, and formulae on spreadsheets."

It occurs to me that 'spread' and 'sheets' are unsuitable terms to use when the topic of sex has reared its head, so I move on speedily.

"It has nothing to do with logic. It's feelings."

The phone rings in reception and I hear Pimpim answer it.

A sly smile crosses Da's lips.

"I think you should kiss me, David."

"What?"

"That's the only one way to tell for sure."

She makes her way round the desk, pushes me back on my chair, and sits on my knee. I smell her perfume, and notice the redness of her mouth. She puts her arms around my neck.

"Kiss me, then we'll know."

"I –"

"Kiss me," she orders.

I kiss her.

Our lips brush. At first, we are tentative, then there is a growing conviction in our actions. I place my hands lightly on her hips, and my body starts to ignore my brain and have ideas of its own. We explore each other slowly. The tenderness is unexpected for both of us. When the kiss ends, my own surprise is mirrored in Da's eyes.

There is a knock on the door.

Da doesn't move. Our faces are still close when she says, "Come in."

Pimpim takes a couple of steps into the office before she notices us. Her eyes widen. In her hand she clutches a sheet of her notepad, but she appears to have forgotten it's there.

"What is it?" says Da.

"*Khun* Piotr called," she stutters.

"I'll handle it."

Da peels herself off me, stands up and brushes her skirt. Unlike the other two people in the room, she is completely unfazed.

"You *will* consider what I've said, David, won't you?" she asks in her best business voice.

I nod dumbly.

"Make *Khun* David a coffee, Pimpim. I believe he might need one."

Da sweeps out majestically, taking Pimpim's note, and leaving our confused receptionist staring at me. Pimpim bows her head and retreats slowly, closing the door behind her.

And there was I thinking that the universe couldn't possibly have any more curved balls to throw at me after Katie's reappearance and the revelation about Jenny.

A proposal from Da. Hell's teeth.

Of course, the whole idea is preposterous. We'd be at each other's throats in a week once reality dawns. But I need to pick the right time to let her down gently, and that will be *after* Polzin is dead.

At least now, if I don't survive my attempt on the Russian's life, there is an upside: I won't have to face the wrath of Da.

25

"To dissociate from your darkness is to lose your power over it."

Jessa Crispin

Manila, 12.30am, Wednesday.

The first city of the Philippines is one of the most densely populated conurbations on Earth. It has been rebuilt as a result of wars more times than Troy, and over the centuries it has rivalled Tokyo in its propensity for natural disasters. Earthquakes, hurricanes, floods and volcanic eruptions are only some of Mother Nature's whimsicalities that have afflicted the Filipinos' capital. Yet, despite its brutal history, to the locals – the Manileños – it is known as 'The City of Our Affections'. For me, Manila is an accident waiting to happen.

To this charge sheet of invading armies and Acts of God must be added choking pollution, crime, dirt, rampant poverty, and a pervasive sex trade. In the spirit of even-handedness, however, I should point out that most of the people are friendly and generous, and that the old walled city of Intramuros contains some delightful architecture. So, it's not all about death squads and blinkered Catholicism. Plus, there are some decent restaurants, and the hookers in the bars tend to be discreet and have good singing voices.

Politically, things are fairly quiet in the Philippines at present. After last year's scandal about poor Filipinos selling their kidneys to rich foreigners, the acquittal of Imelda Marcos on charges of making illegal money transfers, and the traditional smattering of hostage-taking incidents, corruption scandals and seizures of bomb-making equipment, things have calmed down. So far in 2009, there has only been one major series of explosions in Southern Mindanao (blamed on the Moro Islamic Liberation Front) and the kidnapping of three officials of the Red Cross.

OK, that's the briefing done.

Buchanan and I touched down on the Philippines Airlines flight from Bangkok at Ninoy Aquino International Airport yesterday. It was a little before six in the evening.

After a surprisingly tolerable wait to be processed through immigration, Buchanan purchased a temporary SIM card, and we piled into a taxi for the unsurprisingly intolerable journey into Manila. It took us about an hour-and-a-half to travel the ten kilometres to the city centre, during which time we were treated to church choir music from the car's sound system while our driver stroked his rosary beads and tried to persuade us to change our hotel.

We checked into the *Manila Grand*, an iconic five-star hostelry with a view of the South Harbor. Neither my companion nor I were hungry, so we agreed to forego dinner and meet in the bar after unpacking.

Once in my room, I switched on my laptop to see if there was any word from Orlov. There wasn't. I then logged into a few Thai media websites for news of the current situation in Bangkok, which I have been monitoring closely.

Trouble has been brewing there for some time, and in the last week it has spilled onto the streets. Six days ago, about a hundred thousand red-shirt supporters of deposed premier Thaksin Shinawatra marched on Government House demanding the resignation of Prime Minister Abhisit Vejjajiva. Over the weekend, while I was on Koh Phangan, protests had spread to Pattaya, causing the cancellation of the ASEAN Summit. On Monday, the protest leader Arisman Pongreungrong was arrested, and by Tuesday soldiers in full combat dress were firing tear gas and live rounds at demonstrators near the Victory Monument in central Bangkok. TV stations broadcasting footage of the clashes have been blacked out, and several UDD radio stations closed down. We were lucky that there was minimum flight disruption at Suvarnabhumi Airport, although a heavy security presence was much in evidence.

None of this bodes well for our project. If either Buchanan or I find ourselves routed to the Thai capital in pursuit of a Polzin, the city is going to be crawling with police and army.

I made my obligatory phone calls to Katie, Da and Nang. Katie and Wayan were at Singapore's Clarke Quay, Da was on surveillance duty, and Nang was grumpy.

"Do you know when you're coming to England yet?" asked my step-mother.

"No."

"Well, Natalie's funeral is next week, and I *shall* expect you here for it."

I joined Buchanan in the Tap Room Bar, a thickly-carpeted and vaguely gothic drinking hole. Not really to my taste, but it offered greater privacy than the lobby lounge.

My companion was finishing a call when I pitched up.

"Our documents are being delivered in half-an-hour. I'll have to leave you for a bit."

"Very efficient."

"My people know their stuff."

"You have time for a San Miguel first, though, right?"

While we cradled our cold beers, I gave him a news update on the state of affairs in Bangkok. He was less concerned about the demonstrations than I was, and his mind appeared to be elsewhere.

"We need an edge," he suddenly announced.

"An *edge*?"

"If we're going to get this assignment done successfully."

"We *have* an edge. We have surprise on our side."

"Perhaps," he responded, "but I'm not sure that will be enough."

"What kind of an edge?"

He shook his head.

"I dunno."

"You're unusually nervy. Hell, I'm more relaxed than you. Are you always like this before a job?"

"No. Never."

"Then, what's up?"

"This one is different."

"Why? Because you're not being paid for it?"

"No. Because it's personal. Also, I have a partner – you – who doesn't have the slightest idea of what he is taking on, and who has never shot anyone before."

"Do you think I'm going to freeze up when the time comes? That I'll bottle it?"

Before he could answer, a message bleeped on his phone.

"I'll be back in a few minutes. Get me another beer, would you?"

While he was gone, I ordered a second round and resolved not to make any references to trees, even obliquely. I doubted he was in the mood for jokes.

When Buchanan reappeared, he was carrying a plain, A4-size envelope. He extracted a couple of documents and put them into his jacket pocket before handing me the packet. I peeked inside. It contained my fake passport, a few other papers and two rubber stamps.

"What are the stamps for?"

"They're Philippines immigration 'in' and 'out' stamps, depending on whether you're leaving the country as David Braddock or Eric Snow."

"Right."

He narrowed his eyes.

"Can you remember that?"

"Yeah, probably," I responded as carelessly as I could.

We each drank our second San Miguel in silence.

When he rose to leave, he said, "I'll see you at breakfast, and we'll discuss tomorrow's schedule then. Maybe you'll be more receptive after a night's sleep."

"Maybe we both will."

"Good night."

Restless, I hung around in the bar and had a third beer but no whiskies. When I went back to my room, I tucked the fake documents and stamps into the safe, and logged into the Dark Web.

Nothing. Not a sausage.

Unable to countenance the thought of lying in bed staring up at the ceiling, I took the lift down to the lobby and stepped outside for what was only my third Marlboro of the day.

My lungs must be feeling terribly confused.

This morning, and much to my astonishment, I awake refreshed.

My sleeping mind is apparently done with lucid dreaming and phantasmagoria. I guess it's gone back to thinking about sex. I do hope it's not having sick erotic fantasies about Da. That would be the ultimate betrayal.

Buchanan is more like his old self at breakfast: humourless and taciturn. His hesitancy of yesterday has either gone or he is better at hiding it. He is wearing a suit for his legal/illegal business meetings today.

There is nothing quite like formal dress for making a man appear respectable and trustworthy, is there? I, on the other hand, am attired in crumpled linen, and topped out with my Panama. The hat and I have become inseparable in recent months: it must be acting as a comfort blanket for me.

Englishman goes on lethal mission and wears fetching hat. Sounds like a great epitaph.

Buchanan tells me he isn't sure how long he will be out. He is dealing with lawyers and bankers, and they take their own sweet time. We agree to meet back at the hotel at five.

"What will you do all day?" he asks.

"Well, I'll miss you, that's for sure. I'm missing you already."

"Did you check for a message from your contact last night?"

"Yes, and this morning. The wires are silent."

"This contact of yours had better deliver. Otherwise we're wasting our time."

Indeed, he had better deliver. If he doesn't, we are up shit creek in a barbed wire canoe. *All dressed up and nowhere to go.*

Buchanan leaves.

I pick up a map from the concierge. My memory of Manila is fuzzy as it's many years since my only previous visit here. That was on holiday with Claire, a lifetime ago.

What to do? I could join a guided tour, but then I'd have to be sociable.

I catalogue the current state of my health. I'm wide awake and my hands are steady. No alcohol cravings. I do, however, have a cramp-like pain in my chest and down my left side, though it is not constricting my breathing as it has done before.

I'll walk it off. (I wonder if that's what Natalie said to herself when her heart was playing up: "A brisk stroll should cure this. It's nothing.")

I step outside into the morning.

We are in Manila's dry, hot season. It's overcast at present, and though the temperature is predicted to be in the high twenties, the humidity will make it more like the mid-thirties. It's going to be sticky and uncomfortable. Fortunately, I have my trusty Panama and a pair of Ray-Bans.

I turn onto Katigbak Parkway and manage to cross the busy junction with the R-1 without getting run over. To my right is Rizal Park and lots of shade from the trees along Padre Burgos Avenue. I walk at a slow pace for a few minutes, and take a left at the traffic lights by Maynilad Luneta Lift Station. A dodgy operation: as in most parts of Asia, red lights are advisory only.

I soon reach the boundary of the old walled district of Intramuros. Here, I stop for a breather and grab two bottles of water. Despite my slow progress, and the fact that it is still only mid-morning, my body temperature is on the rise. My chest is lighter, though, and fears of imminent cardiac arrest recede.

For the next couple of hours, I amble around the streets, taking in the bleached-white Spanish buildings, the old brickwork and, inevitably, the grubby shacks which have sprung up in the area's less desirable side-roads. Wealth and poverty enjoy an uneasy coexistence here, with native tree species – talisays, molaves, kamunings, and the like – occasionally providing a buffering, like some Filipino DMZ. I wonder if these woody perennials would give Buchanan the willies. Most likely not. They're not European enough to trigger his phobia.

Between them, the Japanese and the Americans flattened this place during World War II, and although many of the famous historical structures have been restored to their former glories, the work was not fully completed. Either the money ran out or someone decided to make a quick buck and sent in the bulldozers.

There is a *lot* of traffic, and I change direction frequently in search of pockets of oxygen. I'm soon lost, but I don't care. I can consult my map later when it matters. *If* it matters.

While my feet wander, so do my thoughts. Half-remembered landmarks and street names stir memories of the walk that Claire and I enjoyed here.

I find myself standing outside San Agustin Church. A young American couple are taking selfies at the exact spot where Claire and I asked a local to snap our picture. I go inside the church, not because I am seized by any sudden religious fervor or sentimental impulse, but because it is one of only two Catholic buildings in the city that has air conditioning. I soak up the ambiance and the chilled wafts. Thank goodness the Resurrection Sunday festival is over, otherwise the place would be teeming with pious acolytes chanting Hail Marys and flagellating themselves when nobody was looking.

Once I've cooled down, I cross myself for the sake of form, and exit. An early lunch is in order.

I stumble across a cheap eatery which has a large awning over an outside area, and some standing fans. Situated in a cul de sac, it also offers a refuge from through traffic. *Good enough*.

I grab a seat, light a Marlboro, and order a cold drink and a plate of *palabok* – rice noodles, shrimp, minced pork and *chicharon*. Locals appear to make up the majority of the establishment's clientele, which I take as a good sign. I don't need gastroenteritis, not even as a diversion from the dull ache around my heart.

A skinny old man and a large woman are sitting a few tables away. He bears the same hangdog expression the Old Monk had when I saw him with his wife, and he is defeatedly gazing into space while his female companion addresses him in a stern voice. His eyes say, *Rescue me*.

That's family for you.

For the first time ever, I'm wishing I'd read my father's manuscript. In disregarding his wish for me to understand him, I've been spiting myself as well, spurning the opportunity to learn about my mother and her life in Malaya.

I contemplate my resentment at Edward Braddock's silence towards me. The apple hasn't fallen far from the tree. I never told him anything of my tribulations in England with Jim Fosse, even though he only lived a few miles away at the time. I deliberately kept him at arm's length during Claire's illness, and shared as little as possible with him of my years on Koh Samui.

When the Polzin affair is over, I resolve, one of the first things I will do is read his memoir.

However, at the moment, there is the pressing matter of deciding how I am going to spend the afternoon. I have finished my *palabok* and don't want another cigarette.

I toy with the idea of picking up a hooker and bedding her – though I wouldn't be undertaking this for the joy of erotic release. No, it would be more a case of being able to show myself as a recidivist for the purpose of sabotaging Da's proposal. If I turn up at the *Agency* drunk, stinking of whisky, and confess to backsliding into congress with Filipina whores, then I would no longer be considered suitable husband and stepfather material. But that is not going to fly because, right now, sex is the last thing on my mind. Well, not the *last* thing, but it's way down the list.

But all such musings are driven forcibly out of my head, because something happens.

Something unforeseen.

Because ...

Because, all at once, the world changes. Again. In an instant. A door slides back to reveal the opening into another world.

For, under the clouding sky of Intermuros, an apparition has appeared. I blink twice, but the apparition does not vanish. It is no mirage.

I should have expected as much, after all the happenings of recent weeks.

There it is.

There *he* is.

My spirit collection is complete.

The sixth ghost, my final visitation. The spectre who will direct me to an alternative future to the one revealed by Natalie: a future of violence and terror to vie with the one of family contentment.

For sure, he has changed since I last saw him. He's lost weight. His attire is smart, though he doesn't wear a business suit or carry a briefcase with a sticker of the US flag. But I'd know that swaggering gait anywhere.

He crosses the end of the alleyway and disappears behind a wall.

Reichenbach was correct. *Jim Fosse is still with us.*

Jim. Sodding. Fosse.

It takes me a few seconds to react. Then I drop some notes on the table and scurry after him.

He is walking at a moderate pace, oblivious to the perspiring Englishman trailing him at a safe distance. My heart has stopped niggling and started thudding. My vision has narrowed to a single imaginary target etched between his shoulder blades.

Where is he going? Home? Most ex patriates in this part of the Philippines – if I remember correctly – live in Quezon City, Makati or Taguig. But he could be headed anywhere. If he raises an arm and hails a taxi, I will lose him. However, there is an intent about his stride, and he pays no attention to the bikes and cars passing by him.

This dance of pursuit continues for a few minutes, during which time Fosse takes several turns, never looking back. He is confident here. *He knows his way around*, I conclude.

We leave Intramuros.

One final right turn and he enters a small apartment building. I run a professional eye over it: white, modern, five storeys, pricey. I give it a few seconds, then cautiously approach the main entrance. Through the glass doors, I can see the lobby. There is no reception desk: it is unmanned. Directly ahead of me are two lifts. The illuminated displays above them show that one lift is on the ground floor, the other lift is on the fourth. I watch these indicators for a minute: they don't change. Fosse must have gone to the fourth floor – there wasn't time for the lift to have stopped at another floor, in my estimation.

I try the main doors. They are locked shut. An electronic access pad is on the wall to the left and, above that, buzzer buttons – one for each apartment. Each apartment has the occupier's name on a card. The five apartments on the top floor have tenants named Enriquez, Peterson, Beltran, and Miller. One of the cards is blank.

No *Fosse*. But then, he's hardly going to be living under his own moniker. Like Buchanan, he is a phantom.

If he lives here, that is. He might be visiting someone. I swiftly dismiss that notion. He had a key card: this *must* be his lair.

I read the names on the cards again.

Enriquez and Beltran sound like Latinos of some sort. No, Jim couldn't pass himself off as Central or South American or Spanish. They're probably locals anyway. Then there are Peterson (Apartment 41) and Miller (Apartment 43): either could be him. Or he may be in Apartment 44, the one with the blank card. That would be Jim's style.

I snoop around. The building has no underground car park. A pity, since that might have been useful for gaining forced access, and a good deal less conspicuous than smashing in the front door. I deliberate whether to confront Fosse immediately, but decide against it.

I make a note of the name *Gaviola Apartments*, and of the road, which I mark on my map. Next, I go and find a bar.

Is my spotting Jim Fosse a case of karma giving me a dig in the ribs? Or is this serendipitous event more geared for the American?

I gaze at the bottle of beer and experience an abrupt drop in my energy levels. Perhaps I should have ordered tequila. My sense of control over recent events is draining away.

The easiest and quickest thing to do would be to email Jim's address to Reichenbach and leave it up to him what he did with the information. After all, James Fosse is not my problem, and I have other things to worry about. However, a half-formed notion is slowly fermenting in the sewage farm of my brain. After two more San Miguels, my embryonic idea has swelled and solidified like scum on the surface of a cesspool.

I pay for my drinks and head back to the *Manila Grand*. As I walk, a welcome sprinkling of rain dampens the city dust.

Once in my room, I fire up my laptop and discover a message from Orlov. Boy, it's all happening today! I wonder what's coming next. A meteor strike destroying all life on the planet? Buchanan being attacked by a tree? My father showing up to tell me his fatal stroke was an elaborate practical joke?

Calm, Braddock, calm. Settle down.

I read slowly through the tabulated words and numbers.

Hmmn.

When Orlov said we wouldn't receive much notice of the Polzins' schedule, he wasn't exaggerating.

Grigory is landing in Bangkok *today*, and will spend three nights at the *Indo-China International* while he conducts a series of meetings (details included). Next, he flies to Macau for two days, then Hong Kong for a brief stopover before returning to Moscow. Mikhail's timetable is even tighter. He lands in Phnom Penh this evening where he will check into the *Grand Khmer Garden*. He has two days of discussions with the family's Cambodian partners, then he will catch a flight back to the Russian capital via Ho Chi Minh City on Saturday morning. Therefore, at no point will the father and son be in the same place at the same time: this accords with the earlier intel.

I drum my fingers on the desk.

If they are going to be more-or-less simultaneous, the two assassinations will have to happen in Phnom Penh and Bangkok either tomorrow or Friday.

Will Buchanan be able to arrange weapons deliveries in Thailand and Cambodia in time? To organise the guns for tomorrow would seem to be a stretch. That would only leave us Friday. One day to get the jobs done. Otherwise, at least one of the Polzins will have to be killed in Moscow: an unappealing prospect.

Then there is the matter of the eureka moment I had this afternoon. Buchanan is not going to like it, I'm damn sure of that. He's going to take some persuading since he prefers everything organised and properly thought-out. Last-minute changes will be anathema to him: he's the cautious type.

Well, tough. Given the Polzins' itinerary, we don't have the luxury of time.

I check the media feeds for the latest situation on disturbances in Bangkok. The protest has fizzled out following Tuesday's arrests, and at noon today it was declared 'officially' over. For once, the authorities are taking a tolerant position, even arranging free transport for some protesters back to their provinces. *What a way to celebrate Songkran*.

Next, I trawl the Internet for any reports on happenings in Phnom Penh. It's quiet. Well, as quiet as it ever is. The only newsworthy event in Cambodia this month occurred on the third of April, when the Thai Army and the Cambodian Army had one of their periodic clashes at the disputed border near the Preah Vihear Temple. Four soldiers were killed, but the sabre-rattling on both sides has since ceased. Until the next time.

Finally, I go through Da's comprehensive notes on flights to the relevant destinations. We have a number of choices, so the travel part of our logistics should present no difficulties. Plus, as luck would have it, Da's recommended hotels in the two capitals are in close proximity to those selected by the Polzins.

The clock may be against us, but the Gods of Politics, Airlines and Convenient Places to Stay are on our side.

I drink three flat white coffees in the hotel lobby while I wait for Buchanan. At a quarter-to-five, he strolls in.

"Business go well?"

"Yes. All sorted." He scrutinises me. "You look excited."

"I'm having a caffeine rush. We've received a message. Let's go to my room."

I show him the schedule from Orlov and he frowns.

"Jesus. This is going to be a sprint."

"True. But today I think I may have found the 'edge' you wanted."

"Oh? And what's that?"

"Not so much 'what' as 'who'. I've seen someone here in Manila who may be able to help us."

"Help us?"

"Yes. An American whom I've come across several times in the past. It's like I'm haunted by the bastard, actually: in Leicester, in Bangkok, even on Samui. A dangerous chap. I know for certain that he's murdered people. His last established killing was in Bangkok, as it happens. So, he's familiar with the city. Useful, that."

Buchanan stares at me like I've lost my marbles.

"He's a psychopath," I add.

My companion controls himself with difficulty.

"And what is this paragon's name, may I ask?"

"Fosse."

Buchanan's eyebrows knit in puzzlement.

"*Fosse?* An American? And, you mentioned Leicester? That wouldn't be *James* Fosse, would it?"

"You know him? Bugger me, but it's a small world. How do *you* know him?"

He hesitates before replying.

"He paid me to kill his wife."

26

"A feast is made for laughter, and wine maketh merry:

but money answereth all things."

Ecclesiastes 10:19

They say you can judge a man by the company he keeps. If that's correct, I'm as good as condemned.

I've been frozen to the spot since Buchanan spoke.

"You killed Monique Fosse? The woman whose body was found in that Yorkshire quarry a few weeks back?"

"Yes."

"How many women have you shot?"

I expect him not to answer, but he holds up three fingers.

"Does Wayan know?"

"No. I offered to tell her everything, but she said she didn't want me to."

I have a million questions, but it's pointless asking them. The disclosure has unsettled me. But I knew what sort of man I was dealing with, I tell myself. Why *wouldn't* a paid assassin kill members of both sexes? *Because he's been brought up properly?* This doesn't alter anything. The ink has long dried on my devil's contract.

"Did you meet Jim Fosse in person?" I say.

"Yes. I don't like to meet clients as a general rule, but sometimes it's necessary."

"What do you make of him?"

He considers.

"Ruthless. Slippery. Egocentric. He didn't strike me as particularly brave. He was definitely nervous of me, scared even. Hardly the man to join our undertaking."

"You'd scare most people when you've got your executioner's face on. That doesn't mean anything."

"Even so –"

"Listen, I want to take Fosse with me to Bangkok. Grigory Polzin will have two bodyguards, and their boss may also be armed. Two against three is better odds than one against three. Jim can fire a gun, whatever his faults."

"What makes you think he won't fire the gun at you if he gets the chance?"

"Fosse only cares about three things: himself, excitement and money. I'll be offering him excitement *and* money. Sure, he's careful and cunning. But, like most sociopaths, he has a low boredom threshold, and is prone to act impulsively. He'll jump at the chance of the adrenaline rush. The cash will be the icing on the cake."

"You won't be able to control him, David."

"Maybe not, but I *can* manage him."

Buchanan remains skeptical.

"Our assignment is tricky enough without introducing a loose cannon like James Fosse into the equation. It could all go dreadfully wrong."

"Or dreadfully right."

He says over-patiently, "Tell me what you have in mind. I want to understand your reasoning *in detail. With justifications.* But I warn you in advance that I'm not going to be railroaded into anything stupid. I'm no fan of half-baked improvisation."

I tell him what I have in mind. *In detail. With justifications.*

When I have finished, Buchanan says, "Let me summarise. You're telling me that Fosse won't know anything about my part of the project. He won't be made aware that I'm going to Cambodia to dispatch Mikhail. He will only be informed about Grigory's assassination."

"Correct. No added risk for you, only for me. So far as Jim is concerned, this is simply the mission of a distressed father exacting revenge for his daughter's death. Nobody else is involved."

"Yeah, a *kamikaze* mission."

"So, I'm going around to Fosse's this evening to put the proposition to him. Do I have your immoral support before I leave?"

"You mean *moral* support."

"That too."

"Pah."

"Now, importantly, can your people get our weapons to Bangkok and Phnom Penh in time?"

"I expect so, though the express delivery is bound to cost more as they have us over a barrel."

"I'll reimburse you."

He snorts.

"Only if you live."

"If I don't, Da has custody of a big chunk of my money. Speak to her and she'll repay you whatever is necessary. She's been briefed on our project."

Buchanan reacts with horror.

"You've told your secretary? Jesus Christ, David. Nobody was supposed to –"

"She's *not* my secretary, she's my business partner," I correct him. "Keep your hair on. Da won't say a word. And, for your information, she loves me. In fact, she proposed to me on Monday."

"Are you always so surrounded by chaos? I'm astonished you've survived this long."

"I was born under a lucky star. Now, take out your phone and give instructions on the guns. And don't forget about the one for Jim."

He puts his head in his hands.

"I can't work like this."

"Suit yourself. But, whether or not you're up for it, I'm going to Bangkok to shoot Polzin."

"How will you do that if I refuse to provide you with any weaponry?"

"Hmmn. Good point."

A sigh of reluctant surrender from Buchanan.

"All right. Let's go with this moronic plan, David. It's your funeral. I sincerely hope it doesn't turn out to be mine too. One condition: you go and see Fosse tomorrow morning, not tonight."

"In case I change my mind after I've slept on it?"

"That might happen, yes."

"But Fosse might have flown the coup by tomorrow."

"He might. That's a chance you'll have to take. It's my final offer. Of course, if you have an alternative source for the pistols, then you can do whatever you like."

To emphasise the point, he pulls out his phone, looks at it, then returns it to his pocket.

"Up to you," he says.

I consult Da's flight notes while Buchanan reads over my shoulder.

"Flights and hotels, hmmn. Did your secretary – sorry, *business partner* – prepare this for you?" he says with heavy sarcasm.

I don't reply.

Buchanan studies the sheet, before announcing, "I'll catch the seven-thirty-five flight to Bangkok tomorrow morning, then it's a quick hop over to Phnom Penh. That will give me valuable time to recce. Not much, but some. Fortunately, I've already done some homework on our likely cities, but on its own it's nowhere near enough. There's no substitute for checking out the place in person. Luckily, I've been to Phnom Penh before, so it's not entirely foreign to me. And, now that we know where Mikhail is staying, and where his meetings are, I can focus on finding the right killing ground."

Killing ground. The words send a chill though me. This is really happening.

There are several flights to the Thai capital later in the day, not all of them direct. If we don't catch the Philippines Airlines departure at two twenty-five, it might be midnight before Fosse and I make it to our hotel. Plus, I need to do homework too, not to mention some rather hasty contingency planning. For the next two days, time will be at a premium.

"Very well," I say with bad grace. "I won't see Fosse until tomorrow morning. But you're making this dreadfully complicated."

"Or dreadfully simple," he replies, echoing my earlier riposte.

"Now, about hotels –"

"I'll make my own hotel arrangements, thank you. However, I have no objection to you following Da's written instructions, if you want. Just don't tell her anything else, David, OK?"

"OK."

"Good. Now, let me make some calls and I'll see you in the restaurant in an hour or so. I skipped lunch so I'm hungry. Write down the details of Mikhail's schedule and meetings for me, would you? Thanks."

He leaves.

As requested, I transcribe Mikhail's information onto the hotel notepad, and add Da's suggested hotel in the Cambodian capital to piss off my companion. Then I make some calls myself.

Vlad is duly updated on my alibi requirements. No names are mentioned, and I have to rephrase several sections of my message so as to lodge in his thick skull what it is that I'm trying to convey to him. Perhaps his English is not so improved as I thought. As a coded conversation, it is not of the first order but, finally, he gets it. I'm grateful he's not involved in the actual assassinations: I'd have to use cue cards. The Thai fixer is sorting him out on the Tim Jennings complication. No incarceration for the big Russian. He'll soon be home looking after mama.

Katie and Wayan are having a right royal time in Singapore. They've done a sightseeing tour, and Wayan has bought some new clothes – we'll make an entitled Westerner of her yet. Later, they're going to the Night Safari.

"What are you and Robert up to?"

"We spent most of today in Intramuros doing touristy things and having a few beers. Dinner in half-an-hour. It's all good, never fear."

"I'm so glad you're rubbing along, Dad." She sounds relieved. "Wayan will be pleased too."

"Tomorrow, we're off to Corregidor Island," I say, reminding myself that Buchanan and I need to continue to keep our stories aligned, "so you might not hear from us."

"No problem, so long as you've having fun."

Oh, we're having fun all right. If it was any more fun, we'd be laughing ourselves to death.

Da is out on surveillance when I ring her.

"Is everything OK, David?"

"Everything is dandy. I'm just calling to tell you that I'm flying to Bangkok tomorrow, and that I'll use the hotel you recommended. Don't be concerned if I don't phone. It's going to be a busy day."

"Will there be two of you going to Bangkok?"

"Yes."

She can assume my travelling companion is Buchanan. That way, she won't be any more uneasy than she is already.

"And will Eric Snow be in Bangkok?"

By this, I take it that Da wants to know whether I'll be using my fake passport at the hotel.

"Yes."

"Ah, right."

"Sorry, Da, I have to go. I'm meeting someone for dinner. We'll talk again soon."

I am about to cut the line when she says, "By the way, David ..."

She pauses.

"Yes?"

"I enjoyed that kiss."

A response is required, so I say, "Me too."

Finally, I speak to Nang.

"If all goes well, I should be in London at the weekend, so I'll make Natalie's funeral. A soon as I've confirmed my flight, I'll be in touch."

"Right." Her relief is evident. "I'll inform Laurette that your doctor has OK'd you to fly from Saturday."

"Can I talk to Jenny?"

"She's still at school, David. Haven't you figured out how time differences work yet?"

Buchanan wolfs down his dinner in the hotel's happily-quiet restaurant. Now that we're no longer waiting on anyone's actions and matters are back in our hands, he's become noticeably energised. *In the zone*, as it were. He has the air of a man gagging to pull a trigger.

After our plates and coffee cups have been removed, Buchanan insists on going through the whole plan again and Fosse's part in it. I give him

Mikhail's schedule, and he slips me a piece of paper in return. On it is written a Thai cell number and the words *LEK*, GATES and *SILK SARONGS*.

"'Lek' is your contact for the weapons," he explains. "Ring him when you arrive in Bangkok. 'Gates' is your name. When you speak to him, mention that you are in town to collect a package of silk sarongs. Continue from there. The guns, suppressors and ammunition will be available for you on Friday morning. I've just done the money transfers online, so you won't have to give your delivery man any cash. Pick a sensible place to rendezvous with him, will you?"

"Got it."

"After tonight, you and I will be in communications blackout with everybody, including with each other – except for essential code triggers. When I reach Phnom Penh, I'll buy a Cambodian SIM card. I'll message you straightaway so you have my temporary number. Once one of us is in a position to act on their target in the next one-to-two hours, that person should send the other one a message: a single *X*."

"Like a kiss?"

"Yes. If the receiver is able to act on *their* target in the same timescale, they send back an *X*. For every extra hour the receiver thinks he will need over that, he should reply with an extra *X*. So, for instance, if you reply with three *X*s, I will assume you could need up to four hours. Then we'll adjust our plans as best we can. This can't be an exact synchronisation, that's not practical, but we *do* want the shootings to be as close together as possible."

"Agreed. It would not be helpful, for instance, if Mikhail's bodyguard were to ring Grigory to tell him his son's been shot."

"Or vice versa."

"We have to kill the bodyguards too, don't we? To avoid complications."

"Ideally, yes," he says carefully.

"Right."

"If the sender doesn't hear back from the receiver within a few minutes of sending their message, the sender should assume the receiver is either dead or otherwise unable to respond, and act accordingly. And if, for whatever reason, one of us has to abort the mission, that person sends an *A*. OK?"

"OK. But neither of us will be sending an *A*."

"Let's hope, eh? Once the deeds are done, we'll meet up back on Samui."

"Good. That's it, then."

"Not quite. There's something else I have to talk to you about."

"Oh? What's that?"

He shifts uneasily in his seat.

"Do you mind if I order a cognac first?"

"Make it two."

"Aren't you off spirits?"

"One won't hurt."

He is silent until our brandy glasses show up.

Then, after a deep breath, he says, "My real name is Ross Gallagher."

When I make no comment, my dinner companion asks, "Does that name mean anything to you?"

"No. Should it?"

He shrugs.

"I thought it might. You see, you are acquainted with my half-sister Adele Darrow, now Adele Fletcher. You and Wayan were at her and Simon's wedding in London last November."

A memory stirs.

"*You* are the black sheep brother? The one Adele had the falling-out with, whom she forbade to attend her wedding? That was *you*?"

"Yes. That was me. Did she tell you why there was a falling-out?"

"No."

"It was because she discovered that I was partly responsible for the kidnapping of Rosie Fletcher in Bangkok. Simon's sister. Adele's sister-in-law-to-be. You see, I was the one who set her up as a drug mule while I was working for the Sangukhon crime family. Adele hasn't spoken a word to me since."

I point a finger at him.

"You were using the name Lauchlan Andrews then, weren't you? I tried to track you down in connection with Rosie's disappearance, but you'd vanished."

"I know," he says with a sad grin. "I've known about you for a long time. *The Samui Detective*."

"So, you *are* Scottish?"

"I am."

"And you're also the hired gun that Interpol is after, aren't you? The elusive and infamous *Captain Nemo*."

"As to that," he replies, "I genuinely have no idea what name the international plods have for me."

I study him for a few seconds.

"Why are you telling me this now, Robert? I mean, *Ross*."

He finishes his brandy and fiddles with the glass.

"I'm in Manila to put my affairs in order, David, in case something happens to me while we're hunting the Polzins. Today, I've organised a number of bank transfers and arranged for my lawyer to amend my will. Many of my liquid assets are now in accounts of Ross Gallagher because he – or rather *I* – is or am the only person who can legally make bequests. It's all dandy being a fugitive when you're alive, but once you're dead it's different. Phantoms can't leave money to people. And in my will, I've left all I own to Wayan. I want to make sure she is looked after."

"All very commendable, but what has this to do with me?"

"I've named Wayan, Katie and you as my executors."

"But Katie is officially dead, and presumably Wayan is unaware of all this."

"Depending how the next couple of days go, Katie may find herself officially alive again. That is one of the reasons we're doing what we're doing, isn't it? As for Wayan, I've left a letter with my lawyer addressed to her which explains everything. If the lawyer hasn't heard from me in two weeks, he is to send it to her."

He hands me a card.

"This is the lawyer. He's English, but he works out of Madrid. If I don't make it out of Cambodia, I want you to contact him."

"It's more likely that I won't make it."

"Well," he replies, "that's true. But you never can tell."

The confidence he was displaying at the start of our meal has evaporated. He suddenly looks disconcertingly vulnerable. *That's great.* I team up with a professional assassin and he chooses now to get sentimental and sappy.

I study the card for a moment.

"But why me an executor?" I ask.

"In case you hadn't noticed, David, I don't have a great number of people around me I can trust. You're reckless, cynical and rather arrogant at times, but I *do* trust you. I realise we're not friends and probably never will be, but you'll do the right thing by Wayan. You are a decent man."

"Yeah, so folks keep telling me," I mumble.

Ross Gallagher leans back in his chair and spreads his arms wide.

"And now you know me. I have removed the mask of Nemo. *Here you may see the tyrant.*"

"That sounds like a quotation from Shakespeare."

"It is. Macbeth. Just before he dies."

"I hope there aren't too many of the wrong sorts of trees in Phnom Penh, Ross."

"Me too, David. Me too."

The man I now call Ross Gallagher has gone back to his room to refresh his memory on Phnom Penh, and to scrutinise certain areas of the city from satellite maps and drone footage. He will be taking virtual walks through the streets of the Cambodian capital through ground-level photography, reviewing weather forecasts, and gathering all the information he can on Mikhail's hotel and its environs. He may have a new name, but the anally-retentive nature of the beast remains the same: consider the options, assess the variable factors, build in contingencies. *Fail to plan, plan to fail.*

I can understand how he is frustrated working with me. I'm more of a seat-of-the-pants guy, though whether spontaneity has any useful place in the art of assassination is a moot point. I guess we'll find out.

In deference to the advice of the Scottish hit man, I *have* knuckled down on the Internet and done *some* research for my own assignment in Bangkok. But my watch tells me it's nearly ten-thirty and I've had enough, so I switch off my laptop.

I have a promise to break.

I'm off to see Jim Fosse. *Now.* Sod the notion of waiting until morning. I'm not going to change my mind about involving the American in the project, so I may as well get on with it.

I grab a towel from my bathroom and make my way to the *Manila Grand*'s gym, where a young Western man is grunting his way through some heavy lifts. He wears a bandana, and his faded vest and shorts suggest he is a dedicated gym rat. The only other person in the room is a bird-boned Asian lady on a treadmill.

I pretend I am inspecting the facilities, and when I am sure nobody is watching me, I wrap one of the ten-pound hand weights in my towel, and exit. If I have to smash my way into Jim's building, or discourage any night-muggers who might be sizing me up as a target, having an easily-swingable lump of metal with me might prove useful.

Outside the entrance to the hotel, I ignore the doorman's puzzled glance at my towel-wrapped package, and get into a taxi.

My journey only takes a few minutes, and the driver drops me off at the end of the American psycho's road. This puts me about a hundred yards from Fosse's apartment building. The street is fairly quiet and well-lit, so the short walk presents no obvious dangers – although it's unwise to let down one's guard anywhere in Manila after dark.

Only two problems present themselves: gaining access to the building, and finding out which of the three apartments on the fourth floor is Jim's.

As to the first problem, I rely on Hollywood movies for the solution. Solution one: buzz one of the lower floor flats and tell them I'm an upper-floor tenant who has forgotten his key card, and hope that the occupant I speak to is credulous and unafraid of intruders. Solution two: follow someone into the building, grin pleasantly and hope they don't object. Solution three: bust in a door or window and keep my fingers crossed that nobody calls the police.

As to the second problem ... well, let's not worry about that now.

Because, here I am, standing on the pavement outside the apartment block, looking shifty and suddenly appreciating why a morning visit here would have been much more sensible. What tenant is going to be stupid enough to allow a complete stranger into their building at this time of night?

Moreover, there are hardly any lights showing through the various windows. Most of the occupants are either in bed or out. And there are *no lights at all* on the fourth floor.

So, it's going to have to be a break-in, I suspect. But I can't even force an entry straightaway. Several cars are cruising by, and two pedestrians have appeared while I've been dithering. Fortunately the walkers are a middle-aged couple, not street punks in hoodies.

I slowly ascend the four entrance steps to the glass doors. To make myself appear less suspicious, I prop my back against the brickwork of the doorway, light a cigarette, and pretend to be talking on my cell phone.

I feel like a right dick. No wonder Ross Gallagher despairs of me. Suppose a passing police car decides to stop and ask what I'm up to? What are they going to make of the ten-pound weight I'm carrying? I really should have thought this through.

I've almost finished my cigarette, and am contemplating finding a cab to return me to my hotel, when the God of Idiots Who Really Don't Think Things Through intervenes.

A taxi pulls up, and out gets Jim Fosse. A tiny Filipino girl with a sprayed-on mini-dress climbs out after him.

Fosse hasn't seen me. He's talking to the driver through the open car window and handing him some bank notes.

I flick away my cigarette butt and step forward.

"Hello, Jim," I say.

Fosse turns and starts at the sight of me. I pull the hand weight out of the towel and flex it up and down casually.

"Can you spare me a few minutes?"

The American blinks several times, then bundles the girl back into the taxi, throws some money at her, and slams the door shut. He passes the taxi driver some more notes, and tells him to take the girl back to where he picked them up. The cab drives off. The street is suddenly deserted.

Fosse stands unmoving on the pavement, weighing me up. I rewrap my metal gym friend, and say casually, "I brought this so I could do a spot of exercise while I was waiting for you. Nothing more sinister than that, I assure you."

The unblinking eye of a CCTV camera watches us cross the lobby and enter one of the lifts. I press the button for the top floor, and Jim gives me a sideways glance.

As we ascend, I ask, "So which one of the tenants are you, Peterson or Miller? Or are you the mysterious nobody in Apartment 44?"

"Miller," he replies. "And Apartment 44 is empty."

"Ah. Good name, Miller. Not the sort of name to attract attention."

"How did you find me?"

"I'm a private detective, remember?"

A bell pings and the lift doors open. We step into the hallway and Jim lets us into his flat.

The lounge and kitchen are of an open-plan design, tastefully coloured in creams and greys. The floor is wood, and every surface is spotless and devoid of clutter. The furniture is modern; both expensive and functional. A large pastoral print hangs on the wall. *It's OCD Central.*

"Nice place, Jim. Two bedrooms?"

"Yes."

"Roomy."

Fosse hangs his keys on a hook and moves into the kitchen area.

"Can I offer you a drink?"

"No, thank you, Jim. The last time I had a drink at your place in England, it turned out to be rather ... complicated."

He pours himself a whisky.

"So, you haven't forgiven me for that yet?"

"No."

"And how about that little mix-up in Thailand?"

"Also, no."

"Ah."

"The British police found your wife Monique's body a few weeks back."

"Yes." He taps the side of his head. "I believe I did read something about that. Poor Monique. Oh, by the way, David, while we're on the subject of corpses, thank you for identifying my body in Bangkok. That was most helpful."

"That's me to a tee. Anything for an old friend."

"Shall we sit down?"

I ease onto the sofa, and place the gym weight within easy reach, just in case I have to bash his brains out.

Fosse slides into the armchair opposite and positions a coaster on the low coffee table. He sets his glass precisely on the coaster.

"You're still a stickler for order and tidiness, I see, Jim."

"*Be regular and orderly in your life, so that you may be violent and original in your work.* My favourite Flaubert quote."

"*Never trust a man who quotes Flaubert: he's bound to be an asshole.* My favourite David Braddock quote."

"Touché." His smile gets nowhere near his eyes.

"Incidentally, I'm sorry to interrupt your romantic evening. Though your girlfriend probably has to be up early for school tomorrow anyway."

"There'll be other evenings."

He takes a sip of whisky and settles back in his chair. He's a cool bastard. Ice-bloody-cool.

"So, what are you doing here, David?"

"It's late, so I'll skip the small talk."

"That would be much appreciated."

"I have a proposition for you."

"*A proposition?* How intriguing."

"I want you to help me kill someone."

Fosse stares at me for a moment, then he throws back his head and laughs.

"How delicious. That's quite an about-turn for you, David. I recall when I put a similar proposal to you ten years ago, you rejected it out of hand."

"A lot has happened since then."

"It certainly has. Tell me, do you expect me to participate in the actual killing, or will I merely be playing a supporting role?"

"The person concerned travels with two bodyguards. I want you to shoot one, and I'll look after the other and the main target."

"*Shoot?* Not strangle or garotte or otherwise dispatch in a more imaginative fashion?"

"No, shoot. You've handled a Glock before, right?"

"On a number of occasions."

"Then, it should be easy for you."

"No murder is *easy*, David. It's always fun, but it's never easy. And carrying out the deed comes with a sizeable personal risk."

"I'll compensate you for that. I'm not expecting you to do it for nothing. I'll pay you one hundred thousand US if you help me."

He whistles.

"Plus expenses?"

"Yes. And I'll supply the weapons."

"Payment in advance?"

"Don't push it. You get your money after the job is done."

Fosse swirls the whisky while he ponders.

Eventually, he says, "You *do* have a proper plan, David, don't you? I wouldn't want to find myself involved in a shambolic shoot-out like in the final scene of some Quentin Tarantino epic."

"Yes, I do. We're not going to be riding into town, guns blazing and hoping for the best. Give me *some* credit. I intend to survive this encounter, and to walk away without a blemish on my name. You see, I enjoy being alive, Jim, and I *wouldn't* enjoy prison. So those two preferences have been factored in."

He is still swirling his whisky.

"What do you say?"

"I say I'm going to require more information than that."

"Like what?"

"Your poet Kipling said he kept six honest serving men: What and Why and When and How and Where and Who. I need you to tell me everything."

"Which I will, when the time is right. What, When, How and Where are for later. For now, you'll have to make do with Who and Why."

"Well, that sounds like a good start."

"I think I will have that drink now."

"Whisky?"

"Yeah. On the rocks."

When he returns, he positions my glass on a coaster.

"I'm all ears," he prompts.

The whisky burns my throat, and I set down the glass.

"The target is Grigory Polzin."

Fosse's eyebrows spring up.

"The Russian oligarch?"

"The same. Do you know him?"

"I've *heard* of him. A powerful individual. Not a man whom it would be easy to get close to, I'd imagine. Why do you want him dead?"

"He ordered the killing of my daughter Katie."

A lightbulb goes on in Fosse's head.

"Ah, yes. I vaguely recall her trial. Last year, wasn't it? It made the international news. She was acquitted of murdering her husband – Polzin's son. But I didn't realise she had been killed."

"Officially, she 'disappeared'. No body has been found. But I know she is dead, and who is responsible for it."

A normal person would offer their condolences at this point. But Jim Fosse is not a normal person.

"Excellent, David. That puts my mind at rest. I was concerned that this was some kind of set-up, but now I understand. It's *revenge*, right? Ah, yes, I can identify with the revenge motive. And you were always the devoted family man, so that explains why you've turned. It's a family thing. A *vendetta*. Great. Perfect."

"I'm so pleased I've put your mind at rest."

The comment goes over his head.

"I've never been into all that sentimental family nonsense myself, as you are aware, but I can now appreciate why someone like you would be sitting here with someone like me discussing what we're discussing."

He sounds cheerful, like he's solved a difficult crossword puzzle. For an instant, I'm tempted to hit him repeatedly with the gym weight until his head is a bloody pulp. But I don't.

Instead, I say, "I'm here because you're the only psychopath I know."

He nods.

"So, what happens next?"

"Are you 'in'?"

"I am," he replies enthusiastically. "I wouldn't miss this adventure for all the world, even if it is paying a measly one hundred thousand."

"Hardly measly."

"To tell you the truth, I've been terribly *bored* recently. You wouldn't believe how long it is since I've killed anyone, so your timing couldn't be better." He wags a finger at me. "You *are* going to have to disclose the details of your plan to me, but I'll be patient. I do, though, reserve the right to bail on you if your scheme is too crackpot. Stimulation is one thing, but I enjoy being alive too."

"Right."

"So, what now?"

"You pack."

"*Pack?*"

"Yes. We're flying out of Manila tomorrow afternoon."

"Where are we going?"

"You'll see from your boarding pass. But you won't need any warm clothes."

"How long will we be away for?"

"Assume a week. I need to know what name you'll be travelling under, your passport number and date of birth, so I can make your flight reservation."

"This *is* exciting. Joseph Miller, Canadian, born June 1, 1962. I'll get the number for you in a minute."

The bastard actually claps his hands in glee.

"I'll collect you here at eleven tomorrow morning, Jim, and we'll travel to the airport together. Be ready."

Fosse's tone becomes sober.

"Out of interest, David, tell me something. What would you have done if I'd said I wasn't interested in your proposition? Clubbed me to death with that lump of metal?"

"No. This was for street protection and for breaking in, if necessary. If you had turned me down, I suppose I could have called your old enemy

Reichenbach and told him where you are, or informed the authorities about you. But I doubt I'd have done either of those things. I'd most likely have just walked away. Your paying for your crimes is not high on my list of priorities. I have an oligarch to kill."

"I am proud of you, David Braddock," he says. "I admire a man with resolve. Especially when it involves homicide. Let me find you that passport number."

Back at the hotel, I return the borrowed weight to the gym.

Because I'm like that.

A decent man.

27

"Vengeance is a delicious fruit, which must be allowed to ripen in order that it may be fully enjoyed."

Émile Gaboriau, File No. 113

Considering that I'm in cahoots with a professional assassin, and that I have, as of yesterday evening, augmented our team with an unprincipled, murdering psychopath, my sleep last night was remarkably unbroken.

However, while my brain is clear, my body is acting up. My chest feels like some internal parasite with sharp teeth is trying to chew its way out. There is a slight numbness in my left arm which stretching and flexing has only partially dispelled. The tremor in my hands is back too. I swallow a couple of strong painkillers, which I ill-advisedly wash down with a miniature whisky from my room's mini-bar. This, in turn, makes me giddy for a few minutes.

Shit. This is no time to fall apart. Not when my goal is so teasingly close.

I have a long shower, and some of my physical ailments tone down a notch. Perhaps food and coffee will help. Today, I'm breakfasting alone as Ross is already on his early flight.

Before I enter the restaurant, I have a quiet chat with the concierge and explain that I require two tickets to Bangkok on the Philippines Airlines afternoon flight and that I want to pay for them in cash. He has a hurried conversation with a colleague, taps into a computer for a couple of minutes, then announces in a whisper that he can assist, though the transaction cannot go through the 'official' hotel channels. We go into a back office where I give him the relevant passport details and hand over the appropriate number of bank notes, slipping him a hundred US for his trouble.

"Are you taking breakfast with us this morning, Mr. Braddock?"

"I am."

"This will all be sorted out for you while you are in our restaurant, sir. Please come and see me after you've finished."

"Perfect. And I'll be checking out around ten-thirty. Can you arrange a car to take me to the airport?"

"It shall be done, Mr. Braddock," he says, beaming at me. "I do hope that you have enjoyed your time with us."

Before I leave the hotel, I empty my room safe and go through the contents of my suitcase.

Clothes, toiletries bag, cigarettes, rope, tape, plastic cable clips, towel, polythene sheeting, gloves.

Ready, Player One.

Jim Fosse and I are sitting in the Philippines Airlines business lounge at Manila Airport. We are half-heartedly munching nibbles from the buffet and drinking copious amounts of water.

The American is in a reflective mood. He is examining his boarding card as if it contains the encrypted secrets of the cosmos.

"We're going to Bangkok," he says in a flat voice.

"Apparently we are."

"Are we flying on somewhere else later?"

"No."

"So, we'll be *staying* in Bangkok?"

"Yes."

"And doing the job in Bangkok?"

"Yes."

"If you continue giving me one-word answers, David, I'm going to be asking you a lot of questions."

"Can we talk about this later?"

"*When* later exactly?"

"After we've checked into our hotel. Then we can talk for as long as you like. Within reason, that is," I add. "I forget you are American."

"It had better be a good hotel," he grumbles.

I open my laptop, go online, and plough through the Thai news sites. The capital remains peaceful.

Fosse picks up my Panama hat and inspects it.

"Do you wear this everywhere you go?" he asks.

"Pretty much. Why?"

"It makes you stand out. You should think about not wearing it."

My hands are still trembling.

I hope Fosse hasn't noticed.

When our flight's boarding is announced, I am about to switch off my cell phone when I notice I have a message: a single letter *Y*. I save the sender's number to my contacts under the name *Nemo*.

The Cambodia end of the operation is rolling.

The receptionist at the *Bangkok Oasis*, the hotel recommended by Da, has a hint of ladyboy about him. His name badge reads *Toi*, which means 'tiny' in Thai. Once the sun has gone down, I suspect, his form of address might be more exotic.

Toi gives the front pages of our passports – that is to say the passports of Eric Snow and Joseph Miller – a cursory inspection, then sets them down on the desk and switches his attention to his keyboard. That's a relief. If he'd bothered to check further and seen that Eric Snow's passport has no Thailand entry stamp, it could have been awkward.

After consulting his screen, he looks up and says, "We do have two Executive Rooms available, sir. Our last two. They are connecting rooms. Is that all right for you?"

"Connecting rooms is perfect. Joseph and I are virtually married anyway. And I'd like to pay in cash. In advance."

Toi throws Jim a sly glance.

"I understand completely, sir. That's no problem here. This is Thailand."

Discreet. Da's research was sound. If the rooms are as welcoming as the lobby, we'll be fine. Plus, we're only a stone's throw from the *Indo-China International*, the place where Polzin is staying.

I have fond memories of the *Indo-China*. That was where, four years ago, Kat Charoenkul and I indulged in some really filthy, disgusting sex and she ...

My inappropriate reminiscences are interrupted by Jim tapping me on the shoulder.

"Was it entirely necessary for you give the impression that we're gay?" he hisses in my ear.

"You should be more comfortable with your sexuality, my friend," I reply.

Toi hands us our key cards and winks at me.

"Come on, Joseph, let's go upstairs. I can't wait to try out the beds."

My bedroom is large and more than satisfactory. I down one of the complimentary bottles of water as I'm running a slight temperature. Otherwise, I feel OK-*ish*. No alcohol this evening, I promise myself, not even beer. I have smoked a few cigarettes today so far. Maybe another Marlboro or two might steady my hands, though the shaking is not as pronounced as it was earlier.

First things first.

I call the number Ross gave me, and am answered with an *Uh.*

"Is that *Khun* Lek?"

Another *Uh.*

"Do you speak English?"

"Yeah."

"This is Mr. Gates. I am in Bangkok to collect some silk sarongs."

"Sarongs?" His brain obviously takes some time to warm up. Assuming he has a brain.

"A *package* of silk sarongs."

"Ah." He gets it. "OK, OK."

"Can you deliver today?"

"No, no. Tomorrow. Morning."

"Early?"

"What?"

I give up on English and tell him in Thai to meet me at a particular stall at the Saphan Taksin BTS Station at seven-thirty, and that I'll be wearing a white hat. I have no idea what the Thai is for 'Panama', so 'white hat' will have to do.

"OK."

I ring off.

I have barely opened my suitcase to unpack when Jim knocks on the connecting door. I open the lock on my side and he steps in.

"Hey, your room is bigger than mine," is his first observation.

His gaze falls on my open suitcase.

"*Rope?*" he says. "What do we need rope for? And is that a plastic sheet?"

"Forget about that for now."

"You booked us into this dump for four nights. Does that mean we're not doing Polzin until Sunday or Monday? And, if so, what was the goddam rush to leave Manila today?"

"The four nights is a contingency. God willing, we're shooting Polzin tomorrow."

"Tomorrow?"

"Yup."

"What's the rush?"

"He's not in town for long."

"You have a copy of his schedule? You know where he's staying?"

"Yes, and yes."

"How did you acquire that information?"

"You ask too many questions."

"But he's already here in Bangkok?"

"He is."

"So why don't we kill him tonight at his hotel?"

I treat him to an old-fashioned look.

"Blood and viscera splattered all over his hotel room? Bangs in a confined space and lots of potential witnesses, not to mention CCTV footage? Even with silencers fitted, guns are not exactly silent. No, no, no. Too messy and too risky. Besides, I thought you were keen to avoid being an actor in a shoot-em-up movie. No, what I have in mind is a more subtle ambush, one where it is easier for us to escape the crime scene undetected."

"Well, that gives me *some* comfort. Still –"

"Anyway," I interrupt, "we can't do the job tonight, even if we wanted to. I don't have our guns yet. Plus, I have some final legwork on the ground to do, double-checking to ensure all goes smoothly."

Fosse scratches the back of his head and frowns.

"When do we get the guns?"

"In the morning."

"Cutting it a bit fine, David, aren't you?"

"I prefer to think of it as employing clockwork precision. You're a businessman, Jim. You should appreciate the workings of a just-in-time system."

"Huh. As long as it's not a just-too-late system."

"Quite."

"So, you're going to share Polzin's schedule with me now, and your cunning plans?"

"Tomorrow morning."

He huffs.

"Why all this cloak-and-dagger stuff, David? Why does everything have to be so last minute?"

"It only appears hasty from your perspective. I've been sweating over this for *months*." I give a shrug. "Anyway, this is how I work. So, as one control freak to another, I say, *Suck it up, bro'*. I'm the boss, and this is my party."

"I could decide to walk away, you realise."

"You won't. This is probably the most exciting thing to happen to you for months. And, there is the little matter of that one hundred grand to consider. For only a few minutes of your time. You can be back in Manila at the weekend having sex with your pubescent girlfriend. Sounds like a great deal to me. All that is required is a little patience on your part."

"You're *enjoying* keeping me in the dark, aren't you?"

"A man has to get his kicks where he can."

Fosse taps his fingers together and sucks his lips.

"All right," he says at last. "We'll do it your way. What time are we going out to visit these locations?"

"*We* aren't going out. *I* am. And I won't be back for hours. In fact, it's highly unlikely I'll be back until morning – after I've picked up the guns. So, we'll meet for breakfast in the restaurant at eight-thirty."

"You're staying out *all night*?"

"Yes. So, don't bother knocking on my door. I won't be in."

Frustration flickers across the American's face.

"Well, I'm feeling rather neglected, David. What am I supposed to do for the rest of the day?"

"Now, let me see: a single man on his own in Bangkok. I'm sure you'll come up with something, or something will come up."

He points at my suitcase.

"At least tell me what the rope is for."

"No."

"Why not?"

"*All good things come to those who wait.* Proverbs are wondrous things, don't you agree?"

"No," he says bad-temperedly, "proverbs are for sheep."

"*Baa.*"

I change my clothes, pick up a city map in the lobby, and hire a taxi. I tell the driver to leave the meter running while I explore a couple of localities and satisfy myself that, should these last vignettes of research prove necessary, I am fully prepared. This takes a few hours, and my fare is enormous. A happy taxi driver drops me outside a low-budget hotel close to Saphan Taksin BTS Station. I have noticed no soldiers on the streets, and police activity seems to be back to business-as-usual.

It is tempting to validate Grigory Polzin's presence at the *Indo-China International*, but I can't risk being seen and recognised. I have to trust Orlov's intel.

There's a lot being taken on trust.

I have no intention of returning to the *Bangkok Oasis* tonight, since I want to keep Fosse off-balance for as long as possible. Plus, I need to be somewhere close to the BTS station for my morning rendezvous with the dull-witted Lek. This place – the *Happy Tourist* – will suffice to keep me off the poorly-illuminated street. It's within easy walking distance of the river, and the desk staff will be untroubled letting a room to a man carrying no luggage, only a plastic bag containing basic toiletries from a *Family Mart*. I only hope I don't get a noisy neighbour because the walls are sure to be thin.

I pay for a room, and suffer the squeaking lift to the third floor. Once I've got the key to work in the antique lock of my bedroom door, I drop onto the lumpy bed, absorb my depressing surroundings, and switch on the tiny TV.

After a few minutes of channel-hopping, I conclude there is nothing worth watching.

How I would like to call someone – anyone – but I can't.

Radio silence, as Ross counselled.

I am alone. There is no one I can talk to, not even Claire.

It is eleven-twenty.

An abyss fills my vision. There is no hint of white light at the end of the tunnel.

The sound of the city fades away.

I am crossing the event horizon of the black hole, becoming human spaghetti.

The singularity approaches.

EVERYONE DIES

Dawn.

06:04.

The sky holds promise of a sunny day.

I rise from the uncomfortable bed. A gecko scurries across the wall.

My body is stiff. I ache everywhere.

My hands are steady, but I have a sack of concrete lodged in my chest. I cough up some phlegm but happily no blood.

The bathroom mirror confirms that I look like shit.

A disposable razor removes the stubble from my chin, but it leaves my face red and blotchy. I scrub my teeth, and stand under a sputtering, lukewarm shower for ten minutes.

I consult the mirror again. *A trifle better*. My eyes are not so red.

My key is duly returned to a dozing Thai at reception, and I step outside to smoke a Marlboro. If the street wasn't particularly appealing last night, in the rosy glow of early morning, it is gaggingly grotty. The walls and shuttered frontages opposite are covered in graffiti, and the unmistakable smell of human piss assails my nostrils. Refuse bags spill onto the pavement, gnawed open by feral animals or particularly hungry beggars. To round things off, my cigarette tastes foul, and does nothing to relieve the constriction in my chest. An ancient and barely roadworthy *tuk-tuk* pootles by, its driver more interested in sleep than in customers.

What an uplifting way to begin what could be my last day on Earth.

Ah, Bangkok, *mon amour*.

My watch informs me it is twenty minutes to seven. There are still fifty minutes until my appointment.

I buy a takeaway cup of instant coffee from a convenience store. It's vile – like drinking scalding-hot diarrhea strained through a sweaty sock – but it dispels the last remnants of my slumber as I amble towards the river.

The city is stirring, coming to life. Bangkok is never completely unconscious, but between the clubs closing and the start of the normal working day, there is the air of a shift change, like the capital is taking a breath before plunging back into vibrancy.

At Sathon Pier, worker bees buzz around in slow motion, their faces blank or downcast. Ferries' engines throb impatiently. The Chao Phraya River sloshes against the pier's cement and wood posts, as it churns and heaves its way towards the distant Gulf of Thailand. I lean against a railing and take out a Marlboro. But it is a habit reflex. I don't want one, so I put it back in the packet.

At seven twenty-five, I take the short walk to the BTS Station, where I collect a sturdy bag from a lymphatic half-wit, to whom I give a thousand Baht for his trouble. The bag contains what must be the heaviest and most lethal sarongs ever made.

I unpack my shopping in my bedroom at the *Bangkok Oasis*.

Wrapped in cheap sarongs and paper are two nine millimetre Glocks, two loaded magazines, two suppressors, and two shoulder holsters. I inspect the handguns, and insert a magazine and suppressor into each one. The balance of the weapon feels significantly different with the suppressor added. Clumsier, awkward even.

I lock the weapons and holsters in the safe, and stuff the packaging in the trash bin. Next follows a *proper* shower and shave, and some fresh clothes. As I leave the room, I hang the 'Do Not Disturb' sign on the door.

Time for breakfast.

Fosse is decidedly ill-tempered over his Full American and coffee.

"I assume you didn't come back last night," he says.

"Nope. But don't worry. Everything is in order."

"I do worry. All this –"

"Let me grab something to eat first."

Jim fumes silently while I help myself to some yoghurt, toast and fruit juice. In truth, I have no appetite, but I need to line my stomach with something.

When his patience is exhausted, he says, "So. Talk to me, David."

I push away my plate.

"All right. I'll meet you upstairs in a few minutes and we'll go through it all in detail. I just need to have a dump first."

"At last," he exclaims. "OK, have your dump, the rest rooms are over there. I'll see you presently."

He rises and strides purposefully to the lifts. The swagger in his stride is back, if indeed it ever left.

I lock myself in a toilet cubicle and pull out my cell phone.

It's ten minutes to nine.

Decision point. There has been no message from Ross, so I'm going to send him one. How many *X*s to send though? One or two?

I run through the memorised schedule for the Polzins. Grigory has his first meeting at eleven o'clock at the *Shangri-La Hotel* – that's close by, equidistant from the *Oasis* and the *Indo-China*. Mikhail's first appointment of the day in Phnom Penh is at ten-thirty. The location for this is also close to his hotel.

I message a single *X* to the Cambodian number and wait. Within five minutes, I receive back a message also containing a single *X*.

Ross is ready to go. We're on.

Jim, being American, has *rode the elevator* to our floor, but I, being English, *take the lift.* Adrenaline is starting to flood through my body, and my heart is thumping. I have to make a concentrated effort to be calm in front of Fosse.

He raps on our connecting door, and I unlock it.

"Tell me what the fuck we're doing," he says without more ado. "Do you have the guns?"

"Yes. We're hitting Polzin this morning."

"When?"

"A little before eleven."

"In two hours?"

"Yes. Polzin is staying at a hotel near us. He has an engagement at eleven o'clock in one of the meeting rooms at the *Shangri-La* – also near us. I have drawn a full floor plan of the business level, showing lifts, stairs, entrances, etcetera. I've worked out exactly where we both need to be positioned and how we'll ambush him and his two goons."

"And you know what other conferences and so on are taking place there today? It sounds like a crowded venue for an assassination."

"Trust me."

He narrows his eyes.

"Show me the guns."

I remove the Glocks from the safe and hand one to him. While he's examining it, I drop mine on the bed, pull out my suitcase, and open it. I have my back to Fosse as I start unpacking the rope and other stuff, but I can hear him fussing and clicking the weapon.

"Turn around, David," he says.

Fosse is pointing his gun at me.

"This is no time for horsing about, Jim. We have to go through the plan –"

"Don't *move*," he orders. "I don't want to shoot you, but I will if I have to."

"What the hell is going on?"

"I believe this is what is called the *twist*. The part of the story where the plot gets turned inside out."

"Listen, if this is about money –"

He cuts me off.

"It's not. Well, not really. Polzin is paying me the same to betray you as you were going to pay me to help kill him. No, it's more to do with ... enjoyment. Like seeing the look on your face now. It's priceless, David, honestly. Plus, I'm not entirely sure you wouldn't have turned me over to the police, or contacted Reichenbach after the job was done. You do have this tedious moral streak in you. So, it's partly about self-preservation too."

"*Polzin* is paying you?"

Fosse shakes his head in mock sadness.

"You made a serious mistake in seeking me out, David, and a worse one in giving me time alone after you visited my apartment. That gave me the opportunity to call Grigory and tell him what you were up to – though I admit it wasn't easy to get through to him, and I had to be persistent. And it helped that we knew each other."

He pauses for a reaction, but I don't open my mouth.

"We worked together on an oil and gas deal some years back, you see. Unlucky for you, but lucky for Grigory.

"At first, he was skeptical about what I had to say. Perhaps he suspected I was trying to scam money out of him, or he didn't believe that you had the backbone to carry out such an undertaking, and it was just a fantasy. But when I mentioned that you had access to his travel schedule, then he became interested. And that's not surprising, is it? Having a spy at the heart of his organisation is a serious matter: only someone very close to him would have access to that information.

"Unfortunately, it didn't help my pitch that I couldn't give him any details, as you hadn't shared them with me. He wanted some proof of my assertions. However, he certainly sounded more convinced when I spoke to him yesterday evening and told him that I knew he was in Bangkok, and that you were planning to kill him today. But even so, he still seemed strangely reluctant to act unless I could produce real hard evidence of an assassination plot. Well, now we have the guns, don't we?"

He waves his Glock around before pointing it at me again.

"Excuse me while I make a call, would you? Oh, and please sit down on that chair, would you? And don't even *think* about attempting a grab for your gun. You'd never make it."

Keeping his weapon trained on me, he uses his left hand to speed-dial a number on his cell phone. After a few seconds of waiting – during which he smiles at me pleasantly – he speaks into the phone.

"Mr. Polzin, this is Jim Fosse. I'm in Room 603 at the *Bangkok Oasis*, and I have Mr. Braddock with me. I also have two fully-loaded guns, one of which is pointing at Mr. Braddock as we speak. Apparently, this gentleman was intending to shoot you at the *Shangri-La Hotel* at eleven o'clock this morning."

He listens to Polzin's reply for a minute or so, without interrupting and without taking his eyes off me. Then he says, "Very good, Mr. Polzin. I understand. We will see you in about half-an-hour. I will do my best to keep Mr. Braddock alive until you get here."

He ends the call.

"You know," he says conversationally, "I'm a little disappointed in you, my friend. In the past, you were a much more difficult adversary. A worthy opponent. But you've become sloppy. Maybe your obsession with avenging your daughter has blinded you to what is feasible and what isn't."

I stare at him.

"Don't you have *anything* to say, Mr. Braddock?"

"You are such a cunt, Jim."

He tuts.

"There is no need for that sort of language, David. I thought you Brits were supposed to be good losers. You should be, you've had enough practice. Now, we're going to sit here quietly while we wait for Grigory. Then the fun can start."

Interlude Number Two

I'm pressing the pause button again, for obvious reasons.

The end is near, as no doubt you will have deduced. But before we head towards the closing credits, I want to say one or two things.

Real life is not like a novel, is it? In fiction, one has the opportunity to de-randomise events, to construct a story with a message, to imbue a narrative with meaning. To give a life *relevance*.

A novel has a beginning, a middle and an end. It has its risings and fallings. Once you have finished reading it, you can look back and – if it's a good book – appreciate the artistry. If it's a mystery or a thriller, there will have been certain features that drew you in, compelled you to suspend disbelief. Credible, three-dimensional characters. Red herrings. Subtle deceptions. The inevitable conclusion that you should have anticipated, but didn't.

A real person's life, though, usually doesn't make sense. Oftentimes, it ends in failure, however much we might wish it were otherwise. Individuals either live too long, or their time is cut prematurely short. It's messy. We have no say in what large happenings occur in the world. We can't influence the camera's shutter speed. Whether it is chance that betrays us, or our friends, or our bodies, ultimately, we don't control events.

Vae victis: woe to the vanquished.

But, that's not to say we shouldn't try. Not all planning is wasted.

Sure, often our schemes will go awry.

But when they go right ... Oh, boy.

Now *that* is a sight to see.

Even if we die achieving our goal.

Sometimes, it's worth it.

It *is*.

Unpause.

28

"Towards thee I roll, thou all-destroying but unconquering whale; to the last I grapple with thee; from hell's heart I stab at thee; for hate's sake I spit my last breath at thee."

Herman Melville, Moby-Dick

The waiting ends. There is a knock on the door of Room 603.

Fosse, still holding his Glock, checks the peephole before admitting Grigory Polzin and his two black-suited bodyguards.

They are confronted by the sight of an Englishman sitting on a chair, with ropes around his torso and his hands behind his back. *Me.*

Polzin looks fatter than when I last saw him, more jowly. The goon to his right has a Neanderthal head and long arms, the muscly one to his left only just fits into his suit: if he moves too rapidly, the seams will give way.

Fosse closes the door.

There is silence as the Russians size up the situation. Polzin appears a little flustered, but then I guess this wasn't how he had envisaged his morning going. He's improvising. None of them is inclined to approach me yet, and they maintain a three-yard distance from their trussed-up captive, their backs almost touching the wall of the bedroom.

Good. Perhaps we can have a cosy little chat without their invading my space, and before events turn nasty.

"Braddock," Grigory says with a heavy sigh and a heavy Russian accent, "I didn't think we would ever meet again. I'm sorry it's not under better circumstances."

"Me too. And, if you hadn't ordered Katie's murder, we might be drinking vodka together and slapping each other on the back at this very moment."

"I suppose it is pointless trying to convince you that I had nothing to do with her disappearance?"

"It is. Completely pointless. You'd be wasting your breath."

"Your daughter was responsible for my son's death, Braddock, whatever that corrupt English judge concluded at her farce of a trial."

"Your violent, abusive half-wit of a son, you mean."

He bristles at this, but controls himself.

"It is fair to say that Alexander had his faults, but that doesn't mean he had to die. In any event, he is – or rather *was* – my flesh and blood. I owed it to my child's memory to even the score. You must understand that. You wouldn't be here now if you didn't."

"At least there is one thing we agree on."

He turns to Fosse.

"You can go, Jim. We'll manage it from here."

The relieved American walks past the grim trio, but as he puts his fingers on the handle of our connecting door, I say, "I'd prefer it if Jim stayed."

Polzin peers at me as Fosse hesitates.

"You are hardly in a position to make requests," he says. "But all right, he can stay. For now."

This prospect doesn't delight Jim, but he releases his grip on the handle and throws me an angry glance. Polzin relaxes a little, but his goons are still on high-alert.

"First, Braddock, you should know that I do not intend to kill you," announces the oligarch. "After we have talked, I intend to hand you over to the Thai authorities. I am sure they will take a dim view of your planning to slay a prominent Russian businessman in cold blood. By the time you get out of prison – assuming you are ever released – you will no longer be a threat to me. And if I consider that you are, I can deal with you then."

"I see. So, what is it you want to talk about?"

He is somewhat disconcerted by my apparent nonchalance, but he keeps his voice steady.

"You knew when I was flying to Bangkok, where I was staying, and where I was having a meeting this morning. That information could only have come from someone in my inner circle. I want the name of the person who supplied you with those details."

"So that you can hand him over to the authorities too?"

"No. I have something different in mind for any traitor in my organisation."

"I'll bet you do. So, what happens if I can't or won't give you a name?"

"Then, things will quickly become unpleasant for you."

One of the bodyguards takes a step towards me and I growl at him loudly. Momentarily startled, he steps back again.

"Come anywhere near me and I'll kill you," I say.

Polzin laughs.

"You're so arrogant, Braddock. Even now."

He leans back against the wall, folds his arms, and regards me quizzically.

"Assuming you had carried out this pathetic attempt at an assassination, how did you expect to get away with it – even if you could have left Bangkok alive? Given our joint family history and connections, you would have been a prime suspect for my murder. Or do you believe the police are that clueless and corrupt?"

"I have a watertight alibi all set up. Yesterday evening, an American ex-soldier of my acquaintance boarded a flight from Bangkok to Samui. He is roughly my build, and he was wearing a Panama hat and shades, and carrying a fake passport with the same number as mine in the name of David Braddock. I almost always wear a Panama and shades these days, by the way. It's something of a trademark. On arriving on the island, he was to be met by friends of mine who will swear they spent yesterday evening and the whole of today with him. That is to say, with *me*. The flight ticket, airline check-in, and CCTV footage will be enough to prove I wasn't in Bangkok when you and your bodyguards were shot."

The Russian tilts his head to the side.

"At least you had thought through *some* of this. Now, to return to your informant –"

"I'm not finished yet," I snap at him. "You see yourself as infallible, don't you? Well, Mr. Big Shot, let me inform you that you're *not*. Your instructions to your assassin to murder my daughter went awry. Katie is not dead. In fact, she is very much alive. What do you think of *that*?"

"You're lying."

"No, I'm not."

A myriad of emotions crosses his face, but after a few seconds they congeal into a cold, hard expression. When he speaks, his voice is icy and tinged with anger.

"I always considered you a stupid man, Braddock, but I had no idea you were this stupid. Thank you for telling me that your daughter is alive.

"After my business with you is concluded, I will set about hunting her down and making sure she does not escape a second time. That shouldn't be too difficult. I would guess she is somewhere on Samui or on one of the nearby islands – to be near to you. And I am sure that, should finding her prove to be difficult, there are members of your family, friends, or people at your office who will know where she is, and can be made to talk by applying the right pressure.

"So, once again, you have my gratitude, Braddock, for that helpful piece of information. And now, if you please, I would like you to tell me the name of your spy."

"It's not happening. I couldn't reveal to you his identity if I wanted to, because I don't know who he is."

"That seems unlikely. Let's see if we can jog your memory."

Polzin says something in Russian to the bodyguard on his right. The goon pulls a handgun out of his shoulder holster, and a suppressor from the inner pocket of his jacket.

"You know, you have poor judgement, Grigory," I say.

"*I* have poor judgement?" he exclaims. "What about *you*? You put your trust in Mr. Fosse. That didn't turn out the way you anticipated, did it?"

"On the contrary," I reply. "It turned out exactly the way I anticipated."

For the first time, a shadow of doubt flickers across the features of Grigory Polzin. I keep one eye on the bodyguard who is screwing the suppressor into his weapon. My timing has to be *just right.*

"You see, I knew that you and Fosse had done business together. I'd done my research. And I know what an untrustworthy little shit he is. Which is why I arranged for a special gun for him. *One that doesn't fire.* He discovered this inconvenient fact soon after he called you, when I picked up my own pistol. I promised Jim I'd spare his worthless life if he went along with this charade of my supposedly being tied up. That's why he is so miserable. You see, *my* pistol *does* fire."

The goon has finished fitting the suppressor, and Polzin makes a panicked grab for the weapon.

Now.

I stand up quickly, and the small piece of tape holding together my binding-rope comes away. At the same instant, I bring up my right arm which is holding my silenced Glock, and fire a round into the centre of Polzin's forehead. The gun spins from the Russian's hand onto the floor.

The bodyguard on Polzin's left reacts immediately, taking the decision to charge me rather than draw his weapon. He tries to get under my pistol arm, but he is too big, and I get my gun awkwardly between our two bodies. As he thuds into me, I only remain standing because I have braced myself and he hasn't had the distance to build momentum. Clumsily, I fire twice into his torso and feel him shudder. The dying Russian slides down me heavily, his slow descent lubricated by the hot crimson gore that now covers us both.

The first goon, meanwhile, is recovering the dropped weapon with surprising speed. I struggle to free my arm holding the Glock from the weight of the other man. With a final heave, I liberate my gun hand, just as the kneeling bodyguard swings his pistol up. We blast at each other more-or-less simultaneously. At point-blank range, neither of us can miss.

A massive pain smashes through my chest, and I am hurled backwards, splintering the chair and landing heavily. It's like my heart has exploded – and maybe it has – but I force myself to sit up.

The bedroom wall is sprayed in blood, and the Russian on the floor has half his head missing.

Fosse chooses this moment to bolt. He discards his useless gun, flings open the connecting door, and hurls himself through it.

Not so fast. Whatever I might have promised him, the world doesn't deserve to have Jim Fosse in it.

I discharge a round into his back. His arms fly out and, for a second, he resembles a stricken starfish. Then he pitches forward onto his bed.

Nobody is moving. They're all dead. *It's done.*

I can't maintain this position for long: the effort is too much. The Glock slips from my fingers as I lie back. Blood is pouring out of my chest. I place my hands over the wound, but I know it's useless. I cough and a stream of blood flows out of the side of my mouth. A red pool forms and grows around me.

I will never get to raise Jenny, to watch her grow up. But if Ross Gallagher has done his job – and I'm confident he has – then Katie will be free again. She'll make sure Jenny is all right.

They'll *both* be all right.

My vision is blurring, and the pain coursing through me is so intense that I'm about to lose consciousness. *Forever.* I can't even tell if I'm still breathing: my mouth and lungs are full of crimson fluid.

There is no Old Monk on hand to grant me a last-minute reprieve. Not this time.

And now ...

Here comes that white light.

Enveloping me. Enveloping everything that is me.

Gate gate paragate parasamgate.

Gone. Gone. Gone beyond. Gone *beyond* beyond.

Whiteness.

Nothing but white.

No more pain.

No more anything.

I'm done.

Post Mortem Report

Mikhail Polzin was killed outside the main entrance of the *Grand Khmer Garden* in Phnom Penh. His death took place within a few minutes of his father's murder in Bangkok. The Cambodian police determined that the young Russian had been shot by a high-velocity rifle wielded by a gunman on the roof of the building opposite the hotel. Unlike Grigory Polzin's messy end, his son's assassination bore all the hallmarks of a professional job.

The international media went into a frenzy over the evidently-coordinated slayings, and the Russian government expressed its outrage over the deaths of two of its prominent citizens. Since it was generally assumed that only someone with power and influence could have ordered the hits, initial suspicion fell on the Thai and Cambodian directors of the casino development company whom the Polzins had flown to South East Asia to meet. In the end, though, no charges were laid.

Meanwhile, in Moscow, Fyodor Orlov was hauled in by the Russian authorities who were well aware of the antipathy between him and Grigory Polzin, and their rivalry over foreign casino investments. No evidence could be discovered, however, linking the oligarch to the Asian murders. *Realpolitik* then took over. Polzin was not coming back from the dead, and Mother Russia needed men like Orlov to assist in rebuilding the economy after the Great Recession. Orlov was advised to make a discreet donation to party coffers, and the case against him was quietly dropped. The planning of the assassinations was officially attributed to 'senior criminal elements in Thailand and Cambodia'.

Polzin's wife Irina now found herself to be an extremely rich woman, and free of all responsibilities. She promptly sold off all the family businesses, and moved to Monaco where, some months later, a trimmer

Widow Polzin was photographed smiling blissfully in the arms of her twenty-five-year-old Serbian tennis coach.

Muay Thai fighter Vlad was obliged to stay on Samui longer than originally envisaged. "Until the noise dies down on the Polzin affair," Orlov insisted. Nevertheless, within two months, the big Russian was back with his ailing mother in Moscow, and taking up a new position in Orlov's organisation which required him to wear a suit. While this was not to Vlad's taste, he was partly comforted by the fact that he now carried a gun, which he hoped he would soon have the opportunity to use, having missed out on all the excitement in Bangkok and Phnom Penh.

For Katie Braddock, all threats to her personal safety had been decisively removed. She flew back to England using her Monica Young passport, where she and the joyful Nang Braddock cooked up a tale. Katie, having had a tip-off that Grigory Polzin had ordered her death, and not trusting the authorities to protect her against the oligarch's wrath, had been in hiding at Nang's house in the Midlands for the last few months. Now that both of the male Polzins were beyond any revenge, Katie announced her official return to the land of the living.

The newspaper coverage was sensational. 'Fugitive of Fear is Free Again' was one of the headlines. 'Suck That Russkis!' bellowed the *Sun*.

The police, though, smelled a rat. DI Zachary took it upon herself to grill Katie and Nang over their 'incredible fairy tale', but neither woman gave an inch. When Nang's faithful cleaner backed up the narrative – testifying that she had from time-to-time seen a young woman with cropped dark hair and Gothic clothing about the place – Zachary lost her cool.

"Do you mean to tell me that after all the TV coverage of Katie Braddock's disappearance, you didn't recognise her?"

"Like I said, she looked very different from her pictures. Nang told me she was a vulnerable drug addict whom she'd taken under her wing, and I had no reason to disbelieve her."

"A vulnerable drug addict?" exclaimed Zachary in frustration.

"That's right."

"You do appreciate that it is a serious offence to lie to the police, don't you?"

"I do," replied the old lady calmly. "But Nang Braddock is a fine woman, honest and straight up. Plus," she added sweetly, "your lot fitted up my Vinny for a burglary, so I don't owe you any favours. Now, is there anything else, or can I get back to my dusting?"

The household's part-time gardener was similarly unforthcoming when questioned.

"Listen, love," he said, "Adolf Hitler might have been living in the house for the last ten years for all I know. I spend all my time with the plants, and never go inside."

Zachary's boss told her to drop it. Since Nang Braddock had never been interviewed over Katie's disappearance, she couldn't be charged with wasting police time or obstructing the course of justice. And what crime had Katie Braddock committed? With the memory of their drubbing at Katie's trial still fresh, and the public on her side, the police - Zachary aside - had no wish to be seen as mounting some vindictive campaign against a victim of domestic violence.

"I don't believe a fucking word any one of them has told me," announced the exasperated DI.

"Neither do I," replied her superior. "Now, let it go, for God's sake."

Swine Flu and ongoing rows on MP's expenses soon displaced Katie Braddock in the media consciousness. Her London apartment was sold, drawing a line under the Polzin saga, and allowing Katie to throw herself wholeheartedly into the matter of Jenny Holland's guardianship.

Ross Gallagher and Wayan Lastri moved to Chiang Mai where they set up house together, and later married.

Ananda, the Old Monk, his report on the shortcomings of *Wat Son* completed, returned to his rural home and the continued benevolent dictatorship of his redoubtable wife.

Sam Trask's affair with Hitomi Tanaka fizzled out. He took a full-time job in his sister's realty business in Greensboro, and Hitomi left New York to work on an anthropological study in Brazil.

And what of David Braddock, private investigator and sometime family man?

Braddock's eventful life ended on the floor of a Bangkok hotel room amidst blood and carnage, when his neglected and oft-abused heart stopped beating.

Following which, in keeping with his contrarian nature – and much against the better judgement of karma – he was resurrected.

White.

Everything is still white.

Is that it now, for eternity? Just – *white?*

But, wait.

A fuzzy, greyish blob is slowly forming. It wavers about a bit then sharpens and resolves itself into a face. It is the face of someone familiar.

"Ah, you're awake," says Nathon Lamphongchat. "About time too."

I am lying on a bed staring up at a whitewashed ceiling with a bright strip light. The walls of the room are white too. There are tubes and wires attached to me, and various machines. I try to sit up, but Nathon restrains me.

"No pain," I say.

"You're full of morphine. Even so, if you move around too much, you'll feel pain all right, and probably start bleeding again. And, don't worry, I've let Nang know you're all right, and your business partner at the *Agency*. She said she'd put the word out that you're OK."

Da will tell Wayan, and Wayan will tell Katie. *Good old Da.*

"I should call them."

"You can speak to them later. For now, lie still."

"Where am I?"

"In a little private medical facility that I set up for my people. It can be awkward using the public hospitals when they've found themselves in an illegal scrape, you see. We're reasonably well equipped here, and have a couple of tame medical staff available on call when required. We don't have state-of-the-art, high-tech stuff, but we do have a small operating room and access to a surgeon who's good at removing bullets."

"Am I in Bangkok?"

"Yes. Near Chinatown. Just off Thanon Krung Kasem. It's mainly food stalls and repair workshops around here, nothing fancy. Plus, in Maitri Chit, around the corner, there are a number of coffin manufacturers – which is handy when our surgical operations go badly."

"As practical as ever, Nathon."

"But, *Where am I?* is not really the question you should be asking, David."

"Why am I alive?"

He clicks a finger and points at me.

"*That's* the question. And the answer is, that you're only alive because of Da Pintaraporn."

"*Da?*"

"Yes. After you told her about your preposterous idea to assassinate Grigory Polzin, she phoned Jingjai who passed her over to me. She filled me in as best she could, mentioned that you might be travelling under the pseudonym of Eric Snow, and asked if I would keep an eye on you if you came to Bangkok. I said I'd do my best.

"As Da was tasked with recommending hotels to you, I told her to make sure that, if you did come here, you would stay at the *Bangkok Oasis*. That's one of *our* hotels. Reception staff were instructed to put anyone registering as David Braddock or Eric Snow into Room 603, and to put their companion into the connecting room. These rooms were to be kept free in the meantime, as was Room 602 which was reserved for my men. We bugged your rooms, and fitted a couple of mini-CCTV cameras so we would know what was going on."

My companion. Since Da assumed I'd be travelling with Robert Buchanan, Nathon would also have believed that Fosse was Buchanan. *Whoops.* But there is no point in enlightening him at this point. We'll cross that bridge if and when we come to it.

The Thai is continuing his narrative.

"Da updated me on your movements immediately after you updated her, so I had men waiting to follow you from the time you landed at Suvarnabhumi Airport."

"Jesus."

Nathon looks pensive.

"She's quite a woman, that Da, and obviously fond of you. She was most insistent that we keep you alive if we could. Is she attractive?"

"You might say so."

"Married?"

"Widowed."

"And, are you and she –?"

"No, we aren't," I reply somewhat too forcefully. "Besides, she's my business partner and much younger than me. *Much* younger."

"Even so, if she's unattached you should grab her quick. Women like that don't stay on the market long."

"Can you stop talking about Da, please, and tell me how I got here?"

"Ah, yes. Well, when there was all that fake tying-up nonsense in your room, my men weren't sure what to do. They could see by the CCTV camera that you were holding a gun, but didn't know what was going to happen next, so they rang me for instructions.

"I was on my way over when all hell broke loose. They scrambled, kicked your door in, and found a gruesome tableau of blood and bodies. And you dying on the floor. The bullet only just missed your heart. But, even so, it actually stopped beating for a while, and we thought we'd lost you. Lucky for you, one of the men I'd assigned to follow you used to be a doctor. He managed to restart your heart, though it was still touch-and-go as to whether you'd bleed out before we could get you here."

"He *used to be a doctor*?"

"Yes, he was struck off after some inappropriate behaviour involving a young female patient."

"Oh, that's karma at its best. Don't tell me my life was saved by a rapist."

"Kob Sook isn't a rapist. It was consensual and the woman was nineteen. No, where he went wrong was having sex with her sister too. That's when the first woman reported him. Then his life spiraled down into homelessness and drug addiction until I offered him a job."

"Murdering people? So much for the Hippocratic Oath."

"Not just that," says Nathon indignantly. "He also organises the rotas for –"

"Too much information. Way too much. But please thank him for me."

"I will. You should rest."

He turns to leave.

"By the way, how old was the sister?"

"Kob Sook didn't say."

"Ha."

He hesitates before adding, "Incidentally, Mikhail Polzin is dead too. He was gunned down in Phnom Penh. They're still searching for the shooter. I suppose that's the part of your plan you didn't share with Da."

"You suppose correctly."

The door shuts behind him with a soft click.

I sink back and close my eyes.

It's black, not white, thankfully.

Good.

I prefer the darkness.

OK.

I guess, at this point, you may be feeling a trifle aggrieved; that I've conned you with those retrospective insights from the hereafter; that I'm not 'dead' in the sense that you understand the term. Although, those of you who know me should be familiar with my reputation as an unreliable narrator, and therefore ought to have anticipated some sort of deviousness on my part. And for those of you who don't know me ... well, now you know me a little better.

True, I am not what you might term a conventional corpse, but I have not lied to you entirely. There is some veracity in what I've said.

I *did* die.

My heart stopped. For a while, there was nobody named David Braddock. He was gone. He *has* gone.

For the Returner who opened his eyes on that hospital bed was a different man – *is* a different man. A man who doesn't talk to ghosts, or plan murders, or make bargains with killers. A man not circled by clouds of guilt and regret. A man with no black cinder of anger smouldering in his chest.

Yes, I died.

And what is more, we *all* die. Every day. Each morning we wake, we are not quite the same person we were the previous day. *You* are not the same person. Science tells us that roughly every seven-to-ten years, every cell in your body is replaced. So, when taken with the continual rewiring of your brain through new experiences, and the constant rewriting of your memories that occurs as a consequence, you are decidedly not the person you used to be. You know that picture of yourself aged nine that you carry in your wallet? It is not you. *You* were never nine. You only exist *now*. That is a photograph of someone else.

In truth, we are all Returners.

You're not interested in this esoteric waffling?

OK, I get that. A few months ago, I doubt I would have been interested either. Or, rather, that person who mutated into today's me, wouldn't.

Let me say, however, before you switch off entirely from this line of reasoning, one final thing.

There is a much-used proverb which asserts that life is not black and white, but many shades of grey. It is a less traditional position that death is the same. But it is. I've been there. Moreover, the boundary between the two is less solid than you might suppose. I've been there too.

Perhaps, if we could understand that we are simultaneously living *and* dying, we might be less fearful of our own extinction and less destroyed by the loss of those we love.

If nothing else, that thought should give us *some* pause. And, maybe, in those difficult times when the night is long and dark, a little comfort.

Nathon shakes me awake.

"Someone to see you, David."

It is none other than Police Colonel Deng Charoenkul. I doubt he has come to bring me flowers and a get-well card.

"Well, Braddock," he says, taking a seat. "You are a difficult man to kill."

"Yes."

"And everywhere you go, you bring trouble. You are fortunate that you have good friends like me to look after you."

I raise an eyebrow.

Nathon says, "We owe Colonel Charoenkul our gratitude, David. I explained the situation to him, and he has been enormously helpful in keeping the little incident at the hotel out of the public eye."

Charoenkul snorts.

"Little incident, yes. Not so *little.*

"Now, I am a man who values justice above all else, Braddock, as you are aware. So, when Nathon told me about how Polzin had ordered your daughter's death, my finer feelings were aroused. I said to myself, *Why should the law punish someone who is simply seeking to avenge a deep wrong done to his family?* And I resolved that such a man should walk free."

I can't come up with any suitable response to this, so I remain silent.

"I did think, however, that having Grigory Polzin's son killed too may have been a trifle excessive. I have no doubt that you were involved in that Cambodian business as well, but we won't dwell on that now. Suffice to say, I have pulled in two red shirts for Grigory Polzin's murder –"

"But you're surely not going to –"

He raises a patient hand.

"Let me finish. The Royal Thai Police is under huge pressure in this matter. The Russians are *not* happy, as you can imagine. So, I had to do something fast to show that we were taking the issue seriously. Giving it due weight.

"Of course, I have no real evidence that these two men were involved, but I considered it would be a salutary lesson to the red shirt movement to understand that their members are not above the law – particularly after those street protests recently in Bangkok and Pattaya. The government decided to take far too lenient a position on the demonstrations. If it had been up to me, I'd have machine-gunned the anarchist scum."

I can't come up with a suitable response to this either.

"However," he goes on without a trace of irony, "Thailand is a civilised and merciful country. The two red shirts will be released in a day or two without charge."

"But with a few bruises."

"Maybe a few," he replies with a grin. "Lessons well taught are rarely forgotten."

Behind Charoenkul's back, Nathon rolls his eyes.

"Now, Braddock, to the reason for my visit. I have saved your skin this time, but this is the *last* time. I want you out of Thailand. You are just too much of a magnet for violence. Bad things happen around you. From today, I give you one month to settle your affairs and to leave the country. This is non-negotiable. If you are still here in a month, I shall have you arrested."

"On what charge?"

"I'll think of something."

"To tell you the truth, Colonel, I sense I have worn out my welcome here. I will be returning to England presently: it is already decided. I have family business there to attend to."

"Good. Then we understand each other."

He rises, but doesn't shake my hand.

"Goodbye, Braddock. Nathon." He nods and goes.

When I am sure Charoenkul is out of earshot, I say, "I used to fuck his wife, you know."

"No, I didn't know, David. And I'm not sure I want to."

He sits down in the chair vacated by the policeman.

"I am sorry about that. The good Colonel insisted on seeing you. And I'm not happy that he now knows the location of our medical facility. I shall have to move it.

"He's becoming a problem for me, actually. As I told you, he is much greedier than he used to be since he took up with Mananya Som. Excessively greedy."

"How much does he want for falsifying the evidence and turning a blind eye to certain facts about what happened at the *Oasis*?"

"A *lot*. And he's already been paid."

"I'll reimburse you, Nathon."

"You bet you will. You might be family, David, but there are limits."

"Still, in fairness to the corrupt old swine, organising a cover-up on this scale can't be easy. Explaining away – or not - four dead bodies is no trivial matter."

"You mean *three* dead bodies."

"No. Four. The three Russians and my associate."

Nathon shakes his head.

"The only corpses we found were the three Russians. Your associate got away." He stares at me in alarm. "What is it, David? Are you all right?"

Despite the pain in my chest, I can't stop laughing.

The psycho American is not dead. *Again*. I only wounded the fucker.

Everyone dies, say the philosophers and priests.

Yes, everyone.

Everyone except Jim Fosse.

But perhaps evil never truly dies. It simply mutates into another form.

When I am well enough to make the trip to Samui, I go straightaway to see Katie. She has already been briefed by Da about the Polzin plot, for which she duly scolds me. I tell her everything – all that I confessed to Da – so that there will be no more secrets between us. She hears about Jenny, and Anna, and the last day of her mother's life. I hold nothing back.

When our conversation ends, we are both raw. She cries for a time and I hold her. She says she forgives me, and she seems to mean it. But she *is* a Braddock, and it's hard to tell with us Braddocks.

I phone Nang to tell her someone unexpected is flying to England to meet her, and suffer the lashing of her tongue. She had to concoct yet another tale of woe to tell Laurette Lang as to why I wouldn't be at Natalie's funeral – but she is relieved that I am alive, and her anger doesn't last long. When the unexpected person formally known as Monica Young turns up on her doorstep, she is overcome with joy. Nathon, bless him, had, at Da's request, not informed Nang that Katie was still with us.

Incidentally, Mrs. Lang – when I do eventually meet her – is charming, and clearly the type to let bygones be bygones.

It is time to take my leave of Koh Samui.

However, I am not the only one deserting the island.

I bid farewell to Vlad before he catches his flight to Moscow, and thank the big lug for his friendship.

Next, there is a tearful leave-taking from Wayan, and a firm, understanding handshake from Ross Gallagher – both *en route* to a new start in the north of Thailand, away from prying and familiar eyes. I wonder if we'll stay in contact.

It's the end of an era.

The *David Braddock Agency* has been sold to the island's headshrinker, Dr. Braun, and Da has agreed to stay on for a month to facilitate the transition of ownership, and to show the new man the ropes.

My last parting takes place at Samui Airport, and the person giving me a hug and sobbing is Da Pintaraporn.

"I'm going to miss you, David," she says.

"I'm going to miss you too, Da."

"It's been a long journey since we first met, hasn't it?"

"It has."

"Koh Samui won't be the same without David Braddock."

"It might be better."

She wipes her eyes and straightens her shoulders.

"But it is only a month, after all, isn't it?"

"It is. You and Pratcha will be with me in England in a month."

Yeah.

Right.

I should probably talk about Da.

Lying in that bed in the gangsters' hospital in Bangkok gave me time to think. And the more I thought about it, the less crazy Da's proposition appeared. Plus, this was a woman whose intervention had saved my life. However, it was not just a sense of gratitude that drove me to say yes to her proposal of a *trial relationship*. Much of what she had said to me about the challenges of raising children struck a chord now that a normal life once again seemed possible.

"If you're happy to have a man who has a hole in his chest, I believe we should give it a go," I told her.

"*Really?*" she said, wide-eyed.

"Really."

She bit her thumb and concentrated for a few seconds.

"Are you well enough yet to have sex with me?"

"I suppose so, as long as it's gentle."

"Then, we should have sex to make sure we are physically compatible."

"Fine. But perhaps we should close your office door first. I don't want us to set a bad example for Pimpim."

"Har-har."

"Seriously though, Da, there is one thing that bothers me."

"What's that?"

"The difference in our ages. Doesn't it worry you a bit?"

"David," she says, patiently. "Most women have a daddy complex. But only some of us are honest enough to admit it. Is that all?"

That night, Da persuaded her cousin to babysit Pratcha, and I booked us into a boutique hotel outside Lamai.

Once in our room, we both undressed shyly and somewhat self-consciously.

As we slipped into bed, Da said, "I don't want to spoil the moment, David, but I have to tell you that I don't do kinky stuff. But I don't just like to do the normal stuff either."

"Got it. Not kinky but not normal either. Sounds perfect. And you can call me *Daddy*, if you want."

She grabbed my nether regions and squeezed.

"Shut up about that, and make love to me."

She looked down at where her hand was resting.

"Well, at least we're not going to have to waste time getting you hard."

It seems we *are* physically compatible.

So, Da and I are giving it a go, initially splitting our time between England and Thailand to accommodate school terms: spending time apart and time together. If we're both comfortable with how our relationship is working, we'll make the arrangement permanent – and she and Pratcha will move to England to live with Jenny and me. It's a shame that Pratcha prefers football to rugby, but one can't have everything. At least he's not into guns.

I don't underestimate the bureaucratic nightmare that awaits us in obtaining British residency for Da and her son – even if we are married – but Katie knows a first-rate immigration lawyer who assures me that it will be sorted eventually.

Well, it can't be worse than the endless administrative processes involved in my officially becoming Jenny's guardian, but that process is also worth it. Every day I spend with my new daughter, my damaged heart heals a little, and her sense of confusion and loss reduces a little.

It's April 2010, and as I compose these words I'm sitting on a beach in Northumberland, enjoying a few days' holiday with my newly-extended family.

Family, as the Old Monk observed, is important: both the family we inherit through blood, and – perhaps more crucially – the family we choose. You can go through your whole life wondering what it's all about but, in the end, it's all about your *tribe*. And I have been fortunate to have found mine.

I take a deep breath of fresh, bracing air. The sky is a dirty blue, the temperature is on the cold side, and a stiff breeze is blowing in from the North Sea. All of this works to our advantage – there is hardly anyone else about.

Nang has retired to a local tea shop and is having a brew with the Chairperson of the local Conservative Association, whom she had met purely by chance an hour ago while he was out walking his dog. I say, 'purely by chance', though these days I am more inclined to attribute events to the wily, unfathomable workings of karma. The two of them will no doubt be discussing the forthcoming May general election, and licking their lips at the prospect of a Tory victory.

Katie, Da, Jenny and Pratcha are fifty yards away from me, digging holes in the sand and laughing. Da laughs a lot more these days, and frowns a lot less. When she plays with the kids, she almost becomes a child herself – and it's lovely to see. Things between us are going well, and I believe we're almost ready to move on to the next stage in our relationship: tying the knot in earnest.

Katie, on the other hand, has acquired some worry lines, no doubt as a consequence of the events of the last few years. Since an immediate return to law practice would have been impossible, and money is not an issue, she is doing some voluntary work in a homeless shelter to fill her time. She is in touch with her former boss Lucien Croft, who gave evidence at her trial. I understand, from something Katie let slip, that he and his wife are separated. Thus far, I am reining in my curiosity. Not keeping secrets is one thing, but Katie deserves a private life after what she's been through.

Da splashes some water over Pratcha and waves at me.

Do Da and I love each other? No, I don't think I can call it love. But there is an ease between us, a mutual commitment, a feeling of closeness. We might fight occasionally, but we soon make up. Many couples don't have that much. And, as for the sex ... Well, that's none of your business.

My health is much improved. No heart murmurs. Da maintains that the scar on my chest is where my old, cynical heart was taken out, and a new kinder one inserted. I only have the occasional strong drink, and the odd cigarette. I've made it a rule never to smoke in front of the children.

I've ticked off all the items on my checklist that I drew up before leaving Samui: tipping off Reichenbach as to Fosse's last-known whereabouts, and visiting Adele Fletcher to put in a plea on behalf of her estranged half-brother. Without disclosing any details, I told her that my daughter would not be alive were it not for Ross Gallagher. She listened patiently, but was non-committal as to whether she would reach out to him. Well, we'll see. I've done all I can.

As I promised myself, I finally read Edward Braddock's manuscript. *Twice*. I learned a lot about my mother, and came to understand why my father's attitude to me was always so distant and critical. I also encountered in the pages of his memoir some interesting and unexpected karmic connections both to myself and to others. But that, as the saying goes, is a story for another day.

And now, if you will excuse me, I am being summoned by my family. Before we go to tea, they want me to help build a sandcastle. It is a Sisyphean task since, within an hour or two, the incoming tide will level it. Unseen by us, its ramparts and towers will dissolve, its paper flags will topple, and all trace of its existence will be washed away by the indifferent sea. This product of our labour will merge into Oneness. Like our own lives, its time will be short.

But it will be no less beautiful for all that.

If, like David Braddock, you would like to read the Malayan memoirs of his father Edward, then keep your eyes open for

LAND OF RED MIST

to be published by Tention Books

About the Author

"Makes a living by travelling, talking a lot and sometimes writing stuff down. Galericulate author, polymath and occasional smarty-pants."
John Dolan hails from a small town in the North-East of England. Before turning to writing, his career encompassed law and finance. He has run businesses in Europe, South and Central America, Africa and Asia. He and his wife Fiona currently divide their time between Thailand and the UK.

All of John's titles are available on Amazon in paperback and for Kindle. If you click on the 'FOLLOW' button on John's Amazon Author Page, you will be kept updated on future releases.

Paperbacks of John's books can also be found on the Waterstones website.

John's website is at https://www.johndolanauthor.com where you can sign up to his Newsletter.

You can also follow John's ramblings on Twitter @JohnDolanAuthor or see his Author Page on Goodreads

Printed in Great Britain
by Amazon

49401529R00258